P9-CQH-012

THE Tehran TRIANGLE

TOM **REED** with SANDY **BAKER**

First edition published 2012

Published by
Black Garnet Press
P.O. Box 2914
Santa Rosa CA 95405

Copyright © 2012 Tom Reed
All rights reserved.

ISBN: 0983238324
ISBN-13: 9780983238324
Library of Congress Control Number: 2011961997

Black Garnet Press, Santa Rosa, CA

Printed in the United States of America.

No part of this book may be used, reproduced, or transmitted in any manner whatsoever, electronic or mechanical, including photocopying, recording, or by any information storage and retrieval systems, without written permission, except in the case of brief quotations embodied in critical articles or reviews. For information, address Black Garnet Press, P.O. Box 2914, Santa Rosa CA 95405.

All the characters in this book, with the exception of several brief mentions of historical or current figures, are fictitious, and any resemblance to actual persons, living or dead, is purely coincidental. Geographic locations, scientific information, and historical events are real and documented.

ALSO BY TOM REED

At the Abyss: An Insider's History of the Cold War
The Nuclear Express: A Political History of the Bomb and Its Proliferation

ALSO BY SANDY BAKER

Mrs. Feeny and the Grubby Garden Gang
Zack's Zany Zucchiniland

DEDICATION

To my cousin, George Bradley, who did not come home from Ie Shima; to his siblings and cousins who flew, marched, and sailed into harm's way during that same conflict; and to his kin who did the same during the forty years of Cold War that followed. We are all deeply in their debt.

ACKNOWLEDGEMENTS

Nuclear scientists can write about A-bombs. We can document the byzantine travel of that lethal technology to irresponsible hands, but it takes true artists to tell a story, especially a tale that connects documented history to an unnerving possible future. Sandy Baker shaped the characters that carry this story. Some of them are based on people I know, from CIA foot soldiers to presidents. She then fashioned others from our knowledge of the Shiite world. Ms. Baker also had the stamina to edit the work and to arrange for its publication in the new world of independent publishing. To legacy-published authors I recommend the trip. It leaves the author in full control, able to quickly produce an absolutely accurate, top quality piece of work tied to current events.

Once created, those characters needed depth: expletives at the right moment, eyes of the right color, an inner compass that drove each to his or her destiny. I thank Mark Nykanen, a wonderful writer of thriller fiction, for bringing these people to life and for providing the subtle connections that linked them into the book's many plot lines.

To return to the beginning, I am indebted to General Robert Huyser, a friend from Pentagon days, sent to Tehran in January, 1979 to stiffen the spine of the Shah's generals. A month later he helicoptered out, under fire, but along the way he had come to know the senior General Gharabaghi quite well. In my office, General Huyser wrote his history of those days and left his files to me. Later, as I structured this book, Prof. Abbas Milani of the Hoover Institution contributed his excellent understanding of post-revolutionary Iran. Prof. Najmedin Meshkati of the University of Southern California brought insight into the current-day Iranian psyche. Ms. Azar

Hadi became a link to the younger generation still in Iran while translating key English phrases into Farsi.

John Coster-Mullen, an enterprising writer without security clearances, gave the public an understanding of *Little Boy* with his book *Atom Bombs*. Friends from my days at the Lawrence Livermore National Laboratory lent helpful, yet carefully protected, insight into rudimentary A-bomb physics as practiced in 1945. Others, such as Danny Stillman from Los Alamos as well as analysts who must remain nameless, illuminated the genealogy of proliferating nations' weapon programs. Scientists from the International Atomic Energy Agency in Vienna, along with their sources and contacts, contributed the details of the Libyan, South African, Pakistani, and Iranian nuclear programs. They also provided insights into the Ulba Metallurgical plant and *Project Sapphire*. These men and women must remain nameless, as their careers, perhaps even their personal safety, could be imperiled. Dr. Hallie Beacham advised on the recovery of heroes and villains from physical assault.

For site-specific information, I thank Kristine Leroux for her insights into Paris and Beverly Hills, Jack Daniel for scouting Gilhooleys, Diane Tatum for touring me through the hazards of El Paso and Juarez a variety of Air Force enlisted personnel for describing life at Al Udeid, and a former Secretary of the Air Force for explaining the details of Predator operations. I've lived and worked in Hobbs, NM; the drilling contractor there was really named J.P. "Bum" Gibbons. The names of the waitresses in the cafes are gone, but their smiles remain.

I want to thank former President George H.W. Bush, Pulitzer Prize winner David Hoffman, Foreign Minister Ardeshir Zahedi, and Secretary James Schlesinger, for the kind words found on the book jacket.

Early encouragement came from Andrew Rothstein, producer of a Nat-Geo TV show on the history of the A-bomb; Chris and Ray Wagner, independent movie producers in Los Angeles; and John Nuckolls, a former director of the Livermore weapons lab.

When it came to production, I am indebted to Phil Schwartzberg for the map of New Mexico; to Martha Kemp for line drawings of *Akhbar-I*; and to my executive assistant Karen McDonald for keeping the non-nuclear world at bay while I wrote. She then facilitated the book's production and promotion. I want to thank Team 1 at Createspace for a marvelous and time-sensitive job of copy-editing, book design, and layout.

My literary agent, Phyllis Wender, has now seen me through three book publications. She helped find the auxiliary writers needed for this work. She is an experienced hand in this business, a real pro. My heartfelt thanks to her for more than a decade of friendship.

As noted earlier, Sandy Baker not only created characters, she edited – demanding sensible writing and full compliance with the *Chicago Style Manual* – and then worked with Createspace to publish. We are both indebted to her husband, Bud Metzger for his enduring support and to my wife, Kay, for her patience and steady encouragement.

T. C. Reed   Healdsburg, CA   February 2012

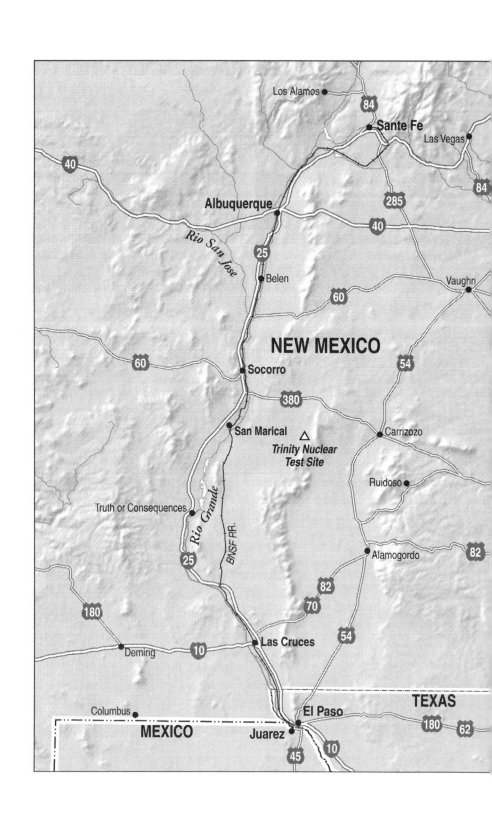

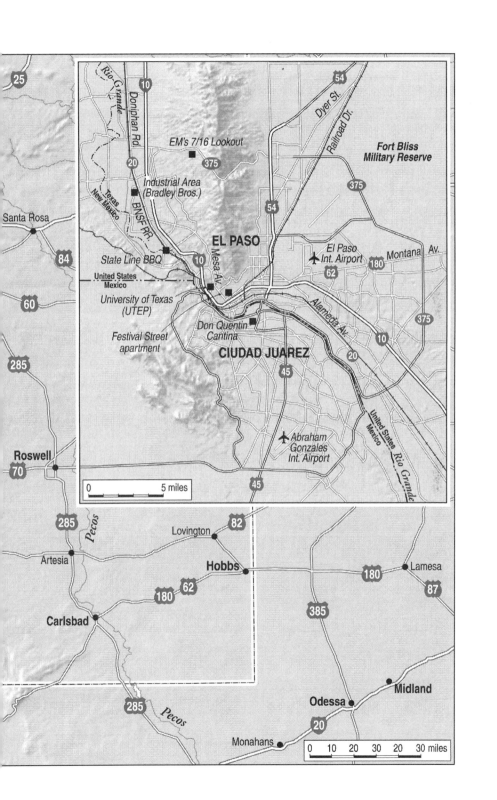

CONTENTS

Prologue xv
Chapter 1   Alchemy at Ulba (*Summer 1999*) 1
Chapter 2   Death, Vengeance and Grief (*Autumn 1999*). 11
Chapter 3   Dancing at the Kremlin (*May 2000*) 19
Chapter 4   Opening the Can (*May - Dec '00*). 27
Chapter 5   9/11 (*2001 - 2002*). 41
Chapter 6   New Venues (*Dec '02 - July '05*) 49
Chapter 7   Girl in the Charred Burqa (*July 2005*). 59
Chapter 8   Al Udeid (*Summer '05 - '10*) 67
Chapter 9   The Road from Karbala (*Dec 2010*) 83
Chapter 10   Tale of Two Cities (*2005 - 2010*) 87
Chapter 11   Invitation to the Dark Side (*Dec '10 - Apr '11*). 95
Chapter 12   Trials (*May - Oct '11*) 107
Chapter 13   Raising the Stakes (*Nov 2011*) 123
Chapter 14   Project 853 (*Dec 2011*). 133
Chapter 15   Home for the Holidays (*Dec '11 - Jan '12*) 145
Chapter 16   Red Flags (*Jan - Mar '12*). 159
Chapter 17   Convergence (*Mar 2012*) 175
Chapter 18   Night Visitors (*Mar - May '12*) 185
Chapter 19   Gilhooley's (*Early June '12*) 205
Chapter 20   Summer Solstice (*Mid - late June '12*) 211
Chapter 21   Hiram Hunts (*Late June '12*). 219
Chapter 22   Independence Day (*July 1 - 6, 2012*). 225
Chapter 23   The Jet Engine Screams (*July 5 - 6, 2012*) 233
Chapter 24   Incubation (*July 7 - 15, 2012*). 241
Chapter 25   Sunrise (*Morning 16 July, 2012*) 259
Chapter 26   Bastille Day (*Noon 16 July, 2012*). 271
Epilogue   (*July - Nov, 2012*). 275
References 283
About the Authors 285

PROLOGUE

A second sun came to Christmas Island fifty years ago. It was not a holiday miracle, a guiding star in the night sky. It was Bighorn, a US thermonuclear device that flooded the equatorial Pacific with a sea of light. The massive flare burned in silence, a universe of nearly incomprehensible heat.

The voice that had counted down to the detonation, that had been dubbed "Mahatma" perhaps without irony, had nothing more to say after the final two words: "Weapon release." After that silent interlude, the skies flooded with brightness, then began to darken slowly as if guilt itself had become manifest, a shadow on the sand and sea.

A young airman turned away. He took off his thick goggles, then glimpsed a startling light show, a veritable ocean of luminosity, with purple and yellow ribbons snaking through swirling, orange clouds. And yet the haunting silence still held. But not the heat.

It seized everyone's attention like a solar engine burning out of control only thirty miles away. The warmth—so welcome at first in the early morning air—soon felt suffocating. It grew more intense with every passing second. A furnace door that just wouldn't shut.

The sonic boom came next. It knocked over unaware bystanders and would have crushed the bones of anyone significantly closer to the explosion.

Only at the end of the Cold War did many of the witnesses at Christmas Island learn of American and Soviet plans to lay down hundreds of these weapons on Moscow and Washington. The harrowing scenario was so shocking to the airman, now an old-timer. He found it inconceivable that anyone would plan to use those nuclear bombs again.

But the new century brought new madness, and other suns now waited, some most impatiently.

One of them sparked to life right behind the old man's back, in a land of trust and faith.

CHAPTER 1
ALCHEMY AT ULBA

September 1999

This was the real Valley of Death. Not a line in an ancient psalm but mayhem in real time. An exhausted Elizabeth Mallory spurred her horse deeper into the barren wasteland of eastern Kazakhstan. She rode past a few hills but mostly flatlands where radioactive waste from Soviet nuclear bomb testing had settled decades ago. It now rose in a poisonous plume, kicked up by Elizabeth's horse.

Dust and destitution, and the signs of death all around her. She plunged past an abandoned cement factory, its round, towering chimney standing cold and forlorn in the wake of a collapsed Soviet Empire. Bizarrely, that cinderblock shop stood cheek by jowl with an equally moribund children's camp. A warped plywood cutout of Tyrannosaurus rex arched over the entrance, an eerie welcome in any language.

One more mile. That's all, girl. She talked to herself when she wasn't encouraging Gunpowder, the strong, gray gelding with his glorious black socks and tail carrying her through the decimated countryside. The crimes of the Kremlin appeared with each glance. An economy in free fall. Privation everywhere. Predators too.

Elizabeth urged on Gunpowder, glancing left, knowing that was where the Ulba Metallurgical Plant stood more than thirty miles away. Once it had been a hub of nuclear production for a Soviet high-tech attack submarine. Then it became a storage facility for unused fissile material, but it was so poorly secured—by a single antique padlock—that a few hours ago

impoverished former workers moved more than half a ton of the highly enriched uranium, mixed with toxic beryllium, to a nearby airstrip. The short
trip in an old ZILtruck marked the culmination of months of negotiations
and planning for the sale of high-grade bomb-making material. Iranians
and Americans both wanted it. Elizabeth and Gunpowder were running
the last leg of the race for the deadly Kazakh chemicals. The finish line was
a dirt airstrip.

Where is it? The runway had a name, the Ust-Kamenogorsk airport, but
that was typical Soviet hyperbole. It was no more than a flat stretch of desert on the outskirts of the dying city. She'd seen the satellite photos. Now
she wanted to see it for real.

But Elizabeth was also looking for *them*: the exporters of thirteen hundred pounds of weapons-grade uranium in trade for thirteen hundred
pounds of Iranian gold. A lethal equivalency. And where the *hell* was the
empty farmhouse? She wanted to get up on that damn roof with the rocket
launcher.

She spotted the apple orchard—*finally*—spindly and half dead in the
dusky light, the sun a urinous-looking ball setting fast.

An aging, fat-bodied Antonov AN-12 cargo plane was somewhere in
the sky. She couldn't see it yet. Touchdown was expected at 7:00 p.m. according to the last CIA communication via her secure satellite link. She
could not be late. She needed to hit that pig of a plane in the air. She didn't
want to bring it down on the uranium canisters being trucked to the airstrip from the old metallurgical plant. People still lived around the airport,
raised fruit and vegetables. Families too, hard as it was to imagine. And it
was painfully safe to assume the bomb-making material wasn't any more
secure in a truck than it had been in the decrepit plant.

She sickened when she heard the unmuffled roar of the AN-12's four
Ivchenko engines. She snapped her head to the right and saw a dark speck
in the sky through the skeletal arms of the sickly apple trees.

Elizabeth and Gunpowder raced out of the orchard. She spied the farmhouse a hundred yards away and smacked Gunpowder's flank hard enough
to sting her hand. Seconds later she reined him in and jumped down, un-
strapping from the tattered saddle a rocket launcher and a pack laden with
two Stinger missiles. She loaded the weapon.

A ladder she'd seen in the satellite photos hadn't moved, and she raised
it in seconds. Wheels down, the plane was making its final approach, ready

to take on the most valuable—and lethal—cargo in its many years of service. Given the eight nuclear bombs Iran could make with the thirteen hundred pounds of enriched uranium, Elizabeth's assignment was as clear-eyed as necessity itself.

She started up the ladder, its wood grayed from many years of use. She made it halfway to the roof before another rotten rung in the failed Soviet system broke and sent her, the rocket launcher, and the missile crashing to the ground.

Iranian Major Ashkan Gharabaghi stood near the end of the dirt airstrip, not far from two tents his driver and pair of security men had set up, obscured by overgrown brush and untended trees. He watched the turboprop heading directly toward him. To be imbued with the spirit of Allah on a mission this critical marked the height of his glorious career and a means to leapfrog over men in the Iranian leadership who were too tepid for his taste. Gharabaghi had helped create the Army of the Guardians, which had protected the Ayatollah Khomeini in the early days of the revolution—and murdered his opponents.

He was also a veteran of the Revolutionary Guard Corps and a man who, by his own account, had fought valiantly against Iraq. If he needed a reminder of his bravery, he could take out his *chimiayee*, the award given to those wounded by Saddam's gas. Or he could simply cough and feel the piercing pain in his lungs from the chemical weapons the US had furnished to the Beast of Baghdad. The injury only steeled his resolve to vanquish his enemies. In Iran he had conceived the use of construction cranes for the mass hangings of political opponents. And here, at the end of a dirt runway, he awaited a means to bring the US weeping to its knees.

He smiled when the howl of the cargo plane's ancient engines slowly reached his ears. A truck waited a few hundred meters away, loaded with the prize.

His index finger smoothed his Clark Gable mustache, a small vanity he allowed himself. Though loathe to admit as much to his fellow Revolutionary corpsmen, he liked to think he resembled the American film star of old. He even quoted the line "frankly, my dear, I don't give a damn," but only to himself in his flawless English. His charms, in his considerable estimation, were not merely physical. He had made persuasive spiritual overtures to numerous men in the Muslim republics of the failed Soviet Union, moving swiftly to fill the void left by weak leadership. In a matter of months, he'd established a powerful network to provide Iran with nuclear materials. Most of the men he'd organized believed in Islam. Others found their faith in gold. Gharabaghi provided the preferred currency, whichever it might be.

All those efforts had brought him to the Ulba Metallurgical Plant three weeks ago. After countless cups of tea and the promise of turning uranium into gold—"Modern-day alchemy," he'd told the miserably poor men with a laugh—he had secured a blessed deal for the Islamic Republic of Iran.

He looked at his watch, figuring the turnaround time for the Antonov-12 would be less than an hour. He would be onboard for the glorious flight to Tehran, although he would not be touching an ounce of the enriched uranium. The Kazakhs had brought their wives to load the pails on the plane. Anything with a pail was women's work. Especially this.

But what widened Gharabaghi's smile—what displayed his perfectly straight teeth—was knowing he'd bested the Americans. They'd been trying to buy off the Kazakhs too, but they were slow, burdened by their bureaucracy and arrogance. Yes, they had won the Cold War, any fool could see that; but the new Islamic Caliphate was rising and the West was doomed to lose. You could not fight the will of Allah on earth any more than you could in heaven.

Still hundreds of feet in the air, the cargo plane lined up almost in front of him now. The loud engines were a symphony, the sweetest sounds Gharabaghi had heard since leaving the boudoirs of Tehran. But as loud as those engines were, they only hinted at the screams destined to rise halfway around the world—in the very heart of the Great Satan—when Project 853 was complete.

Jesus frickin' Christ. The rocket launcher smashed down right beside Elizabeth. If the Stinger missile had gone off, it would have hit the farmhouse a few feet away and blasted it and her into oblivion. She heard those old engines grinding through the air and knew the cargo plane had to be damn near landing.

She climbed to her feet, looked at the roof, and realized she had to jettison any plans to use its modest peak to shield her while she aimed the Stinger.

With thirty-five pounds of rocket launcher on her back, she rushed around the corner of the house and saw the AN-12. The sunset threw off streaks of gold as bright as the highlights in her Rumpelstiltskin-spun hair and lit a face with baby blues that more than one beau had declared unforgettable. But right now she had eyes only for an old Russian—the bucket of nuts and bolts that flew under the name of Antonov.

She positioned the rocket launcher and winced. Not over the way the setting sun singled her out like a spotlight, a *target* for whoever was providing security for this horrific exchange. No, as daunting as that prospect felt, what made her gut grind with fear was the way the sun lit up the Stinger and overpowered the infrared sensors in the missile. She could not get a lock on the heat emanating from the Ivchenko engines.

Blinding as the light was, she held steady. Knowing an unseen AK-47 could take her out at any second, she held steady.

Patience, she said to herself. *Patience*. Said like a prayer, and maybe it was, the only kind an agent not long out of Langley could make in a moment like that. She watched the AN-12 descend. The world between Elizabeth and her target felt emptied of everything but dread. Only trees on a hill loomed a mile away.

The gnarly, old Russian turboprop bellowed so loudly she barely heard the rocket launcher beep when the plane dipped below the tree line, where the sun could no longer taunt the Stinger's sensors. But there was no mistaking the rocket launcher's audible signal that commanded her to fire.

Elizabeth obeyed. For seconds—or was it years?—she held her breath. She even thought of loading a second missile. No need. The Stinger destroyed one of the turboprop's engines. The plane flew apart and crashed, scattering a cloud of fine, gold dust on the hills west of Ust-Kamenogorsk.

Above the explosions and crackling fire, as she headed toward the corner of the farmhouse, she heard another sound, even more ominous: a man screaming, "Get her!" She glanced over her shoulder only long enough to glimpse a dark-haired man stepping from behind brush and pointing directly at her. Bullets buzzed her head like bees.

"Patience," she whispered to Gunpowder. The horse's eyes were widening; he looked like all he wanted was to bolt.

She shared the impulse, strapping the rocket launcher across her back, bandolier style, just before she lifted herself up onto the old saddle. She nestled the pack with the extra missile against the pommel and kicked her heels. Not that she needed to: Gunpowder took off as fast as the explosive for which he was named.

Elizabeth's cover was blown, as she'd known it would be. It had taken her weeks to move into position, but she'd managed it with her impeccable Russian and a nom de guerre to match: Elena Milo. *"Ya bezhentsev,"* she had told the curious; they heard hearing the beseeching tone of "I'm a refugee" with every syllable.

She'd morphed into a Russian version of an Australian sheila: dusty jeans, a well-worn, tight T-shirt, and a sweat-stained hat, all adorning a woman in full command of any horse she came near. She was a long way from the desk she'd occupied as a secretary-receptionist at the embassy in Moscow. The beautiful Harvard grad had spent her evenings in the company of Moscow's emerging elite, gathering intelligence on the new Russia by recording their vodka-fueled attempts to impress her. Elizabeth had handled herself with aplomb. And why not? Agency life was in her blood. Her father had been one of Langley's steadiest analytic hands during the Cold War.

But even he would have tensed up if he could have seen her now, racing back into the apple orchard with the growl of a car engine reaching her ears. She glanced over and saw a battered Mercedes station wagon speeding along a dirt road that ran parallel to the orchard about a hundred feet away. Bullets snapped the tree limbs overhead, but as long as she remained in the orchard she would prove a poor target. She had no more than another minute before that protection ended and she would burst into the open. Whoever was firing the Kalashnikov—that was what it sounded like to her trained ears—wouldn't hesitate to shoot Gunpowder out from underneath her.

Maybe I can't outrun the Benz, much less those bullets, but I can outmaneuver the vehicle in tricky terrain, she decided.

Elizabeth pulled hard on the reins and rode Gunpowder back toward the farmhouse just long enough for the Benz to reverse itself—a cumbersome move executed by a driver clearly trained for only high-speed chases.

Knowing this she gave the vehicle a few seconds to accelerate fully, then she nimbly reversed once more, this time sprinting for the end of the orchard. The old cement plant could give her cover. When she'd passed it earlier, she'd noticed truck bays commodious enough to accommodate her horse.

She'd been an equestrian since early childhood and had picked Gunpowder with care. Only a few days earlier, she'd found him in a broken-down corral in the Russian border village of Gornjak. Her first glance had revealed dozens of undernourished, wormy-looking horses. After several minutes a few came up to her, including a palomino, but she couldn't risk a horse that flashy in the drab Kazakh countryside. Then Gunpowder sniffed her hair and nudged her. He looked healthier than the others. She ran her hand down his legs. Solid enough, with trimmed hooves. He had broad trail-riding feet and big nostrils for taking in air on a long, hard run. Both qualities were tested as she rode him hard now, glancing over her shoulder to see that the Benz had turned around and was fishtailing as the driver tried to catch up to her.

Elizabeth raced from the orchard and angled toward the factory, on her left at ten o'clock. She hadn't counted on the rubble from a collapsed wall, scarcely visible in the dimming light.

Gunpowder slowed as they came upon the scattered bricks. She pulled out her 9mm Makarov semi-automatic pistol. Turning, she found the Benz racing toward her. She fired three times, shattering the windshield. But it didn't slow the car or send it wildly careening.

Gunpowder lunged into the bay, and she dismounted. The horse breathed heavily as she took his reins and rushed him out of view. He was a steady creature, and she thought he would have been a fine police horse—patient and quiet in the chaos. Then she realized he might have been bred from a long line of police horses before being sold off, like so many other resources—including enriched uranium—in the old Soviet Union.

She peered out of the bay as she dug out the last Stinger and setting up the rocket launcher.

The Benz had stopped seconds earlier. In the twilight she saw dust drifting from the sudden braking. But the cracked windshield and poor light veiled any view of the occupants—if they were still inside. Were they already creeping toward her in the plant? They easily could have rolled out of the car and scrambled to the far side of the factory. Undoubtedly her pursuers could get into the cavernous structure through any of the doors or compromised walls. Heavy equipment long gone to rust cast dark shadows she couldn't see past.

She listened for footsteps, movement of any kind. Gunpowder's breathing was still loud, giving away their presence. His broad torso expanded and contracted like a bellows.

Nobody had left the car since she'd first looked. They had to have scurried to the factory. Glancing round, she saw a door about fifty feet behind her, a gray rectangle in the dark. It looked big enough for Gunpowder.

She loaded the second missile. The horse stirred uneasily. She grabbed his reins, then peered toward the far end of the factory, where she thought the men might have entered. She was tempted to fire the rocket launcher to cover her retreat but saved the missile in case a more tangible threat beckoned.

Elizabeth led Gunpowder toward the door quickly, the *clippity-clop* of his hooves ringing loud as death in the gloomy building. The two of them paused behind the carcass of an orphaned cement mixer, the kind carried on trucks. It lay on its side like a dead beast. She listened for the men who'd chased her.

Where are they? How many?

They had to be outside the plant. That was all she could figure. But then she heard a boot or shoe skid on the concrete floor as if in response to her thoughts. *Just one?* Whatever their number, they'd be hard pressed to chase her if she could get out of the factory with Gunpowder and make it to the hillside.

"Easy, boy," she whispered to the horse. And then she heard another footstep. She fired. The missile struck a wall that was much closer than she'd realized, perhaps one hundred feet away. Fierce heat enveloped her, crisping the fine hairs on her arms. She squinted from the bright light, saw a body lift ten feet off the floor in a ball of flame, and ducked as bricks flew into the air.

Gunpowder whinnied. She sensed his growing panic, tossed aside the now useless rocket launcher, and led the horse directly out the door. She looked around and didn't see anyone, but the oncoming night was stingy with reassurance.

A clear, metallic *click* issued from the darkness to her right, and Elizabeth fired the 9mm repeatedly. There was no return fire. She mounted Gunpowder and took off.

Another car sped toward the factory. Headlights swept across the rubble-strewn ground ahead of her. She rode Gunpowder into the shadows of the trees as hard as she dared, then started up a gentle hill. The horse shuddered, and she sensed the creature's barely controlled panic. Then she heard gunshots and threw herself forward, gripping Gunpowder's neck, no longer daring a muzzle flash that would pinpoint them.

The horse navigated rugged terrain, taking them past scrawny trees and across ditches as they headed uphill. He paused for an empty pool she hadn't seen, and she realized they were crossing through the children's camp.

"Good eyes," she whispered to Gunpowder.

The horse edged around the pool's concrete skirt and moved back into the scanty trees, climbing once more. Nothing but another equestrian or a dirt biker could follow them now, and she hadn't seen evidence of either.

By the time they reached the top of the hill, night fell over them as thick as an old, Russian blanket. She leaned close to Gunpowder's ears and spoke softly: "You were magnificent, boy. You really were. I wish I could take you home with me."

By morning she'd traveled through miles of forest, finding her way to a small Kazakh farm. She sold Gunpowder for a pittance to an old man with a kind face, then paid far more for the man's old Lada than it was worth. But it was time to dust her trail with largesse. She pulled away from the smiling, nearly toothless old man with billows of black smoke rising behind the rattly car.

Elizabeth's careful getaway arose from her firm belief that the men she'd foiled at the airstrip would try to chase her down. But she couldn't possibly have imagined the gruesome vengeance an Iranian major would extract before he made his own way out of eastern Kazakhstan.

CHAPTER 2

DEATH, VENGEANCE, AND GRIEF

Autumn 1999

A crust of sweat and dust coated Elizabeth's skin and hair by the time she rolled into Gornjak just north of the eastern Kazakhstan border. She was tempted to nap after her sleepless night on horseback but didn't dare.

She found the Cape Fear Café, where she was supposed to rendezvous with Colonel Myer. Elizabeth parked the junky, old Lada right where she could see it. With a judicious use of gold coins and her fluent Russian, she'd made it across the border with few questions from the grateful guards. Money bought everything in the new Russia, including people and passage.

She couldn't wait to get out of the old car. It reeked of diesel, tobacco smoke, and the sweat of men too weary to bathe. But she still felt exhilarated by her success in Kazakhstan. Her first mission in the field confirmed her feeling she was vastly overqualified for her embassy post as a secretary-receptionist cum femme fatale. She was certain she'd proved otherwise by putting all her arduous training to good use. And she felt no qualms about killing the men in that plane and whoever had perished in the old cement factory when she'd used the rocket launcher. Before leaving for Kazakhstan, she had wondered if the murderous side of spycraft would leave her struggling with post-traumatic stress disorder.

Not hardly, she assured herself as she spotted Colonel Myer, lean and sturdy-looking as a steel post. He rose and welcomed her.

"You must be starving," said Myer who'd escorted Mallory from Moscow to the Soviet-Kazakh border with instructions to await her return.

She allowed that she'd worked up an appetite, and the two of them, joined by the colonel's aide, Major Tiplady, settled into a meal of sausage and onions.

After Elizabeth snagged a shower at a downscale hotel in Gornjak, Major Tiplady took the wheel of a Land Rover for the two-day drive north to Novosibirsk. The vehicle was notably more spacious than the old Lada, which Elizabeth guessed had been stolen within an hour of their departure.

Later the next day, a consulate officer delivered a parcel to Colonel Myer in the parking lot of the Novosibirsk train station. In minutes Elizabeth and the two marines were scheduled to take a train to Moscow. The man from the consulate spoke softly, and Elizabeth didn't catch any of his message, which was clearly intended for the colonel only.

Novosibirsk's celery-green station had been built in the glory days of the Russian Revolution, before Stalin's crimes became apparent to most of the world. The city was a major stop on the Trans-Siberian Railway, and the station reflected the early elegance of pre-WW II. Elizabeth took weary note of the ornate chandeliers as she hurried with Colonel Myer and the major onto the train that would take them across the steppes of Russia. After her night on horseback and two days on the road, their mini-stateroom, with its four bunks, looked as alluring as a suite at a Four Seasons hotel.

The wiry Major Tiplady locked the door immediately and roped it shut. He warned her against wandering the train.

"If you need the facilities," Myer told her, "the major will escort you. People get mugged and thrown off this train all the time."

Elizabeth stayed awake until the train passed the outskirts of the city, where the steppes ceded their autumnal colors in a palate worthy of Isaac Levitan and other great Russian naturalists. The train's rhythmic rocking lulled her to sleep. When she awoke, Colonel Myer asked her if she felt ready for a debrief. It lasted almost three hours, and then she let the hypnotic motion of the train claim her once again.

The next time she awoke, the colonel eyed her closely and opened the parcel that his assistant had given him back in the parking lot.

"This got dropped off at the US consulate this morning," he said. "It's repugnant, but you'll need to see it. And because of your background, this might be harder for you to take than it is for those of us without a long association with horses."

"What did they do to Gunpowder?" she demanded at once.

"That was his name?" Myer asked. She nodded warily. "Sorry about that," he said, handing over the envelope. He let her fish out the color photos. Eight by tens. A series taken with a motor drive, showing a powerfully built man holding the horse's reins tightly while another man drove a metal stake into Gunpowder's left eye. The next photo showed the horse's legs buckling as they were shot out from under him. The series then showed Gunpowder whipping his head around as the torture continued.

Elizabeth looked up, trying to steady herself with controlled breaths. "They couldn't catch me, so…" Her voice trailed off. Colonel Myer nodded, then told her to keep looking.

"It gets worse."

How? she wondered. She saw quickly that the horse had been shot, but saw more photos documenting the same treatment of the nearly toothless old farmer with the kind smile.

"Do we know who?" she asked.

"Why? Do you plan on avenging their deaths?" Myer asked. "We wouldn't approve of that."

"No, I'm not going rogue on you over a horse and a farmer I met for ten minutes," she said. "I would just like to know."

Myer shrugged. "We're not sure. As you can see, they didn't show their faces."

"No, they wouldn't, would they?"

"But it's clearly a message, Elizabeth. From our intercepts they knew they were chasing a woman, which didn't do much for their egos. You did a great job."

Myer smiled for the first time. But Elizabeth's newfound ease had vanished when she'd seen the first photo.

The next morning Major Tiplady escorted her to the bathroom at the end of the train car. This had become a routine. So were the words Elizabeth said to herself while she endured the filthy commode: *Not the Orient Express.*

She'd heard the expression "bone weary" many times but had never experienced it until that train ride to Moscow. The colonel debriefed her two more times in the course of the day and then she slept until the next morning, when he woke her a final time with the rich aroma of coffee. She blinked her eyes open and found the beloved elixir, a Turkish pastry, and a plate of sliced apples that had been spritzed with lemon juice.

"The ambassador will want to see you as soon as you have a chance to clean up," he told her.

Still groggy, she sipped herself into awareness, ate the sweet confection of phyllo and honey and almonds, and disembarked. She trudged through the magnificent surroundings of the Moscow station with only a passing awareness of the arched ceilings and marble floors.

A dark-suited man drove Elizabeth to her apartment, where she scrubbed herself clean after days without a bath. Then he sped her to the embassy. She found Colonel Myer waiting for her in the ambassador's office.

The career diplomat handed her a lush arrangement of Russian roses, kissed both of her cheeks in a distinctly European fashion, and continued to treat her like a returning heroine. Without further ado, he guided her into a surveillance-proof bubble in the embassy's basement.

The salt-and-pepper haired man closed the door and informed Elizabeth the director of Central Intelligence had authorized an inscribed Intelligence Community Medal for Valor for her.

"And I'm obliged to tell you, Elizabeth, you must guard the details of this award as a secret for some time to come."   "I understand," she responded with a broad smile.

"The president sent a note to your father," the ambassador added.

"That was gracious. I'm sure my father appreciated that. So I can talk to him about it?" she said.

"Oh, yes, your father's cleared."

She thought so. He still consulted at Langley, long after he'd retired officially.

"So what's my next assignment?" Surely they would use her clearly demonstrated skills.

Surely they had no such plans: "We'd like you back at your desk, Elizabeth. Of course."

"Secretary? Receptionist?" She felt herself bristle so hard she thought she might have blurred before his eyes.

"Well, there'll be more debriefing, and we'll call on your expertise when we need it. But we'd like you to continue to gather intelligence on the alpha males taking over this country."

She slumped visibly.

"Oh, cheer up, Elizabeth. You're twenty-six years old. You've just had a brilliant start to your fieldwork. You're on your way."

She forced herself to brighten.

Autumn proved tumultuous in Moscow with the changing of the guard. Yeltsin was losing whatever alcoholic hold he'd had on the country in the 1990s and a new corps appeared to be emerging, led by Vladimir Putin. He'd been a KGB officer during the Cold War and the mayor of St. Petersburg for much of the past decade.

While Elizabeth followed the events around her closely, she also kept abreast of Project Sapphire, the competing American effort to retrieve the Soviet-enriched uranium in Kazakhstan. Three United States Air Force C-5 planes landed at Ust-Kamenogorsk airport with the approval of the Kazakh government, but still with great secrecy.

American technicians repackaged the uranium-filled pails into 448 drums to comply with environmental and safety concerns, then airlifted the entire consignment back to Oak Ridge. The reason the Kazakhs proved so pliable? Twenty-seven million dollars for their lethal prize, which was about what Major Gharabaghi had offered to his prospective partners, a treasure still strewn about the Kazakh hills.

Interesting, but the truly memorable event for Elizabeth was the call she received from her father in November. He said her mother had passed away. She had suffered from Alzheimer's for almost a decade, and for the last few years hadn't even recognized her daughter. So when Elizabeth heard her father's husky voice pass along the news, her sadness was tempered by the knowledge that she'd grieved her mother's loss years earlier—and the even more painful understanding that in a very important way, her mother had never known her.

Carolyn Mallory had tried to raise the perfect daughter, but her husband had been the perfect agency man. Who could have competed with him in the eyes of the teenage Elizabeth, an athletic young woman who excelled as an equestrian, a track star, and a field hockey forward? While her mother wanted her daughter's pleats to be pressed, the young Elizabeth wanted her cleats to be sharp, her arms strong, and her legs ready to carry her as far as necessary.

But Elizabeth felt bad for her mother, for she had belonged to a generation of women often tormented by their times. They had borne children right after feminism's second wave assaulted the social order and called into question all the assumptions they had come to believe. So many women fled their marriages and built new lives. Elizabeth's mother never changed. She lost her daughter because of her own temperament and the tumult of that unprecedented era.

"I was there with her, Lizzie." Only her dad got to call her that. "Like President Reagan, she'd been going downhill for a long time." He'd served the fortieth president well.

"At least it's over, Dad. Are you okay?"

"I'm fine, Lizzie. No need to rush home."

"Are you just saying that? Because I can be out of here on the first thing smoking."

He laughed, and she knew he hadn't lied: he really was okay.

"The family's here, all of Carolyn's sisters and brothers. Your Uncle Charley's here too." Her dad's brother. "I'm well cared for. We'll hold a service to honor your mother around the Fourth." He meant Independence Day—her mother's birthday and favorite holiday.

"I'll see you before then, Dad."

"By the way," he said, his voice turning husky again. "I got a nice note from the president a few weeks ago. I'm proud of you, Baby Bear."

She croaked out a good-bye, then cried after she hung up. Not for her mother but for her father, alone in Bethesda.

An unexpected note of cheer occurred the very next day when a young man at the embassy gave her a chummy elbow on the elevator and said, sotto voce, "So you're the Kazakh killer."

She rolled her eyes as if she had no idea what he could possibly be talking about, but inside, where Elizabeth kept her secrets safe, she was pleased. Mostly, though, the reminder of Kazakhstan made her want to get her hands on the man who'd ripped two creatures of kindness from the world: Gunpowder and the old man who had taken the horse into his care.

Only a week later, she found herself back in the bubble with the ambassador.

"We've got to stop meeting like this," she said to him.

He smiled but it had an obligatory gleam, confirmed when he crossed his arms and sat on the edge of his broad desk. "You may have an opportunity to advance the work you began in Kazakhstan a few months ago. The Iranian who ran that nasty little operation is a Major Ashkan Gharabaghi."

"The guy who had the horse tortured too."

"I doubt anything that happened in Kazakhstan took place without his knowledge or approval. He's a control freak. So I'd say the answer is yes."

She nodded, but her face must have given away more of her homicidal impulses than she intended, because the ambassador shook his head.

"Elizabeth, we need you to keep very cool. He's coming to Moscow for Putin's inauguration and the ball. You fit a profile—and I mean that in every sense of the word—a profile that he finds clearly desirable. We'd like you to make nice with him, if that's possible."

"What does *that* mean?" she asked.

"Our agents don't do honey traps," he responded quickly. Carefully, too, she decided after deciphering his words: the agency would use women, but not its own, to ensnare targets sexually. "But if it's possible," the ambassador went on, "and we recognize it's a long shot, we'd like you to insinuate yourself into his good graces."

She took a deep, obvious breath. "Wow. I tried to kill him. He tried to kill me, and now—"

"He doesn't know it was you. From your debrief it appears he didn't step out from the brush until you hit the plane and turned back toward the farmhouse. And from our intercepts, all they refer to is a woman. No description beyond 'blond.' But see how he reacts when he sees you. Make sure you catch the first glance he throws your way." And then, with a wicked smile, the ambassador added, "Because I'm absolutely certain he will. He'd be a fool not to."

What a flirt, Elizabeth thought. "Why me?" she asked.

"You mean besides your appearance, intelligence, and quick wit?"

"Please don't undersell me," she responded, even though clearly he was doing double duty: flirting with her and, perhaps incidentally, briefing her as an agent as well.

He offered his most toothy smile. "Because you have the requisite attributes. You speak Russian, as he does, and we need a young woman."

"Because of the young woman's intelligence and quick wit, right?" she bantered.

"Because this investigation could go on for years. It could consume your life. We don't want someone superannuating before it's over."

She offered a puzzled expression.

"The Iranians want the bomb, Elizabeth Mallory." He used her full name, which to her ears added to the portent of his message. "And we can't let them get it. We have all kinds of people in place. You're not the only one. You may end up on a desk, but they're moving people like chess pieces and so are we."

"So am I a pawn, a knight, or a queen?"

"We think you could be a queen."

She looked him in the eye, wondering if he were still flirting. She didn't think so. But he was certainly seducing her for the assignment: the honey trap for Major Ashkan Gharabaghi—without the sticky wicket of sex.

CHAPTER 3
DANCING AT THE KREMLIN

May 2000

On a chilly spring evening, Elizabeth left her Moscow apartment on the arm of Colonel Myer to attend Vladimir Putin's inaugural ball. At noon he'd been sworn in as president of the Russian Federation.

A limousine whisked them under a large arch, through the red fortress walls, and into the vast Kremlin complex, leaving them off at the Kremlin building itself. Colorful cathedral domes, scores of government buildings, and an impressive array of towers were lit brilliantly under the night sky, drawing the attention of scores of dignitaries heading to the celebration. But the striking American couple also turned heads as they entered St. George's elegant ballroom. And why wouldn't people stare? The colonel looked resplendent in full dress uniform arrayed with medals earned as an artilleryman in Vietnam. But Elizabeth, dressed with unusual flair, drew even more attention. Her russet-colored dress clung to every curve and stood in sharp contrast to the other ladies' beaded and sequined gowns. Her streaked, blond locks were swept back in a chignon and wisps of hair framed her face. She wore a single strand of dark-amber beads with drop earrings to match, all provided by the ambassador's vault—a little-known perk of the spy trade.

Despite her appearance with the colonel, Elizabeth had no romantic interest in him. In the past few years, she'd been surprised to find her taste in men had started to run a generation ahead of her age. While Myer quali-fied in that regard, she liked more spontaneous guys, with an irascible touch to their manner. Besides, her romantic indifference to Myer was matched by his devotion to his wife. He'd been teamed with Elizabeth for one reason: to provide security for her as she worked to strike up an acquaintance with Major Gharabaghi.

The celebration of Putin's formal accession also contained its own thinly veiled secrets, most notably the restoration of power to Putin's old KGB allies. The new president had been director of Russia's Federal Security Service, the main successor agency of the notoriously thuggish KGB.

But this evening threw a veneer of order and respectability over a history of assassination, torture, extortion, and abduction. The Russian army chorus sang, vodka flowed like water from the famous St. Basil fountains outside, and buffet tables groaned under platters of caviar and fresh foods unimaginable to the impoverished citizens left to brave the cold night.

As an orchestra played the opening bars of Tchaikovsky's "Sleeping Beauty Waltz," Colonel Myer asked Elizabeth to dance. The well-matched couple assumed a subtle course under the crystal chandeliers toward the Iranian delegation clustered in a corner of the grand ballroom. When the music stopped, Myer bowed formally to Elizabeth and offered to get her some champagne.

She stood alone, feeling adrift as other couples left the floor. The feeling intensified when she realized she had, indeed, fallen under the scrutiny of Major Ashkan Gharabaghi's unblinking, black eyes. She recognized him from the mug shot at the embassy, which even she had to admit did nothing to suggest his considerable physical presence.

Catch his first glance. That had been the ambassador's admonition. *See if there's recognition.*

So Elizabeth, trying mightily to feel like a queen in this nuanced game of nuclear chess, turned her eyes to the man holding court at the Iranian table. What she saw were his dark eyes, as focused on her as hers had been on the Antonov-12 last summer. If her intuition meant anything at all, he found her alluring. She had seen the look before but only rarely responded with a smile. She did now, though.

Without looking away from her, he rose from his chair. His underlings looked up, caught the trajectory of his gaze, and turned their sights on Elizabeth as well. As he approached her, he spoke in a language she did not understand. He tried again: *"Tanets?"* Dance?

"Da," she responded in Russian.

Then, in excellent English, he introduced himself: "I am Major Ashkan Gharabaghi of the Islamic Republic of Iran. Would you dance with me?"

Elizabeth smiled and took his proffered hand without reciprocating with her own name; silence and a scintilla of mystery might have provided additional allure.

As they swirled past the candelabras of St. George's, she was grateful his medals prevented any close physical contact. While attractiveness often proved disarming, she could not gaze at his Ken-doll looks—hair slicked back, mustache too perfect, posture unbending—without seeing the photo of the dead farmer. And when she forced herself to look into his eyes, she flinched inwardly at the torture he'd inflicted on Gunpowder. But the man was undeniably handsome, with the ruthless charm of a Cobra.

After the orchestra took a break, she told him her name, as if the smooth way he'd glided her across the dance floor had won him the first of many concessions.

He led her to the white settees ringing the room. "Tea, Ms. Mallory?" he said. "Or vodka? We Muslims don't imbibe, but I would be happy to get it for you."

"No, thank you. Not tonight." Elizabeth's initial tension was supplanted by her professional focus. She felt no fear, only the pleasure artful cunning can bring.

They spoke in short phrases about the weather, the most tiresome of all subjects, until he asked the question she had been waiting for: "*Kofevarka zaftra?*" Tea tomorrow? "*Metropol?*"

She hesitated and gave him an appraising look. "But we have just met, Major—"

"Major Gharabaghi," he said straight away.

"Yes, right, Major *Gharabaghi*," she repeated as if testing the sound of his name might have offered her a hint about his character.

He might have thought so because he piped up immediately: "I am man of honor."

She certainly knew better, but she nodded and asked, "May we meet for lunch?" Without saying as much, she wanted him to think she preferred daylight to the unspoken demands of a nighttime date. But her main goal was a start earlier than teatime, to give her a few more hours for interrogation.

They settled on the Metropol as Colonel Myer returned, handing her a flute of French champagne. She introduced him to Major Gharabaghi, noting pointedly that the colonel was a friend. And while keeping her eyes on the major, she sipped from the crystal glass, leaving the crimson impression of her lips. Elizabeth watched Gharabaghi's gaze follow the flute down to her side.

Myer acknowledged Gharabaghi with a slight nod, then escorted Elizabeth around the ballroom. They spent another hour chatting with members of the US and British delegations. Elizabeth also ran into several Russian men whom she'd dated. But her mission with Myer had been accomplished earlier when the Iranian major had invited her to tea, and both she and the colonel thought it best to leave before Gharabaghi's libido settled down. They did not want him changing his mind.

When they slipped back into their limousine, Myer asked if the Iranian major had been a good dancer. She knew he did not refer to Gharabaghi's ability to waltz.

"Graceful," she said. Elizabeth waited until he walked her to the door of her apartment before offering the more telling details of her tête-à-tête. She had assumed the limo was bugged. "He's smooth, clearly a well-trained insider, already sent to language school. We've got a prime target, Allan."

At noon the next day, Elizabeth strode into the dining room of the Metropol Hotel, stunning in a mid-length, black gabardine skirt, a brown sweater, black boots, and a purple-and-black checked silk scarf. The maître d' took her long, elegant, sable coat and led her to Major Gharabaghi's table, discreetly distant from the door and prying eyes. Two men in navy suits stood against a wall. No telling whether they provided muscle for him or an economic kingpin seated nearby; security had become important in Russia's nouveau riche capital.

The major took her extended hand but rather than shake it, he kissed it like a prince in a fairytale. She tried not to shudder at the brush of his mustache against her skin and conjured a smile for his uplifted eyes.

A waiter in black tuxedo pants and a vest glided up to the table. Gharabaghi looked at Elizabeth expectantly.

"Coffee, please," she said, settling across from him.

For almost two hours, they lingered over a lunch of whitefish, parsley potatoes, and wild asparagus. The conversation alternated between Elizabeth's careful remarks and the major's strongly worded responses. He was a man who appeared to think a woman found a man appealing in direct proportion to his bombast.

In response to his claim to have been a horseman of great repute, she said, "So you were an equestrian…" She halted before saying "too." Better not to suggest she knew the first thing about horses. Right now a woman on horseback would probably make him think of the Kazakh killer. Instead, she sighed. "Oh, I've always wanted to ride horses." She offered him an admiring gaze to go along with her wistful tone. "But they're so big. Are they dangerous?"

Naturally he made riding noble mounts sound as dangerous as picnicking with a Komodo dragon.

As with most men Elizabeth had known, the major was content to talk about himself. He told her he'd been born in Tehran in 1960. That was a full fifteen years before Elizabeth's birth. His father, he noted, had been a captain in the shah's regular army.

"One of my earliest memories, Elizabeth, was a trip to Persepolis. Nineteen seventy-one." Gharabaghi smiled, and she thought he'd begun a wistful reminiscence. "It was October of that year. The shah staged a gaudy celebration of the founding of the Persian Empire twenty-five hundred years earlier. Even at age eleven, I thought the whole show absurd." His voice began to rise again. "Outside the tent city, the SAVAK arrested hundreds of my older friends."

SAVAK was the shah's secret police. They were widely known to have tortured and executed the despot's political opponents. Iran had long been saddled with tyrants of one political stripe or another, but none more frightening, in Elizabeth's view, than its current rulers.

"*Oni byli nyeuvazhitel 'no.*" The major resorted to Persian to say his older friends had been accused at the celebration of being disrespectful. "The whole Persepolis show was intended to legitimatize Shah Reza Pahlavi, the heir to Cyrus the Great. *Finny!*"

She smiled at his use of the expletive "bullshit." And when she saw the major whipping himself further into a froth, she took quiet delight in imagining what his face must have looked like when she'd escaped his clutches in Kazakhstan.

"I went home to the mullahs," he continued. "They hated the shah's plan to westernize Iran. Father"—the major's hand fell to the table hard enough to rattle the silverware—"stayed on the shah's senior staff." Gharabaghi shook his head disapprovingly. "I met with Khomeini in Paris and then I welcomed him to Tehran a year later. *Veliiki den!*" Great day!

A highly contestable contention, given the deplorable impact of Shiite rule on Iran, but Elizabeth listened with the body language of a young woman much enamored of the drivel to which she was being subjected. Dating in Washington had prepared her for this. At last she took her leave to use the facilities, where she checked her remote mike hookup. She put her fingers over it while she relieved herself.

When she returned to the restaurant, she found the major holding her coat. He made a point of saying he had paid the bill, a statement both tacky and unnecessary; he did not fit the profile of a man who would dine and dash, at least not on a first date.

He suggested they stroll to the nearby Kremlin museum. Having studied Russian art history along with the language at Harvard, Elizabeth managed to quiet his almost ceaseless need to talk about himself by commenting on the magnificent collection of bejeweled eggs and cigarette cases. She noted a good friend of hers had a great uncle who made the cases for the House of Fabergé. The major could not have been less interested. Rather he found the museum as a reason to lament loudly the Arab invasion of Persia 1,400 years earlier. He pointed to an egg made in honor of a czar and said, "*Our* most cherished relics disappeared," as if that particular egg were among them. "But we still have our heritage, our language, and, most of all, our honor!"

Where's a Stinger when you really need one? Elizabeth forced her thoughts from blasting the bombastic man into oblivion by asking, in her most innocent voice, where he thought Iran would move in the twenty-first century.

"I do not *think*—I know. Soon, *Inshallah*, we will retake control of Mecca and Medina. The Twelfth Imam *will* return. *Kogda on eto delaet, yadernyh pozharev budet rabotat yego voli!*" When He does, nuclear fires will work His will!

She took note of that comment, guessing the agency's electronic eavesdroppers did as well.

When they stepped into the dusky chill, the major coughed convulsively, bending his estimable frame forward and gripping his chest. Elizabeth paused, but then placed her hand on his back. "Are you okay?"

Slowly, he straightened, scowling. "It's a gift from your country." His voice was hoarse, his face now flushed with anger.

"I beg your pardon," she said, surprised by the major's most obvious loss of composure.

He reached inside his navy-wool jacket for a lozenge. "Saddam's chemical weapons did this to me, and they were a gift from Reagan. Saddam used them against us during the trench warfare days. You Americans supported Saddam. How could you?"

Elizabeth took a breath, knowing he wouldn't understand anything less than a stalwart defense of her country because that was what he would do if the tables were turned. "Well, let's see. I believe you took several dozen Americans hostage. These were people serving in our embassy, trying to build relations between our countries. You held them for over a year. What did you expect us to do? Send flowers?"

"That doesn't matter," Gharabaghi shouted. "We gave them back the day Reagan was sworn in! But I spent weeks in hospital. Doctors say half my lung tissue is burned away. I must see doctors all the time," he continued between hacks, sounding more petulant by the moment. Maybe he realized this as well, because he forced his shoulders back, sucking hard on the lozenge, and drew in a deep breath. "I will see you back to your apartment."

"Are you sure?" she asked, sounding convincingly solicitous.

"Of course," he said, failing to suppress a cough. He lifted his hand and waved without looking. A Mercedes limousine pulled up seconds later, and she realized he had never been without security. He directed the driver to her precise address, then glanced at her as if to say, "I know this and so much more about you."

When he walked her to the lobby door, he took her hand and pressed his lips, so recently the recipient of so much spittle, to her skin. He looked up and said, "I will see you again."

But she heard no kindness in his voice. His farewell sounded like a threat. Or maybe she was conflating his tone with the sound of her silent riposte: *You certainly will.*

But what resonated most in her thoughts as she neared the end of her Moscow assignment were the words she'd eked out of Gharabaghi only minutes earlier: "The Twelfth Imam *will* return. *Kogda on eto delaet, yadernyh pozharev budet rabotat yego voli*!" When He does, nuclear fires will work His will!

The Twelfth Imam was the messiah long prophesized in Shiite belief. To hear an Iranian of Gharabaghi's stature link such a revered figure's return to Iran's nuclear ambitions only confirmed the dangerously intractable course the country had taken.

Over the Memorial Day weekend, Elizabeth headed home. She locked her apartment behind her, knowing the Iranian leadership had fused their geopolitical ambitions to their religious beliefs as surely as they hoped to fuse atoms for a devastating bomb.

CHAPTER 4
OPENING THE CAN

May–December 2000

Elizabeth took a chauffeured black Town Car from Dulles Airport to the house she would share now with only her father in Bethesda, Maryland. She wanted to live with him again, at least for a few months, to keep a close eye on how he was faring as a widower.

As the driver navigated the lushly treed suburban streets, she realized she'd missed cherry blossom season. It reminded her that Washington was Moscow's antipode in climate as well as politics.

Before she could climb out of the backseat, her father stepped from the brick colonial and hurried across a flagstone path to the driveway. She wrapped him in her arms, and though he was a few inches taller than she was, and certainly thicker of torso, Elizabeth had the most peculiar sensation of feeling stronger than her dad for the first time. She realized her mother's death had pained him far more than he'd let on while she was in Moscow. But of course he wouldn't have done anything to compromise her mission, and she understood that now.

His smile lit up his rubicund complexion, which seemed to whiten his hair even more. "Good to have you home, Baby Bear."

The endearment sounded so familiar and loving. Elizabeth was glad she'd never denied him the pleasure of using his favorite nickname for her, not even during her early adolescence, when it had made her want to scream.

"How are you, Dad?"

"I'm okay, Lizzie." He nodded, appearing deep in thought, then added, "She was ready to go."

"Long as you're not," Elizabeth responded with mock sternness. Internally she winced because her response spoke so clearly about who had always been her favorite parent.

If her father noticed, he let it pass. "Don't you worry about me. I'm an old war horse. I'm still going strong. I was at the gym this morning, and I'm still cycling."

"Good. We'll pump some iron together and get some kilometers in."

He grabbed one of her two large trunks and rolled it inside, saying, "You look tired, Lizzie."

"I am! I'm feeling kind of burned out. Wait till you hear about Kazakhstan."

He made her a vodka martini—"In honor of your first mission!"—and listened closely to her description of taking out the AN-12. He clapped loudly when she told him how the Stinger had destroyed the Ivchenko engine and downed the plane. His ebullient reaction made her feel for a moment like she had Gomez, from the Addams Family, for a father—but only when she looked at the colloquy as an outsider might see it, meaning anyone not in the intelligence services.

As she described racing through the orchard and finally making her getaway through the old cement factory, he moved to the edge of his seat. Then he got up and said, "I think I need another one." He went to mix a second martini.

When he sat back down, he read her the note the president had sent him. He so clearly relished divulging the communiqué, she didn't let on that she already knew of its contents.

"So what's next, Lizzie?"

She noticed that every time she returned home after a long trip he used her name a lot, as if he needed to say it aloud to convince himself she was really home. It felt good to be loved like that. He'd always made her feel like she could conquer the world.

"I'll be heading out to Langley on Monday. They want me to review all the debriefs for errors or omissions and to develop an overview of the situation in Iran."

"It's not good," her father said. "Those mullahs are bad business." Elizabeth nodded. "But I've got something to take your mind off the blue meanies," he went on. "I'm going to barbecue some lamb shanks. I've had them marinating all day."

"You? Cooking? *Marinating?*" She could scarcely believe it.

"Somebody's got to be a little domestic around here, so I took a couple of cooking classes." He pointed an accusing finger at her, but with a big smile. "I knew Baby Bear wasn't going to take over."

She laughed. He got that right. But then again, he usually did.

On Monday she merged onto the beltway and headed to Virginia, remembering how when she was a child her father had commuted to Langley by driving to Cabin John, just north of Bethesda, with his canoe. Then he'd paddled across the Potomac and walked up the hill to headquarters. Faster and a lot more fun, but security had gotten a lot tighter over the past two decades.

After driving past a twelve-foot-high piece of the Berlin Wall, an iconic reminder of the agency's successes during the Cold War, she passed through the hydra-headed CIA security system, replete with name badges with magnetic strips that permitted her access through steel turnstiles.

Elizabeth headed to Deputy Director Chris Roberson's office. The bald bulldog came out from behind his desk, offering his hand, intense eye contact, and a broad smile. "Ms. Mallory, you did a commendable job in Moscow and Kazakhstan. Not many—"

Girls. Go ahead, say it, she dared him silently.

"—your age are handed the Medal for Valor."

Nice recovery. But Elizabeth was more than willing to shrug off the DD's unspoken faux pas. She knew most of these old dogs were doing their darndest to adjust to a new era in the military and intelligence worlds.

"I'm delighted to meet you in person," he added.

"Thank you. I appreciate that, sir."

"We appreciate all the memoranda you sent us about Iran. You had your ears to the ground."

"I tried, but I still don't think our leaders really understand the dangers coming from Tehran."

"That's what I want to talk to you about. Quite a few of us here think our next president will need to deal with the Iranians in a serious way."

The 2000 Bush–Gore presidential campaign was in full swing. Roberson gestured for her to sit in a leather chair in front of his desk, then returned to his seat. "So we want you to collect and compile what we know about the Iranian nuclear threat and then boil it down into a secret-level briefing for the staffs of the nominated candidates. After the election, we'll want you to provide all the details, from every compartment, to the national security advisors attending the forty-third president of the United States."

"I'd love to," Elizabeth said. "It would be an honor."

"I know you hold an array of SCI clearances." That was spook-speak for sensitive compartmented information. "But we've added access to the Iota compartment for you. It will allow you access to our intercepts of Iranian cell phone traffic *within* Tehran. It's fragmented stuff, but we're finding interesting clues in there."

"How are our human assets?"

He smiled. "The best and the brightest Iranians are getting out if they can. I feel for these people. Their world is getting turned upside down by these Islamists. We've got defectors along with businessmen and penetrating agents. We'll arrange interviews for you. But keep in mind, some meetings will need to be in a social environment. We don't want to spook them."

"So to speak."

He chuckled. "We'll have you debrief others right here in the SCIF." That was an acronym for Secure Communications Intelligence Facility. Or, as Elizabeth thought of it, a set of rooms, walled off within a larger building that was swept for bugs and considered reasonably secure.

"The Iran library is at your disposal," he said as if he were ending the meeting. But when she started to stand, he added, "I'd like to see an outline of our briefing for the candidates' staffs as soon as possible. The end of September?"

"Yes, sir," she responded quickly.

"With the full NSC paper, along with an excerpt for the president's daily memo, by the end of October. And Elizabeth?" Before she could "yes, sir" him again, he said, "Thank you. You *earned* that medal. I'm really glad you made it back."

Summer passed in a blink of ever more exotic meals with her father, who was newly inspired by the Cooking Channel. She'd known him as a man of omnivorous interests but not appetite. And she'd never imagined him cooking sweet potatoes with beet chips and garlic rosemary salt—as a side dish no less. She encouraged his culinary interests and choices of wine, and loved the fact that she could talk to him about her work, joking at one point about "the family that spies together." But she'd clammed up right then because the ending to that saying—"dies together"—could have come out so easily and would have cut far too close to the bone.

She couldn't tell him everything about her work for Deputy Director Roberson, just the broad strokes. The most telling details she confined to the well-secured chronicle she was writing for the agency. On a Saturday afternoon in late August, she went in to work and settled at her desk to review an entry written right after she'd met with Vasily Gorelik at the Metropolitan Club in DC. Like its counterparts in New York and other major cities, the club offered a plush setting for fine dining with lots of room between tables for discreet conversation.

Gorelik had been a division chief in the Soviet Ministry of Atomic Energy. A dour, overweight Russian with a huge head of hair, he possessed a wanton appetite for food and pretty women. He tried to indulge in both with Elizabeth over lunch. He succeeded only in inhaling two plates of crab cakes and lots of vodka straight up. She sloughed off his double entendres and kept him on task even as he grew more openly inebriated.

He'd been living what he clearly saw as the good life since 1993, when he'd fled Russia, lured by US money set aside precisely for the purpose of buying up the suddenly unemployed Soviet nuclear talent. But in the years before the Soviet Union imploded and he embraced the West's fulsome lifestyle, his ministry produced fissile materials. The finished products—weapons—were then turned over to the Soviet Ministry of Defense.

"Those guys at Minatom"—the Ministry for Atomic Energy of the Russian Federation—"were cowboys," Gorelik sputtered, adopting the lingo of his host country as he raised his glass and downed yet another export from the one he'd left behind. He explained that many of his coworkers at Minatom had become "consultants" for countries seeking to develop nuclear weapons. Not a bulletin to Elizabeth, but it pleased her to see how readily he provided such an offering.

"Which ones?" Elizabeth asked, leaning forward, painfully aware his eyes had settled on her cleavage, exactly as she had intended them to. But even that provocation couldn't get him to divulge the names of more than one nation. That revelation, however, proved to be a zinger and made it into her report, which she sat in her desk chair rereading now: "One of Gorelik's friends gave an Iranian agent a complete directory of all fissile material storage sites in the former Soviet Union. His comrade also provided an estimated inventory at those sites."

When Gorelik had told her that at the Metropolitan Club, pausing only to devour an entire crab cake in a single bite, she had come to understand the twisting trail of events that had marked her life. It had begun with the dismantling of the Berlin Wall, which she'd watched on television as a young teen, and led her to Kazakhstan with Stinger missiles on her first mission for the CIA.

Where's the trail going next? she wondered. She sat back in her desk chair and gazed out her window at a lone leaf that had already turned red. It fluttered, and she remembered that the crimson color was always there. It just couldn't come out until the leaf started to die.

Like blood, she thought with a start.

She met Peter Gallagher when she joined her coworkers for an evening of pizza and beer in Georgetown. He was boyish and cute, with male pattern baldness before age thirty. Elizabeth ended up sitting next to him in a restaurant that featured wood-fired ovens and a casual atmosphere. Peter let on quickly that he was a graduate of the Massachusetts Institute of Technology. Elizabeth realized he'd been about a mile downriver while she was attending Harvard. But his interests were in science, and they'd taken him to the Treasury Department's security division.

"*Security's* a pretty broad term," she said to him. "What specifically do you do?"

"It's not just your agency that requires discretion," he volleyed.

"Is someone from the CIA at this table?" she whispered in his ear.

He rolled his eyes but relented, as she'd guessed he would. "Well, everybody thinks the Secret Service pretty much protects the president and makes sure nobody's counterfeiting the precious dollar. But guess what?"

"What?" she said playfully.

Now he whispered to her, and she felt his warm breath on her ear. "We help the CIA counterfeit *other* people's money."

"That is so bad. You should be ashamed. What hypocrites."

It took Peter a couple of beats to understand she was kidding. While he recovered, Elizabeth thought it would be nice to thank him for the handsome *tenge* notes she'd used on her excursion to Kazakhstan. But of course she couldn't.

"So tell me, Elizabeth," he whispered, "do you like bad boys?"

Now it was her turn to roll her eyes.

The following week the agency asked her to meet with Gerhardt Mertens, a strapping, six-foot-six German construction contractor. He insisted on a walk along the Potomac, and the way his dark blue eyes darted about, she could tell he was worried about eavesdroppers. Oddly, though, he never thought to ask if she were wired. Perhaps he simply assumed she was. If so, Mertens was correct. But he clearly had concerns about other ears, making no secret of his obvious surveillance of their immediate surroundings.

Unlike Gorelik, Mertens, with his thinning, white hair and the notable fitness of a man who had spent his life working hard outdoors, eschewed any small talk. And he spared her the sexual overtures and undertones that had pocked the Russian's conversation.

As they started walking, Elizabeth realized Mertens's English, while accented heavily, would read smoothly in transcription. He unabashedly admitted building underground bunkers all over the Middle East. He didn't add "for tyrants," though the addendum occurred readily enough to Elizabeth.

"Easy work. Good money," Martens said. "Those Arabs, they love their pyramids."

Several runners moved past them, silencing him at once, as did a woman with a jogging stroller for a toddler. But otherwise Mertens spoke easily.

"I am a builder. None of it bothered me. But I will tell you, that changed when I went to Iran."

He nodded emphatically, and she gave him the prompting he clearly wanted: "What happened there?"

"Two years," Mertens said, raising his fingers as if he were offering her the peace symbol. Most decidedly, he was not: "That's how long I spent building concrete boxes all over the place. And not just boxes. Oh, *no*. Every one of them we protected with layers of reinforced concrete, dirt, and then *more* concrete and rebar. Then *more* dirt and more concrete."

"Why all the layering?" she asked. She had a pretty good idea but wanted to hear it from him.

Mertens eyed a Middle Easterner with open suspicion. The dark-skinned man in a turban turned away. Elizabeth wished Mertens hadn't done that. Some of the agency's most valuable hands came from the Middle East, and they needed more of them. For all she knew, the man might have been a colleague.

"To protect against penetrating bombs," Mertens said. "Those places? I began to see they weren't really just rooms. More like hangars or factories—the kind of stuff Hitler would have liked. Creepy."

He scowled, and seconds later peeled away from her. "I'm going now. You didn't hear this from me."

She thought he had an unnecessarily dramatic flair, but his information was consistent with what the agency had been hearing from contacts in situ. Bunker building? Attempts to buy or steal nuclear bomb-making materials? A lot of breast beating against the Great Satan? You didn't have to be a foreign policy wonk to add that up. And you didn't need to be paranoid to be scared.

Over Labor Day weekend, Elizabeth and her colleagues from Langley fled to a rented beach house on the Delaware shore. Someone—she didn't know who—had also invited Peter Gallagher and given him the room next to hers. But from the way he lit up when he saw her, she knew at once where he really hoped to bed down.

The first evening, after he'd had three drinks of courage, he slipped his arm around her lower back as they stood in the large kitchen of the beach house along with half a dozen other revelers.

"Don't do that," she said softly, not wanting to embarrass him. He withdrew his arm, but the next day he finagled her as a doubles tennis partner. After they retired the competition, they played against each other. Elizabeth was good, but so was he. She thoroughly enjoyed the face-off.

And if she could have kept him at racket's length, she might have enjoyed his company as well. But as soon as they took a break, he cornered her with a monologue about currency engraving. She imagined telling her father that one could not overestimate the boredom induced by the details of ink, paper, and presses. She escaped to shower as one might duck a conversation at a party by heading to the bathroom, but Peter reappeared over barbecued chicken to tell her the less than fascinating tale of counterfeiting rupees.

"Millions of them!" he exclaimed.

She couldn't imagine that his bosses at Treasury would have approved of his using state secrets as a tool of attempted seduction. Painfully, Elizabeth realized she would have to report him to her own agency. Talk about a loose cannon. She could just imagine the headlines in *The Times of India* if he kept up his patter. But she also knew better than to give away *her* game by sounding censorious, so she joined in the playful repartee.

"Rupees? Who cares? How are you with Benjamins?" she joked. He laughed but wagged his finger as if reproaching her.

Elizabeth feigned fatigue and retired early with a history of the Cold War. It kept her awake far longer than she'd expected, and when she heard a soft knock on her door she realized her bedside lamp had thrown too much light.

"You awake?" Peter asked softly.

"Yes." The impatience in her voice was measureable, but Peter wasn't thinking with his ears.

"You had to play really hard to keep up with me, so I thought I'd make it up to you by giving you a massage."

"No," she said, shaking her head for emphasis even though he couldn't see her.

"Because I—"

"No."

When she heard him turn the door handle anyway, she said, "Now you're risking dismemberment."

The handle turned back the other way.

"Maybe you should give this Peter fellow a chance," her father said when she got home late on Labor Day proper and told him about the weekend. They'd retired to the deck in back and clinked beer bottles in a silent salute. "We could use a good counterfeiter in the family," he added, reminding her of Gomez Addams again. They both laughed.

"He's a bore. A pest."

"You finding anyone you're interested in?" he asked.

She shook her head. "What's strange to me is I'm finding myself more interested in older guys."

He put aside his beer. "I don't want a son-in-law my age."

"Don't be ridiculous," she shot back. "I mean guys ten, fifteen years older. But most of them are taken."

"It'll happen when you least expect it, Lizzie. You'll see."

Lately the only unexpected experience she'd had was a ladder breaking while she was lugging a Stinger missile up to a roof. An omen of the unexpected? She hoped not.

Elizabeth's assignment to write a chronicle of Iran's attempts to build a bomb took her into a SCIF, one of the agency's most secure rooms at Langley. The austere chamber had no windows, and the walls and ceilings were built of masonry, not studs and wallboard. Moreover they were filled with sheets of metal foil, which would stop any unauthorized bugging. There were motion detectors in the corners of the ceiling to detect off-hour intruders. The room appeared barren, with a conference table and chairs. Nothing else.

Elizabeth was not permitted to bring her laptop. She would use the one provided for her. As for a cell phone or camera, no way. Even to enter the compartment was a procedure. A woman from the agency's security office gave her a briefing on the man awaiting her arrival. Often the identity of an informant was kept secret, but that was not the case with Jack Rosengren, a former Los Alamos physicist now transferred to the UN's International Atomic Energy Agency in Vienna.

After the security officer told Elizabeth all the dire consequences she would suffer if she leaked any of the information she learned in the SCIF, the stern-looking woman had the young operative sign a document confirming her receipt of the briefing—and the threats.

Rosengren, an older man with ample hair and an intelligent demeanor, had been part of an IAEA team that traveled to South Africa in the early

'90s to oversee that country's withdrawal from nuclear weapons status. Elizabeth saw very quickly he possessed an unusual blend of paranoia and iconoclasm. In short he made it clear he didn't believe anything without verification, which left him with little regard for overseas sources.

He offered his own disclosures about the South Africans with blunt efficiency: "When they announced an end to nuclear production and the closing of all the plants, the engineers at ARMSCOR"—the Arms Corporation of South Africa—"were not pleased."

Back in 1989, Elizabeth noted to herself.

"It's the same problem we're still having with a lot of the Soviet scientists. The guys at ARMSCOR wanted millions to retire. Right to our faces they threatened to sell the technology if ARMSCOR didn't pay up. But a few payouts here, a few more there, and we thought we had the situation under control. Then a Pakistani by the name of A.Q. Khan started recruiting them right out from under our noses. We felt like the Dutch boy with his finger in the dike. And we did okay except for one guy. You're going to want to note this name: Lowell Hout."

"Nuclear physicist?" she asked. Rosengren nodded. "What happened to him?" she followed up.

Now Rosengren shrugged. "Have no idea, but from the time I met him I knew he'd go to the highest bidder. Some place with a lot of *oil*."

"Someplace like Iran?"

Rosengren nodded again. "*Exactamente*."

A few days later Elizabeth met with Massoud Naraghi in an anonymous motel room on the outskirts of Fairfax. The fidgety, dark-haired man was a defecting Iranian engineer who confirmed only what the growing body of evidence pointed to: Iran was making an enormous effort to build a nuclear bomb.

Naraghi began to pace as he told her the war with Iraq had exposed Iran's military weaknesses, and the Iranian mullahs had authorized him to talk with the ubiquitous Khan.

"So where and when did you meet with him?" Elizabeth asked.

"Dubai, thirteen years ago. This was right after we heard Kahn would sell us what we wanted."

"Which was?"

Naraghi took an obvious breath. "Uranium enrichment technology." He said those words like he was reading from the Koran, and Elizabeth recognized the reverence a man of science could have for the unbridled power of the atom.

"And what did you want the enrichment technology for?" She pressed him for absolute clarification.

"A nuclear bomb."

Bingo!

"So you were willing to pay him?"

Naraghi confined his response to a quick nod.

"What was Khan like?"

"Intense. He wanted a decision from us fast. I thought he was on a deadline."

"Okay, so what did you tell him?" Elizabeth asked.

"That we were ready to pay him, and we did. We wanted to enrich uranium or breed plutonium in our country. But we were already looking at stealing it from the former Soviet republics or—"

"Steal it?"

Naraghi nodded again. "We had agents going all over the 'stans." The nickname for the former Soviet Muslim republics ending in the suffix.

"What other approaches were you taking?"

"We would have bought it from China or North Korea if we could have. We were looking at every option."

"But you couldn't?"

"Not then. I don't know about now."

Elizabeth left the motel feeling lightheaded. Naraghi was the real deal: an Iranian insider with firsthand knowledge of his own country's nuclear ambitions and the shadowy Khan.

She rendezvoused with the field men who'd wired her along with the security officers who were tasked with preventing any assassination attempts on Naraghi or her. One of them drove her back to Langley. Neither of them spoke of the momentous meeting.

Meantime the agency was pulling in phone intercepts showing Iran had already established a nuclear weapons lab north of Tehran. Not a science lab, as Iranian leaders were claiming, but a nuclear development center with high-explosive test facilities. It was known as FEDAT. But what the reports intercepted from those attending indicated was that Iran, curiously, was not not bent on terror. Its leaders wanted nukes to reach four principal objectives: to use as deterrents to keep the US at bay; to have devastating power to gain control of Middle Eastern oil—half the world's supply; to overwhelm their Sunni neighbors, especially Iraq; and to take back control of the holy cities of Mecca and Medina.

The fact that the intercepts indicated no interest in terror would have been reassuring but for all the mullahs's edgy talk about "God's will" and "the end of days."

What does that *mean?*

The real keeper among the intercepts was that the religious leaders driving Iranian policies wanted their first live nuclear test to be a stunning *political* statement. They wanted to keep casualties to a minimum yet upset the international order in an unforgettable manner. Chillingly they referred to America's downing of Iran Air 655 as presenting an acceptable casualty level for "the other side." There had been 290 people aboard that flight.

Tit for tat? Elizabeth wondered.

Before she wrote her report for the senior agency staff, she met with two young Basiji militants in a small room at the venerable Willard Hotel in downtown Washington. This time she was not told the identities of the informants, though she knew right away they would have bristled had they known they'd been classified as traitors.

The pair, both thin and bespectacled, openly disdained Elizabeth but were happy to take agency money. Without any hesitation they stated they did not trust their current president, Mohammad Khatami. Hearing their brazen denunciation of their elected leader made Elizabeth think the military had plans to dump the moderate Khatami—and soon.

"Why are you unhappy with him?"

"He does not want to see the nuclear program continue," the shorter of the pair said.

"And that is why we will have one of our own as president in 2005," his cohort said with obvious pride, noting the year of the next Iranian election.

The interview ended after Elizabeth endured half a dozen citations from the Koran. Nonetheless, she thanked them curtly. They shook their heads like she was a fool. They might as well have said they planned to return as victors.

❀ ❀ ❀

In late September Elizabeth presented her conclusions to the agency's senior staff. Seven men and two women faced her in another Langley SCIF.

"What we're finding"—she used the editorial "we" out of modesty— "is Iran poses by far the most serious politico-nuclear threat to the stability and economies of the Western world."

After putting that kettle on high, she continued: "Pakistan has tested nukes and is clearly beholden to fanatics but has no real government. North Korea is a Chinese substate charged with annoying the West. It's already a serious supplier of nuclear technology and missiles to other proliferators— people who are harvesting plutonium from their fuel rods. Even so North Korea is not going to attack anybody. They're broke, starving, in the worst of straits.

"As for Iraq, that county is as good as dead. Saddam is all blow and no go. But as I said." She paused and looked at her listeners. "Iran poses the real long-term danger."

She dotted a lot of i's and crossed a lot of t's before she finished. Elizabeth believed she'd done a good job of convincing her audience. Deputy Director Roberson congratulated her, and other senior staff joined in.

Two other notable briefings followed. In early October Elizabeth held separate meetings with the designated transition aides of the two major candidates. Whoever won—and from the polls the election looked like it would be tighter than a noose on a traitor—she was in line for a non-partisan, intelligence-community job in the new administration. She was thrilled by the prospect of working in the heart of Washington, so close to the seat of power.

Who wouldn't be? she asked herself in an exuberant moment.

But Elizabeth had no idea how twisted and perilous that path would become for both herself and her country.

CHAPTER 5
9/11

2001–2002

It didn't become clear which administration would employ her until December, when the US Supreme Court confirmed the election of George W. Bush. A week later the president elect identified Condoleezza Rice as his national security advisor.

During the transition Elizabeth developed a strong relationship with Rice. They were both serious athletes, and Rice made no secret of her real ambition: to become commissioner of the National Football League. Fitting, given that she reportedly snuggled with a football in her crib.

Condi was twenty years older than Elizabeth. The younger woman took heart in seeing that Rice was single, successful, and plenty driven. *Sounds like me,* she thought. *Happy, too.*

Often at dawn the two women donned running shoes, sunglasses, and ball caps to jog along the Potomac in anonymity. Condi was kind and offered advice Elizabeth considered worth remembering, including, "Be careful of close attachments."

Once Bush was inaugurated, Rice took over management of the National Security Council staff. Elizabeth's mandate was to handle part of the intelligence portfolio for the NSC. This charge included welcoming her old friends from Moscow—men now searching for safe havens for the wealth they'd plundered from their floundering nation.

A former date took her to dinner at the Hay-Adams, one of the city's most venerable bistros. With a pianist offering artful jazz standards and classical music, the Russian expat told Elizabeth Moscow was a different place now.

"Putin is hazardous to our health. He offers us a deal. We get to keep our wealth and stay out of prison but *only* if we stay out of politics. He's collecting power like crazy, Elizabeth. He wants to be the new tsar. He *is* the new tsar. I'm just glad I have an anchor to windward at the Bank of New York."

She reported everything she learned from the Russian émigrés, but her attention remained fixed mostly on Iran.

Like all good NSC staffers, Elizabeth came to work right after her early morning run. While sipping strong coffee, she read reports from the other side of the world, where friends and foes had been busy during their own daylight hours.

By 8:00 a.m. on a clear September morning, Elizabeth had started preparing options for the president's responses. She could breathe a little easier because Bush was travelling in Florida. There would be no 9:00 meeting. But she did have to focus on the summaries Condi would send along to Air Force One.

Those summaries never made it. A little after eight a message came from the Situation Room in the White House: "Hijacking in progress."

At quarter to nine, NORAD—North American Aerospace Defense Command—scrambled two F-15s from Otis Air Force Base on Cape Cod to intercept and interrogate an American Airlines flight out of Boston. But the F-15s were too late: American flight 11 had just hit the North Tower of the World Trade Center. The scene came to life on American TV screens. Fifteen minutes later United flight 175 hit the South Tower.

Condoleezza Rice sent a message to the president, who was sitting in a schoolroom in Florida: "America is under attack." The most chilling words Elizabeth had ever read.

By nine thirty the Secret Service had rushed Vice President Cheney to a bunker under the East Wing of the White House. Loudspeakers and emergency communication links directed the NSC staff to evacuate: "Now, on the double!"

In minutes Elizabeth saw that everyone in the White House complex was on the run. She kept pace with the equally alert Rice as she sprinted across the south lawn.

"Over there," Elizabeth cried out, pointing to another huge cloud of smoke. "The Pentagon's been hit too!"

"Everything's changed," Rice said.

No kidding, Elizabeth thought.

She promptly joined her CIA colleagues on three planning fronts: air attacks on the al-Qaeda camps in Afghanistan; support of the native Northern Alliance military forces there; and, finally, the insertion of US troops into the fight.

The Taliban fled Kabul in November and were driven from Kandahar in December. US Special Forces had Osama bin Laden virtually cornered in the Tora Bora Mountains by the end of the year. Communication intercepts confirmed he was there. It seemed to Elizabeth, at her desk in Langley, that the mastermind of the 9/11 attacks was finished thanks to a strong US response by armed CIA detachments. But the secretary of defense bewildered her—and many others in the intelligence community—by declining to block the exit routes from Tora Bora over the pass into Pakistan. Officers in the field were dumbfounded. Predictably, bin Laden escaped.

Elizabeth, along with other members of the NSC staff, helped formulate the Axis of Evil concept President Bush would use in his State of the Union speech to identify Iraq, Iran, and North Korea as America's newly identified enemies. She felt uneasy with that formulation because, in her view, as far as a threat, Iran stood head and shoulders above those other two economically collapsed states.

Her uneasiness intensified when she was asked to brief troops from the CIA's Special Activities Directorate as they headed to Iraq. The men and women were going overseas to try to convince Iraq's generals in the field that their best interests would be served by flipping over to the US side *when* the invasion came.

Then an explosive allegation came from an Iranian exile group, the National Council of Resistance. The Washington press corps assembled at the Willard Hotel on August 14, 2002 to hear a startling statement from the group's spokesman.

"Iran is planning to enrich uranium at a secret facility in Natanz," the older man told his rapt listeners. "They look to their still-incomplete nuclear reactor at Bushehr as a future source of plutonium." The spokesman provided documentation and maps.

Elizabeth and the NSC staff noted these Iranian disclosures with keen interest, but the White House focus was on Iraq. In fact some on the NSC, along with the White House speechwriters, were already working on a presidential message to the United Nations calling for an assault on Saddam's government.

Once more Elizabeth found herself on the back deck with her father on Labor Day, but this time her lament wasn't over a young man. It was over the profound mistakes the Bush White House was making in the Middle East.

"Dad, these guys have their eyes on the wrong ball. All this WMD stuff in Iraq is baloney. The so-called evidence is fabricated. Iraq doesn't have any nukes. They have no route for getting any nukes. Iran, though, *is* marching down the nuclear path. And North Korea is breeding plutonium *now*. Our vice president has his head up and locked!"

"You're right, Lizzie. They're picking the wrong war in the wrong place at the wrong time. And there could be real hell to pay."

But the message from the White House was clear: Iraq was the target, not Iran. A profound mistake in Elizabeth's view. Iraq did not possess weapons of mass destruction. The UN inspectors had done their jobs and the US-imposed sanctions had turned Iraq into an empty shell. But Iran— *My God!*—was pursuing a game-changing nuclear bomb. Elizabeth grew so desperate, she wished she could have parachuted into Tehran and found the real smoking gun that could have produced a real mushroom cloud, not the chimera her old friend Condi Rice was chasing. But there was no reaching Rice now, not literally or figuratively. Their last encounter was at an NSC staff meeting, when Rice turned to the NSC staff and declared, "We need to know how the Shiite civilians will react when we invade Iraq." Not *if* but *when*.

A fait accompli, Elizabeth realized.

Rice then spelled out the background of Iran's first revolutionary president, Abulhassan Banisadr.

"He comes from a leading Shia family from both sides of the border." She meant the long-embattled Iran-Iraq border. Banisadr, she noted, had been a street demonstrator during the Mossadegh crisis of '53; the US and UK had backed a coup that toppled the democratically elected leader. Banisadr was arrested twice, wounded once, and then fled to Paris, where he grew close to the Ayatollah Khomeini. He returned to Tehran on the Ayatollah's jet in '79 and a year later was given the presidency of the new Islamic Republic. But two years later he suffered a fall from grace and was removed from office by the Majlis, the legislative body in Iran. Realizing he was now a candidate only for assassination, Banisadr fled back to Paris, where he became a reformist voice in the growing Iranian exile community.

Elizabeth knew the history well, including the fact that the agency had built ties to Banisadr during the hostage crisis twenty years earlier, which Condi was addressing at the very moment.

"But that was when he got on the wrong side of Khomeini," Condi added a second later.

To say the least, thought Elizabeth. The ex-president, disguised as a woman in chador, had been forced to flee for his life aboard a defector's 707.

"Elizabeth." Condi turned to her. "Let's get Banisadr's take on how the Shiites in Iraq are likely to respond to our invasion. I'd like a private visit before the end of the year."

Elizabeth tapped away at her laptop as Rice went on,

"I think he'll confirm our thinking that when we knock off the Sunni scum in Baghdad, we'll be greeted as heroes, just like the Americans entering Paris in '44. The Kurds and Shiites hate Saddam, but let's get some confirmation from Banisadr." She looked directly at Elizabeth. "Keep me posted."

The momentum for an invasion of Iraq had grown only more powerful since that meeting. Now Elizabeth finished her homework on Banisadr by pulling yet another of the CIA's Iranian Revolution files.

TEHRAN, JANUARY 1979

The more successful Iranian citizens have long since fled, many to California and Texas. The oil companies and their contractors are doing their best to escape the chaos. The city of Tehran has become an armed camp; the city of Qom is an epicenter of religious fanaticism.

Military officers remaining in Iran are calculating their odds. Some are hoping for a coup; others are planning to switch sides.

Our confused administration in Washington is sending mixed messages and divergent envoys. The American ambassador is to deal with Khomeini; the Pentagon's man is to stiffen the spine of the military. Within this bedlam the Shah's Armed Forces Chief of Staff, General Abbas Gharabaghi, sits firmly athwart the fence.

A-ha, thought Elizabeth. That was precisely what that Major Ashkan Gharabaghi character had admitted in Moscow: that his father had been an opportunistic whore.

She quickly unearthed another memo, dated August 1981.

When Khomeini and Banisadr arrived at Tehran's Mehrabad Airport in February 1979, it was General Gharabaghi who assured their safe travel to the arms of their allies downtown. A week later order collapsed; the troops began to mutiny, shooting their officers. Only Abbas Gharabaghi, the chameleon general, survived. He was tolerated by the new regime and now enjoys a gracious retirement in Paris as a guest of the ever-accommodating French.

Mr. Banisadr was ousted last week. He was accompanied into Parisian exile by his family. They all settled into a secure enclave managed by the French security service at Versailles. They are supported by the Compagnie Talleyrand, the world's largest and most successful oilfield services firm. Talleyrand's operations in Iran survived the '79 revolution. Tallyrand worked both sides of the street quite well. They are still there.

With the last of her research completed, Elizabeth contacted the CIA station chief in Paris. Using encryption, she wrote: "Condoleezza Rice wants to talk to Abulhassan Banisadr on the QT. Agenda is classified, but I'm sure Banisadr is smart enough to figure it out. Can you arrange for him to visit DC this fall? Fund citations to follow." The latter referred to the payment Banisadr would receive. Elizabeth guessed it would be substantial.

At the end of the week, she received the answer Condi Rice wanted: "Your client, code name Albert, is willing to come to the US if he can bring his wife and son and, after meeting with Rice, he can spend the holidays in Houston with his younger brother, a fellow refugee who fled aboard the 707."

The communiqué continued by noting Banisadr's brother, Reza, and his wife, Genevieve, had emigrated from Paris to Houston, probably to assure US citizenship for their expected child. The station chief added, "We helped them with visas and green cards. Reza went to work for Talleyrand as a well-paid field engineer. We will ticket from here."

So a powerful chapter of Iranian history, in the personage of Banisadr, would arrive about the same time Santa Claus made his rounds. Elizabeth considered the imminent appearance of the former Iranian president a gift of the first order. But even the finest wrapping can shroud the most disturbing treachery.

CHAPTER 6
NEW VENUES

December 2002–July 2005

Abulhassan Banisadr sat across from Elizabeth in one of Washington's favorite barbecue joints. To her delight the Iranian expatriate and his family preferred down-home fare to the exclusive eateries of Georgetown. The former president of Iran handled his ribs like a cowhand accustomed to a chow line.

Now he took a damp cloth, dabbing sauce from his lips and just below his apple cheeks. After wiping his hands, he sat back as a waiter swooped low to remove the remains of his dinner. His deferential Muslim wife followed his cue immediately, although half her ribs were uneaten. But his son, Mehdi, glared when the waiter asked if he'd like him to remove his plate, then swatted the air above his plate as if he were disgusted with what he'd just consumed.

Intrigued, Elizabeth watched him closely. Mehdi, all of seventeen and awkward in appearance—a child who *might* grow into his prodigious nose—had shaken his head at the café's surrounds and muttered, "America" so softly she might have missed the way her country's name had been used as an epithet. He had bowed his head and prayed before eating, which gave pause to his parents, who followed suit; but then the boy plundered his plate and sucked down three root beers. He seemed as balled up in contradictions as many American teens. Elizabeth wondered what would win out in the end: Mehdi's delight in America's unabashed consumer culture or his rigorous adherence to Islamic precepts. No telling at his age.

"That was, how shall I say it? Delightful," his father said. Abulhassan's wife nodded quickly. His son shook his head as if his father were a wart.

"How about some dessert?" Elizabeth asked. "Cheesecake?"

His wife, whimsically named Ozra, watched him closely. As soon as he said, "Oh, I couldn't," she shook her head. But Mehdi brightened, if only for a moment.

"I want some," he then said gruffly.

With blueberry topping, as it turned out. He devoured a piece of cake, as large as the Lincoln Memorial, with his cell phone at his ear.

"Are you looking forward to the meeting tomorrow?" Elizabeth asked Iran's former president. Banisadr would be conferring with Vice President Cheney and Condoleezza Rice in the Old Executive Office Building. Elizabeth—*Argh!*—had not been invited. But she thought she might garner a preview of his views right here in one of Washington's less tony districts.

"Yes, it will be an honor to meet your vice president," Banisadr said formally, his eyes looking past her from behind the dark, rectangular glasses he had long favored. She glanced to the side and saw the shapely form of the waitress who had lured the Muslim's eyes.

"Do you think the Shia in Iraq will support an American invasion of their country?" She hoped not—anything to put a brake on that dismal development. But she also knew it was a fool's mission to think the Shiites wouldn't back the US. Their support for an invasion would come despite the sect's bitterness over what its leadership viewed as a betrayal at the end of the Gulf War in 1991. The US had called for a Shia insurrection, but US military support never came. When the Shiites did rise up, they were promptly cut down by Saddam's helicopters and hoods.

"Do I think my brethren will support the Americans this time?" The former president repeated the gist of her question. He nodded, but his actual words proved ambiguous: "My brethren will do the right thing."

She considered that phrase typical of the Arab world: not an answer, but not an impolite rebuff either.

The elder Banisadr turned to Mehdi, who was still on his phone. "Are you done, my son?" The disagreeable young man answered by flicking his fingers at his plate again.

Elizabeth grabbed the check. The next day she learned Banisadr had, indeed, entered the Old Executive Office Building and told the vice president he could expect Shia support for an invasion of Iraq. Which no doubt pleased Cheney as much as it made painful sense to Elizabeth. Iraq was ruled by tyrannical Sunni Muslims who had long persecuted the Shia, the actual majority in that country. Of course Shiites would let bygones be bygones if an invasion, promoted partly as an attempt to spread democracy in the Middle East, would put them in power. But wouldn't that strengthen Iran's hand? To have their so-called brethren in control next door?

That much-more vexing question was never asked by the VP, according to Elizabeth's sources. Neither was the exploration of other complex Middle Eastern issues that might have undermined the will for war. Elizabeth was beginning to feel like she'd landed in the middle of the Hans Christian Andersen tale about an emperor who wore no clothes.

Three days after arriving in Washington, the Banisadr family flew to Houston. Mehdi appeared ecstatic at the prospect of meeting his cousin, Rosincourt.

Seventeen years earlier, Rosincourt Sadr, a squalling, dark-haired baby boy, had been taken home from hospital to the exclusive River Oaks section of Houston. Spanish moss hung from the oaks shading the estates, including the manse where a throng of Iranian expatriates had gathered to greet the infant swaddled so lovingly in a soft, white blanket. The crowd celebrated with cookies and cakes, fruit juice and candy.

Rosincourt grew up with the advantages of wealth. He spent the 1990s at St. John's, a university-preparatory school, becoming as fluent in Spanish as he was in his native Farsi. He also did exceptionally well in science.

Despite his Muslim background, his father wanted the young man to attend a proper Christian school in the heart of upscale Houston to assure his son's acceptance in the Texas establishment. But at home Shia teachings prevailed. The boy led what might have appeared to be a spiritually divided life, but while he was respectful of his Christian peers, his home life inoculated him against the larger culture that competed for his attention.

Rosincourt's mother discouraged his participation in athletics. She didn't want him to get hurt. Neither did she encourage him to form close friendships at school. With his dark complexion and black hair and eyes, Rosincourt appeared like any other friendly immigrant child. A budding all-American. But he was a young man who was socially isolated, and when he did engage with peers he was never a leader; even in a crowd he remained a loner.

Tinkering in the family garage—which was larger than many homes in more modest sections of Houston—was Rosincourt's *raison d'être*. Clearly he was a skilled mechanic or engineer in the making. His father noted this and took him out to the oil fields of East Texas and Southern Louisiana when his company was logging a well.

When the Banisadr family visited, Rosincourt and Mehdi were both seniors in high school yet had never met. Over the holidays their parents enthusiastically exchanged stories and photos of their children, but as the visit grew to weeks it became clear Mehdi, who had come of age in Paris, was the golden boy of the extended Banisadr family. His high school years in France had been filled with accomplishments and academic awards while Rosincourt was said to have been "finding himself." Left to themselves, though, the teenagers were equals with their own worlds to explore.

Mehdi urged Rosincourt to show him around the city. With the Texan navigating from the passenger seat, the sophisticated Parisian took the wheel of a his father's rented SUV and drove them to places in Houston that Rosincourt had never seen—barrios with gang graffiti on highway overpasses and school buildings.

"Look around, Rosincourt," Mehdi said more than once. "This is the real America."

The real America? Rosincourt wondered what he meant. His America was far preferable to this. He shrugged and suggested they visit San Jacinto, where a towering obelisk stood high above the stars and stripes and the Lone Star State's own flag. The world's tallest war monument honored the battle that had freed Texas from Mexico. Nearby they also toured the battleship *Texas*.

"It fought in both wars," Rosincourt told Mehdi.

"Which ones?" the Parisian snarled. "The Gulf War or the one they're planning?"

Mehdi lightened up when he had a chance to chase young women down in Galveston, where the beaches, on this warm January day, attracted local girls. But his avid interest was returned with only tepid smiles, and he announced they were "not nearly as pretty as the chicks in Paris."

Near the end of Mehdi's visit, the boys spent an evening on the Banisadr veranda, where the more outspoken young man talked about the future of

Iran. Rosincourt found his cousin anxious and intense when he paced and spoke about his fellow Shia. A zealot, actually, which was a word his own father had used to describe some of the extreme Christian fundamentalists in America. Mehdi seemed kind of like them. He couldn't talk about the rise of Islam without clenching his fists and punching the night air as if he had just declared victory in some war for the heart and soul of his religion.

"My father"—Mehdi suddenly stopped walking and his face loomed inches from Rosincourt's—"is too careful. He's too caught up in the past. Stuffy," he said, as if it were a curse. "He is a wimp. Do you know that word?" he asked Rosincourt.

"Sure."

"That's what our fathers are. They have become too westernized."

What about you? Rosincourt wondered. Day after day he'd watched his cousin revel in all things American, and he appeared to love Paris. The last time Rosincourt checked, France was sure part of the West.

But Rosincourt also understood the appeal of the simpler life promised by his cousin's brand of Islam. It was uncluttered by the confusion of America. But mostly Rosincourt wanted a nonpolitical life and a challenging job designing machines.

As 2003 dawned Abulhassan Banisadr loaded his family into the big SUV for their trip to the airport and their flight back to Paris. As they drove away, Rosincourt watched the window come down on the front passenger side, where Mehdi had long ago replaced his mother. She now sat by herself behind her husband and son.

"Hang in there, Roz," Mehdi shouted. "A new Iran is coming!"

What the hell does that mean? Rosincourt wondered. *I was born here. Who cares?*

A new Iran was all too real to Elizabeth. She thought the Iranians had to be jubilant over seeing their enemy, Iraq, so clearly in the crosshairs of the US. To justify an invasion, the Bush administration was leaning heavily on phony documents about yellow-cake uranium from Niger and conveniently mislabeled aluminum tubes from China. She, and others in the intelligence community, rued the secretary of state's eloquent but unsupportable speech to the UN in February. Elizabeth couldn't bear to be part of that intelligence debacle any longer. She asked to be transferred from the NSC to the 9/11 Commission starting work in New York. But she could not get away from the Iranians: National Security Administration phone intercepts, unearthed late in the 9/11 investigation, revealed a significant Iranian role in providing logistical support to the hijackers. Tehran, it turned out, had facilitated the travel of the conspirators to and from Afghanistan and Pakistan as the 9/11 plot developed. Ten of the fourteen Saudi terrorists aboard the hijacked planes had travelled into and out of Iran between October 2000 and February 2001. Coincidence? She thought not. But those NSA revelations, as startling as they were to Elizabeth and others on the 9/11 Commission, led to conclusions the Bush administration did not want to hear. Its focus remained on Iraq.

Elizabeth and the others tried to rewrite the panel's conclusions, but the commissioners wanted no further delay. They appeared exhausted. The report they issued in August 2004 ignored Iranian involvement. Disheartened, Elizabeth returned to the National Security Council in Washington to prepare for the next transition.

With the coming of George W. Bush's second term in 2005, Condi Rice was nominated to serve as secretary of state. She asked Elizabeth to join the team. Elizabeth declined. She believed the invasion of Iraq had set off a horror story in that country. It would surely be fueled by Iran's ambitions.

She felt like she'd plunged into Alice's rabbit hole, where nothing appeared as it seemed. Not even her friendship with the self-absorbed Peter Gallagher. In the Spring of '05, he came flitting out of her past to invite her to dinner.

"Sure," Elizabeth said. She'd heard of the restaurant, 1789, but knew little of its reputation as a wonderful place for a mood-enhancing dinner date. When Peter escorted her past the heavy wooden doors and she spied the large hearth, beamed ceilings, candles, and cozy atmosphere she felt a jolt of discomfort, which was not alleviated by Peter's whispering, "Romantic, isn't it?"

She said nothing, suppressing the flip response that came almost immediately to mind: "The *restaurant* is." Was he delusional? She'd spurned his every romantic advance, from an arm around the waist in a beach-house kitchen to his ridiculous offer of a back massage proffered because she'd had to work so hard to keep up with him at tennis. Which was a joke. As she recalled they'd been so evenly matched she'd worked him into a froth.

Well, maybe in more ways than one. After they settled and Peter conferred with the wine steward, he cleared his throat. She could tell he was about to make an announcement. *Dear God, don't let it be a proposal.*

When was the last time she'd seen him? It had been at least a year. *What's going on?*

"I've accepted an assignment on the front lines, Elizabeth."

The front lines? What is this? Rick's Café in Casablanca?

"I won't be seeing you for a while. We need to get on with our lives."

She choked on her first sip of merlot and almost sprayed the table. He reached out and patted her shoulder. "You'll be okay, Elizabeth. I know it's all a bit sudden, but my country needs me. The currency people want *me* to move to Seoul to get closer to the counterfeiting factories up north. We want to intercept their phony bills the minute they cross the border, or when they leave China. It's critical work. I have to go. But I will miss you, Elizabeth, and I'm sure you'll find someone else. In time." He patted her again. "I'll keep in touch. Don't worry."

She wanted to scream. *Get a grip, get a grip,* she warned herself. She took a deep breath.

"Peter," she began, "have you noticed I've never let you kiss me or even hold my hand? I'm happy you've got a good career move in the making, but why do you think your departure means anything to me?"

"Elizabeth," he said patiently, furrowing his brow with concern, "I saw how you almost choked on your wine. You don't have to deny your feelings for me. They're very clear. They always have been."

"I was choking, Peter, in disbelief that you could think I would ever have any of those feelings for—"

"Look," he said, suddenly impatient, "if denial makes you feel any better about my leaving, then go into denial. I understand."

Elizabeth stood, the better to look down on him. When he started to rise, she put out her hand and he sat back down like a well-trained dog, though she was certain he lacked the emotional complexity of even the most simple-minded canine.

"I am leaving, Peter. Whatever you've been smoking, you should stop right now, before your delusions deepen."

She stepped out the doors she'd graced only minutes before and hailed a cab. As the driver pulled away, he said, "Didn't I see you walk in there a few minutes ago with some guy?"

"You did indeed."

"That's the shortest damn date I've seen in a while."

"Not short enough," Elizabeth replied.

When she arrived home, her father was sympathetic, but she knew her mother would have fumed with disapproval. She could almost hear Mom calling from the grave, "You'll never find a nice young man that way." How many times had Mother repeated those words to her? But they nagged at Elizabeth now, and even one of her father's vodka martinis couldn't take off the edge.

"Maybe I'm never going to meet anyone, Dad. But the nerve of that twerp."

Her father laughed, but gently. "Just be grateful, Baby Bear. He could have haunted you forever. He'll probably find a nice little wife who will indulge his every fantasy."

"Yeah, well, when am I going to find a nice little hubby to indulge mine?"

Her father eyed her over the rim of his glass. "I don't think I want to hear about your fantasies."

"Don't worry. Besides, they're in cold storage."

Even during her teens, Elizabeth had found herself impatient with her male contemporaries. She could never let them win, whether she was on her appaloosa in the Maryland countryside or swatting a tennis ball on neatly trimmed grass courts.

Yes, there had been ballet lessons thanks to her mother, but from the vantage point of adulthood she saw they'd only prepared her for gymnastics when she made it to Harvard. That and cross-country running at sunrise along the north side of the Charles River.

"Did I make that drink too strong?" her father asked her.

"What? No, not at all."

"Because you're looking kind of dreamy."

"Maybe I was. But it's nothing, really."

"Lizzie, you're good with languages. You want some career advice?"

"Go to the language school?" she replied, referring to the Defense Language School in Monterey, California. "Because if that's what you're suggesting, I've been thinking about it. Russian was great back in your day"—meaning during the Cold War—"but I could use Farsi a lot more now."

Her father nodded and offered a wicked smile. "Just don't go getting too enamored of the culture. I don't want to have to look at you through a veil."

"Oh, right, Dad, can't you just see me in a chador?"

He smiled, clearly amused by the absurdity. "Of course you could put in for the Korean language school if you really want to impress that boy of yours."

"Stop! Let's not even joke about it."

Elizabeth's request for a transfer and admission to the Defense Language School was approved quickly and actually applauded by the CIA hierarchy. She was all set to make the move later that summer, but then she received an urgent summons to see Deputy Director Roberson.

"Have a seat, Elizabeth," he said gravely. He turned his computer screen around so she could see it. "I want you to take a look at this."

The amateur video was blurry, but she had no trouble deciphering the images: people pushing, shoving, and screaming inside a train car. And then the camera zoomed in on a young woman in a burqa, smoke and flames rising all around her.

CHAPTER 7
THE GIRL IN THE CHARRED BURQA

July 2005

The burqa made Soroya Assaf cringe. Why was that woman wearing it? Couldn't she see the nasty looks she was getting on the Paris train? Soroya was worried someone might punch the woman. Even with chopped-off, green hair, Soroya didn't warrant a glance, but every time she looked back at her fellow Muslim traveler she could feel the hostility directed at the burqa. It was as real as the heat and humidity in the packed commuter car. *And people say the French are so civilized.* Soroya couldn't wait to get off at Versailles.

If anyone were likely to be sympathetic, it would have been Soroya Assaf, who had arrived in Paris six weeks earlier from Beverly Hills. But the French had made themselves clear enough on the subject of women in burqas when the National Assembly condemned traditional Muslim outfits that left women covered up and veiled. More to the point, the French had banned them in public places. But the fines were tiny and enforcement was feckless. The French as much as said, "Wear it, but be prepared to be shunned." And these Parisians were sure doing their fair share of shunning. Traveling tourists, on the other hand, were unconcerned.

Soroya could always pick out her fellow Americans. Big. Bright, floral shirts. Polyester. The French would have been shunning *them* but the locals were too busy aiming their animus at the woman in the burqa. Or was she a girl? Who could possibly tell? Could have been a man.

Soroya noticed the veiled person shifting in her seat and reaching down. Soroya thought she moved like a young woman. Agile and feminine. And she appeared to be traveling alone, as silently censorious in her suit of clothes as the people staring at her.

Whatever, Soroya told herself, relaxing back in her seat. She'd get off the packed train in a few minutes and visit the Sun King's palace—French classical architecture at its best. She'd seen plenty of photos, and now she was about to see its golden hues for real for the first time.

The train's gentle movement was enough to induce sleep in the young American, who had been making love to her Algerian boyfriend late into the night. But seconds later her somnolence was shattered when the girl in the burqa began to shriek.

Soroya spun around and saw the dark clothing in flames a dozen seats away. An older woman pulled the emergency cord. Screams, smoke, and panic filled the passenger car. Soroya leaped across the backs of the intervening seats, shouting in English at a tourist to smother the fire with his raincoat. Then she yelled in French to a commuter to grab the extinguisher at the end of the car. To a Latina, she screamed in Spanish for *agua*. Water.

In less than a minute, the combined efforts doused the flames, but the damage to the burqa-wearing girl was ghastly. Soroya saw third-degree burns and a puncture wound to the abdomen. She grabbed the girl's intestines as they started to spill out. Soroya wasn't sure how the fire had started. Had some angry Frenchman set the young woman aflame? But then she saw a packet of PETN explosive powder and a container of acid, along with a faulty igniter. All of it was hidden beneath the charred and shredded outer garment. Soroya sickened. An assault on the girl, as bad as it would have been, would have been less damaging to the reeling image of Islam than a young, burqa-clad, would-be suicide bomber on the Paris Metro.

The girl was now hysterical with pain. Soroya heard wailing emergency vehicles pull up beside the tracks. One was an ambulance, the other a police car. Both disgorged teams of men, all focused on the identity, connections, and survival of the girl who had fumbled her own suicide bombing.

The emergency medical technicians injected the girl with morphine. Even then, perhaps in fear the girl would die, police began to question her. She gasped that her name was Danielle Kasravi. "Twenty-four," she added.

Perhaps Danielle also feared she would die because she quickly told the police of her desire to join her brother in heaven, saying the mullahs had assured her safe passage if she removed an apostate from this mortal world.

Just anyone? Soroya wondered before Danielle uttered a name: "Banisadr." Danielle said she was going to the Café des Deux Chien, where the former president of Iran had coffee every morning, often with other members of the Iranian exile community. Radicals from Iran had brought a suicide vest to Danielle's apartment.

The girl and her revelations disappeared into the back of the ambulance. Only then did Soroya look at her hands. They were covered with blood.

Four groups of people noted the attempted suicide bombing. The first was the media. *Le Monde* carried screaming headlines about a terrorist bomber on the train to Versailles. A companion article named the bystanders, including a young American of Iranian descent, Soroya Assaf.

The second group to take note was the extended Banisadr family. Abulhassan Banisadr now understood he had returned to the radicals's hit list. He wanted to meet the Assaf woman. She had kept Kasravi alive so the police could get her story. The former president of Iran sent word to Soroya and they met at the targeted coffee shop a week later.

Over steaming café au lait, Banisadr asked about the assailant. Soroya was able offer little information aside from that provided by the news agencies. But she might have been guarded as well. If so, Banisadr didn't appear to notice. He talked about his brother living in Houston and offered to write a letter of introduction to him for Soroya.

"Thank you." She didn't think a letter from a former president could hurt her career prospects, and she enjoyed the company of Iranians newly arrived to the States.

The coffee consumed, Banisadr stiffly said good-bye, and Soroya retreated to the apartment she shared with her Algerian boyfriend.

The third group following the bombing and its aftermath was the Basiji militants and their station chief in Paris. He was the man who had brought a suicide vest to the ill-fated Danielle. They paid special attention to Soroya Assaf's meeting with Banisadr. The station chief sent a message to the offices of the Revolutionary Guard in Tehran:

> Soroya Assaf, age eighteen, second generation Shia, now resident in Paris with Algerian (Muslim) man. Soon to return to her home in Los Angeles. At some risk tried to save the life of one of ours. Stay in touch; could be useful.

He attached a copy of the story from *Le Monde*.

The fourth group to study the failed plot was the American intelligence community, especially Elizabeth Mallory. She had yet to head off to the Defense Language School in Monterrey when word of the plot against President Banisadr came to the world's attention. She not only had a personal connection to the man but she was deeply versed in his role in post-shah Iran, including Banisadr's abrupt removal from office in 1981.

But twenty-plus years later, Iranian politics took an even darker turn. In May 2003 Elizabeth watched as hardliners seized control of Tehran's city council, using their votes to circumvent any legitimate election. They installed Mansoor Alizadeh as the mayor of Tehran. A forty-seven-year-old populist and civil engineer, he was widely reputed to be a religious fascist even by the standards of Iran's overtly reverential capital city.

Bad blood's in the air. That wasn't simply a figure of speech for Elizabeth. During the 1990s Alizadeh had governed Ardabil Province, but in 1997 then-president Mohammad Khatami, a moderate, had removed him from office. Now, with a base in Tehran's city hall, Mansoor Alizadeh was the logical candidate to oust Khatami and win the presidency for the hardliners.

That election was two years away, but Elizabeth knew from following Iran's nuclear chess moves that the Islamists planned years in advance. Already Alizadeh's supporters were packing the Interior Ministry—the police and election services—with allies and were beginning to murder domestic opponents with vigilante attacks. For their overseas rivals like Banisadr, they had turned to covert action.

The Iranians were forming yet another formidable Islamist front. Elizabeth's colleagues in other American intelligence services had recently foiled an attempt by al-Qaeda to ship explosives into the US disguised as printer cartridges. They had also encountered the underwear bomber aboard a Northwest flight from Amsterdam to Detroit. All of these terrorist attempts, including the attack on Banisadr, were clearly designed to kill people as visibly as possible.

Ruthless as the Iranian plotters in Kazakhstan had been, Elizabeth realized a younger, even more dangerous generation of radicals was seeking power in Tehran. More than ever she was glad she was heading off to learn Farsi; it could prove a critical tool for an ambitious operative. But before she could leave for the West Coast, a CIA operations executive asked her to travel to Paris to get a firsthand report from Banisadr on why the Basiji in Tehran wanted to kill him.

"While you're there," the man went on, "see if you can find this Assaf woman. What is she all about?"

Two days later Elizabeth had to pass through layers of security to gain access to the Banisadr apartment. Early afternoon light flooded the old-world Persian ambience, from a well-worn, intricately woven carpet to ornately carved hardback chairs. Abulhassan Banisadr's living room was as remarkably formal as the man himself.

Elizabeth had dressed in a conservative, slate-gray suit with a muted, blue-and-gray floral headscarf wrapped loosely around her blond hair. She waited, sitting erect on the hard, wooden chair, as Iran's first revolutionary president entered the room.

Despite the easy informality of eating barbecued ribs with him in Washington two years earlier, they engaged in only the most formal reintroductions now, and she was reminded of other instances when America's casualness was quickly adopted by visitors and just as quickly jettisoned when she met them on their home turf.

Tea was served. After sweetening hers with honey, Elizabeth mentioned their last visit. "I enjoyed your company and Ozra's very much. How is Mehdi?"

"Mehdi is fine," Abulhassan said, pointedly not answering her query about his son any further.

"Did you have a good trip to Houston, sir?"

"Yes. The whole family enjoyed the holiday. Thank you for those arrangements, Ms. Mallory."

All right. Let's get down to business. "You had a close call last week, Mr. President. Why do you think that Kasravi woman was sent to kill you?"

"I don't know her, but it's the same old story." For the first time, Banisadr appeared to relax. "The Mesbah-Yazdi crowd does not like the idea of a republic." Mesbah-Yazdi was shorthand for the Grand Ayatollah Mohammad Tariq Mesbah-Yazdi, who believed in the imminent return of the Lost Imam and thus the end of days. It was the opinion of experts on the Iranian extremists that a nuclear exchange between Iran and Israel and/or the West would be fine with the Grand Ayatollah. Certainly it would be compatible with his beliefs. He'd actually written dismissively that "some people imagine violence has no place in Islam." Alas, he was Alizadeh's religious mentor.

"If not a republic, what do they want?" Elizabeth asked Banisadr.

"They want to install their man, the Islamic fascist Alizadeh, so they can conduct business the way they do in Zimbabwe: one man, one vote, one time. No *majlis*, no republic, no consent of the governed, just an Islamic dictatorship. I don't agree, as you know, and I don't mind saying so to the press. Those people in Tehran don't like that."

"So does Alizadeh subscribe to everything his mentor, this Mesbah-Yazdi, says?"

Banisadr shook his head. "I don't think Mansoor's that unbalanced. He's just a power-hungry demagogue. I hope we can stop him next month." He was referring to the presidential election. "Hashemi Rafsanjani is a good man."

"Are you safe, Mr. President?" she asked. "Is there—"

"How easily did you get into my apartment?" Banisadr smiled.

"Point well taken, but there are clearly some dangerous elements trying to chase you down here."

He nodded. "We keep our eyes on them. One of Alizadeh's men arrived here last week. We keep track of who comes and goes. This one is part of an official Iranian delegation. I understand you once danced with him in Moscow."

"Major Ashkan Gharabaghi?"

Banisadr smiled, apparently pleased to have intelligence that hadn't reached Elizabeth yet. "Yes, that is correct. I tell you, the radicals are getting stronger all the time. *You* need to be careful too."

The next day Elizabeth tried to track down Soroya Assaf, but the trail led to a warren of narrow streets lined with crowded apartments filled with

Algerian immigrants. The blond-haired woman in the dark business suit drew malevolent stares from men lounging on stoops. The CIA station chief in Paris had warned her people in these poor neighborhoods felt aggrieved, but she had declined his offer of a security man. She hadn't wanted to look like she was part of an invading force. But now Elizabeth felt violence in the air, undirected and ready to explode.

Go on, she urged herself. *You took on bona fide killers in Kazakhstan.* But Elizabeth stopped and retreated. Another voice deep inside warned her to get the hell out of there. She wasn't surprised when a few months later those streets erupted in American-style rioting and violence. The anger felt that palpable. But as real as it would prove to be, the fury of the backstreets of Paris wasn't the most dangerous threat Elizabeth faced at that moment.

When she returned to her hotel, she was greeted in the lobby by Ulysses Valdez, the American embassy man who had escorted her to Banisadr's building the day before.

"Ms. Mallory," he said in a hushed voice. "Get your bag. Let's go."

"Why? What's going on?" Elizabeth was tired, still jet-lagged, and was looking forward to a tasty room-service meal and catching up on some sleep.

Valdez glanced around them. Still speaking softly, he explained, "We know the prime reason you came to Paris. That interview has been accomplished. But it has set off an unpleasant and highly informal Iranian response. Some professional hit men, all speaking Farsi, are looking for you. We need to get you out of Paris immediately. I'll provide security for you up to your room and all the way to the airport. Get your bag and let's get out of here."

His urgency jolted her into full awareness. They rode the elevator to the fourteenth floor and she packed and cleared out of her room in minutes.

On the way back down, he informed her she was booked on United's flight 915. "It leaves in one hour. The armored embassy limo is waiting for us outside. There's another security man in it, plus the driver. Once I get you inside security at Charles de Gaulle, you should be safe, but we'll stay on hand until takeoff to make sure you're okay."

With his eyes everywhere at once, Valdez rushed her to a large, black Citroen, which sped her to the airport.

As soon as she settled in on the plane, she wondered what had triggered such keen, murderous interest in her. And then she realized it was no coincidence the threat had come within days of Major Gharabaghi's arrival in Paris. Just as Elizabeth had gained intelligence on him since they had first faced off in Kazakhstan, no doubt he had learned she wasn't the demure secretary-receptionist at the US embassy in Moscow. No young woman of such lowly professional stature would have shown up in so many places in the intervening years. And now she'd been in Paris to meet with Iran's former president, himself a target of assassins.

Elizabeth sat back in her seat in business class, smiling at the thought of how furious Gharabaghi must have been when he'd figured out that she was the Kazakh killer, the woman who had destroyed his plans to return to Tehran with a shipment of highly enriched uranium. Even back then the CIA had intercepted intelligence showing that the Iranians at the airport had glimpsed a blond-haired woman—and that they were incensed she had shot down an Antonov AN-12 with the same skills once displayed by their fellow Muslims in Afghanistan. A woman, co-opting *their* tactics.

So he put two and two together, and they added up to "fool."

Elizabeth remembered his squiring her about the dance floor and then Moscow. He had been plenty angry when he'd coughed and blamed the Americans for his bad lungs. She could only imagine how he'd felt when he'd realized the woman he'd tried to woo, who had the audacity to marvel over his tales of equestrian skill, had actually escaped him on a horse.

So he'd called in the professionals. As she took a glass of wine from the flight attendant, she remembered vowing to herself that she would see Gharabaghi again. But she'd always thought she would do it on her terms, not his. And there she was, taking flight once more.

It made her think of Gunpowder. It made her vow revenge.

CHAPTER 8
AL UDEID

Summer 2005–Summer 2010

*B*eh madreseh zaban defaei khosh amidad.

"Welcome to the Defense Language Institute?" That was Elizabeth's best guess at translating the sign at the Presidio of Monterrey, California. She was far less flummoxed by the mission-style architecture that grabbed her attention as she drove onto the campus. The buildings, leafy trees, and lushly green lawns were simply beautiful.

She felt great to be landing there and found herself singing along loudly in her car to Steppenwolf's "Born to be Wild": "Get your motor running..." A couple of factors prompted her sudden exuberance. For starters she was glad to be out of Washington and immersed once more in an academic pursuit. And she was belting out a classic rock song because it would be the last smidgeon of English she would be permitted to use. From that point on it was Farsi day and night till she dreamed in it.

Elizabeth settled into a dorm room, then endured a week of orientation and language lab, capped by endless homework in the evenings. She dined alone, feeling isolated by the proscription against socializing with the much younger enlisted men and women, not to mention the severe limitation on communication imposed by her rudimentary Farsi.

She found an outlet in early morning runs under clear, blue skies. She could talk to herself in English but surprised herself by slipping into colloquial Farsi. Studying yet another language brought to mind a joke one of her Russian professors at Harvard had told his class: "What do you call someone who speaks three languages? Trilingual. What do you call someone who speaks two languages? Bilingual. And someone who speaks one language? American."

"Not me," Elizabeth shouted out as she ran along a path threading through conifers high above the Pacific Ocean, smelling the sweet scent of pine. Running was the best preparation she could think of for sitting on her butt for eight hours a day in language lab.

It felt odd to be so much older than her classmates, some of whom ran together in small groups. She'd always been the prodigy and now she was running with these military up-and-comers, all so serious but pretty damn cool too.

The central California coast hosted an array of academic institutions, not just the language school. There was also the Monterey Institute of International Studies and the Naval Postgraduate School. All kinds of fit folks out running in the a.m.

She darted out from under a towering Monterrey Pine and in minutes had moved down along a seawall, where she smelled the salt and heard the hungry cries of gulls. She overtook a pack of naval officers and was only a meter past them when she heard a mellow, Midwestern voice say, "Good morning, Ms. Mallory."

She looked over her shoulder and saw a guy about her age, cropped hair and a tanned, smile-lined face.

"Name's Frank Snyder, ma'am. I'm a student at the postgraduate school." Every sentence was an achievement as the young officer labored to draw even with her. "Information sciences, C4I."

Elizabeth knew the acronym by which he'd defined himself: The four Cs were command, control, communications, computers. The I? That was easy: information systems and compartmented intelligence.

Elizabeth looked around, then just nodded at him. He had an inviting smile, and she really wanted to talk to him, but language school had strict rules.

"It's okay," Snyder said to her. "I'll do the talking. We heard you were here, Ms. Mallory, but the language school won't let us talk to you. We figured"—puff, puff—"that we'd see you out running. Kind of chilly for a conference." He laughed. "But it's the best we could do." Still puffing, he added, "We confirmed your clearances. We have a SCIF, and we'd welcome you at our intelligence briefings. You'd bring some real-world perspective to us sailors."

"I'll look into it." That was all she allowed herself to say.

Elizabeth knew a fair amount about the Naval Postgraduate School. It hosted hundreds of students from across the US and allied countries for graduate work in technical and political studies. The school tried to run an open campus, so she was delighted to learn of an intelligence center where she, a fully cleared CIA hand, could go for updates on matters of interest. Her mentors at the Defense Language School initially frowned on her escapes into the English-speaking world, but after a month of lectures and drills, she was doing well. Given her seniority and the Navy's strong interest in her participation, the language school relented, allowing her to visit the Naval Postgraduate School one morning a week.

Her timing for the first briefing couldn't have been better. Mansoor Alizadeh had just ascended from mayor of Tehran to Iran's presidency and was the subject of the briefing by a naval officer. The SCIF was as Spartan as the ones she'd used at Langley and for the same reason: fewer places to hide bugs.

"Alizadeh had never actually been elected to anything before he won the presidency," the blond, buzz-cut briefing officer told them. "He was appointed to the mayoralty of Tehran. That's because he was—and is—the chosen instrument of the hardliners. He was a civil engineering student at the University of Science and Technology during the fall of the shah in 1979. He was active in the streets and, some say, in the subsequent occupation of the US embassy. He never joined the Revolutionary Guard, but those people are his close friends."

Close friends like Major Gharabaghi, Elizabeth thought. The major had been in the Guard Corps and done a lot more than occupy the embassy. Gharabaghi had been murdering opponents of Khomeini.

The briefing officer went on, "Alizadeh is active in the Guard's militia, known as the Basiji. They recruited teenage suicide bombers for the war with Iraq. And they were the street toughs who turned out the vote for Alizadeh last month."

So it's going from bad to worse over there, Elizabeth thought as she left the SCIF. Frank Snyder eased up beside her.

"Could I take you to lunch?" he asked.

"Yes, you could," she said. Elizabeth was tired of dining alone, and if the language school had given her an exemption for the briefing then she would extend the briefing—if only in her mind—to a meal.

They went to the Paradiso restaurant down on Cannery Row; the strip now bore little resemblance the subject of John Steinbeck's famous novel. Frank, she was pleased to see, had stopped calling her "ma'am." The word made her feel about a hundred years old.

You do have a few years on him.

Without saying as much, they eschewed all classified talk and praised the rockfish with spaghetti marinara. But when he took her hand to lead her down by the seawall, she gave him a gentle squeeze and withdrew it. Frank was a nice guy but he didn't get her motor running. As they walked along, awkwardly silent, she could all but hear her mother yelling, "What's *wrong* with you?"

Really, what is wrong with me? Frank's nice enough.

But nice enough was never enough.

They did make a date to run the next morning, and a friendship blossomed as they changed routes and did intervals every day, each pushing the other.

In late September the briefings at the Postgraduate School turned to Hezbollah's war with Israeli troops in the backstreets of southern Lebanon. Elizabeth startled her peers with her understanding of the Hezbollah command structure.

"Hezbollah is simply a guerilla arm of the Iranian state," she put forth. "They are tough, well armed, and competent. I'm appalled, but not surprised, that Hezbollah won and that the Israelis are pulling out."

It wasn't that Elizabeth saw the fingerprints of Iran everywhere. It was that the Iranians were reaching out effectively—and chillingly—in every manner possible. One of Snyder's fellow officers confirmed her suspicions.

"Iran's Hezbollah proxies apparently took control of the Israeli drones overflying the combat zones," he told her.

Elizabeth was inspired to study Farsi even harder. Her instructors drilled her in Persian pronunciation and grammar. Productive seeds took root over the course of the fall.

She spent Christmas day with Commander Snyder and a dozen of his shipmates.

"As soon as we get a break in the weather," he said with a smile, "we'd like you to join us for some real sailing."

The prospect delighted her. Elizabeth had sailed on the Chesapeake Bay in her childhood but never enough to satisfy her taste for salt spray.

The weather warmed up enough by February to go out with Frank and a dozen other sailors on one of the forty footers the Navy maintained. Frank was the skipper; his name was Commander Snyder, after all. Elizabeth drew jib-sheet duty. She relished the feel of the sails filling, the whispery sounds of wind and water. And when the entire crew, wet and happy and boisterous, hit the Whaling Station on Saturday evenings after an invigorating day on the water, she caught her reflection in the bar mirror and saw that her smile was as bright as the sunlit sea.

June brought orders for Elizabeth to relocate to the National Security Agency headquarters at Ft. Meade to start work as an intercept translator. It was her post-doc training session, a chance to polish her new Farsi language skills before being transferred to an operational assignment overseas. At Ft. Meade she'd be only an hour's drive from her father. Commander Snyder received orders to proceed to Japan. He waited until he was alone with Elizabeth at the Whaling Station to break the real news about his next assignment.

"I'm to become communications officer aboard the USS *Vincennes.*"

Elizabeth stiffened. The *Vincennes* had shot down an Iranian airliner a few years earlier and would always remain both a target and a rationale for terrorist retaliation. She said as much to Frank. He nodded.

"I know. The ship has an extra burden."

"Two hundred ninety of them," she said softly. The number killed, including sixty-six Iranian children. "A terrible disaster," she added, shaking her head. A naval court of inquiry found that the Iranian airliner had repeatedly failed to respond to ID challenges from the *Vincennes*, so there were plenty of people in the military who felt the captain had been justified in firing. Elizabeth didn't agree with them. She subscribed to the considerable school that thought the captain had been trigger-happy. In any case the US had settled a decade later by paying $200 million to the families of the victims. But, as Frank quickly noted, those people never forget.

"Red, right returning?" she said, using nautical shorthand to wish him a safe trip home.

"You got it," he replied.

Before reporting to Ft. Meade, Elizabeth received approval to follow up on the American student, Soroya Assaf, the volunteer at Médecins Sans Frontières who had acted quickly to save Danielle Kasravi's life on the Paris Metro. The fact that Elizabeth had never contacted Assaf in Paris still hung in the air, and Beverly Hills was just a quick drive south. At the very least, Elizabeth wanted to fill in some blank spots, perhaps even meet the woman.

Elizabeth contacted an old Quantico classmate and tennis partner, Azar Hadi, who now worked the terrorism beat for the FBI in LA. As a young girl, Azar and her parents had fled revolutionary Iran. Not surprisingly they'd ended up in Beverly Hills, now a de facto Iranian city.

Azar returned Elizabeth's call quickly and offered a verbal nod when Elizabeth brought up Soroya Assaf's name.

"Yes, she comes from a terrific family. I know them."

"You heard about Soroya's actions on the Paris commuter train?"

"Affirmative," Azar said. "We have a file on that. She had an Algerian boyfriend who we think was an Islamist, but that remains unconfirmed."

Elizabeth's blood quickened. "Has she stayed in contact with him?"

"Not that we know of. There's no record of his entry into the country and no record of her rendezvousing with him over there. Might have been a fling during her stint with Doctors Without Borders."

"If I came down there, would you have time to give me a rundown on the Iranian expats in your neck of the woods? And whatever you have on Assaf?"

"Sure, just get the clearances to me and I'll make time."

"Tennis anyone?"

"Yes! And that too." Azar laughed.

Over the Independence Day weekend, Elizabeth bid farewell to her friends graduating from the Naval Postgraduate School. Frank and his classmates looked so handsome in their dress uniforms, white gloves, and caps.

It was a flower-bedecked event on the top floor of Hermann Hall, a jewel of Spanish architecture that served as the school's administrative center. Elizabeth took part in toasts, hugs, and kisses and watched the men and women of the US Navy and the intelligence community go their separate ways.

The next morning she headed for Los Angeles. By evening she was settled into the Century Plaza Hotel on Santa Monica Boulevard. She awoke early and headed down the street to meet with Azar Hadi at the FBI office. After coffee and updates about their respective careers, Elizabeth asked about Soroya Assaf.

Azar lifted her dark eyebrows. She was a handsome, fit woman, Persian at a glance with dazzling blue eyes. "Let me put it this way," she said slowly. "I'm glad I'm not *her* mother. Until recently she was a real handful for her parents. Her father is a pediatrician. They got out of Iran in the mid-seventies as the situation over there got out of control. They're devout Shiite Muslims, very conservative, but absolutely no radical activities. Complete pillars of the community. Their social circle is what you'd expect—medical colleagues, neighbors. No unusual outsiders."

Elizabeth knew Azar had just outlined the standard-issue experience for the first generation of Muslims to immigrate to the US. Most were amazingly resilient and resourceful. "And the second generation?" she prompted.

Azar nodded knowingly. "Soroya had a normal upbringing. She was very strong academically at Beverly Hills High. The family seemed close. She had one romantic attachment in high school that's worth noting. She and David Borookhim hooked up and stayed that way through graduation. He's a charming kid, also from a very successful Iranian expat family. His father develops commercial real estate in West LA—like half his neighbors." Azar and Elizabeth both laughed.

"So we have two popular kids who got together?" Elizabeth said.

"That's right. But my sources told me that as high school graduation neared, the two sets of parents started getting antsy because it looked like the relationship was getting really serious. The Borookhims are Jewish. They also emigrated from prerevolutionary Tehran, and both families brought with them their old-world constraints, to put it neutrally. None of the adults wanted this mixed Muslim-Jewish relationship. It's the old story—Romeo and Juliet, only now they were alive and well in Beverly Hills.

"Now, keep in mind, Elizabeth, this high school romance is more than just background. It relates directly to what happened with Soroya Assaf last summer because once the grad parties were over for the class of '05 and the summer jobs were starting, Soroya's parents sat her down and laid down the law: You're Muslim. He's Jewish. Life will take a terrible toll if you try to continue with him. Oh, and by the way, Mohammed will pass harsher judgment in the future. Then Dr. Assaf really lowered the boom. He told her if she ever communicated with David again, she would no longer be considered a member of their family."

"And across town?" Elizabeth asked.

"Same thing. Mr. and Mrs. Borookhim were telling David it was over with the Muslim girl."

"So who took it harder?" Elizabeth asked. "Soroya or her young man?"

"Soroya by far. From what I heard, David was relieved. After 9/11 he'd been getting grief from his buddies about having a Muslim girlfriend. He went to work for his father in the construction business and never looked back. But Soroya was furious. She came down to breakfast the next day with her hair chopped off and dyed green. Then she headed off to Paris to do her volunteer gig with Doctors Without Borders. From all reports she and David never even had a chance to say good-bye, although I've got to think they snuck in a call or two. In the fall they went off to different colleges. He entered USC and Soroya went to UCLA, where she was totally rebellious. She's been in the front line of every antiwar, anti-Bush political rally and demonstration that takes place anywhere in Los Angeles. I hear she's handy with a paint brush and banners and pretty damn brazen with her slogans."

"What do you mean?" Elizabeth couldn't let that one slip by.

"Well, I think the one that really mortified her parents was the video— which went viral—showing her carrying big poster that said, 'The only Bush I trust is my own.' The drawing after the word 'Bush' left nothing to the imagination."

Elizabeth laughed. "No, I can't imagine her parents were happy to see her marching down the street with that one."

"Conservative Shiites? Seeing their daughter holding *that* up? But here's the good news, in terms of the girl settling down. She looks like she's on the rebound. She's involved with a good-looking, out-of-town young man. He's also Muslim, a second-generation Iranian, and he has a job, so if you listen closely right now you can probably hear her parents sighing with relief."

"Who's the lucky guy?" Elizabeth asked.

"A student from the University of Texas in El Paso by the name of Rosincourt Sadr."

"Hey, I know about that family. Tell me what you've heard."

"Only that he's a mechanical whiz in his senior year at UTEP." University of Texas at El Paso. "I guess he's good enough at what he does that he's already gotten offers from the aerospace industry out here. He landed a summer job at a high-tech machine shop right in Santa Monica last year. I do background checks for their new hires, so I know all about Sadr. He was working with a bunch of bright young kids, most of them just out of Caltech, UCLA, or USC. They seem to like him, and he sure loves the beach. So what do you know about the Sadr family?" Azar asked.

Elizabeth told her about playing host to President Banisadr's family in Washington and arranging for them to visit the Sadr clan in Houston. "Banisadr's son, Mehdi, was not the most pleasant kid I've ever met, but he must be about the same age as Rosincourt."

"That must have been an interesting meeting," Azar replied. "I'm not surprised Banisadr wanted Houston on his itinerary. The Iranian community is very tight. We're always reaching out to one another. It was no different for Rosincourt. He got on the horn to the Assafs as soon as he arrived in LA. I heard about him within twenty-four hours of his arrival. You can imagine how happy the doctor and his wife are now. A pleasant, well-educated, Muslim boy with a high-tech job dating their daughter? That's a dream come true for them."

"And the anti-Bush rallies?" Elizabeth asked.

"Soroya still goes, but"—Azar chuckled—"no more naughty references to her pubis. Even so, you better not connect. A surprise visit from a Farsi-speaking Anglo woman almost twice her age might set off a lot of bells."

With the coming of autumn, Elizabeth settled into two different worlds: a new one at Ft. Meade and the old, familiar one in Bethesda, where she decided to continue living with her father. She knew it was odd for a woman of her age still to live at home, but her father had morphed into her closest friend. She wasn't sure how that had happened. But at heart she knew that even during her most rebellious days of adolescence she had admired him—and now more than ever. Though retired from Langley, he was still sought after as a consultant in times of crisis. Suffice it to say he wasn't at home much given the drumbeat of bad news out of Iraq. Some of the old hands were getting called in to see what could be done to rectify an increasingly disastrous situation. The Pottery Barn rule—you break it, you own it—was proving hard to implement in Iraq, which was riven by more rivalries than the reptile house at the National Zoo.

So while her father scooted off to Langley in his Prius as if he'd never retired, Elizabeth made the easy commute to Ft. Meade. Her new world confined her for most of the day to a small, windowless cubicle with sound-absorbing walls. It was a teensy fraction of the huge, black buildings that constituted the headquarters of the National Security Agency, an amorphous-sounding name that had not appeared on any Defense Department organizational chart until the end of the Cold War. The NSA provided security for US communications. It also made stunningly successful efforts to penetrate the communications of others, both sovereign nations and the nastiest nonnational players such as drug dealers, terrorists, and financial manipulators. Its storied British counterpart during World War II had been Bletchley Park, where code breakers contributed mightily to the Allied victory and shortened the war by at least two years.

The usual civil service rules did not apply at Ft. Meade. The staff was given regular polygraph tests because communication intercepts were the crown jewels of intelligence work. Fail them or the agency in any way and an employee could be fired with minimum delay.

Elizabeth found the work surprisingly dull during her first few months, but thankfully it could also prove intellectually challenging. The NSA was home to a juggernaut of computational power, and she relished the wonders it could work. One of the agency's old hands leaned over a cup of java and told her one of the NSA's most important precepts: "The best news in our business is when an adversary thinks his codes are impenetrable."

Elizabeth started analyzing fragmentary intercepts from southern Lebanon. She realized that in achieving victory over Israel, Hezbollah had broken codes, employed simple but high-tech weapons, and drawn support from a horde of impoverished native Muslims. Hardly a ragtag group of militants.

Her comprehension of Farsi improved daily, and her interpretations brought her to the attention of the NSA's senior staff. With the president's announcement of a planned surge in Iraq, which she guessed her father had helped devise, she figured she'd be sent overseas. Indeed, at the end of 2007 she received her orders to report to the CENTCOM forward headquarters in Qatar, a small emirate on the western side of the Persian Gulf.

Qatar, about the size of Massachusetts, was fully endowed with oil and gas reserves. Since 1995 the Al-Thani family had provided rational leadership and looked to the US for security. The government of Qatar built the Al Udeid Air Base to attract a major US presence.

Elizabeth arrived in December to temperatures with daytime highs in the seventies. She was assigned to the NSA station, where her responsibilities grew as the Iranian involvement in Iraq became clearer to the high command. From her point of view, it had been terribly predictable from the start.

As part of the surge, Colonel Emmett Gourdine had been assigned to Al Udeid. He was as much a rising star in the American military establishment as he had been a track-and-field record-breaker back in Bossier City, Louisiana, where he'd earned his nickname: Flash. His exploits as a sprinter had brought him to the attention of the US Military Academy. A milk-chocolate complexioned teen of Creole-Cajun heritage, Gourdine graduated from high school with honors in 1984, then worked in the Gulf fishing industry for a year as his West Point nomination wound through the congressional maze.

He entered the academy in 1985 and left four years later a six-foot-six, reed-thin young man. Fitting into an M1 tank proved challenging, but he preferred to ride with his head and shoulders above the turret anyway.

He served as a platoon leader during the Desert Storm rescue of Kuwait in 1991, earning the respect of his men and a bronze star for his leadership during the American Army's Hail Mary sweep across the Iraqi desert. Ten years later Major Gourdine was serving in the Pentagon when hijacked American Airlines Flight 77 hit the west side of the building. He was soon dispatched to Afghanistan.

In 2003 Lt. Col. Gourdine led his tank battalion into a firefight in Fallujah, earning a purple heart when an improvised explosive device—

an IED—on the road to Baghdad blew a hole in his armored vehicle and injured his left arm.

In recognition of his leadership, Gourdine was soon promoted to full colonel. He returned to Iraq as part of the surge, where he became an expert on a new generation of roadside explosive devices: EFPs, or explosively formed projectiles. A far more lethal weapon than an IED, an EFP was a carefully machined piece of large-diameter pipe filled with explosives and then capped by a copper disk. Detonation transformed the disk into a molten jet of hot metal capable of penetrating several inches of armor. "Like a hot poker through putty," one expert said.

Gourdine had an uncanny knack for spotting and then defeating EFPs. After two years in Iraq, he was transferred to CENTCOM forward headquarters in Qatar, where he was to train others in this highly hazardous line of work. He was an Army man: never married, always in harm's way.

But upon his arrival at Al Udeid, Colonel Gourdine encountered a different challenge: Elizabeth Mallory.

At age forty-one, Flash was still an excellent runner. He'd added muscle to his lean sprinter's frame while his long, handsome face remained mostly unlined. To stay in shape, in the evenings he ran the five-mile circumference of the base with the air wing troops at the base.

"Better watch out for the blond, old man," his fellow joggers warned him. "You'll be sucking her dust."

Gourdine only laughed, but not for long. After hoping to meet this Mallory character, he managed to see only the numbers on the back of her sweat suit.

"Well, ah'll be damned," he said, laughing good-naturedly. "Come awn, Ms. Mallory," he offered in his south Louisiana cadence. "Ah'll treat you to some iced tea."

Elizabeth never paused. She'd noticed him on the run, but only in passing—in the most literal sense. But now as she looked into his dark eyes, and saw his enticingly long lashes, she realized immediately she would *like* to have iced tea with him, very much so. Moreover, when he smiled at her again she felt a distinct, almost alarming softening deep in her core.

What's this all about? Are you daft, woman? she scolded herself. *It's about him.*

It most certainly was. From those first moments, her attraction grew. And when he said "Elizabeth," all four syllables rolled off his tongue like he enjoyed her name more than anything else in the world. He was self-confident, professional; happy but not goofy. He possessed a Colin Powell-like ease that struck a favorable chord within her. The world might have been going crazy, but he was rock steady and nine years older than she was. Very appealing. He reminded her of the Denzel Washington character in *Courage Under Fire*, leading his tank regiment across the Iraqi desert with head and shoulders held high above the turret.

The next night they dined together at the mess hall, ran side by side in the evening, and talked for hours about Iran's designs on the Muslim world. Though from different racial backgrounds, they became close in the ensuing days, laughing when one outran the other, holding hands, and—when she could restrain herself no longer—kissing quickly and deeply. The melting she'd felt when she first met him now spread through her. She wanted him. And while the likes of Peter Gallagher, or even Frank Snyder, had never tempted her, she felt her body speaking a demanding language of its own. The force of attraction was so strong, it was as if their species had drawn them together for its own higher purpose. The way he held her firmly at the waist, with his fingertips pressing down on the top of her bottom, made her want to whisk him away. So that was precisely what she did.

One evening, without a word, she took his hand and led him into her room. They fell onto her bed as if it had been the target of the whole evening's trajectory.

Flash was a treasure.

Elizabeth's winter in Qatar passed wonderfully. Her work intrigued her more than ever, and her evenings with Flash became increasingly intimate. He also became a good buddy. She felt unpressured around him; she found him well-grounded and self-assured but self-effacing at the same time. Unlike other men he didn't rage when he heard the ugly reports from Iraq. And he had a Southerner's gentle manners. She found herself graciously stepping aside while he opened doors for her. It felt uncomfortable at first, but then she began to realize she was falling in love with Gourdine.

In April, when the sun started to burn hot again, she experienced a huge jolt: Flash was ordered to return to Iraq for a few weeks of temporary duty. The neophyte Iraqi security forces were losing men to the new EFPs. Elizabeth experienced an entirely new fear: the loss of someone she loved.

They sat on her bed together that night. She took his hand and kissed his fingertips. "I'm going to miss you something fierce, Colonel Emmett Gourdine." She said his whole name for the first time in weeks, as if it were a way to lay a deeper claim to him.

"I'm not just going to miss you, Elizabeth. I'm going to miss someone I love very much."

He'd had the guts to say it first. She choked up, drew his hands to her chest, and held them tightly against herself. With her eyes tearing, she said, "I love you too. And I'd *never* say that if I didn't mean it."

He tapped his chest and pointed to her. "Me too."

Shortly after he left for Iraq, Elizabeth was given the life-or-death responsibility of CIA overseer at the Predator ground station at Al Udeid. The unmanned but armed aircraft operated thousands of miles from their home base, loitering for a full day until finding a target. They were flown by teams of US Air Force operators, some of them sitting in darkened trailers at Al Udeid. But ultimate authority for the decision to fire, to *kill*, was vested in the director of Central Intelligence in Washington, then delegated, along with specific rules of engagement, to his senior CIA agents assigned to the trailers. Elizabeth was now one of those agents. Her track record in Kazakhstan and fluency in Farsi made her a natural choice.

A week later her Colonel Gourdine missed a cue and his Humvee was hit by a well-hidden EFP. The molten projectile punched a hole through two inches of steel, killing the Colonel's driver instantly. Gourdine survived but his life hung in the balance. Parts of his left arm and leg had been ripped away. Shards of steel penetrated his abdomen. He was evacuated to Heidelberg, where surgeons worked to save his life. This time Flash's wounds were horrific.

Elizabeth received the devastating news at the Al Udeid command post in a brief e-mail from a field hospital in southern Iraq. It advised that Colonel Gourdine was in critical condition.

An eternal week later she received a call from Gourdine's commanding officer. As soon as Elizabeth heard his voice and the mention of Flash's name, she knew the worst the world could offer.

She hung up the phone and wept. Blind with tears she made her way to her room and curled up on her bed, drawing her pillow to her face. She smelled Flash's scent, the one she'd clung to every night. The pain that shot through her could have been lethal. It felt sharp enough to core out her insides and left her feeling empty as a husk.

When the news spread, she was relieved of her duty at the trailer. A fellow female officer came in and sat beside her. Elizabeth asked to be alone. She remained that way for the next two days, unable to eat. When she could finally breathe without convulsions, she called back Flash's commander to ask for details.

"The colonel hung in there for a week," he said, "but the flying steel destroyed his internal organs. There was no chance. His remains are headed home, first to the Port Mortuary at Dover Air Force Base, then to rest in Bossier City."

"The mortuary?" Elizabeth cried out in pain. "What the hell for? You know what killed him. Let him go home. Let him rest in peace!"

"Well, Ms. Mallory," the kindly general responded, "we learn a lot by studying the remains of battlefield casualties. Like where did the lethal weapon come from? I'll give Dover your e-mail. They'll keep you posted."

Her voice softened to a whisper. "Please let him rest in peace." Tears ran down her cheeks as she replaced the malevolent instrument in its cradle.

A week later grief turned to rage. A short e-mail from a tech sergeant at Dover Air Force Base attached a painfully detailed autopsy report. In a cover memo, he noted, "Colonel Gourdine was killed by flying shrapnel fragmented and accelerated by a roadside explosively formed projectile. The steel fragments were from the Humvee's walls, but the copper in that projectile came from a machine shop in Lavisan."

A town north of Tehran!

Two seconds passed before Elizabeth screamed "Shit!" at her computer.

Her fight with Iran was now personal. She closed down her computer and strode to the operations center, ready to resume full control of her Predator squadron. She felt like she was made of steel—the kind that would never melt.

CHAPTER 9
THE ROAD FROM KARBALA

December 2010

Four men sped south at eighty miles an hour in an old, beige SUV. They had just departed Karbala, an Iraqi shrine community, behind the lead vehicle—a dusty, white Toyota pickup. Their security team, in a black minivan, trailed half a dozen car lengths behind. Ashura, a Muslim day of mourning and remembrance, had drawn the motorcade to this holiest of Shiite cities. Now the vehicles hurtled toward Basra on Iraq's Route 9, an immaculate, four-lane, divided blacktop highway that traversed a wasteland of brown rock in an arrow-straight line.

Mehdi Banisadr sat in the backseat of his SUV, discussing with a trusted lieutenant his infiltration of Iraq's oil distribution system. Mehdi had become the mastermind of Iran's oil thievery, executing it on a grand scale. Every day several million barrels of Iraqi petroleum flowed down pipelines to loading barges in the Persian Gulf. Mehdi, the paymaster, used his clout to divert a third of all that crude to vessels headed for Iran or her customers.

He enjoyed blueblood status within the Iranian revolutionary community. His father, Abulhassan, although now discredited as a reactionary, had been the first president of the Islamic Republic of Iran. A more distant, still revered relative, Muhammad Baqir-al Sadr, had been a respected ayatollah in the Shiite Muslim world. In 1980 Baqir had led an unsuccessful assassination attempt on Saddam Hussein's foreign minister, a Sunni Muslim. Al-Sadr was captured and killed by Saddam—the first ayatollah executed in modern times. Shia Muslims throughout Mesopotamia vowed revenge. They got a taste of it once Saddam was driven from power and they could name Sadr City, the Shia slum north of downtown Baghdad, after Baqir.

Young Mehdi had been born into that vendetta. Upon his graduation from the University of Paris in 2007, the heir to the al-Sadr dynasty had returned to his roots in Iran. In his eyes, his father had long ago gone soft on the question of Shia supremacy in the Muslim world. Mehdi wanted a resurrection of Persian glories and a new Islamic Iran to overpower the Sunni kingdoms across the Persian Gulf.

Mehdi's companions on the road from Karbala were older Iranians, yet they were openly subordinate to their well-educated young leader. All were engaged in the covert penetration of postwar Iraq. Mehdi's boss was not in the vehicle. He was Assam Suleimani, the Iranian general secretly running the Shia network in Iraq.

A heavily bearded aide in the front seat of the pickup opened his cell phone to report in. He spoke Farsi, but his words would have been ambiguous in any language.

"Red Dot One has departed the temple. Returning to base. There by sundown."

In the rear seat of the SUV, an animated Mehdi still chatted with his highly focused lieutenant about their diversion of Iraqi oil.

At an altitude of 20,000 feet, another traveler—an unidentified drone aircraft—stalked the three-car motorcade. A young man directed the unmanned plane from a console 800 miles to the south. The screen before him showed trenches by the side of the highway, dug by a backhoe. They reflected attempts to find water. Nearby, a lone cemetery honored the elders of the ages, not the recent wartime casualties consigned in huge numbers to large, unmarked graves. To the west of Route 9, the young man saw only desert. To the east small farms reached to the Tigris River for water. The buildings were made of concrete blocks. All had rebar extending upward from unfinished second floors—an Iraqi tax dodge: Incomplete buildings avoided most government levies; finished factories and farmhouses were fully assessed.

"Play that telephone call for me again," Elizabeth Mallory said to the young man. She listened carefully, knowing from sources on the ground that Mehdi Banisadr was in her crosshairs. He had been on the CIA's most-wanted list for a year. Nearly a decade earlier, she had shared dinner with him in a barbecue joint in Washington. He'd been an abrasive young man, ostensibly spiritual. No surprise to her that he'd matured into a hardliner. He had done huge harm to the stumbling Iraqi economy, and his henchmen had murdered dozens of innocent Sunni longshoremen. But what focused Elizabeth most of all was knowing Mehdi was also importing explosively formed projectiles from Iran into southern Iraq. Flying steel energized by one of those projectiles had crippled Colonel Emmett Gourdine, leading to his death after a week-long struggle.

Elizabeth recited the Persian epithet about revenge: *"Faramoosh nemisha-vad,* Mehdi." Never forget.

The young controller at al Udeid piloted the Predator drone, which moved quietly and unnoticed above the vehicles. At an adjoining console, a sensor operator noted a reference to the Red Dot One message on her screen. It followed and was correlated with other messages from observers and sensors on the ground in and around Karbala.

The trailer was quiet except for the clicking of computer keys, the hum of fans, and the squeaking of chairs. All eyes were on a variety of monitors and controls. Then the young woman who'd noted the Red Dot One message on her screen spoke out.

"Supporting reports confirm a three-car motorcade with quarry in the central SUV. Security follows in black minivan."

"Got 'em,'" the pilot/controller responded. "I'm tracking target SUV visually. Permission to fire?"

Elizabeth stood in that darkened room behind the two operators. Her headphones, benefitting from sophisticated computational support, were tuned to the cell phone within the speeding SUV. Her azure eyes never left the consoles. A sweat-soaked shirt and wrinkled scarf protected her from the ventilators; bifocals hung on a cord around her neck. Her look and accessories all bore silent testimony to years of dedication to her job and country. But today she had an intense personal interest at stake.

"Is the motorcade well clear of Basra?' she asked. "What's the spacing between the vehicles? Who else is in that beige SUV?"

"The highway is clear," the female sensor operator responded. "Motorcade is on open road with light traffic. It's still early in the day. There are about a hundred yards between the vehicles front and rear. Target and his lieutenant are in backseat of the center vehicle with driver and one other in front. No women or children onboard."

Elizabeth remained cautious. She had never made a mistake with a drone, but others had. Robotics made warfare impersonal. It could be too easy to fire. She was concerned about collateral damage, especially pilgrims leaving an Ashura observance in a country where American involvement was supposed to have ended.

"Let's see the bloom image," she ordered as she sipped on a now-cold cup of coffee.

A computer-generated diagram of projected damage from the blast and debris appeared on the screen. Elizabeth studied it with great care and then stood erect.

"Okay, execute mission."

"Roger that," the controller responded. He turned a key and flipped a switch. Forty seconds later the beige SUV and its four Iranian passengers were flying fragments, then ashes falling to the desert floor.

"Nice shot," Elizabeth said as she turned to pour herself a fresh cup of coffee. Under her breath she extended a more personal message: "Colonel Gourdine sends his regards, you bastards."

CHAPTER 10
A TALE OF TWO CITIES

2005–2010

Hobbs, New Mexico, stood half a world away from Basra, Iraq, but they had much in common. Both were oil towns in the desert. Both were deeply religious, although Baptists and Muslims appeared on opposite ends of the theological spectrum. And, soon enough, both Hobbs and Basra would have a killing in common.

Justin B. Bradley, known affectionately to his friends as Bum, hitched up his pants and pulled on his old, chapped Tony Lama boots. He looked like the classic portrait of a Western man: lean and lined as an old saddle, hair gray as shale rock, a smile bright and quick as dry lightning.

He grabbed a straw hat with a dipped front brim that made him look like an aging outlaw and headed down to a coffee shop that had never been violated by a barista.

Bum had spent twenty years in the US Air Force as a mechanic. He'd seen a nuclear bomb test near Christmas Island, then watched far bloodier action when stationed at a hangar in Thailand during the Vietnam War. Half the aircraft he'd kept ready for duty sooner or later failed to return. Young men, not much older than he had been, flew suicidal, low-altitude bombing runs against heavily defended targets. It was grim business bidding a possibly permanent good-bye to those flyboys.

The tragedies didn't slow till the first laser-guided smart bombs arrived. Bum was glad to install them and help end the wanton loss of so much life, but he'd never forgotten the fresh-faced young men who had arrived too early and died too soon.

Then he'd taken part in Operation Baby Lift in 1975, helping to evacuate thousands of children from Saigon—without their parents. After witnessing that heartache, he decided never to have a family. "Too much to lose," he once confided to his brother, Hiram.

Bum retired from the USAF in 1981, then joined Hiram in building a business headquartered in Hobbs. The two of them serviced oil rigs throughout the southern part of the Permian Basin, where oil and natural gas were pumped out of a sedimentary rock formation spread across 75,000 square miles.

The Bradley Brothers Company had done well, but when the brothers turned sixty they began to focus on the future of their firm. For starters they moved the equipment division to El Paso so they could better serve their increasing number of clients on the Front Range of the Rockies.

Then they gave consideration to who would eventually take over the company. Hiram's daughter, Sarah, had always been a bit of a tomboy and had turned into a terrific oilfield hand, so she was a sure pick for the front office. But Bum had never married, much less had children, so the brothers also had to look for young talent from outside the family. In 2007 Bum found their best prospect in Rosincourt Sadr, a bright, young fellow from UTEP. Rosincourt, with a sparse but shaped beard, was a natural mechanic and fully knowledgeable about the digital technology that was starting to befuddle Bum. Sure, Rosincourt was a bit standoffish, but the multilingual young man could talk to all the Hispanics working for the company.

Bum had always thought he could pick the winners at the starting gate, and *manager* might as well have been branded onto Rosincourt's brow—it was that obvious. Bum was also glad to have outbid an aerospace firm in LA. The young wizard had worked for them for a couple of summers, and the company wanted him bad, but Bum upped his offer and the boy was smart enough to say yes. Bum reckoned Rosincourt's future was as endless as the wide--open spaces around Hobbs.

Rosincourt also had a helluva sparkplug for a girlfriend—Soroya something or other. Much as Bum could figure, it didn't pay to learn her last name because it would soon be Sadr. She was a good Muslim girl; Bum didn't feature her keeping her own name. In bits and pieces he'd gleaned both kids, as he thought of them, had been raised by conservative parents.

And when the gal graduated from UCLA, she moved to El Paso to be with her beau. Bum and Hiram also hired her. She'd majored in biophysics at UCLA, so they started her as a lab tech.

She and Rosincourt shared a two-bedroom apartment on Festival Street, a few blocks from the El Paso Islamic Center on Paragon Lane. But Bum supposed if they were like most kids that age, they spent the lion's share of their time on a mattress, not a prayer rug. Hey, he was happy for them. Outside of the Islamic Center, Roz and Soroya could have felt like the odd ones out. But they had each other and good jobs, and if they worked hard they'd probably end up with the company as well.

That's America for you, Bum thought as he straddled a stool and watched a spry, older woman fill his cup with coffee and his face with a smile.

Soroya spotted Rosincourt overseeing the repair of an oil well drill bit in the new shop in El Paso. His parents had left an urgent message with a secretary, and Soroya wanted to flag his attention. Rosincourt's folks wouldn't have confided in her even if she had picked up the phone. His mother had remarked more than once that they were "living in sin."

Then talk to your son, she'd wanted to yell at her. He was the one balking at marriage.

Rosincourt was leaning over Juan Ortiz, pointing to something on the base of the bit. Soroya could wait. Both she and Roz had a more relaxed schedule since he'd gotten the Bradley brothers to move to El Paso. Even speeding, the drive to Hobbs took two and a half hours. The move also meant Bum wasn't around so much. He and Hiram were both making noises about getting away from day-to-day obligations. Sarah Bradley, Hiram's daughter, had already taken over the oilfield services division. All her old man did was some marketing, and Bum just kept his eye on the books.

Rosincourt had started working for them on July 5, 2007, right after the Americans celebrated Independence Day. Even though Soroya had still been at UCLA back then, she remembered that date every time she and Rosincourt drove down to Juarez. A smiling billboard of George W. Bush peered down at them from beside the freeway, asking, "Do you miss me yet?"

No! she always said to herself. Often she added any number of colorful expletives, but she also kept those to herself. Rosincourt didn't like it when she swore and had been aghast when she'd showed him the video of her parading with a poster that said the only bush she trusted was her own.

Seeing Bush's mug also made her think of Iranian president Mansoor Alizadeh. Yes, he looked like a freakin' nerd, but she liked his boldness. And he'd brought such a magnificent sense of purpose and destiny back to Iran. She'd minored in Persian history at UCLA and believed in the return of the Persian Empire, rejuvenated by technology and national pride. Oil could buy a lot, including a restoration of that magnitude.

On her first visit to southwest Texas, Soroya couldn't have imagined living out there in the dusty desert, but by the time she'd graduated from UCLA in 2009 she'd been ready to exit the stifling, self-centered atmosphere of Beverly Hills. And she'd wanted to see if Roz was really serious about her. She admired his technical brilliance, his generous nature in bed, and his political pliability. She'd even managed to get him to smoke pot. He'd been resistant at first, but once he saw the aphrodisiac effect the drug had on her, it had become a nighttime routine for both of them. But there was no getting around the one big drawback to El Paso and everything northeast of it: this was George W. Bush territory, and the folks there loved him.

It was assuredly not the place to walk into a science building and announce, "It's fun to blow people up," which, astoundingly, was what Ahmad Ibrahim Fares-Hammad, an electrical engineering student from Qatar, had done at UTEP. Rosincourt had met Fares-Hammad on the Internet and then had sipped a few cappuccinos with him at Starbucks, so he and Soroya had felt obliged to help him make bail after he'd been arrested for "maliciously making false information concerning alleged attempts to injure, kill, or unlawfully damage or destroy a building by means of explosive." Basically, for scaring the shit out of people.

What an idiot, Soroya said to herself when she recalled the incident. *What did he expect would happen when he walked in with a bunch of wires sticking out of a box?*

This was red-state America. If you were from the Mideast, you kept your head down. She sure didn't walk around with green hair anymore. She kept her black locks pulled tight at the nape of her neck and used just enough makeup to soften her looks. The political atmosphere of the whole country had darkened. The 2010 midterm election had repudiated the new American president, which had angered and depressed Roz and her. Then there'd been the indictment and trials of three Muslims—the 9/11 mastermind, the Detroit Christmas bomber, and the Times Square terrorist—which had produced a thunder of anti-Muslim rhetoric. In the South, a pinhead preacher made a big deal of burning a Koran. And overseas, air strikes in Afghanistan and on the Pakistani border left a trail of innocent civilians dead.

She flagged Rosincourt's attention, mouthing, "Message. Mother. Im-*por*-tant!" He nodded, and she returned to the lab, none too happy with him either of late. They'd been living together for more than a year. Wasn't this supposed to lead to…dare she say the word? Marriage. But Roz wouldn't even discuss it. She was beginning to worry that Bum Bradley might have been Roz's mentor in all things, not just business.

And look at that geezer. Perfectly happy and content living without a family. At times Soroya wondered if Roz was so old world he'd put her in a chador if he ever had the chance. It was one thing to take a hit of herb to fire up your libido or pop a little speed when you were working late hours, which Roz had done any number of times, but a little open-mindedness about drugs didn't make you believe your Muslim girlfriend would ever have a say equal to yours.

Soroya honestly wondered if things could get much worse. Then Roz came bursting into the laboratory, phone in hand. He was crying, more bereaved than she'd ever seen him.

"He's been murdered," Roz cried.

"Who?" she said.

"Mehdi, murdered by one of those drones." He threw the phone against the wall, shattering it, then fell to his knees.

She helped him to his office, and while he grieved openly she checked his e-mail to see if there was any news from his family overseas. She found a message from his Uncle Abulhassan, the former president:

From: BANISADR@AOL.FR
TO: REZAB@SPEAKEASY.NET
CC: ROSINCOURT@SPEAKEASY.NET
Date: Sun, Dec 19, 2010
Subject: PAINFUL NEWS FROM BASRA

Reza:

My son, Mehdi, has been murdered outside our holy city Karbala. He was en route from observing Ashura to Basra, where he was working toward Iranian ascendancy in southern Iraq.

He died as a result of a drone missile. Looks like the bombings earlier this year in Tehran. All had Mossad or CIA fingerprints all over them. Those people never sleep.

This is very difficult for us, but I want you to know what happened. As I learn more I will keep you posted. In any event, Inshallah.

With love, your brother, Abulhassan

Soroya called Bum and left a message, saying a death in the family was forcing them to leave early. She reached Sarah Bradley and repeated the same words, adding only that Roz was inconsolable.

"Go home, absolutely," Sarah said. "I'm so sorry to hear that."

Soroya pictured Hiram's thirty-three-year-old daughter, the phone headset pressing down on her red hair. "Thank you. I will."

Roz was curled up on a chair, shaking his head, wiping his eyes.

"Come on," she whispered to him. "Let's get out of here."

"Mehdi, Mehdi, Mehdi," he mumbled.

When she got him to stand, he moved like a man of eighty. She drove him home and wasn't surprised when he grabbed a can of Budweiser from the fridge and pulled out the pipe they used for their nightly indulgence. She did not admonish him; if ever there were a time to anaesthetize oneself, this was it. But she didn't join him. Somebody had to be clear-headed if one of the brothers called, even if just to offer condolences.

But what she really wanted to do was take some kind of action—get even with Mehdi's murderers. But how do you get even with unmanned planes that kill at the flick of a remote switch?

Not with posters or demonstrations. The biggest antiwar march in history had taken place in dozens of cities all over the world before the US had invaded Iraq, and it hadn't done a bit of good. But maybe in the end that was a good thing. She recalled Mehdi's talking to them from Paris soon after the US had rolled into Iraq. Roz had put his cousin on speakerphone and said, "Listen to this, Soroya. It's important."

Then Mehdi had said something she'd never forgotten: "The Americans are doing Shia business for us, Soroya. They're destroying the Iraqi army. They're not destroying a Muslim nation. Saddam's tanks are the only force standing between Iran and the Persian Gulf states, between us and the holy cities of Mecca and Medina. Between us and half the world's oil. Don't you guys worry about the war in Iraq. Just like Bush says, bring it on."

You were right, Mehdi. They did our work for us.

But that was Iraq, she reminded herself. *What about the United States?* she wondered.

They were the ones who murdered you.

CHAPTER 11
INVITATION TO THE DARK SIDE

December 2010–April 2011

Soroya watched Rosincourt stare at the papers on his desk. Since hearing about Mehdi's execution—that was what it had been, another American execution without the benefit of a trial or jury—she had also lost her edge. Imperfect work had slipped by her as Bradley Brothers' employees strove to meet their year-end production targets. She'd had to snap herself out of a funk and make the culprits do their work over. Lost time. Lost money.

She dragged Roz out to lunch and they came back marginally rejuvenated, managing to extend *"feliz Navidad"* greetings to their senior employees. They made a similar feint at a Christmas party that evening, but by mid-week in late December they gave up. The grief over Mehdi was too great, especially for Roz. They handed over management responsibility to an old-timer from the Hobbs days, and finalized their own holiday plans: Soroya to Beverly Hills, Roz to Houston.

Now at the terminal in El Paso, he gave her a good-bye hug no more heartfelt than his empty holiday greetings at work had been. And he didn't kiss her either.

"You going to be alright driving?" Houston was a twelve-hour, numbingly boring trip.

"Yeah." He was starting to look and sound pitiable. He hadn't bothered to trim his beard, and his stubble was taking over. His head hung down so much it could have been a deflated balloon.

"Hey, I mean it." She grabbed him. His response was not reassuring. He pulled out a small, white pill and popped it into his mouth without bothering with water. She'd never taken amphetamines, but he made a point of buying them every time they went to Juarez. Those little, white pills hadn't done anything for their sex life. At least it wasn't crystal meth.

"Don't overdo it," she warned him.

He walked off without a word, leaving her in the terminal.

Amateur hour, she said to herself when she shoehorned her body onto the flight to LA. It happened every Christmas when seasoned travelers suddenly found themselves cheek by jowl with the folks who flew only once a year—and then insisted on taking most of their household belongings with them, along with bags bursting with gaily wrapped gifts.

Soroya knew her mood had soured, but as far as she was concerned, she had ample reasons of her own to be depressed. Mehdi was dead and, truth be known, she'd had a crush on him. She'd never met him, but they'd talked on the phone, and she'd seen lots of photos. *And he's doing something.* Or was, she reminded herself. *What's Roz doing?* She imagined him staring at the highway, white-line fever burning up his brain.

Soroya's mother welcomed her with the warmest hug Soroya had known in days, but the older woman appeared anxious, peppering her with questions about how Roz was handling the news of his cousin's death.

"Roz? How about me, Mom? I knew Mehdi too."

"Did you? Did you meet him?" Mrs. Assaf asked as if in awe of that possibility, her Iranian accent still as strong as it had been on the day they'd fled Tehran.

"I talked to him on the phone. A lot."

"But Roz was his *cousin*. This is a terrible thing. Mehdi should have stayed in Paris."

"Mom," Soroya said sternly, "he was fighting for Persian pride. Don't you understand that?"

Her mother waved her hand. "Oh, you and your politics, and only trusting your own you-know-what." She gestured at her daughter's privates, which made Soroya glower. "I do not want to hear about such things."

Welcome home, Soroya said to herself.

Her friends from high school and college still appeared shell-shocked by the success of the Tea Party in the fall elections. She met half a dozen of them at one of their favorite watering holes on Sunset Boulevard.

"How is this happening?" asked a blond woman who had taken two political science classes with Soroya. "They're working people voting against their own self-interest."

Working people? Soroya looked at the brass and walnut surroundings, the crystal tumblers and mirrors, and heard the soft, cosseting music. *What do we know about working people? We grew up in Beverly Hills.* Her sour mood still stamped her.

"The whole country has turned into a bumper sticker," she replied. "They're dumber than stumps."

"Maybe," said a frizzy, auburn-haired guy she'd known since her freshman year at Beverly Hills High, "but they're winning." He raised his glass, a gesture more suitable to a wake than a gathering of old friends. Nobody else said a word. It was clear to Soroya politics was not on the table at this gathering, and certainly not the debacle in Iraq. She made one more attempt to vilify American actions in the Middle East but there were no comers—and these were friends who'd demonstrated with her. Nothing but shrugs and stony silence. It was as if they were saying, "Sure, the CIA is the devil. Tell us something we *don't* know."

"It's Christmas," a pixyish girl said. "Everything else," she added, "is just bullshit."

Soroya's longtime neighbors hosted equally bland social gatherings. Most of them were of Iranian heritage. Alizadeh's name came up, and he was quickly denounced. He was called a fanatic, a crazy man, as if insults were all he deserved—the only man brave enough to take on the West and Israel openly.

Soroya simmered.

Rosincourt drove. After leaving Soroya at the airport, he headed eastward. That first night he made it as far as a roadhouse outside Ft. Stockton. He'd settled into his second beer when the bartender announced he'd put together a top-ten list of America's most patriotic songs.

Oh, no, Roz said to himself. He looked around uneasily. He was the only guy in the bar not sporting a Western hat. Right about then he wished he'd borrowed one of Bum's.

Roz's eyes dipped. He saw nothing but boots, and they looked pointy and damaging, and this was the kind of music he loathed: Tim McGraw and Trace Adkins and Lee Greenwood and Merle Haggard.

The fightin' side of me?

Was it Roz's imagination, or was he getting jostled every time someone walked by him? Uh-oh, he just heard a guy say he'd like to kick some Iraqi butt. But it might have been the song, with lyrics about putting a boot up somebody's ass.

Like mine.

Roz didn't dare move. So he ordered another beer. And another. Pretty soon. his bladder was singing its own song, and it wasn't about fighting Iraqis. It was about peeing his pants.

He glanced around. "Where's the bathroom?" he asked the barkeep.

"The bathroom?" the big guy bellowed. He looked like a weight lifter. "Back there." he pointed.

Might as well have yodeled that the rag head was heading for the can as far as Roz was concerned. But he *had* to go.

He eased off the stool, got bumped again. Did someone say "sorry about that?" He wanted to think so.

Man, he was fucked up. He brushed by a crowded table, inadvertently elbowing a woman with long, red hair in a white-straw cowboy hat. He apologized profusely. All he got from the guys and their dates was stink eye.

I'm pulp, he told himself, remembering photos of wood mash from some class at UTEP.

He felt safer in a stall. He locked the door. Lots of traffic in and out. He peed for an hour, maybe two. When he came out, he caught some glances but washed up and headed back to the bar. It felt like an island of calm. Or maybe it was the beer.

The songs were still playing. Each time the barkeep would say, "Remember this one?" Or, "Man, this one gets me *so* bad."

What are you doing here? Roz asked himself. He figured he'd better get out before the music whipped the locals into a frenzy. Not a dark face in the place except for his.

But as he paid his bill, the bartender gave him a nod and said, "Come on back anytime you want. We got room for you. You hear what I'm saying? And do yourself a favor, son, don't be driving."

Roz nodded. A few moments later he climbed into the backseat of his car and passed out.

He awoke with a raging hangover, glad only that he had gotten some sleep. Between those little, white pills and all the grief he'd been feeling, sleep had come in fits and starts. But last night, thanks to his old friend Bud, he'd banged out some Zs.

He climbed over the seat and opened the glove compartment for a couple of extra-strength something or others. Popped them without water too, like a real pill-head. Then he poured himself out of the car, aware that he was cold. He spotted the bar, dark at dawn, but across the way he saw a breakfast place and wandered over.

Revived, he drove a few more hours before nodding off in a rest area. He drove the rest of the way to Houston in silence. No radio, no country music *please*, just thinking. At sundown he exited Interstate 10 for the festive streets of River Oaks. Christmas lights wrapped every tree, and gift-laden sleighs appeared on half the lawns—in a town where it never snowed.

Roz made it just in time for a traditional and bountiful Christmas dinner. His mother had roasted a wild turkey one of the neighbors had bagged on a recent hunt. The rich scent activated Roz's appetite, which had gone dormant what with the little, white pills becoming an everyday habit. But he'd held off on them today because his mother and father had a way of seeing right through him. It never felt good to catch their gaze when he'd taken pills or smoked pot or hoisted another Bud.

No one mentioned Mehdi over dinner. The family gathered in the large, well-lit dining room, joined by their mostly Christians friends. But Roz had to admit they'd never spurned his family. All of them were connected to the oil industry in one way or another and most were technically trained. After his mother served up a special Christmas spice cake and the guests left, Roz and his father settled down to talk about Iran—and Mehdi's grim fate.

His dad led him into a study lined with bookshelves packed with all manner of literature from Iran, Europe, Asia, and the States. His father had always been a great reader of fiction, Roz less so. Roz preferred technical books and eschewed tales real or imagined.

"Mehdi was a victim, son," his father said, "and I feel terrible about what happened to him. You can't imagine the pain Uncle Abulhassan is going through. But his boy made some mistakes. He let his anger at the past blind him to the tragedies of the present."

"What?" Roz already felt impatient with his father. Why was he insinuating there was anything tragic about Iran nowadays? But before he could gather his wits to respond, the young man was surprised to hear his father criticizing the CIA.

"They toppled our *democratically* elected government in 1953. I was a little boy, Roz, but I saw it happen. They forced the shah down our throats, and that's the way it was for a quarter of a century. The Americans, Brits, and Israelis ran our country through the shah and took whatever they could, including our wealth. And then the Americans sold the shah all the military hardware he wanted. For what?"

Roz had no answer. It pained him to realize his father knew more of this shameful history than he did.

"To keep down his own people. So when the revolution came in 1979, it offered us hope. That's what Uncle Abulhassan thought when he went back to Tehran, but events ran out of control. That's when the hardliners took over. Those of us who had hoped for a true republic had to leave, and I'm glad we did, Roz. If we had stayed, it would have been horrible. The CIA did everything it could to cripple the economy over there. Then they sided with Saddam Hussein during the ten years of war that killed a million of our people. A *million*. You weren't even alive for most of that, but it was so hard to live here in Houston knowing that our taxes were helping to pay for the guns that were killing our own people. But what could we do?"

That was the question Roz had been asking himself—*What can I do?*—ever since he'd heard about Mehdi's murder.

"Uncle Abulhassan made mistakes too," his father went on. "He let himself get too close to the wrong people—Reagan's men and the Bush family. But Mehdi went too far the other way. Did you know he joined up with Alizadeh's friends in Paris? And then, after he graduated from university, he moved back to Tehran?" Roz nodded. "Did you know he joined the Basiji?" Roz nodded again. "Those are scary people. *He* should have been afraid of them, but instead he was deeply involved in Alizadeh's campaign for reelection, which was a farce. There was no way the Iranian people were going to make him president again. The economy was sinking. Unemployment was over twenty percent. Inflation was out of control. They didn't even have gas. How pathetic was that? A big oil producer and they didn't even have enough gasoline to run their own country. So those people stole the election."

Roz figured he must have blanched because his father nodded emphatically.

"That's exactly what they did. They stole it. And Mehdi and his Basiji friends did the dirty work. They intimidated voters, destroyed voting machines, then in the poorer parts of Tehran and in the outer cities they paid voters to stuff the ballot boxes for Alizadeh. Hossein Mousavi really won, the whole world knows it, but Iran got that religious fascist again. Your cousin was on the front lines. That was no secret, son. He did a very thorough job of beating up, torturing, or killing any Green Revolution demonstrators he could find."

Roz shook his head. "I do not believe Mehdi would have done those things. He fought with honor. They killed him."

"They did not kill him, Roz." His father looked around the room. "The country we live in did that."

"And we helped pay for his murder," Roz jumped back in, echoing what his father had said moments earlier about Saddam Hussein.

"That's true, but Mehdi had blood on his hands. Listen to me. When the Revolutionary Guards took over the government, guys like your cousin got huge promotions. He was working for General Qassem Suleimani, the commander of the Quds Force. That's why Mehdi was on his way to Basra. The Quds sent him there to export Iran's revolution. They got him smuggled into the Shia neighborhoods. He was organizing them to take over Iraq when the Americans left. Uncle Abulhassan told me all of this. He's heartbroken, Roz, like I would be if anything ever happened to you. But he's not kidding himself about Mehdi. The boy had his heart in the right place, but he sided with the wrong people. He sided with the men who drove your uncle and me to seek refuge in France and here. Do you understand? It's not simple, Roz. I want *you* to understand that because Mehdi never did."

Rosincourt spent the following week trying to figure out who *he* was. American? Muslim? Iranian? He was all of those things. Which only confused him more until he asked himself what ranked highest in anyone's life. Was it a country? Or God? Of course it was God. Then he realized, first and foremost, he was a Muslim, a Shiite. And as a Shiite, Iran was as critical to him as Israel was to a Jew.

For the first time in his life, Rosincourt felt clear about his allegiances. He was stunned he hadn't recognized this sooner. Shiites were not Sunnis. Sunnis were the men who took over planes and flew them into the World Trade Center towers. And they were mostly from Saudi Arabia. They committed acts of terror for what seemed like the flimsiest reasons. *But we who come from Iran look at things differently.*

His thinking grew only sharper on his drive back to El Paso. Twelve hours to mull over his recognition that he was a Shiite first, an Iranian second. American? That was an accident of birth, but his religion was ordained by God. *God!*

When he walked into the apartment on Festival Street, he found Soroya sitting at the table, reading the copy of the Koran that had been on a bookshelf for too long. He hadn't taken a single white pill or smoked pot. He hadn't stopped for beer. He was thinking clearly. That was why he knew, when he looked in her eyes and nodded at her, that she would nod back.

And she did.

But old habits are hard to break, and the fierceness of Roz's insights might have paled entirely if what appeared to be a chance encounter hadn't taken place. Since Soroya had come to El Paso they had been going down to Juarez to hang out at the Don Quintin, their favorite cantina. The restaurant and saloon lay just south of the Rio Grande and across Chamizal Park. They both knew the drug war in Mexico, with its scores of macabre murders, made any visit to that notorious city dangerous, but the allure of the outlaw life in the border towns also titillated them.

Three months earlier they'd arrived within minutes of a real gangland slaying. But the proprietor had ushered them past four shot-up bodies as if the dead were a minor inconvenience, and Roz and Soroya had been seated alongside locals more inured to the violence.

Now, after they drove across the border and saw the ambulances and heard sirens and watched the drug lords' black SUVs cruising the streets like sharks, they experienced a peculiar thrill. Roz wasn't even surprised to hear Soroya start singing an old Lou Reed song, "Walk on the Wild Side," as they pulled up to the Don Quintin. After all, the drug lords were fighting the Americans too. If that wastrel of a country a few miles away had not turned into a nation of drug abusers, these poor Mexicans wouldn't be slaughtering one another for the right to service the craven needs of the *norteamericanos*.

Roz had begun to refract everything in the world, even the wanton violence of drug kingpins, through the prism of his disgust with America.

They walked inside—no bodies to step over today—and the handsome, mustached owner greeted them like the oldest of friends. Roz ordered a tall-neck Bud, telling himself it was just so the alcohol could clear his tongue of the hot peppers in the salsa and mole. He had cut back his drinking a lot. He'd begun to believe his fate was to return to Iran, and he couldn't go back to such a sacred land with bad habits. So one beer. *That's all.*

He was nursing his third Bud when a couple they'd met at the Islamic Center stopped by their table. They were very pious, and it surprised Roz to see them in the bar. Surprised Soroya, too, by the look on her face.

The husband, Irwandi Bereueh, was a tall, broad-shouldered man in his forties, a visiting professor in the Geophysics Department at the New Mexico Institute of Mining and Technology in Socorro, a center for high-explosives research. He always looked rumpled, the quintessential academic, but for his eyes. Roz had noticed the man's focus was intense, as if he were determined to peer right through him.

Marshanda was Irwandi's wife. Both were of Indonesian heritage. After Roz and Soroya had seen them half a dozen times at the Islamic Center, they'd dubbed the couple Adam and Eve because they seemed inseparable. They were in the States as part of a cultural exchange by a private organization that aimed to bring together the oil-producing cultures of the world. Adam and Eve did mention at one point they were from Aceh. Roz noticed at the time that Irwandi had paused after he'd said the name of their home province, as if it should mean something. It hadn't, so Roz Googled it when they got home from the center.

Quite an eyeful greeted him on the screen. Aceh was a restive region on the northern tip of Sumatra. Very different from the rest of Indonesia. It was thought to have been Islam's first toehold in the equatorial land area that lay between the Pacific and Indian oceans. He wasn't surprised to find it was rich with oil and gas, or that ExxonMobil was the major operator there. The corporation, he read, had hired and trained locals and promoted them to positions of considerable responsibility. Roz would have bet a paycheck that Irwandi Bereueh was one of the beneficiaries.

So he Googled him as well and found, sure enough, ExxonMobil had once awarded Irwandi a scholarship to study petroleum engineering at the University of Southern California. But Irwandi, from what Roz could gather, had returned from laid-back Los Angeles to a province radicalized by Muslim resentment of the Suharto regime. The Jemaah Islamiyah, or Islamic Congregation, had taken root there in Irwandi's absence. The JI, as it was called, was a Shiite military group focused on overthrowing the Suharto regime and expelling all Western influence from Indonesia. Roz wondered what Irwandi and Marshanda, who was an ExxonMobil secretary, thought about JI, which had turned virulently violent by the late 1990s. According to the reports Roz read, the Islamists had hooked up with Osama bin Laden, and by the early years of the new decade had targeted high-profile tourist areas with horrific bombings.

Roz wondered if Mehdi or any of the other Iranians in the Revolutionary Guard had taken notice and tried to recruit the JI. As fellow Shiites they would have had a lot in common.

He and Soroya invited Irwandi and Marshanda to join them at their table. What else could they have done? Roz didn't want to spurn them, even though the censorious glances they were throwing at his Bud meant he would soon be switching to the lemonade Soroya favored. At least he wasn't blasted on Bud and bud. He smiled at his private joke.

Adam and Eve ordered tea and plates of chicken enchiladas.

"They're so good here," Soroya enthused after the waitress, in colorful native garb, took the order. "We had some the last time we were here."

That brought up talk of the dead bodies they'd had to skirt to get into the Don Quintin.

"These poor people," Irwandi said. "They are being destroyed by the depraved appetites of all those drug addicts."

Roz detected a guarded manner in Irwandi's words, as if he might have said "all those *American* drug addicts" had he known his audience better.

"Do Americans even realize how much they're hated?" Roz said bluntly. It was not a question.

"I doubt that very much," Irwandi replied. "They are too self-absorbed."

"They're narcissists," Soroya chimed in. "Like little children standing in front of mirrors, always looking at their reflections, never at their real selves."

"Who would want to look at that?" Marshanda replied.

With that many-layered exchange, Roz knew the foursome had settled the key question that haunted so many encounters with other Shiites in America: did any of them approve of the Great Satan? Most Iranians liked America, so one had to be careful; but clearly Adam and Eve loathed their host country. Roz felt everyone relax.

A mariachi band came out, and soon the Don Quintin came alive with dancing. By the end of the evening, Roz felt he and Soroya had made wonderful new friends, and that he'd misjudged the couple. From Soroya's beaming face, he could tell she liked them too.

When Adam and Eve suggested meeting with fellow Iranians in a couple of weeks, Soroya said, "That would be great. We could go dancing again."

Roz asked if he and Soroya already knew these Iranians from the Islamic Center, "Like we know you guys."

Irwandi shook his head and said, "Better to keep this to ourselves."

The younger couple drove back across the border to the Great Satan with Adam and Eve trailing right behind them.

CHAPTER 12
TRIALS

May–October 2011

In the spring of 2011, a new and far more effective drone had been introduced into the surveillance war along the Pakistan-Afghan border. *Something's up* Elizabeth thought. These new birds, known as Sentinels, were flown by teams of her peers in separate trailers, so the sudden increase in Sentinel flights puzzled her. The full magnitude of Operation *Neptune Spear* became clear only during the first week of May when a dozen navy SEALS invaded Osama Bin Laden's Pakistan hideout and soon dumped his dead body into the Arabian Sea.

When the news arrived at Al Udeid, she and the rest of the base burst into a spontaneous celebration. It wouldn't bring back Flash or the thousands of others murdered in attacks planned by the al-Qaeda mastermind, but it announced to the world that nobody was secure if they committed those kinds of crimes, not even if they had the protection of the Pakistani military and intelligence agencies, which was becoming increasingly obvious to Elizabeth and others.

Intelligence officials realized very quickly that bin Laden's death's left them with no time to lower their guard. Quite the opposite because the huge intelligence haul from Abbottabad forced those officials to recognize the need for a terrorism triage. Not those words exactly, but the emergency room image occurred to Elizabeth when she was quickly reassigned to El Paso. It might have sounded like a dreary posting to some agents, but she knew better: Iran's Hezbollah cells had begun to metastasize throughout Mexico, a country greatly weakened by a savage drug war. Intelligence reports said Hezbollah's careful dispersing of guerilla units—so successful in Lebanon—now appeared to be the modus operandi in Mexico. Elizabeth, with her fluency in Farsi and encyclopedic knowledge of the Iranian players, was an ideal agent to confront this emerging threat.

By the start of summer, she was working out of the El Paso office of the Bureau of Alcohol, Tobacco, Firearms, and Explosives, known colloquially as the ATF. She settled into a spacious apartment in the hills above the city, and in the evenings she enjoyed the sunset over the Rio Grande River and the mountains to the west.

Her days were spent in a covert federal complex amid the strip malls, motels, and gas stations on one of the city's main streets. Across the border the CIA had established a network of eyes and ears among the women who worked in the maquiladora. Elizabeth chortled when she found out what some of these informants manufactured during their long shifts: shawls for sale to Muslims in the US.

Some things you just can't make up, she said to herself, still beaming over the irony, but her smile slipped away when she learned that America's new Sentinel drones were now in the skies over Iran. Her thoughts returned to earlier briefings at the Naval Postgraduate School. *Had Iran's Hezbollah been able to spoof Israel's drones? What if they took control of a more sophisticated American prize over Iran? What if they could land one there? Not good!*

Two weeks after the soirée with Adam and Eve at the Don Quintin, Rosincourt and Soroya drove back across the border to the Plaza Consulado Motel, located a few blocks away from their favorite haunt.

Irwandi and Marshanda Bereueh met them in the parking lot, but the convivial smiles that had marked their recent greetings at the Islamic Center were gone.

"Come with us," Irwandi said, escorting them up rusty metal stairs to an unkempt and foul suite on the third floor. Once inside they found a local technician conducting an electronic sweep of the room.

"What's going on?" asked Soroya, who received a stern head shake from Roz, as if she'd committed a grievous wrong by having the temerity to speak up.

"We want you to meet someone," Irwandi said.

"A fellow Iranian," Marshanda added, still not smiling.

This is no party, Soroya thought.

If she had any remaining doubts, they disappeared when a tall, dark-haired man with a hard face walked into the room displaying a permanent scowl, imprinted on his face the way a handprint is set in concrete. He reviewed the sweep of the room before nodding at Irwandi, who then introduced him.

"Rosincourt, I would like you to meet Colonel Ashkan Gharabaghi, a senior officer in Iran's Revolutionary Guard Corps."

A startled Roz stuck out his hand. Colonel Gharabaghi shook it firmly. He glared at Soroya. The young woman was so stunned by this obvious affront she merely stared back, taking in a lot quickly. His manner of dress was not what she associated with a military man. He wore Levis and a snug T-shirt that flattered his hard torso. *A vain man*, she decided. This became even more apparent when she noticed his hair had the scantiest gray roots.

With the introduction completed, the colonel dismissed the Bereuehs as so much furniture. Soroya considered it a victory that she hadn't also been banished.

When Adam and Eve closed the door behind them, the colonel looked Roz in the eye and said, "You must be clear, when I talk to you or you"—he allocated a glance in Soroya's direction—"you must never speak of this to anyone."

When they both nodded, the colonel continued, "The new president of Iran is my lifelong comrade."

Soroya, astonished to be in the same room with one of Alizadeh's closest friends, eased aside her sense of insult and listened to the colonel carefully.

"Mansoor and I served together on the front lines in the Iraq-Iran War. We scouted the deserts of Kazakhstan. We got rid of the *kafar* when they tried to take over Iran's government. I got Mansoor in as mayor of Tehran. I worked on his first election for president. I made sure he had the votes for reelection two years ago. I took care of those Green Revolution people."

I, I, I. It's all about him, Soroya thought. *What an egomaniac.* But what made her shiver was the last comment about the Green Revolution. He might as well have said he'd imprisoned, tortured, or killed everyone he could find who was protesting the transparently fraudulent presidential election returns of 2009. She hoped his sharp eyes had missed her shudder.

She thought they had. He spoke almost entirely to Roz. Soroya wondered what Rosincourt was thinking.

Gharabaghi confirmed his authority within the military chain of command: "I am a colonel in the Quds Force."

Soroya knew this was the intelligence arm of the Revolutionary Guard Corps.

"General Suleimani is my boss."

That comment appeared to register with Roz, who nodded.

"What do you know about the great general?" Gharabaghi asked immediately.

"My cousin, Mehdi, spoke highly of him," Roz said.

The colonel nodded. "That is why we are talking to you. We know about you from Mehdi. He said you are a very skilled engineer. We were so sorry about his death at the hands of the murderous Americans."

Roz nodded vehemently now. Soroya thought he looked spellbound. Perhaps he was, especially if he'd realized, as she had, that Colonel Gharabaghi had set out specifically to reach Roz. That could set any young man's head to spinning—to learn the president of Iran's best buddy wanted you. Running into Adam and Eve, she realized, had been no accident.

"What do you think of what the Americans did to your cousin?" the colonel asked Roz.

"I hate it," Roz said. "He was working for all Shiites, and the Americans cut him down like a dog."

Colonel Gharabaghi nodded. "Mehdi said if anything ever happened to him, we should make sure we contacted you. He said you understand the importance of blood. You come from the same family seed. Is that true?"

"Yes. I felt like my arm was cut off when I heard what happened to Mehdi."

"It was," the colonel said. "Every time we lose a brave solider of Shia, we lose another limb. But every time we strike back, we build a stronger body for all true Persians."

Much as Soroya had been put off by the colonel's chilliness toward her, she was impressed by those words. Shiites had been horribly abused. *But we're getting stronger.* And these older men—she glanced at Gharabaghi— they were just slow to adjust to women in a changing world. As if to confirm this further, the colonel ordered her to go lunch with Adam and Eve.

"I must talk to Rosincourt alone."

On the walk to Don Quintin's, neither of Soroya's newfound friends would discuss the colonel or what he might have been saying to Roz. They remained as taciturn after ordering lunch. Soroya had to make do with her chicken enchiladas in mole sauce, and the recorded love songs of heartsick Mexican singers.

Then, in the afternoon, the colonel met alone with Soroya, querying her about her background.

"You used to protest a lot. I have seen a video of you on the 'net. It is a disgrace. Immoral. Is that your true self? A sinful woman who will parade around in public with a sign about her private parts?"

"I was a different person then," she said.

"Were you? You wanted to stop the US invasion of Iraq. Why? That would have strengthened our enemies. The US did us a great favor. Were you too stupid to see that?"

"I just thought it was wrong. I didn't know any better. I see now why it was good."

"It is better than good. We are taking over Iraq. The US broke it apart, and now we are putting the pieces back together the way we want. The Great Satan"—he shook his head—"was so stupid it defied reason. Never in my life would I have even hoped for such a gift, and Allah gave it to us. *Inshallah*, they will suffer dearly for their mistake. But for you, is coming here just another way to protest?"

"No. I want to help."

His dark eyes stared at her. "Tell Rosincourt to come back in. You may stay too now."

When Roz sat back down, the colonel said, "I will check a few things. Come back in two weeks. Irwandi will tell you where and when. But do not speak to him or Marshanda about anything, and if they ask you questions about what we have said inside these four walls, you must tell me. If you speak of this meeting to anyone, even if the Americans torture you, we will find you and make you beg us to return you to the bloody hands of your tormentors."

Soroya left the Plaza Consulado Motel feeling scared and shaky but honored. She had just joined the long line of great Persians who had dedicated their lives to the Shia cause, to the greater glory of God.

They waited for two weeks. Marshanda accosted Soroya just as she was leaving the Islamic Center.

"Congratulations," the older woman said. "I *think* you made it. The colonel would like to talk to you some more. Can we all meet over there in Juarez next Friday? Ten o'clock a.m. in the parking lot of the Villa del Sol?"

"Yes, absolutely."

After receiving directions, Soroya was tempted to joke about looking forward to more of the colonel's lighthearted humor, but she remembered his admonitions and thought better of it.

She hurried to her car, eager to tell Roz but also wondering what "made it" meant. What did it entail? The same mixture of excitement and fear she'd known upon first leaving the colonel's company suffused her limbs now.

Soroya felt much the same way when she and Roz met Irwandi and Marshanda in another dusty parking lot to climb another set of rusty stairs. This time the Bereuehs were dismissed immediately, and Soroya assumed the room had been swept before they'd arrived. The colonel met alone with them again, his greetings as perfunctory and unsmiling as they had been three weeks earlier.

"*Mekhham dar bareh shoma beshtar bedanam.*" I want to learn more about you, he said in Farsi before switching to his impeccable English. "But I'll let the Americans do the work." The hint of a grin crossed his face. Soroya was not pleased to see this but couldn't have said why.

"I'd like to see if you can get approved by Los Alamos. Let's see if they will accept you as a small business contractor. It's called the Central Contractor Registration database. I want *them* to look for arrest records or any other bad things on you. I'll let *them* tell *me* if you are clean. If they approve you, we'll also know you're not under any suspicion by the US government. That is critical."

Soroya wanted to ask why but knew better. The colonel had been clear that his organization, whatever it was in Mexico, functioned on a need-to-know basis only.

He gave Roz copies of the Los Alamos application forms and wished him well.

"This will take a couple of months," he concluded. "People in the US Department of Energy are bureaucrats. They do not want a bunch of Muslims in their club, but that's okay. They are thorough and very picky. If you are approved, tell Irwandi. Then we'll set a date to meet again here in Juarez."

When the colonel stood for a handshake, Roz shocked Soroya by actually asking him a question: "Why do we always meet in Mexico?"

For a moment Soroya thought the colonel would smack him, but then that slight grin of his reappeared, along with Soroya's uneasy feelings.

"My associates and I have no plans to visit the USA. We use Chihuahua. It's simpler to move around here, as long as we have guards. Travel to the US? A hassle."

The colonel ended the conversation with a brisk *Huda hafiz*. God protect. In less than thirty minutes, their second meeting with the man was over. The colonel had barely acknowledged Soroya's presence.

"Do you notice the way he treats me, Roz?" she asked on their way back across the border. "I might as well be invisible. Doesn't he realize I'm an equal part of this thing?"

"Take it easy, Soroya. He's fine. You know how these guys are."

I sure do, she thought.

One week later Rosincourt and Soroya dutifully drove their minivan to Los Alamos, one of the largest science and technology laboratories in the world. Nine thousand people worked there, and about six hundred fifty contactors did business with the lab. Roz and Soroya hoped to become two of the latter. Bum and Hiram Bradley loved the idea of expanding their operation, congratulating the kids on taking the initiative to become contractors at that impressive facility.

Roz and Soroya drove past thousands of acres of burned forest that had threatened Los Alamos the previous summer, then spotted a large, stone sign that greeted visitors and employees alike. Soroya wondered if it had been installed long ago enough to greet the scientists who had worked on the Manhattan Project during World War II—the men and women who had developed the atomic bombs that were dropped on Japan.

Guards admitted the two of them to the unclassified part of the laboratory for an interview with a surprisingly amiable woman who reviewed the application as they sat there. She brushed jet-black bangs from her eyes and smiled.

"We'll have to inspect the Bradley Brothers plant. Are you aware of that? We'll be going through it with a fine-tooth comb."

"Yes, we understand," Soroya said while Roz sat unspeaking, as if they had something to hide.

Sure enough the inspection proved every bit as thorough as the interviewer had suggested. The Bradley Brothers Company passed and was quickly certified to perform unclassified contract work on mechanical fabrication projects for Los Alamos.

Within twenty-four hours Adam and Eve dropped by Soroya and Roz's apartment to pick up the certification documents. Two weeks later they again knocked on the door. No phones were ever used.

"It appears you're both clean." Irwandi beamed at the two of them. "At least in the eyes of the Americans. We'll let the colonel's friends worry about your loyalty to Muhammad." These words sent a chill down Soroya's spine.

Just as she thought Irwandi was through, he put his hand on the door-frame as if to forestall her closing him out of the apartment. "Before your next meeting," he went on, "the colonel would like you to take your car down to the Buenos Neumáticos Garaje on North Mesa. Our security people are suspicious of GPS trackers attached to cars. They want to do a scan."

"Sure thing," Rosincourt said. "Good idea."

"I'll make a date for you on a Thursday afternoon," Irwandi offered. "Then you should head over to Juarez early the next morning. The Plaza Juarez Park Hotel this time on Avenida Lincoln y Coyoacan. See you at the usual hour? Ten a.m.?"

"Done deal," Roz said.

Two weeks later Roz took his minivan to the Buenos Neumáticos, an unusually spotless garage. The Hispanic manager, dressed in a white lab coat, said Roz could come back after supper. "We'll be done by then. It's tedious. Takes time."

Roz wandered over to an Indian restaurant to kill time over lamb curry and Raj beer. When he made his way back to the garage, the manager handed him the key fob.

"What do I owe you?" Roz asked him.

"No charge. That's been taken care of. *Está bien.*" The manager smiled.

Roz walked into the Festival Street apartment looking relaxed. When Soroya kissed him, she knew why: beer.

"How many?" she asked.

"Just two."

Which means three or four, she thought. "You're going to fuck up and get a DUI," she said to him.

"Don't say 'fuck up.'"

"Why? You do. Oh, but I'm a *lady*? Is that it?"

"Just don't do it. It could slip out around him."

Roz didn't even need to say Gharabaghi's name. And as much as Soroya resented the warning, she knew Roz was right.

"Fine," she snapped. "But don't drink and drive. What did they do to the van anyway?"

"Checked it out for the GPS, I guess."

"You guess? Didn't you stay and watch?" she asked him.

"No. He said I could leave and come back, so I did."

Soroya was immediately suspicious. How could she not be? she wondered, looking at Roz with his beer buzz. El Paso was a crossing for tons of drugs. But then she reminded herself the drugs flowed north to the appetites of the decadent Americans, not south to the suppliers. *Relax.*

Marshanda, aka Eve, came by moments later. *Not a coincidence*, Soroya realized when the older woman reminded them Soroya and Roz were to drive over to Juarez the following morning, the start to the Labor Day weekend.

"There's going to be a huge line at the border," Soroya complained.

"That's when he wants to see you," Marshanda replied.

The next morning, as they sat in the fume-choked line pointing south, Roz at the wheel, Soroya noticed the minivan had been vacuumed. "Did you clean this?" she asked him.

Roz glanced around. "No, but the garage was immaculate. They probably do that as part of their service.

What service? she wondered.

Her unease intensified as they inched closer to the border station. What if the Mexicans found something?

What? she kept asking herself. *You're not moving drugs, for chrissakes.* If this had happened on the other side of the border, Soroya would have refused to drive across. She figured she was just getting uneasy because every time they met with the colonel the stakes appeared to get higher, and sooner or later something really big had to be on the agenda. Why else were they going through all of this? Hadn't the Bereuehs sought out Roz?

Didn't the colonel remark specifically on her boyfriend's engineering skills? *So you're not some mule. Relax. They're not going to find anything.*

"They" were the mean-looking Mexican border guards who ordered them out of the van. Every other car had moved right through with a guard's glance at passports and a minimum of conversation. Getting ordered out of their vehicle had never happened to Soroya and Roz before.

"Stand over there," said a guard with the belly of a man who had entertained too many combination plates at the local cantina.

Two guards inspected the bottom of the car by running mirrors all along its sides. Another guard pored over the interior.

Oh, shit. Soroya spotted a German shepherd and his handler approaching. She glared at Roz. *You better not have fucked up.*

The dog looked frighteningly alert. It sniffed the van like a bone might have been behind every bumper and wheel. This went on for at least five minutes, which Soroya figured cost her five pounds of water weight. Hot and scared and sweating in the broiling summer sun.

The guard with the dog said something quickly in Spanish to the big-bellied commander, who glared at her, then said, "Go."

Roz, who looked like he was ready to keel over from the heat and a hangover, handed her the keys—a rare event.

She took them gladly—anything to get moving—and they navigated a narrow backstreet in Juarez until they spotted a veritable greeting committee. Adam and Eve, of course, but a Mexican man with dark hair and a white suit was also with them along with a local security guard. The bulge from his shoulder holster gave away his role.

After the briefest greeting, Irwandi said the men needed to conduct a complete check of the minivan. "Mr. Acuña here would like to borrow it for half an hour while you have coffee with the colonel. He's waiting for you upstairs in room 305. Pablo"—he indicated the security guard—"will make sure nothing disappears from your car."

"Okay, no problem," Roz mumbled, but Soroya heard his unease, which echoed her own.

She handed the keys to the suited man, Mr. Acuña. The dark van soon disappeared into the warren of Juarez streets, the bodyguard riding shotgun.

Adam and Eve herded the younger couple up crumbling concrete stairs. Soroya had noticed that so much of Juarez appeared to be falling down.

They entered a spacious suite where Colonel Gharabaghi immediately had them all sit around a chipped-veneer table. He served them coffee, then asked Roz and Soroya more about their personal lives, including details contained in the Los Alamos certification report he had before him.

"What you do for fun?"

Fun? Mr. Serious, Mr. Torture and Murder the Green Revolution, was asking what they did for *fun?* Something was up—Soroya just knew it. The curious chitchat continued for almost an hour before the door swung open without a knock. Mr. Acuña beamed ear to ear and gave the car keys back to Roz, and a small slip of paper to Gharabaghi.

"It's all there, sir," he said with a laugh.

Gharabaghi also broke into a broad grin. "Nice work, Rosincourt. You passed a second screening test. We now trust you. And you earned respect from friends we need."

"*What* test?" Soroya asked pointedly, which drew the colonel's first glare of the day.

"Well, son," Gharabaghi said only to Roz, not replying to her, "Los Aztecas have a problem." The colonel had just named a notorious Mexican drug gang with roots in El Paso and an estimated 5,000 members in Juarez alone. "How do they bring home cash they earn selling drugs in the US? You just brought over a quarter million dollars for them, sixty thousand inside each tire." The colonel's smile broadened. "Not much by their standards, but enough that I'll bet you had a nice, firm ride down Juarez's potholed streets."

Roz laughed. Soroya blanched. She hated Mexican gangs. LA was filthy with them. They raped and murdered and forced young girls into prostitution. And she was bringing their money back across the border? A frickin' *mule* for *them*! And now she could be criminally charged in a conspiracy involving those scumbags.

While Soroya tried to control herself, Adam and Eve, along with the crisply attired Mr. Acuña, left the room.

Gharabaghi's smile slipped away as he turned to Rosincourt. "*Ta hala khilli khob bodeh.*" So far so good. "In time we will need your help on a project of historic importance. You two have proven your worth." He threw Soroya a glance like he might have tossed a bone to a dog. "And you are now part of our operation."

We sure are. Fully implicated, which sickened her.

"We are encountering problems in assembling the parts needed for a project," Gharabaghi added. "But while we deal with that problem, there are other scores to settle. And it will give us a chance to learn more about your engineering skills."

Roz shrugged. Soroya thought he looked like a kid, but he did speak up. "What do you have in mind?" he asked the colonel.

"Do you know how the CIA and Mossad are murdering our scientists?" Roz nodded. So did Soroya. It was a grotesque history of assassination. Six times in the past year key scientists in Iran were murdered, apparently because they were part of the country's nuclear program. The dead included Professor Majid Shahriari, who had been the target of a car bomb in downtown Tehran. He was killed on the spot, and his wife was badly injured. The assassins had also bombed Fereydoun Abbasi, who'd been in charge of defeating the Stuxnet virus—a CIA-Mossad plot to destroy the computer programs used by the Iranians doing nuclear research. More assassinations followed.

"Just last month," the colonel went on, "they did it again! Two men on motorcycles gunned down Professor Darioush Rezaei as he left his home. His wife was shot too, but she was saved. Rezaei was our number-one man on neutron transport. What do you think of that?" he asked Soroya directly.

She worried he might have noticed her disgust over Los Aztecas, but she rallied easily now because she found the assassinations of Iran's top scientists so unfair and so typical of the Zionists and Americans.

"It's wrong," she said earnestly. "They have no right to do that."

"And you?" he asked Roz.

"I hate that. It makes all of us vulnerable."

Gharabaghi nodded. "That's right. What would you say if I told you there's a way to strike back right where you live? It wouldn't be getting even, but it would be a start. Alizadeh himself would know of your bravery. Would you want to hear about it?"

Roz nodded, but Soroya wondered if the colonel were planning a debacle like the one that had just made international headlines. Some ne'er-do-well, American-Iranian over in Corpus Christi had just been charged with trying to recruit Mexican gangbangers to assassinate the Saudi ambassador to the US. Those crazies had planned to blow up a restaurant and didn't care if a hundred innocent people were caught in the crossfire or got chewed up by shrapnel. Stupid as that was—*Mexican gangbangers to kill a major dip-*

lomat?—what really made Soroya uneasy was that investigators were linking that massive bit of incompetence to the colonel's buddies in the Quds Force.

"How do we know it's not going to be like that mess with Arbabsiar?" she asked. Mansour Arbabsiar was the American of Iranian descent whom investigators said was at the center of the plot.

Gharabaghi glared at her and shook his head. "You believe the American lies." She thought he looked murderous as he continued to glower. "American propaganda," he thundered. "Quds would never do anything that stupid. That was a complete setup by the Americans. We would never work with Arbabsiar or idiots like him." He sure sounded like he knew the guy. "When Quds works, the enemy never sees us coming."

But you are working with Los Aztecas. Not exactly the national brain trust. But Soroya didn't remind him of his most recent revelation; she was too scared.

"Do *you* want justice for the Iranian scientists murdered by Americans?" Gharabaghi demanded of Roz, who nodded. The colonel turned to Soroya. She nodded too, then said "yes" loudly because she did want justice. She just didn't want anything to do with Mexican drug gangs. *You mean like smuggling their money?* She winced inwardly.

"You will be part of a team that will hit Dr. Sig Antonovitch, director of the Los Alamos Laboratory, with a bomb as he commutes to his home in Santa Fe. The date will be November twenty-ninth, exactly one year to the day after the American attack on Majid and Fereydoun. Others will track the target. Another man will fire the device. We want you to shop for fertilizer and ammonia, then assemble the explosive in a drum and add the detonators we'll provide. We'll place this IED by New Mexico's Route 502 coming down Pueblo Canyon from Los Alamos. We will strike in the heart of evil."

Soroya wondered if Roz was thinking about Mehdi being blown away on the road from Karbala. She sure was. This retaliation was the first real chance they'd have to even the score. It seemed more than fair and was much different from hauling drug money over the border.

Now she saw the colonel lifting his heavy eyebrows at her—as much as saying, "Well, what do *you* think?" Slowly she gave him an approving nod. For a second the air seemed to leave the room, but an undeniable thrill raced through her body. This Sig Antonovitch worked for the Zionists, she just knew it. They all did. He might even have been a Jew.

Gharabaghi handed Roz an accordion file, then reached in and flipped open the first folder.

"Here's the recipe for the explosive. I know this is simple for an engineer like you, but we'll see how you handle this. Buy the ammonia, fertilizer, and fuel in small quantities from many hardware stores and gas stations in many separate towns. Do not take any shortcuts. And keep your back to the surveillance cameras. Always use cash." He stared at both of them. They nodded. "You'll need to buy an oil drum. Get an old one from a scrap dealer. You do that," he said to Roz. "It would be strange for her to do it. You buy ammonia," he said to Soroya. "It's a cleaning supply. That's what a woman would buy."

The gender-based assignment didn't bother her; operationally it made sense.

"Here"—he pointed to a diagram—"is how it goes together. Always wear gloves. Do not let hair or other DNA-bearing matter touch the bomb. Irwandi will bring detonators to your house in a plain package. He will not know what's inside, so don't ever tell him. That will be in mid-November. We will check in with you to see how you are moving forward. We will have a final review here on the Friday after Thanksgiving. Then you will place the device over the weekend that follows. That will be November twenty-sixth and twenty-seventh. Once you make a final cell-phone check, you will place the drum by the side of the road. Cover it with rocks and get out of town. Both of you go to Houston. We want you in the company of others far away, with witnesses to provide alibis. One of our men will be on the mesa overlooking Route 502. He will have a cell phone and will do the firing. *Barnum in ast.*" That is the plan.

The colonel handed Roz a cash-filled envelope. "You are a Shiite soldier now. You are paid directly by God. This money is for the supplies."

They walked down to Roz's minivan, which sported a new set of tires. Soroya barely noticed. They had just accepted a role in assassinating a man. *Not just any man*, she reminded herself. *A killer. A man who makes bombs that kill our people.* She didn't subject her thoughts to any scrutiny. She thought only of cause and effect, the murder of Iranian scientists and the response that would now follow. That *had* to follow.

"You miss me yet?" The George W. Bush billboard stared down at them as they drove into El Paso. But this time Soroya didn't get angry. She smiled because she was getting even. Not just for the assassinated Iranian scientists, but for all the Great Satan's murders.

CHAPTER 13
RAISING THE STAKES

November 2011

Los Alamos lab director Sig Antonovitch walked toward his Crown Victoria limousine after a long day of discussions and planning. He had been hosting an international conference on the peaceful uses of plutonium. The brisk, twilight air of the desert brought a smile to his face. So did the company of Dr. Simon Hall, a professor of engineering physics from the Weizmann Institute of Tel Aviv, who was to join him for dinner at home. Sig's wife, Rose, was cooking crab quesadillas, which she would serve with homemade salsa. He called to let her know they were running a little late.

"I love you too," he said before hanging up.

A Los Alamos chauffeur opened the door of the white limo, and Sig and Dr. Hall settled in the generous backseat. Both men looked tired but satisfied. The Israeli professor gazed at the Los Alamos sunset.

"It looks a lot like the Negev Desert," he said.

"Someday I'll see that," Sig replied.

"And I will have the honor of showing *you* around," Dr. Hall said.

The limousine picked up speed as it descended from the mesa. The road cut through a red-rock canyon toward the main highway that ran adjacent to the Rio Grande. The storied river caught the light and looked like a shiny streak of orange dividing the desert, so dazzling they never noticed a large pile of granite on the right side of the narrow ravine.

"So what's the best time of year to visit you in the Negev?" Sig asked his visitor. "When do I get to visit *your* bomb lab at Dimona?"

Those were his last words. As the limousine rolled past, the innocuous heap of granite turned into a rapidly expanding fireball.

There were no survivors.

The phone rang shortly after eight in the evening. Elizabeth had just finished eating—and missing her father's cooking—when she picked it up and heard the duty officer's voice.

"Ms. Mallory, this one looks serious. The lab director at Los Alamos was just killed en route to his home in Santa Fe. Looks like a professional job, done by a roadside IED."

What are we turning into? Iraq?

The duty officer went on: "A visiting Israeli scientist was in the car with him. Both passengers, along with the driver, were killed. State troopers are on the scene."

With the FBI en route, she figured. They were the forensic experts. In time—a very short period of time, she hoped—they should have been able to say where those bomb components had come from and how the device had been fired, and exactly when.

Elizabeth abandoned her dinner dishes and headed to the office to monitor the investigation, but she had little doubt about the source of the attack because this read like a typical Iranian operation.

Confirmation arrived even sooner than she expected. The next morning an FBI staffer stepped into a conference room where the bombing task force had set up shop. The young man handed Elizabeth an e-mail received at the Los Alamos communications center only minutes earlier.

To the families of Dr. Antonovitch and Dr. Hall:

Please accept our sympathies in this difficult time. We know how you must feel.

With sadness, the families of Dr. Majid Shahriari and Dr. Fereydoun Abbasi

She keyboarded quickly and saw it was the one-year anniversary of the bombing of the two Iranian scientists. With these confirmations in place,

Elizabeth called for a review. An FBI agent summed up with what his bureau knew.

"It appears a lot like the Oklahoma City bombing, Ms. Mallory. The explosive was ammonium nitrate fertilizer drenched with diesel fuel. Detonation was initiated by blasting caps and triggered by a cell phone. We're analyzing the debris to identify the suppliers."

By early afternoon a break in the case might have appeared: a New Mexico State Police sergeant called in to report that a vacationing couple, hiking along the north side of the Pueblo Canyon the day before the bombing, had noticed a Honda parked along the rim. Elizabeth put the sergeant on speakerphone for the benefit of two of the agents working by her side.

The officer continued: "They first spotted the car at sunrise when they started their trek, but it was still there in the late afternoon when they got back. They thought the car might have been stolen, so they wrote down the license number. They planned to call it in this morning—got right on the horn when they heard about the bombing."

"That could be a great break, Sergeant. Have you checked the vehicle's ownership?"

"Yes, we did. Those hikers were right. It was stolen."

"Thank you, Sergeant. Do keep us posted."

Elizabeth hadn't really expected to hear the trooper say they had an address and ID, not if the bombing had been executed by Hezbollah operatives. They were too cunning for that. This was going to take careful leg and laboratory work. The first results of the latter came in the next morning, delivered by a young chemist sitting at the oval conference table. She toyed with her blond bob before Elizabeth asked her to report on what she and her team had found.

"The fertilizer seems to have been purchased from a variety of Home Depots and other landscaping stores around Albuquerque. There's not much indication of the buyer's ID, though there were a few fertilizer purchases made with credit cards. We're checking those out."

And we won't find anybody connected to the attack that way, thought Elizabeth, though she knew every door that opened had to be entered.

"The diesel could have been bought anywhere," the chemist continued in a chirpy voice. "It originated in the refinery over in Lovington. The blasting caps, interestingly enough, seem to be of Chinese origin, but a lot of those are used on construction and excavation all over the Southwest. The cell phone at the detonation site was stolen from a parked car two weeks ago. The original owner had disabled the service, but a new SIM card had been installed."

"Thank you." Elizabeth looked at an official from the motor vehicle department. "Do you know if we've found the car yet?"

"Yes, we have, Ms. Mallory. The Juarez police found it abandoned on one of their side streets earlier this morning.

"Naturally," Elizabeth said. She ended the review without saying a word about Hezbollah—but as far as she was concerned, the presence of the terrorist group had thickened the air.

Blocks away, Irwandi Bereueh was sitting in Rosincourt and Soroya's apartment when the two returned from their alibi-building trip to Houston. His presence startled them.

"What are you doing in here?" Soroya demanded. "How the hell did you—"

"*Rosincourt*," he said, avoiding Soroya's eyes. "The colonel told me to tell you he approves. He wants to see both of you tomorrow, this time at the Maria Bonita Hotel at ten."

"We'll be there," Soroya said, refusing to be ignored. But she didn't press the question about his uninvited appearance in their apartment. It felt like her private life was getting shaved away and soon enough it would be bare as a bone.

Soroya followed the near-constant news reports about the "assassination" of the Los Alamos laboratory director. CNN, FOX, and all the major networks provided tons of coverage—not that they had much to say. Investigators appeared stymied, which made Soroya feel a real sense of pride over helping to even the score. Next time the US and the Zionist settlers might think twice about killing a Persian prince of science.

But Soroya also felt badly for Rose Antonovitch, the widow of the lab director. She was seen weeping at her door when FBI agents visited her home in Santa Fe. But Soroya remembered that somebody great once said, "You can't make an omelet without breaking some eggs."

Three days after the explosion in Pueblo Canyon, Rosincourt and Soroya again traveled to Juarez. Adam and Eve waited for them in the street outside the Maria Bonita, which, despite its name, looked like a dump.

Otherwise the routine appeared familiar: stairs; the *knock knock* at a door on the top floor; and Gharabaghi greeting them as a man finished an electronic sweep of a spacious but worn-looking apartment. But this time there was one significant difference: an older, grumpy-looking, overweight Anglo with a moon-like face and thinning hair sat on the far side of the room.

When the security man departed, Colonel Gharabaghi introduced Roz and Soroya to Dr. Lowell Hout.

"He is our very knowledgeable scientific advisor."

The man barely looked up, but he was a near-perfect caricature of an old-time Monopoly banker, a self-important, cigar-smoking elder who had never seen the inside of a gym. He showed few signs of familiarity with either sunshine or fresh air.

Given the introduction Soroya thought the man's presence would be explained. *Scientific advisor?* But Gharabaghi had other plans, a warning he delivered with a tone so even it sounded routine, and therefore more threatening than anything he had said to them yet.

"Rosincourt and Soroya, you are fully vetted. Now you will be trusted with the most important secrets and plans of the Islamic Republic. You should understand that *any* disclosure of what you hear will result in your death, and it will be terrible. Your parents will suffer as well, first in knowing of your torture and killing, then they will suffer the same for bearing such treacherous children."

Why are you saying this? Soroya wanted to demand. *It's not necessary. We proved ourselves.* Instead she felt herself shaking, even more so when Gharabaghi showed them Google maps of her family's home in Beverly Hills, and Roz's in Houston. Then the colonel pulled out gruesome photos of inmates in Tehran's Evin Prison, men with broken legs left to die of pneumonia in the prison courtyard. She turned them. She couldn't force herself to keep looking.

"The leadership of the Islamic Republic of Iran wishes to build and assemble a nuclear device within the United States," Gharabaghi said. "We will detonate it as a demonstration, without big casualties. It will make clear that Iran has nuclear weapons and the ability to fire when and where we choose. The threat of more Iranian weapons hiding in the country will stop any kind of nuclear answer from US."

Soroya saw Roz's mouth gape, then realized her own jaw had dropped as well.

Gharabaghi offered his flinty grin when he saw their reactions. "If the Americans do strike back, that will be the end of days that Grand Ayatollah Mesbah-Yazdi foresees. You know, Rosincourt, every good Muslim looks to a chosen spiritual leader. Mesbah-Yazdi is our president's guide. They are very close. Both anticipate an immediate return of the messiah. At every cabinet meeting an empty chair awaits him. So, either way, we win. This project is Project 853."

He paused and stared as if he wanted them to ask about the operation's name. *Do it*, Soroya said to herself.

"Why does it have that name?"

Gharabaghi nodded—in appreciation, Soroya thought—and continued:

"In August 1953, Mohammad Mossadegh, the elected prime minister Iran, was removed from power by a British-organized coup, assisted by the CIA. That day of the shah's restoration to power is a date of infamy that lives in every Iranian mind. Thus, 853: eighth month, 1953."

Leaning across the table, the colonel looked straight at Rosincourt, then Soroya, and told them there were only five people and one operating group with full access to the details of Project 853. People cleared for this level-one material included Iran's Supreme Leader Ayatollah Khamenei, President Alizadeh, Minister of Defense Vahidi, the minister of foreign affairs, the minister of nuclear energy, and a core working group within the Revolutionary Guard's Quds Force, Section 853. He, Gharabaghi, was that section's boss.

With a nod toward the rotund man in the corner, the colonel advised Roz and Soroya that the weapon in question had been designed by Dr. Hout in South Africa, was being reengineered and cold-tested in Tehran, and would be built and assembled in the US.

"That is where you come in, Rosincourt," he said. "Although you have already been in this role for a long time. The construction will take place in the Bradley Brothers shop."

He explained that only fifteen enriched uranium discs were needed for this weapon. Each weighed a few pounds, with dimensions measured in inches. They would be fabricated in Iran for smuggling into the US one at a time, via a courier chain.

"The technology is old, so the weapon is big," Gharabaghi said with an emphatic nod.

Soroya felt like gravity had let go of her; she was rootless and scared but also clearly aware she was on the sharp cusp of history. She listened intently as the colonel said the weapon would surely work, and once it was assembled the four-ton device would be loaded onto an Atchison, Topeka and Santa Fe railroad flatcar for shipment north. It would look like any of the other oil-gas separating tanks the Bradley Brothers shipped to Denver. The colonel did not disclose the intended detonation point or any other targeting information, but he made it clear he would be on hand to bring about the explosion with an encrypted cell phone link.

"You will get out of US just before the bomb explodes," he revealed. "You will have a comfortable cottage in a highly secure, Mossad-proof, VIP compound at Ramsar on the Caspian Sea. That is where the shah built his beachfront home. It is a home for real heroes now."

He assured them they would have enough funds to live comfortably for the rest of their lives in a resurgent Iran.

Soroya watched Rosincourt smile, but she felt more unmoored than ever. Live in Iran? With only Roz? *For the rest of my life? What about my parents?*

The colonel went on to explain the level-two clearance category, which encompassed weapon design and construction but not operational plans, included Rosincourt and Soroya as well as Dr. Hout. The South African scientist would oversee technical matters, especially the insertion of the enriched uranium parts into the weapon. And he would certify the device as ready for shipment.

Level-three clearances involved those handling other logistics: finance, the purchase of materials, the transportation of those materials, and the maintenance of security.

At the end of his briefing, Colonel Gharabaghi asked Rosincourt and Soroya to reflect on what they had heard. "You understand the consequences of betrayal? Please confirm you are part of Project 853 when we meet next. You must *never* discuss this with Professor and Mrs. Bereueh. They have no idea why they recruited you. They are not cleared for the project. They only serve as recruiters and a communication link."

The colonel also prohibited any talk of this project by telephone or e-mail. "The American National Security Agency is too good at tracking communications everywhere," he warned, "even if we speak in Farsi. Bin Laden's courier used a phone." Gharabaghi shook his head as if he still couldn't believe that act of stupidity.

Soroya listened as the colonel offered a few more details: Meetings would take place in Mexico because Iranians and those traveling on European or Indonesian passports could enter and exit the country easily. Also the FBI had no authority in Mexico, where law enforcement was lax or altogether ineffective. At their next meeting, Gharabaghi said, the two would have to confirm their commitment to Project 853 and begin the discussion of details. They would all rendezvous a week later, on December 9, at the Hotel La Teja a few blocks away.

What confirmation? Soroya asked herself. *Didn't he just tell us we're as good as dead if we try to back out?* She had no doubt he'd have them killed.

"We will start at ten o'clock a.m. sharp and continue throughout the day," he added. "You will then adjourn to Don Quintin, the excuse for your regular trips to Juarez. I want the American border-control people to see you as a couple of hippies running a local machine shop during the week and then commuting to Juarez for drugs and alcohol on the weekend. It's not right for Muslims"—he grimaced—"but we need to blend in. We must beat the infidels at their own game."

He also informed the couple that if he wanted a special meeting, he would send Rosincourt junk e-mail from an odd source, but with a five-digit string of numbers contained in the message, like a price quote for a shipment of Viagra.

"The first four digits will identify the day and month of the meeting. The last digit will identify the hotel in Juarez." He said he'd give Rosincourt a numbered hotel list from Expedia.

Exhausted and overwhelmed, the couple headed to Don Quintin's after the meeting. Oddly they didn't say a word at first, merely sat across a table from one another sipping beer. Soroya, who didn't particularly care for alcohol, joined in, even thought she would have to drive. The cold liquid and its taste were a welcome distraction.

"We're caught," she finally whispered to Roz. "We can't back out."

He looked stunned. She nodded to drive home the point. But that wasn't why Roz looked so shocked.

"I don't want to back out," he said so vehemently she had to hush him. He went on in a strong but softer voice. "Here's an opportunity to really do something. We can avenge Mehdi and I can build my own A-bomb."

Oh, Roz. She shook her head, dizzy with dread because she knew there would be no escape for her either. She'd played a key part in bombing and killing three men. If she were caught, they'd kill her. Soroya already felt netted as a butterfly and feared she would soon be pinned to a corkboard by the failure of her conscience.

For three days Elizabeth hunkered down with investigators from state and federal agencies in the conference rooms on North Mesa Street to pore over reports from the bureau's top agents. Jack Barry, the CIA station chief in Mexico City, was by her side the whole time, as intense and driven as she was. Neither had a clear idea who specifically was responsible for the Pueblo Canyon bombing, but from the after-shot message from Tehran there could be no doubt the orders had come from Iran. It contained elements similar to the Quds's plot to murder the Saudi ambassador to the US and to bomb the Saudi embassy. That scheme had been exposed in October by federal law enforcement agents, including informants for the Drug Enforcement Administration.

As the week drew to a close, the task force had little to show for its work. They'd heard about fertilizer purchased all over New Mexico—but no hint of a buyer. They learned the detonators came from China. So? Nothing unusual about that. And they confirmed, as Elizabeth and Jack both had suspected from the start, the cell phone used to set off the explosion had been stolen and a new SIM card installed. But there were no fingerprints. No strands of hair. No witnesses. And all of that added up to no suspects, not even any persons of interests. The media, from the locals in Albuquerque to the networks in New York, were hounding everyone and digging like crazy—to no avail.

Elizabeth suggested she and Barry adjourn to El Paso's State Line Steakhouse, a fine bistro of renown. They had a trivial jurisdictional issue to settle, resolved with a few text messages to DC while en route to the eatery.

Jack and Elizabeth had been classmates at Quantico. They had dated briefly before realizing they preferred the easy conviviality of friendship.

Now they settled at a booth where Jack ordered a whisky straight up, Elizabeth a bottle of Coors.

"This is Hezbollah at work, I know it," Elizabeth said as she sipped her beer. "The killer's car ends up in Juarez. I think we can safely assume he was not over there for the music. I'll tell you whom I'd like to talk to—the ladies in Juarez. I'll bet you a full platter of ribs the guys who planned the bombing are hanging out over there, drinking beer and laughing."

"Shiites?" Jack said, lifting his tumbler for a good mouthful of the sauce he'd always favored.

"You know what I mean. Look, our senoritas will know who they are. Let me take a look. I can talk to them."

Jack swirled the amber liquid around, staring at it before he looked back at Elizabeth. "I can't let you. You know that. You are not permitted to visit Mexico. The Department of Homeland Security operates in the US. That's you, girl. The CIA has jurisdiction outside the country. That's me. Never the twain shall meet." Elizabeth scowled. "Furthermore, you firebrand, I do not want you, my dear friend, wandering around Juarez alone. It's one of the deadliest cities on earth. Forty-three hundred murdered in the past two years alone. Nationwide, we're talking more than forty thousand dead since Calderon launched his attack on the drug gangs. That's a civil war. We won't say it publicly, but you know the old line: if you walk like a duck and you quack like a duck, you're a duck. Mexico has the murder rate of a full-scale war. And we don't want you blowing the cover of any of the ladies in the factories, because then you'd all be dead meat."

Elizabeth drained her glass of beer and nodded for another when the waiter looked at her expectantly. He served up her New York strip and Jack's ribs, but after a few bites of her favorite cut, her appetite faded. It wasn't the chef's fault. Her only real hunger was to know who killed Antonovitch and Hall. To satisfy that she'd claw through a barbed-wire wall if she had to. An American and a visiting dignitary assassinated on US soil? Somebody would pay. Would they ever.

But there was no avoiding the obvious obstacle: much of the investigation would have to take place in the murky, murderous blood lands south of the border.

CHAPTER 14
PROJECT 853

December 2011

While Elizabeth paced the conference room, infuriated by an absence of firm leads in the Pueblo Canyon murders, only blocks away Soroya and Rosincourt burrowed into rewarding archival research about building atomic bombs.

Roz sat in a stuffed chair intently researching how the bombs worked. Soroya leaned over his shoulder, marking his progress with Robert Serber's *The Los Alamos Primer*, which he'd found at the UTEP bookstore. It was a compilation of notes the professor had used in April 1943 to orient newly arrived scientists and engineers at wartime Los Alamos.

"Gun barrels, plates, and tampers," Roz said without looking up. "All made of stuff I've never seen before. This is great."

Soroya stroked his hair, trying to reach out to him emotionally as well. They had embarked on an act of terrorism unprecedented in the annals of history: the detonation of an adversary's atomic bomb in the heart of the US. Yes, America had dropped two of them on Japan—and historians were still debating the merit of their use—but at least they had been fired to end a war. Iran's current ambitions reflected a war for souls, and Soroya had to force herself to remember the spiritual dimension of the endeavor whenever she felt her resolve waver.

As a biophysics major, she had become absorbed by the science behind the bombs. In three days she burned through an old but seminal book, published in 1946: *Atomic Energy for Military Purposes* by Henry D. Smythe.

He had been chairman of the Physics Department at Princeton University. But much of what she read proved unsettling, and she felt herself wavering again. *Inshallah, Inshallah,* she had to remind herself. God willing. *Leave it up to Allah.*

Those were her self-administered admonitions on Friday, December 9 as she and Rosincourt stepped from their apartment into the crisp, morning air. Skies were clear, the city quiet, the drug gangs still asleep.

As they drove into Juarez, Soroya smiled at the Christmas lights blooming everywhere she looked. But the glow vanished when the couple showed up at the dreary Hotel La Teja. The same bulky security man, sporting the same bulge from his shoulder holster, met them in the parking lot. Once again he led them silently up two flights of stairs to a tasteless suite. The room reeked of tobacco, which Soroya found particularly offensive, and the carpet showed a variety of stains, some disturbingly dark. But the room was private and secure. The security man closed the door behind them after nodding at Colonel Ashkan Gharabaghi and Dr. Hout.

"Good morning," the colonel said. "Coffee?" He gestured toward a table. Even as they settled in, he continued, "You have come, so you have made your decision join Project 853?"

"Yes," Roz said. Soroya echoed his response but privately questioned whether they had any choice after killing three men for the Quds. Those soldiers of God could track them down anywhere and tear them apart piece by piece.

"You understand," Gharabaghi went on, "in the course of your work you may become martyrs. So much can go wrong. You could get killed. You and your families could suffer terrible consequences. And there can be no leaks," he added, shaking his head.

"We understand," Roz replied.

Gharabaghi recited by rote all the insults Iranians had suffered at the hands of Americans, most prominent among them the 1953 ouster of Iran's elected prime minister, Mohammad Mosaddegh. Then he noted how his own father and Rosincourt's uncle had risked their lives to get rid of the shah. "Now it is the time for Iran to take its rightful place as a major power. We will take control of the oil wealth that feeds and supports Western infidels. We will remove *illegal* settlers from Palestine."

He emphasized the critical importance of nuclear weapons to Iran and made a point Soroya found indisputable: "Look what happened to Gaddafi.

He trusted the Americans. He actually gave up nukes in 2003. Then, eight years later, the bombing started. Look at Kim Jong Il. He kept his nukes so he could sink other people's ships whenever he wanted. Nukes count for a lot. We must have them!"

For the first time, the colonel formally introduced the rumpled-looking man by his side. "We are fortunate to have Dr. Lowell Hout here. He built South Africa's first A-bomb in 1982."

So that was the background of the man previously known only as a "knowledgeable scientific advisor." Soroya thought the flaccid, old guy looked bored, especially as Gharabaghi spelled out the sanctions that had forced the fall of John Vorster's apartheid government. But Dr. Hout was roused to speak when the colonel noted the decision of President F.W. de Klerk to end both apartheid and his country's nuclear weapons program.

"De sanctions now tretening Iran are nothing bud a recycling of de blunt political weapons dat brought an end to apartheid in my country. Und now de Americans have a black president of dere own! To hell wid dem!"

No doubt Hout felt great umbrage over the idea of Barack Obama as president of the United States, but Soroya had read of broader problems in South Africa. Many more of that country's nuclear scientists and engineers still deeply resented their government's refusal to give them a million dollars in severance pay—after putting them out of work so ignominiously. Some had even threatened to sell their secrets to the highest bidder. Others had joined up with their counterparts from the collapsed Soviet state to form a corps of underemployed nuclear mercenaries.

Apparently Dr. Hout had found gainful employment with the Iranians. After the physicist denounced de Klerk and others, he smiled for the first time as he recounted what he called a "historical irony."

"We got our start wid de Israelis. Did you know dis? Dat is right. We promise de Jews uranium, and de Jews give us enough tritium and nuclear secrets to build our weapons. So *dink*," he thundered, "Israeli nuclear technology will soon arm Iran, which is focused on de eradication of dat miserable state. I can't tell you, dis feels *so* good. De Americans and dere kaffir president are going to get a dose of dere own medicine. I can hardly wait."

His threats and insults over, Dr. Hout turned directly to Rosincourt. "Mr. Sadr, your machine shop is to build de casing and all de mechanical parts for a simple fission-type bomb, based on America's World War II Little Boy weapon. We refined dis design and did de proper safety and production engineering in South Africa tirty years ago, but de fundamentals are all Little Boy, so let's start dere."

He rolled out drawings of that weapon, explaining how the cordite explosive, a slow-burning propellant, drove nine enriched uranium rings down a gun barrel until they surrounded six highly enriched uranium plugs. "Dat now supercritical assembly waited for de buildup of de neutron population until de energy released blew de assembly apart. Dose tungsten carbide tamper rings were dere to reflect neutrons and to hold de supercritical mass in place for as long as possible. Do you understand?" Dr. Hout looked only at Roz, who nodded.

"Dat's good. Design tolerances were tight, and dey will be again on Akhbar-I."

Great One. That's the name of our bomb, Soroya realized.

"De materials you will need are not readily available on de open market, but when you get Akhbar-I put together, we are quite confident of success. Dough it was never tested, Little Boy worked just fine. It gave fifteen kilotons on its first firing over Hiroshima.

"Next," Hout continued enthusiastically, "let's take a look at Melba, my pride and joy."

What's with the names? Little Boy and Melba? They reminded Soroya of the Teletubbies she'd watched as a child. *Why not just call them Dipsy and Laa-Laa and Tinky Winky?*

"We built half a dozen in South Africa based on dis design. Then that de Klerk"—he scowled every time he mentioned his former president's name—"had each one destroyed."

Gharabaghi firmly tapped the drawings of Melba, the South African bomb, as if to say to Hout, "Hurry up."

The physicist took a moment to turn his scowl on Gharabaghi, then resumed his explanation. "So Melba design will work. It will yield about fifteen kilotons, just like Little Boy. But now we come to Akhbar-I." Dr. Hout raised his eyebrows, actively warming to his subject, and rolled out a layout—printed on pink paper—of the new bomb.

Soroya watched Roz run his finger over the design. He looked entranced. A boy with his toy.

"It's very similar to the others," Roz said to Dr. Hout. His finger kept moving. "Just as big."

"Dat's right. It will be eight feet long, tree feet in diameter, and weigh about eight tousand pounds."

Roz studied some figures and looked up smiling. "And fifteen kilotons, just like the others."

"Smart boy. You must build or buy de casing and all de parts exactly as we specify," the portly émigré demanded. "Do not get creative. Do not freelance. No need to study de physics, and *no* shortcuts. Just build it!" His eyebrows now danced for several seconds.

Gharabaghi spelled out the time frame. "Slow and deliberate, please. We do not want any suspicion. We do not want you buying any odd hardware—you know, a lot of cordite, tungsten carbide, and gun barrels—all at the same time." The colonel raked his dyed-black hair with his fingers and cleared his throat. "Besides, there are a few small problems back home. They will take some time to solve."

"What problems?" Soroya demanded. Roz cringed, but the colonel said nothing about her impertinent tone, perhaps consumed by what he was about to say.

"The enrichment plant at Natanz is not efficient. Production is slower than we expected. It's not our fault. The CIA and Mossad are damaging our industrial supply chain. They're substituting defective parts for those we order secretly."

Hout harrumphed and took over. "Dose machines spin at one hundred thousand rpm. De slightest imbalance, a speck of dirt or a tiny scratch, will lead to disastrous high-speed disassembly—an explosion. De Europeans have been damaging de rotors, ever so slightly, before dey are shipped to Tehran. But we deal with dis. We have enlisted de help of scientific colleagues in Pakistan. We are also developing our own in-country supply chain."

"That is not the only problem," Gharabaghi said, sounding weary or maybe uncomfortable with his explanations. "Those people, Israelis and Americans, are also waging cyber-war. They've created a computer virus call Stuxnet that worms its way into the centrifuge control systems. Then the rotors spin out of control. On any day only half the centrifuge units are up and running. But we will solve these problems." The colonel seemed to rally. "We will get enrichment up over ninety percent soon. The fissile parts *will* be delivered in the spring. We *will* meet the shot date."

Turning from the drawings, Gharabaghi rose to explain the broader significance and urgency of the planned bombing. "This is not a scientific test. We know Akhbar-I will work. This is a political statement. Like the Madrid railroad bombings in 2004."

He reminded Rosincourt and Soroya that three days before Spain's general elections that year, Moroccan Islamists had fired ten bombs on Madrid's commuter trains. Up till then the consensus had held that Spain's pro-US government would win, but the bombings changed that. The Socialist Workers Party walked away with the prize and promptly withdrew Spanish support for the American war in Iraq.

"Only one hundred ninety-one people were killed on that train." The colonel wagged his finger at them. "Like the deaths aboard Iran Air flight 655. But they changed history. So will we. We will shoot Akhbar-I in the middle of the American political conventions. We will make it very clear that we can set off nuclear bombs where and when we want. This time we will hold casualties to a few hundred. We will not take out an entire city."

Gharabaghi lowered his voice. "We also have our own election deadline. Alizadeh's presidential term ends in 2013. Without a great political success, it may be difficult to keep control back home. We believe the Supreme Leader Khamenei will get fatally ill early that year. Maybe from Quds poison? Or a Quds bullet?" A stingy grin appeared. "We will see. We will get a new supreme leader, perhaps Mesbah-Yazdi, to abolish the elections and keep Mansoor in power. Up north"—he glanced toward the border—"a new American president may take over in a year. The new one may be more of a problem, so we need to move now."

With an air of finality, the colonel then made his announcement: "July 16, 2012 is the shot date. That is the anniversary of the first American atomic bomb test."

Six months to build it. That sounded painfully ambitious to Soroya.

"Where do you intend to fire Akhbar-I?" She figured he'd want to set it off in one of the convention cities. Getting rid of W and Cheney and all those other clowns might have been worth it, she thought. But Denver? Neither convention was planned for the Mile High City, but that was where the Atchison, Topeka and Santa Fe train went.

"Ms. Assaf, you are not cleared for that information," the colonel replied tersely. "You have only a category two clearance. Targeting and operations are highly compartmentalized. They are not your concern."

"Yes, they are," Soroya challenged. "Tell us where you plan to fire Akhbar-I or we quit. Your secrets are safe with us, but if we're not full members of the team, we're not going to play!"

Rosincourt visibly shrank into his chair with horror. The colonel and Dr. Hout stared at Soroya. Hout shook his head and smiled. Gharabaghi reached to his hip, as if for a gun he might normally have holstered there. Then he leaned that hand on the table. She expected the worst and wondered why she was always shooting off her mouth. At home. At school. At university. At Bush. And now at the wrong man.

He shocked her, but not as she expected:. "You ask appropriate questions, Ms. Assaf. I will ask Tehran for approval of a category one clearance for both of you. I will get back to you at our next meeting."

"Thank you," Soroya said, only now aware of the adrenaline flooding her system.

He looked her in the eye and blinked slowly, and the moment ended. He turned to Roz.

"You must use great caution when you buy material. Compagnie Talleyrand will help by hiding the purchases." A huge French company with shadowy links to Iran's rulers, Talleyrand had decades of involvement in Mideast oil exploration. "Most people at Talleyrand are not cleared to know. Even top management thinks Project 853 is really a pulsed-power scheme to defeat IEDs. The rank and file has been told the equipment is for extra-low frequency exploration. Talleyrand will manage the funding. Their Houston office will give Bradley Company contracts to develop an ELF-driven geophysical system."

"Who's going to pay the bills?" Roz asked.

"Talleyrand will fund the device fabrication on a time and materials basis," Gharabaghi assured him. "The cash will originate in Tehran, and that is where Compagnie Talleyrand will be paid for contract work in Iran."

Dr. Hout jumped back in to explain Roz's role in the cover story. "You can be a little creative on de exterior of Akhbar-I. You should weld some pipes and valves onto de outside of de bomb case to make it look more like de oil-gas separators you make for other people."

"Good idea," Roz said. "But how do you plan to get that fissile stuff to my shop? It's a long way from Natanz. That won't be easy."

The colonel took his question. "The only material to be imported into the US is six discs and nine rings. They will make up the fissionable assembly. Each one is fabricated in Iran and then they're shipped one at a time to northern Sumatra aboard aircraft operated by our Ukrainian friends. Given our problems at Natanz, we are also working on plan B. That is what you call it?"

Soroya nodded, surprised to hear Gharabaghi admit he was hedging his bets.

"We have other friendly sources—the North Korean government or Pakistani insiders. But those deals are tough to pull off. One way or the other, we will start landing enriched uranium rings, machined to our specifications, at the airport in Aceh Province early next year."

Where Adam and Eve are from, Soroya recalled. A militantly Islamic region.

"Once in Indonesia, the fissile parts will then be transferred to a Talleyrand jet ferrying well-logging equipment to and from Pertamina and Pemex." Indonesian and Mexican national oil companies. "Each of these bomb pieces will be the size of a human hand and weigh maybe ten pounds. They will end up on my desk in Chihuahua."

"How are you going to get them to me?" Rosincourt asked.

Me? Soroya eyed him. *Who am I?*

"We might ship them as auto parts," the colonel said. "Or we might disguise them as ashtrays stamped with the Talleyrand logo—one the many gifts Talleyrand will bring for our friendly Mexican custom officials. In that case the drug lords will provide transportation in Mexico and across the border. Talleyrand already has a nice relationship with them."

Soroya thought he sounded vague about the smuggling of the uranium after being so specific about so many other details. "Can't they detect fissile materials crossing the border?" she asked him.

Roz shook his head and started to respond, but the colonel silenced him with a wave of his hand.

"Uranium, even highly enriched, is not radioactive on a human time scale. It gives minimum identifying signals to monitors. Not much at all if each part is buried in a box of auto parts crossing the border as part of a regular weekly shipment from a maquiladora."

Now Roz was nodding in agreement. It made Soroya uneasy to see him in such sync with such a killer, even if the colonel was working for Alizadeh. Roz looked so enthralled—that was the only way she could put it—with the technical challenges of building Akhbar-I, she wondered if he'd thought about the ultimate toll his creation might take. It would be comforting to know that he had *some* misgivings even though they were moving ahead with the plan. She wasn't sure why she felt that way.

Her own concerns were not eased the next day when she sat on her couch with her laptop and came across *The Effects of Nuclear Weapons*, a 730-page report by Samuel Glasstone. All of it was now declassified and available on the 'net. The scientist, once employed by Los Alamos, included charts that spelled out the blast, fire, and radiation damage expected from nuclear weapons of various yields at various distances from ground zero.

Soroya learned that if a bomb were detonated well above its target, the explosion would achieve maximum blast effect, destroying buildings and infrastructure miles away. But if it were set off on the surface, the fireball would suck up huge quantities of dirt, irradiate it, and then redeposit it downwind. The radioactive fallout from a ground burst would lead to the most grotesque casualties. The lengthy report also included gruesome photos of victims.

Soroya started clicking her way further through the Web. Scores of online publications made it clear the Hiroshima bomb—exactly what she and Rosincourt were building—had delivered devastating effects: 135,000 people had been killed or injured by the initial blast, a detonation 1,900 feet *above* the city. Twice that number died later as burns and radioactivity took their grisly toll.

The photos of Hiroshima, the statistics on the slow deaths from radiation, and her awareness that Akhbar-I was to be a surface burst—producing far more fallout than was ever seen in Japan—made her try to talk to Roz about her worries. But he barely took the time to listen to her.

"We're making history," he snapped, pausing only briefly from his study of the Akhbar-I designs. He was so intoxicated by the prospect of building the bomb he'd stopped drinking beer and even put aside his nightly tokes from their pipe.

"Yes, I know," she said. *Making history.* She'd told herself those very words only days earlier, but she was developing what Americans called cold feet. She wasn't so sure she wanted to step into the even colder climes of colossal death. The colonel had said he wanted only limited casualties, but this was an atomic bomb they were going to set off on American soil. Wasn't that the very definition of chaos theory? Anything could go wrong.

Millions could die. And Akhbar-I was becoming more real every day. Right in their apartment.

She looked at Roz making notes about the design and clicking away at his computer. Her eyes were drawn to his fingers, then her own. They had blood on their hands. It felt so real she thought she might see red drips falling to her lap and onto his keyboard.

Click. Click. Click.

She was sure their hands would get even bloodier.

The next Project 853 meeting took place on December 16. Colonel Gharabaghi presided over a series of appointments with knowledgeable engineers in yet another anonymous-looking Juarez hotel suite. At least the carpets didn't look like they'd borne the wages of torture. Soroya understood some of what each man spoke about, but Roz appeared completely clued in. He asked questions and typed away.

Each briefing dealt with one aspect of Akhbar-I, such as the dimensions and tolerances of a given component, the alloy needed for certain bolts or screws, and the surface finish required within the gun barrel or tamper rings. None of the engineers had been given the big picture, and Dr. Hout was not present at the meeting.

"He's irrational, a non-Muslim mercenary," Gharabaghi explained. "He's needed in Natanz to get the damn rotors running. That way he will stay out of our way until we need him for the bomb assembly."

When the last engineer departed, the colonel turned to Soroya and said he had permission to answer the question she'd raised at their last meeting. She'd thought he'd forgotten about it.

"Ms. Assaf, the supreme leader of the Islamic Republic of Iran wishes to build and assemble a nuclear device in the United States and fire it in such a fashion that it makes clear Iran has weapons along with the ability to fire them whenever and wherever it wishes. At the same time, we want to reaffirm Iran is not a terrorist state. The detonation will take place in a remote location. Casualties will be limited to the scale of the Iran Airlines shootdown in 1988—a few hundred people. Our restraint, the reparations we will pay to the families of casualties, and the threat of more Iranian weapons in hiding will stop any American nuclear response. But who knows? Even that could mark the messiah's return. We will see."

Much of this she'd heard from him already. "You said it would be loaded on the Atchison, Topeka and Santa Fe railroad to go north. Where? To Denver?"

He peered at her. So did Roz. Her boyfriend also had the same look on his face—not pleasant.

"Why are you so worried about Denver?" The colonel shook his head. "Akhbar-I is to be fired outside the ghost town of San Marcial in central New Mexico. This is on the Santa Fe line directly west of America's first nuclear test site, called Trinity. Journada del Muerto Desert."

This was definitely news. And San Marcial sounded familiar, but so many Spanish names sounded the same to her. They were all *San* this or *San* that.

"No one lives in San Marcial now other than stray dogs," Gharabaghi added. "Ground zero will be in a small canyon. That will further limit the damage to the surrounding countryside. We will shoot on July 16, 2012, the big anniversary of the first Trinity shot. We will demonstrate our ability to fire at any time and place we choose. I"—he pointed to himself— "will be here in Juarez to trigger the detonation of Akhbar-I. I will use an encrypted cell phone link once I'm assured the device is at ground zero."

A cell phone. Just like the Pueblo Canyon bombing. The mention of the murders made her glance at her hands. But Roz had a different reaction.

"Very cool."

The colonel asked where they would be over the holidays. "With your families?"

Roz said he was headed to Houston, Soroya to Beverly Hills.

"Have a good trip. The new year will bring a new world."

The next day, as Soroya packed for the flight to LA, she thought about Akhbar-I's ground zero. *A ghost town.* Eerie. She recalled that the US had fired an atomic bomb at White Sands decades earlier. Also a surface blast, and nobody got hurt. Maybe it would not be chaos theory writ large. Maybe the Iranians had thought this one through after all.

Maybe she could stop thinking of blood every time she looked at her hands.

CHAPTER 15
HOME FOR THE HOLIDAYS

Late December 2011–Early January 2012

Elizabeth was loathe to leave El Paso and greatly discouraged by the lack of progress on the Pueblo Canyon case, but how many Christmases did her father have left? Jack Barry had strolled into her office a few days earlier, asking when she was leaving.

"For what?" Elizabeth had said.

"For the holidays," Jack had growled. "Go home and spend some time with your old man. I know you want to. I can hold down the fort for a few days, and I use the word 'fort' advisedly."

"What about your family?" she replied. She presumed they were in Mexico City. He had two teenage boys and a nine-year-old daughter. But she presumed wrong.

"They're in Fairfax," he said, "safe and sound. It's way too dangerous down *May-hee-ko* way for anyone related to me—or anyone else in the agency. I'm having them fly in here. We've got a suite at the Radisson for the week and some extra operatives to watch over it. You've got a bed in Bethesda. Go!"

So she went. At Dulles her father greeted her right outside the terminal security perimeter and gave her a great big hug.

"Oh, I missed you Baby Bear."

"Don' t go getting all misty on me," she said, but her own throat felt stuffed with something the size of a cabbage, and it was she who wiped away the first tear. As Elizabeth wheeled her carry-on out of the terminal, she detected a slight limp in her father's walk.

"You do something to yourself? Still trying to run down impalas out on the savanna?"

He chuckled. "It's not a big deal. I took a fall cycling last month. It's slowed me down. Tiny foot fracture is all."

"You didn't tell me!"

"You've had bigger fish to fry, Lizzie. It was right after they killed those guys from Los Alamos and all that crap about the Quds trying to kill the Saudi ambassador," he said quietly, with a reflexive look around. "I wasn't about to bother you with news of a few bruises. Besides, I'm back stronger than ever. But that's the last time I ride on damp pavement."

"Should we stop on the way home for a bite?" she asked him. "My treat."

"Noooooo. *My* treat, and it's at home."

Indeed it was. A savory aroma filled the house. Chicken, she thought, and something else, too.

"Should be almost ready to go," he said with an impish smile. "I used the oven timer. Can I offer you an aperitif? Pinot gringo?"

"Bring it on." She laughed. "To quote an unmentionable."

"Oh, he wasn't that bad."

She said nothing, but raised a skeptical eyebrow and then gave her father the broad strokes about the Pueblo Canyon case.

"I'll tell you, Lizzie," he said, handing her a glass of the vino, "what worries me about that case most of all is what it says about the goings-on south of the border. It's one thing to see them eating one another alive down there, and I feel for those people, but it's another thing when they start exporting that violence. It's no accident the bombing took place near a border city."

"Hezbollah, Dad. There's a political vacuum down there. They're moving freely."

"Hard intelligence on that?"

"Mostly my gut, but I'm afraid the evidence is going to become clear."

"Then I'd say you better trust your gut."

He served up roasted chicken breasts with cherry tomatoes, thyme, and goat cheese. Elizabeth was in heaven and remained there for the next three days. He wouldn't let her call a car for Dulles, and on the drive out he said he had a confession to make.

"Okay, but I'm not sure I want to hear this."

"Oh, I'm sure you don't, but what worries me most, Lizzie, is that you're going to go over to the other side."

"The bad guys?"

"No! I mean that literally: the border. Mexico is pure madness. I couldn't bear you getting caught up in that lunacy."

"Dad, nominally I'm ATF now. I'm not permitted down there."

"Nominally? That's what I mean."

"CIA station chief has already warned me."

"I know." He smiled at her. "Soon as I heard about the bombing, I asked him to."

Ten years earlier her father's interference might well have set her off. Now she reached over and squeezed his arm. But she still said, "Back off, bud."

Rosincourt had a less joyous holiday. He arrived at Hobby Field in Houston as if he'd just touched down from the dark side of the moon. He appeared quiet and mysterious to his parents, not the young man they'd raised so carefully and with so much love. Roz had never been outgoing, but now he spent the holidays, including Christmas, on his MacBook looking at Islamic Web sites all over the world. In the evenings he deigned to dine with his parents, but they couldn't engage him. Talk of local or state politics, which had always roused some kind of response, garnered little more than shrugs.

Still his mother tried. "Texas and New Mexico just elected a pair of conservative, no-nonsense governors, son. Things are looking up, don't you think?"

No, Roz said to himself. In Austin the voters had just returned another cowboy to a third term. The creep shot a coyote it the city park with his personal sidearm. And now he was running—badly—for the Republican presidential nomination. In Santa Fe a Hispanic woman, of all things, had been sworn in as governor. *Soroya sure loved that.*

His father mentioned the Tea Party. Rosincourt offered little visible response, but internally he thought, *Doesn't much matter who's in office. Not with my plans.*

"What's wrong, Roz?" His mother asked. "You're sitting there like you're in another world. We missed you!"

"I missed you too," he mumbled.

"What did you think about bin Laden?" his father asked as soon as Roz seemed to stir.

"Great," he said, replying with real feeling for the first time. "No great loss with that Sunni gone. He was just a hater, a goofy old man watching himself on TV. Shiites have real vision."

Roz wanted to say, *I'm part of the new Persian Empire, Dad. It's happening, and I'm the brains behind it.* But of course he kept his silence, more so when his mother brought up the Pueblo Canyon bombing and deaths.

"That was so sad," she added.

He nodded, but what was so damn sad about killing a nuke lab director and his Israeli buddy? *Served them right. And here I am, hiding in plain sight.*

His mother was asking him another question. He missed it completely, lost in thought about the Akhbar-I firing circuits. "What?" he snapped.

"Honey, I was just asking about your summer vacation plans."

"I'll be at the beach."

"Padre Island?" his mother asked.

"No, Ramsar," he said without thinking.

"Ramsar? That's on the Caspian Sea, isn't it?" she said. "Where the shah had a home. What are you talking about, Roz?"

He froze, then closed the clamshell that had become his mind. *Pay attention.* "Yes, Padre Island," he declared. He looked at her, making eye contact to soften her up. "Just dreaming." Which was true, but he would have to keep his hunger for justice for Iran well hidden. Evin Prison awaited those who were careless.

He excused himself and borrowed his father's Lexus, knowing the old man would have died if he'd known what his boy was up to. But Galveston was a nice drive, and the ladies of the night were better company than his parents. They didn't talk constantly, hector him with questions, or dare to lecture him. And the ladies of the night disappeared back into the dark.

Right after the first of the year, he packed his large duffel, said good-bye to his discouraged mother and father, and insisted on taking a cab to the airport. He felt conflicted because of happy memories from his childhood, but those days were over. He planned on never seeing his parents again. They could have their America. They could have the son they thought they knew. The real Rosincourt was now someone they'd never recognize.

In a word Soroya found Los Angeles *depressing*. Her activist friends from Beverly Hills High School and UCLA had turned from politics to making their livings; to planning weddings, which Soroya found especially galling; and to hosting baby showers. How banal could life get?

Numb yourself. What choice did she have? She could rail against the Dark Empire, her favorite term for the US, or she could zone out with her mother in their home theater. Spend some time reinforcing her good-girl image to cover up the doppelganger that increasingly defined her.

Right now, though, her mother had cornered her in the living room of their Tudor-style mansion, proving herself more tiresome than ever.

"How's Rosincourt?" Mrs. Assaf inquired.

Soroya knew that more than anything her mother wanted to hear her daughter's relationship with her boyfriend was on track to marriage and babies. Bad enough her only child was living in sin. "Such a scandal that would be in Tehran!" Mother had told her more than once. Soroya knew anything short of marriage and grandchildren was her Muslim mother's worst nightmare.

Hence Soroya delivered only good news: "He's fine, Mom. We're both doing interesting things at work." Soroya allowed herself a smile, which her mother found encouraging for all the wrong reasons.

"So you love him?" Mrs. Assaf said, shifting her eyes in a flirty manner that made her daughter want to scream.

"Yes, Mother."

Truth was, she thought Roz would rather make love to an atomic bomb than her, which had led Soroya's own affections to grow decidedly indifferent. When he'd stopped smoking pot before bed because he had to keep his head clear for work—for *bomb building*—she'd known she'd lost him. And he'd been aghast when he'd caught her trying to satisfy herself discreetly.

Soroya turned the subject back to the Bradley Brothers. "We're lucky to be working for them. We're doing a lot of propellant chemistry..." Her mother's eyes glazed over, as Soroya knew they would "And quality control in a high-tech machine shop."

A few more seconds of boilerplate and her mother said, "Let's begin our movie festival."

Soroya agreed. Watching movies with her mom was a tradition that harkened back to Soroya's earliest childhood, and she wanted to appear as normal as possible so nothing would seem amiss to her parents. Her father, Dr. Assaf, always considered his wife and daughter's passion for classic Hollywood films a moral weakness. But he picked his battles over piety wisely and never protested the appearance of films like *An American in Paris*, which Mrs. Assaf cued up on the huge flat-screen that filled the wall in a room that had once hosted the likes of Lana Turner, Clark Gable, and Gene Kelly himself.

As Kelly's visage appeared, Soroya felt transported back to that magical city and her own affair with the seductive Algerian. But Kelly was more like David Borookhim, which was the reason she'd been exiled to Paris in the first place. She wondered how David was doing and was surprised to realize she'd never once wondered about her Algerian Säid, or his life back in Oran.

The Assaf family film festival continued through the Christian holidays unless Soroya darted out to catch up with an old friend. But their tales of domestic bliss or horror—as was the case with a few friends—could not compete with the fantasy world she shared with her mother. She had even begun to find Mrs. Assaf's company desirable—as long as she didn't bring up Rosincourt or ask too much about work, which conjured up the near future and the specter of a nuclear explosion.

One night Soroya and her mother settled in with popcorn hatched in an antique cooker salvaged from an old Hollywood movie palace. The machine lived on, as did the Hitchcock thrillers *Rear Window* and *Vertigo*—Mrs. Assaf's double bill for the night.

Soroya loved being able to pause movies, as she did right now. "This is amazing stuff, Mom, seeing San Francisco as it was a half century ago. Look at those seaplanes." They were cheek by jowl with the city. Soroya wondered if the secretaries and shop girls back then really had those views of the bay from their apartments. What a wonderful, peaceful, uncomplicated life they had. Then she remembered a nickname for San Francisco that felt painfully ironic: Baghdad by the Bay.

But what jangled her nerves to the core was her mother's offering on New Year's Eve: the 1959 nuclear tragedy *On the Beach.*

What's with mothers? Soroya couldn't believe she'd have to sit through this one. *Do they just download from the ether whatever ails you the most?*

On the Beach had plenty to ail Soroya. In the film Gregory Peck navigated his submarine around the Pacific, ending up in Australia, looking for signs of life after a nuclear war. The death and devastation he found everywhere were not the products of a hydrogen bomb blast and fire. The fallout was killing everything and everybody—*slowly.*

Soroya realized she was shivering as she watched the last Aussie couple give suicide pills to their baby and then themselves.

Mrs. Assaf put her arm around her daughter. "You okay, honey? It's just a movie."

That's when Soroya realized she was crying—really boo-hooing like a big baby.

"I don't know why this stuff gets to me," she said to her mother, wiping away her tears.

Yes, you do. You know exactly what fallout does

As the credits rolled, she tried to remind herself nobody seemed to have suffered from the wartime detonation at White Sands.

She needed a respite from the scary movies her mother had been playing of late and pulled *South Pacific* from their extensive collection. The two of them stayed up till two in the morning for the happy ending. This time both of them cried, Soroya weeping with happiness. Then more tears spilled from the grim understanding that she'd never find happiness on her current course of action.

The season's big party for Soroya came on January 2. The 2003 graduates of Beverly Hills High School had decided on a second quadrennial reunion to follow all the religious holidays. They planned to convene at the Zanzibar, a popular Santa Monica late-night spot with live music. Dinner, drinks, and life stories—some perhaps even true—were on the agenda. Dozens of classmates had signed up. They would congregate in a private area to mingle, gab, and, in some cases, apologize drunkenly for past transgressions.

Soroya's eagerness to go surprised her. Then she thought of David Borookhim—again. Though she couldn't say the words to herself, she hoped he'd show; she was curious about his life. *It makes sense,* she assured herself. *You haven't seen him in eight years. You can handle it.* But that last reassurance was no more effective than a smoke alarm in a home for the hearing impaired.

But David wasn't there, and Soroya sat with old friends and listened to their litanies of successes, both real and imagined. It seemed more of the latter appeared with every pitcher of margaritas. Then David walked in. She scolded herself for the song that started playing in her head, but she could not turn off the soundtrack from *South Pacific*: *"Some enchanted evening, you may see a stranger...across a crowded room..."*

It did not please her to see that he looked as good as he always had. *No, better*, she admitted to herself. He'd grown into his body. Oh, God, had he ever.

David's wavy, dark hair graced the tops of his ears and neck, and when she noticed this she remembered her lips on his skin and his wonderful soapy scent. His chocolate eyes, bright and alive as ever, landed on her, and he nodded in acknowledgement. She couldn't help but notice, as he pulled out a chair and sat down, that he was fit, either from the gym or hard work. And now he gave her another look, the one that had first melted her heart a decade earlier. If she'd been a cartoon character, a big, red valentine would have *boom-boom-boom*ed from her chest, leaving pink streaks in the air.

What was I thinking? When she'd let her parents end the relationship. *That's when I should have set off a bomb.* She was already joking to herself, effervescent enough to make light of a nuclear device.

She counseled herself to take a breath before she spoke. Didn't help. Her voice still sounded embarrassingly high and then cracked when she said, ""Well, David, wh-*at* are you up to these days?"

Soroya tried to recover with a nonchalant toss of her long, black hair over her shoulder, which, not incidentally, showed off her bright-red décolleté dress to great advantage. When his eyes lowered for an instant, she knew she'd lured at least a tiny bit of the beast who had once been a boy.

"Nothing too exciting," David responded, eyes dipping again. "I made it out of USC with a degree in civil engineering..."

So he's building things too, she told herself without recognizing the irony.

"And then I started with my dad's real estate development company. So right now I'm supervising the construction of our new clothing accessories store on Rodeo Drive."

Not exactly scintillating, but it still sounded a lot better to Soroya than shacking up with Roz and his atomic bomb designs. Buoyed by margaritas, she asked, "How's your love life?"

"Nothing serious, Soroya. How about yours?"

She *so* wanted to dodge the question, but she'd already mentioned to others at the table that she was living with a guy, so she tried—oh, yes, she tried *very* hard—to sound indifferent when she shrugged and said, "I'm living with a nice Muslim boy, just as my parents always wanted." She could not have discounted the relationship with Roz more if he'd been a fingerless leper with putrescent wounds.

David was the one. Roz is no fun. David was the one. Roz is no fun. What an inane jingle, but in her inebriated state it played over and over in her head like a scratched-up, old LP.

A friend of David's asked him a question, and the banter at the table soon turned to summer plans.

Mine? Oh, I'm going to set off a nuclear explosion in the New Mexico desert. What about you? Got something good going? The dialogue she was subjecting herself to was worse than the inane jingle.

A cheerleader she could barely stand in high school actually did ask about her plans. Startled, it took Soroya a few seconds to respond.

"I'm going to be staying in hot and dusty El Paso. We've got a big project we have to deliver in July."

Did you have to be so specific?

"What's the project?" the girl asked. "Something fun, I hope."

Oh, God. But before she could come up with a good lie, David jumped into the conversation.

"Hey, I'm heading out New Mexico way. Remember my grandpa Navon?" He was looking right at Soroya, who tried to hide her shock because yes, she did remember his grandpa Navon. Not that she'd ever met him, but he was the reason David had gone out to New Mexico the summer after his junior year—to spend time with his favorite relative, who was a Sephardic Jew. Like other émigrés from the Basque region of Spain, he had a sheep herd. Now she knew why San Marcial had rung a bell when Colonel Gharabaghi mentioned the "ghost town." It was not exactly a ghost town.

"I remember you talking about him," she finally managed to say.

"Dad's going to spring me loose so I can spend some time with my *zeidy*. He's really getting on, and he's going to be closing down his operation. He'll be moving out here by Labor Day. Talk about an adjustment."

"So when are you going to be there?" she tried to ask as casually as possible.

"Oh, probably from right after July Fourth to early August. That's all the time we can spare, but I should be able to help him get ready to move. He's a great guy. I went out last summer too, but only for a week."

Fuck! She didn't like that word, didn't even say it to herself very often, but it threatened to become a chant with David's bulletin. And then, right on cue, "Throwing Stones," a Grateful Dead classic, started playing on the bar's sound system:

**There's a fear down here we can't forget.
Hasn't got a name just yet.
Singing ashes, ashes, all fall down.
Ashes, ashes, all fall down.**

Soroya, full of tequila and remorse—and filled with visions of ashes from Akbar-I falling on David and his grandfather only a few miles west of San Marcial—blurted out, "Don't do that. That's a really bad idea."

"What?" he said, clearly puzzled. "I've been there a lot."

"But it's *so* hot," she managed. *Really hot.*

He shrugged. "It's not that bad. At least it's dry heat."

"That's what everybody always says," Soroya volleyed, "but a hundred fifteen is a hundred fifteen. It's like an *oven*," she added with great emphasis.

David reached across the table and took her hand. "I'll be okay, Soroya. Really. But it's nice that you care."

Everybody at the table looked at the way he held her. Soroya stared at his hand too. It felt so good. She wanted him to pull her closer, hold her, but instead she stood and grabbed the only available excuse for her outburst: "I think I've had a little too much to drink. I'm going to grab a cab and go home."

"I'll take you," David said.

"You sure?"

He nodded.

"O-kay," she squeaked, voice cracking again.

A strange silence greeted David's rising. Had two old lovers ever fled a reunion more obviously? Soroya doubted it. The silence from their classmates made it all the more awkward.

As soon as they climbed into his BMW, they threw themselves at each other. An hour later, after he'd swept her into his luxurious apartment in the Hollywood Hills, she lay next to him, ravished and smiling and filled with remorse. This was not how a good Muslim woman behaved. Even one who lived in sin. But an even deeper regret loomed, so she tried to warn him again.

"Just don't go," she whispered to him.

"Where? What are you talking—"

"San Marcial. Promise me."

"Promise me something," he replied.

"What?"

"You'll see me again. This"—he looked at the rumpled bedding and gently lifted her mussed-up hair from her face—"should tell us something. Don't you think?"

She nodded. But she said nothing more because what her feelings told her most of all was that she'd made a terrible mistake—and it wasn't in a bedroom in the Hollywood Hills.

There's no way out. Even as she thought those words—and realized how it made them sound like lovers trapped in a bad movie—she knew she really was trapped, and no deus ex machina could ever come to the rescue.

Even an old flame who carried a torch for her might turn to ash in an instant.

Colonel Ashkan Gharabaghi also headed home in mid-December, glad to leave behind Juarez and its seedy denizens. In Tehran he visited his pulmonary specialist. The young, voluble, mustachioed doctor checked his lungs and advised him, as he always did, to stress them as little as possible.

"You still have some oxygen capacity. Not too much," the doctor hastened to add. "You need to breathe clean air. Stay away from cities if you can, Colonel." He nattered on about the benefits of fresh air. Gharabaghi wanted him to shut up because his future held only the choking pollution of Juarez.

He left the doctor's office wondering why he bothered to see that man. Each visit revealed less lung capacity. The specialists had told him the damage from Saddam's chemicals might stabilize, but not yet.

Maybe when I'm dead.

The colonel's spirits were hammered even harder when he ran into an old rival on the streets of Tehran. Amir Ali Hajizadeh was in charge of aerospace engineering for the Revolutionary Guard Corps. He offered a big smile, always a herald of bad news.

"So you are still a colonel, Ashkan?" Hajizadeh shook his head in mock sympathy. "I just made brigadier general, you know."

The promotion was obvious from the shiny new stars on Hajizadeh's shoulders.

"My men just brought down one of those fancy new American drones. Landed it outside Kashmar. Once we took control of its brains, we could land it like a toy. Interesting stuff inside. How about you, colonel? How's your 853 coming along?"

The implied put-down was insufferable. The men parted with an exchange of salutes. The colonel's spirits lifted only when he reached the Saadabad Palace. He was there to meet his old friend, President Mansoor Alizadeh. The palace didn't offer the whimsical touches of so many others in the Middle East and Europe, but Gharabaghi filled with pride as he gained the entrance and spotted the familiar murals, portraits, and furnishings.

Mansoor, so much shorter than the colonel, always ushered him to a seat in the presidential office as soon as they met. Gharabaghi suspected he didn't like to have to look up to him. This afternoon, though, the president appeared agitated, and while this wasn't entirely unusual the cause was different this time.

"The leaders who fell." Mansoor shook his head. "They were all soft."

So that was what it was, the colonel realized. The Arab spring worried his old friend. He needn't have been concerned. "Those men," Gharabaghi told him, "like Mubarak, they didn't have the Revolutionary Guard Corps. We are your good friend, Mansoor."

"That's right," the president replied quickly. He sat down, laid his foot on his knee, and bobbed it up and down annoyingly. "They cozied up to the West. And where is the West now? Watching them hang. Or helping to kill them, like Gadaffi. Fool! He had nuclear weapons and he gave them up." Alizadeh sounded astonished, as if he still couldn't get over any leader making such a self-defeating concession to the unconscionable West.

"He trusted them," the colonel said, equally astounded.

"That's right. We know better." Mansoor jumped to his feet. The colonel was glad to see that stupid foot quit bouncing up and down. "All the others, they fell for that human rights crap. We'd still be stuck with the shah if he'd been made of sterner stuff. That's why we're counting on you, Ashkan." He pointed an unnaturally long finger at him. "But I don't have to tell you about the insults they have visited upon you. How are your lungs?"

Ashkan told him about the latest examination, dismissing the comments of the doctor.

"Maybe that doctor needs to stop telling you where to breathe your air. Do you want me to make him catch *his* breath?" Mansoor asked.

Gharabaghi considered this before shaking his head no. "He's good at what he does. Maybe he should just say less."

"He will say a lot less, I promise you. The Americans did that to your lungs, just like their sanctions are choking our banks. Acts of war!" Mansoor wheeled around, staring out a tall, mullioned window at the featureless sky. Then he turned back and looked down at the colonel, who knew better than to stand. "I have very good news for you, for Project 853," the president said. "The Russians will fuel and operate Bushehr." An old nuclear reactor on the Persian Gulf started by German contractors thirty-five years earlier.

The colonel smiled, knowing they'd now have a second source of fissionable material. Plutonium *and* uranium. "That is great news, Mansoor." Gharabaghi thought of Kazakhstan, the An-12 blown up in the air, leaving half a ton of enriched but unacquired uranium in trucks on the ground. *Now we'll have plenty of stuff.*

"The Maghreb will not succumb to these infidels. Each of these revolutions weakens our enemies." Mansoor paced as he talked. "And this is good. But we are stronger than ever. We will keep the peace here at home, I promise you. Your brothers in the Corps won't let any Green Revolution start up again. We will grind them down." Mansoor made a fist and pounded it into his palm, working them like a mortar and pestle. "And once we make it through the summer, when the glory of Akhbar-I lights the hearts of all true Iranians, we'll be safe, Ashkan." He raised his ungainly index finger and shook it furiously. "We'll get a new supreme leader, and no one will dare defy us. Not even the Great Satan. I will make a speech, and I will name *my* Axis of Evil." His head bobbed like a buoy in a turbulent sea. Gharabaghi noticed spittle on the president's lips. "The United States and the European Union: the Axis of Infidels!" Alizadeh smiled as he articulated the slogan of his creation. "They will never rest easy again."

Mansoor dismissed Ashkan with thanks and a firm handshake. The colonel left the palace knowing that everything he had just heard, from the preeminence of Persia to the detonation of Akhbar-I, was predicated on his success in Mexico. He felt honored, and more determined than ever to raise a mushroom cloud over the United States that would forever shadow the wicked with the real threat of nuclear annihilation. He, a simple man of faith, would bring the land of shameless sin to its knees. That newly minted brigadier would only stand in his shadow.

CHAPTER 16
RED FLAGS

January–March 2012

Bum Bradley sauntered out of his favorite coffee shop full of ham, eggs, and caffeine. Then he headed straight to his '64 candy-apple red Mustang convertible. He still rode horses, hard when he had to, but truth be told the old cowpoke loved this pony even more.

For his trip to El Paso, he had the top down and the heater on high. Man, he felt great. The sun was shining, the air was crisp, and he was glad to be alive. He just wished he didn't have to go quiz Rosincourt about all the damn purchases coming through the shop. He liked giving his newly appointed manager plenty of rope so Roz could lasso every bit of work possible and cinch it all nice and tight, like a calf roper at a rodeo. But he had to go over some of the recent bills. They were strange ones. He hoped Roz would make sense of everything because the kid was the best employee he'd ever had.

What do they call those guys who bring in the big money at law firms? Bum had to think for a moment. *Rainmakers, that's it.* Well, Bum figured Roz must have had his own special rain dance because he was bringing in big deals with those Frenchies at Compagnie Talleyrand. Problem was Bum couldn't make hide nor hair of what Roz was doing for them, and asking questions on the phone had left him more bamboozled than ever. At first Bum's brother, Hiram, had been of the same mind: leave Roz alone, let him take the initiative. Company's growing, so why complain?

But Bum felt such a devil of an itch that he could not keep himself from scratching. Besides, the mint-condition, red Mustang needed a ride. Blow some carbon crud out of the twin exhaust pipes.

The ragtop had a nice rumble. It should have, what with the 289 four barrel and a generator, not that funky alternator they put on the '65s and '66es. This pony could definitely gallop. Bum liked that. Liked the wide-open roads, too. Didn't get a senior discount on his car insurance because the Mustang drew highway patrolmen like a barn drew flies, but Bum paid the price and didn't whine. And then he smiled wide as a Texas sunrise when he blew the doors off all those teensy imports.

Some of his buddies loved to sound like bumper stickers: "When I check out, somebody's gonna have to pry my cold, dead hands off my .45." Not Bum. He knew he'd be clutching the keys to his Mustang.

He wore his outlaw cowboy hat with the brim dipping down in front and caught the eye of a red-haired honey in a Chevy pickup. Pretty. Young, too, about forty. Threw him a smile that he tossed right back. Then he laid a little rubber as he headed down the highway. He could do that in all four gears, but by the time he shifted to second she wouldn't have noticed. *Damn mating games never stop.*

Bum had flowers for Soroya on the shotgun seat along with his briefcase, hand-tooled leather like his Tony Lama boots. He'd brought along copies of Rosincourt's purchase orders for tungsten carbide discs from a firm in China. First time Bum saw the order, he'd signed the checks. Second time? That was when he wondered, *What the hell do we need those kinds of discs for?*

Next it had been cadmium plating from a contractor north of Dallas. Bum had never seen cadmium used in an oil field, and he'd been around derricks so long he might have been nursed on crude.

When he'd called Roz about it, his whiz-kid manager had said it was for a "proprietary project" for Compagnie Talleyrand. Then he'd given Bum a bunch of mumbo jumbo. Hell, on the one hand Bum was glad the kid was so smart he could talk that language, but it also made him wonder whether Roz was larding it on.

Bum's briefcase also contained a copy of an order for an eight-foot-long pipe with an inside diameter of over six inches, and walls more than an inch thick. That sounded like a gun barrel to the Air Force retiree. As if he had any doubt, Bum then found an eBay invoice for a gun breech to go with that barrel. Bum had called him on that as well. Got right to the point.

"What the hell are you doing buying gun barrels and a breech? You planning to launch a war against Mexico?"

Talk about mumbo jumbo. It was so thick, Bum took notes. Roz's answer went something like this: "We're building an extra-low frequency geophysical exploration system for Compagnie Talleyrand. And I don't need to tell you how seriously those people take secrecy. But I can tell you this: the power supply for this unit is a magnetohydrodynamic generator that will produce megawatts of power for milliseconds of time. The generator will blow apart unless I encase it in thick steel. Gun barrels work best."

Huh? A magneto-what?

Even then Bum fed out the rope, making sure Roz felt free to use his genius, 'cause that was what the young man was—a certifiable g-e-n-i-u-s. Even brother Hiram agreed. But then came the purchase order for cordite. Not illegal, but it would raise eyebrows all across the oil patch. It sure raised Bum's back in Hobbs, New Mexico.

"I don't understand those kids." That was Bum's opening lament to Hiram about the cordite order.

Hearing about the explosive made even Hiram wonder. "Maybe you better saddle up and get over to El Paso after all. Roz is bringing in great money, so go easy on him, but yeah, it's probably worth a look."

Bum checked the speedometer as he approached the Texas border: 110, and the engine was hardly straining. Chassis and alignment felt as tight as they had on the day he'd driven it off the showroom floor.

Don't make 'em like this anymore.

Most folks who knew Bum felt the same way about the old mechanic at the wheel of his pride and joy.

People meeting in El Paso could have answered all of Bum's questions—and raised red flags aplenty. Since the beginning of the year, Soroya and Rosincourt had met several times with Colonel Ashkan Gharabaghi in Juarez. The rooms were always different but looked the same. Only the subject matter differed.

First they'd focused on the tamper rings needed to reflect neutrons back into the exploding core of Akhbar-I, and to hold that core together for as long as possible. Machining these would be a tough challenge because tungsten carbide is a hard and brittle material that can be trimmed only with diamond cutting wheels or lasers. Gharabaghi told them to contact the Mudanjiang Northern Alloy Tool Company, a metallurgy shop in northern China.

"They make sintered tungsten carbide parts ready for machining," the colonel told them. "They do good work for us." Soroya took notes.

At the next meeting, Gharabaghi had brought up a rather simple-looking piece of hardware: a two-foot-long, one-inch-diameter steel rod, threaded at both ends.

"Specs call for thick cadmium plating," he told them. "That will not be easy. Cadmium is toxic, but it absorbs neutrons. It's useful in reactors—and weapons." He smiled.

By the end of January, Soroya had tracked down a cadmium-plating company north of Dallas. But then in February Gharabaghi proposed a purchase that really made her uneasy: a gun barrel. Eight feet long.

"It could be assembled in pieces," the colonel explained, "but the internal tolerances are very tight. The bore needs to be smooth, no rifling. This is where fissile materials will be brought together at high speed using cordite propellant. There are lots of reliable suppliers of high-quality pipe in the oil fields. But the gun barrel may be a challenge."

Ya think? Soroya said to herself.

Sure enough, Bum had called the shop to talk about the gun barrel, and she'd listened to Roz do a verbal version of a Mexican hat dance as he threw polysyllabic terms like "magnetohydrodynamic" at the old guy. Bum seemed to buy her boyfriend's bullshit.

Gharabaghi's coup de grâce was still to come: cordite powder. Soroya thought that would surely set off alarms with Bum, but the colonel said it was indispensable. He introduced them to an explosives expert from one of the former Soviet Muslim republics, who explained why. Gharabaghi never disclosed the man's name.

In perfect English the bespectacled, bearded visitor said, "In old days nitroglycerin was used to shoot a well." That meant using the highly unstable nitro to fracture the formation at the bottom to promote a better flow of fluids and gas. "A lot of people got blown up carrying nitro to the wellheads." He laughed. "But we do it better now. We use pumps and compressors. But some people still do it the old way."

The explosives expert went on to explain that the propellant for Akhbar-I would be the cordite—a more stable explosive employed in many construction and other commercial applications.

Soroya was hardly surprised when Bum called again, this time to say he would be paying them a visit.

She steeled herself not to equivocate in front of her boss. That would be a challenge because she had uneasy, even sickening concerns about Project 853. She'd continued her investigation of nuclear fallout, still driven by her first concerns about the "limited" bombing going out of control. Her research inevitably brought her around to the nuclear disaster at Chernobyl. The fire and meltdown in that Soviet-built reactor, operating just north of Kiev, killed dozens on the spot and perhaps 10,000 more during cleanup operations. A few days earlier she'd found a Greenpeace study, published in 2006, that estimated 100,000 fatal cancers would occur in the Ukraine and Belarus alone as a result of Chernobyl. Fallout from the reactor had spread all the way to Scandinavia. A more recent paper claimed nearly a million deaths worldwide would eventually result from the accident. Project 853 was taking on much darker dimensions to Soroya.

A million people! Those folks in Scandinavia had done nothing to offend the Soviets. And now Japanese scientists were finding evidence of widespread radiation after the Fukushima failure.

Neither of those contraptions were bombs, she reminded herself. Just nice, "friendly" power plants.

Soroya also worried about David. Since they'd made love, they'd been e-mailing each other, sometimes three, four times a day. Their affair felt more torrid than ever. Back in high school, they'd been kids. Now they were in full bloom—and feeling it. But Soroya feared Roz would find out about her affair. *Then what? Kill me?* He sure hadn't thought twice about plunging ahead with an atomic bomb. Or maybe he'd tell Gharabaghi there was a security leak, which could bring down the full wrath of the Quds on her and her parents.

Worst of all David was still planning to spend most of July and part of August near ground zero to help his grandfather sell off his sheep herd, close down his ranch, and move to LA. Short of telling David about the devastation planned for that region of New Mexico, she couldn't imagine how to stop him. If she told him about Project 853, he'd undoubtedly warn others, like his grandfather and the old sheepherders with whom David had spent so many summers. The whole world would find out, and it would be a death sentence for Roz and her. And she still had *some* feeling for the guy she slept with every night.

Okay, so she *had* thought about warning David and running away from Roz, leaving him in the grip of the Quds. But how long could she—or her parents—escape the vengeance of those highly trained killers?

Complicating her thoughts even further was her culpability in the Pueblo Canyon killings. There was no easy way out. And underlying all of her thoughts was her belief that Akhbar-I could, in fact, deliver some justice to the US to offset the abuse and disrespect visited on Iran.

Then there was Bum, whom she genuinely liked. If George W. was the devil personified, Bum was the other side of the Texas coin. He always brought her flowers, inquired about her life, and made sure the couple's health insurance was adequate. None of which Roz appreciated in the least. He was now thick into John Coster-Mullen's self-published manual, *Atom Bombs*—a handbook, with drawings and photos, about building an A-bomb. Roz's *bedtime* reading.

Buck up, she told herself. *You've got no choice. You've got to find a way to get David and his grandfather away from ground zero and at the same time you've got to see this thing through.*

Bum pulled up in front of the Festival Street apartment complex. Typical El Paso architecture, which was to say it displayed a gaudy pastiche of Spanish influences, from useless stucco arches to blindingly bright orange roof tiles.

He checked the brilliant blue sky but still pulled up the ragtop. Didn't want to tempt some kid to jump in and try to hotwire it, which was what Bum had done himself almost fifty years earlier when he'd spotted his first hot rod. Police hadn't caught him but the owner had, which was far worse. Gave the young Bum a thrashing he'd never forgotten.

He pressed the doorbell. He smelled lamb roast as Soroya opened the door.

"Here you go, señorita," he said, handing her the flowers he'd been holding. A nice, tasteful arrangement. He hated those monster-sized bouquets that made a woman look like she'd won the Kentucky Derby.

"Come in, Bum. It's so good to see you." She gave him a big hug. "Look who's here," she called to Rosincourt. With a startled expression, he snapped shut his bomb book. "Bum brought us flowers."

Roz nodded but darted back to the second bedroom, which Bum knew they used as a home office. He hurried back out minus the book. So he'd been working, Bum realized. Kid sure was devoted to the job.

During dinner Bum avoided the subject of the peculiar purchases for the shop. He wanted just to see if they were the same kids he'd known in the past. Seemed that way, he realized pretty quickly. Soroya might have been a little anxious, but then lots of women were when they were serving up dinner to the boss, all worried about whether you'd liked their cooking. Liked her cooking? He loved it. Wished she'd open a restaurant in Hobbs, as a matter of fact.

But the two Muslims were as abstemious as ever. Bum would have liked a nice rioja with dinner, but he knew intoxicants of any sort were a real no-no with these two. So he made do with cranberry juice and seltzer water.

By the time Soroya cleared the dishes, he was ready to get down to some serious talk. He started by asking Roz about Talleyrand.

"They are everybody's dream customer," the young man replied. "They pay on time, they know what they want, and they mind their own business..."

Is he trying to tell me something? Bum wondered.

"They expect similar discretion from their suppliers."

He sure as hell is.

"Now, Roz," Bum started slowly, "those guys at Tallyrand have been customers of ours for years. I've got buddies at their Midland and Houston offices. That's where your dad works, right? In Houston?"

Roz nodded. So did Soroya.

"Anyway, Talleyrand's business style is not news to me. But your being all secretive about them is. I don't get that. Neither does Hiram. What gives?"

"Nothing, except they're being super careful. They've got some devices they're having us work on that will revolutionize things in the industry. That's what they say, but I don't know the whole picture either. Only that everything's getting encrypted within a program they've devised. I'm really sorry."

Bum stared at Roz, who'd never held his gaze for long. Didn't now either. Bum understood proprietary interests, even the need for keeping commercial work secret. But still it irked him to have something this big, apparently, going on right under his nose and not have a hint of what it was all about.

"Why is Talleyrand spending all this money, Roz? Now don't get me wrong. We love having all this cash flowing in, especially during these tough times, but Hiram and me, we're worried about what kind of exposure we might have, legally speaking."

Roz waved off Bum's concern. "Well, boss, you know these guys. They really don't want us talking about their new schemes for seismic exploration."

"Bullshit!" Bum exploded.

Roz literally jerked his head back but soon resumed his gibberish about shooting ionized particles down a gun barrel, surrounded by a magnet, to produce megawatts of power for a few milliseconds.

Bum wasn't convinced, but neither could he understand much of what the engineer was talking about. Didn't get any better when Roz launched into a monologue about working on extra-low frequency radio waves to bounce off geologic strata at great depths, precluding the need for expensive and disturbing acoustic systems. Bum grasped the concept, no problem, but the tech talk was beyond him. Finally he just interrupted the spiel.

"Roz, this is my store. I need some straight answers in nice, simple English. What the hell are you building for Talleyrand?"

Christ, another half hour about computer algorithms followed, along with talk-talk-talk about signal processing that left Bum completely perplexed. "Can you show me some drawings?" Bum asked. "Something I can make sense of?"

More mumbo jumbo, and then this: "Everything is in electronic format, boss. You've got to have approval for passwords. Even she doesn't have them." He glanced at Soroya, who nodded. Then Roz concluded with a simple plea: "Can you just trust me on this one, boss? You won't be disappointed, and when we're all through we'll be seeing more business than ever."

Bum nodded, wondering what he was worried about. Roz was already bringing in big contracts. He was a rainmaker, so of course he was generating some storms.

Leave him be.

Another strained conversation was taking place 700 miles away in Los Angeles, where David Borookhim had just told his father he was seeing Soroya Assaf again. The two of them were watching workmen screw siding onto the new accessories store they were building on Rodeo Drive.

Saeed Borookhim closed his eyes slowly at the news, then opened them aimed toward the ground, his head shaking.

"This is not good," he told David. "It will kill your mother to hear this. A Muslim for a daughter-in-law."

"Dad, who said anything about getting married? I'm just seeing her again."

"But that is what your mother will think. I know these things."

"That is what *you're* thinking, you mean."

"I thought we forbade you ever to see this girl again."

"That was when I was in high school. I make my own decisions now."

"But not such good ones," Saeed said, still shaking his head.

The two of them stared as a cherry picker lifted two construction workers up to the building's second level, where they started putting up faux stone.

"So what is this Muslim girl doing now? You say she lives in El Paso?"

"With her boyfriend, but I think that's going to end. She doesn't love him."

"But she stays with him. What does that tell you?"

"It tells me she has parents like I do, and it's tough to break out of their grip."

"Nobody's holding you, David. You can do what you want, now that you're all grown up. Even make terrible mistakes."

"Dad, stop it."

"So I guess you talk to her a lot?"

"Not so much. E-mail."

"Because you're worried she'll be caught with you on the phone, because she has an insanely jealous Muslim boyfriend."

David laughed; he couldn't help himself. "Basically that's right. I've got to give her some time to take care of that."

"So you'll see her this summer, right, when you go to help your *zeidy*?"

"I'm planning on it. I'm not sure she really wants to see me then. She's actually kind of freaked out about my going to New Mexico, like it's a big deal to be there in the summer."

"Maybe she's afraid her crazy boyfriend will find out and shoot you two."

"Maybe."

Or maybe it's something else, Saeed said to himself. He would be the first to admit he had a prejudice against Muslims. "So what?" he'd said to David, when the boy, filled with teenage righteousness, had accused him of intolerance ten years earlier. "They want to kill us," Saeed had said to him then. "They *are* killing our people. Why should I like them?"

"Not all of them are bad," David had protested. "Not Soroya or her parents. Her father is a doctor. He takes care of everybody. He's not killing anyone."

Saeed hadn't said another word back then, just as he'd finally silenced himself a few minutes ago. But that didn't mean he was through. Not at all. Saeed had been brought up by a mother who'd barely made it out of Birkenau. Those inherited horrors had left him seeing the darkest possibilities.

Whatever the reason, Saeed made a call as soon as he climbed into his white Escalade. To an old friend. A man who always got answers.

The Project 853 meeting in late February in Juarez involved an electronics geek who spoke fluent English but with a strong German accent. Colonel Gharabaghi did not offer his name or anything about him when they all met in yet another drab hotel room. The German looked as thin—and hard—as a drafting pencil, with silky, blond hair that covered the tops of his ears.

"He will tell you what we need," Gharabaghi said.

"Do not use a stolen cell phone," the German began.

That's what set off the Pueblo Canyon bombing, Soroya recalled. But the visitor stared at them with pale-blue eyes and continued with a shake of his head.

"This is what you use," he explained, handing Rosincourt a slick brochure. "A phone with GPS features and two-channel links. It is very popular. Millions sold. But to be extra safe, pay cash in store without surveillance cameras. Say nothing to anyone," the German added, though Soroya thought he sure appeared to be in the loop. *How many others are too?* she wondered.

The question she'd asked herself dovetailed strangely with the colonel's next admonition: "Never talk at Bradley Brothers about anything even remotely related to this."

She and Roz had already told everyone in the shop that *all* oil field work was proprietary to the customer. Roz nodded; belatedly, Soroya did, too.

A few hours later and a hundred miles away, another conversation took place, this one at an outside table at the Tortuga Café in Chihuahua. It was a casual bistro with widely spaced tables on a tree-adorned patio—perfect for private conversations. That was precisely the reason the Talleyrand executive and one of Mexico's most notorious drug lords had chosen the Tortuga.

Compagnie Talleyrand had long since made its peace with the Federation, the umbrella organization overseeing Mexico's drug empire. Before President Calderón had launched his war on drugs, a clutch of senior crime barons had maintained order for years, minimizing bloodshed by allocating turf for the benefit of all. In exchange for a generous retainer, the Federation's subordinate gangs had made sure Talleyrand's equipment remained undamaged, their engineers unharmed while in-country. But those carefully organized arrangements—and the hierarchy that favored the overlords—had fallen apart once Mexico's war on drugs exploded. Anarchy, widespread torture, and murder now reigned.

The man from Talleyrand stood to greet Enrico, once a junior member of the Federation who had risen quickly in the ranks thanks to Mexico's mayhem.

"Nice to see you again," the executive said to the suave, dark-haired Enrico. "But where are Eduardo and Cruz? What has happened to the jefes?" The bosses.

"Ah, well." Enrico smiled, looking left to right at his obviously armed security men standing only feet away. "The problem is the Mérida campaign." That was the US-funded drive to crack down on drug trafficking in Mexico.

"Four years ago the American Congress allocated four hundred million dollars to disrupt the drug gangs, money laundering, and other organized crime in our country. The turf wars killed thousands and made headlines around the world. All about macabre murders and dismemberment.

"But you need to understand, señor," Ernico went on, "that half the problem lies on the demand side of the equation. The Americans"—he patted his ample stomach—"have a big appetite for drugs. With all the arrests and shootings, our leaders got hit hard. We started shooting back and got some American agents, so some of our friends, like Cruz, are no long with us. But we are still strong. Everything is getting sorted out now. We can still take care of you."

"Are you sure of that?" the Talleyrand executive asked as he slipped a fat envelope across the table. "That's to settle up for past work. And there's more if you have the people to do it, Enrico."

"I just said we *will* take care of you. I do not speak lightly."

"Alright. We have a new project. It's not drugs or guns. We need your help smuggling gold into the US. It's coming from my tax-avoiding compatriots back in France. They're worried about the economic collapse in southern Europe and maybe France too. So we will be bringing their goods into Chihuahua in small packages, one at a time, via the weekly Talleyrand flight. We would like to arrange shipment into El Paso via your Juarez connections."

Enrico smiled. "Gold?" He shook his head as if to let his listener know he would accept the official line, even if he didn't believe it. "Of course, señor. We still have a reasonable relationship with Los Aztecas up north. They will take care of you in Juarez."

"Good, but what about help with logistics in-country, like meeting the plane and transporting the goods to the border?"

Still smiling, Enrico said, "I know the man for this. Miguel Acuña is perfect. He has been with us for almost ten years. He is a gentleman. This is his specialty, smuggling documents and artwork across the border. I think he will like this. A coat-and-tie man with perfect credentials. The border people think he is a banker. But most important, I trust him absolutely. Miguel has been in this game a long time, and he is rich enough that he does not need to steal from anyone. And he is a survivor, like me." Enrico leaned forward. "Tough as nails. That's what he is. I could tell you stories, but maybe you don't want to hear?"

"I don't," the executive replied. "But I like the sound of this Acuña."

A week later the two men reconvened at the Tortuga Cafe, but this time Miguel Acuña joined them. He wore a buff suit, a button-down blue shirt, and a yellow tie with the same ease that some men wear a smile. Acuña looked to be in his late forties, with a trim, black mustache and an ample head of hair. His unusual gray-green eyes focused on each man as he spoke.

After introductions Enrico repeated his endorsement. The executive from Talleyrand asked Acuña a few questions, but even the most casual listener would have known he was moving forward based on the federation's judgment. With a firm handshake, the deal was done. Acuña, as sophisticated as he appeared, was trusted by thugs. That was what seemed to count most to the man from Talleyrand. He told Acuña he would e-mail him the arrival times of the flights that would bring in gift-wrapped boxes with ten-pound trinkets inside.

"And from there, who guarantees my safety?" Acuña asked in a gravelly voice.

"Los Aztecas will give you an armed escort to the border," Enrico replied. "Then you simply drive over the bridge from Juarez to El Paso with the *gift* on the front seat."

"And if they're examined?" Acuña asked. "What will they find inside?"

Talleyrand's executive smiled broadly. "A nickel-plated ashtray with a Compagnie Talleyrand logo stamped onto the plastic cladding."

Acuña was to deliver each to a private mailbox in El Paso. Payment would be made to Enrico back in Chihuahua after each delivery was completed.

The last link in the chain from Tehran to the Bradley Brothers shop— now an atomic bomb factory—had been forged, hammered out with enough care to withstand the heat of the Mérida furnace.

Saeed Borookhim's old friend was Leon Parsky, the Mossad's man in Los Angeles. The city's Jewish community was tightly knit, and the Israeli intelligence service had a strong presence in southern California. Parsky—wiry, pockmarked, and middle-aged—suggested an eight a.m. meeting at the Beverly Hilton the next day.

After parking his Toyota outside the hotel, he and Saeed exchanged pleasantries, then walked through a park that ran along a stretch of Santa Monica Boulevard. It was a quiet winter morning with clear, blue skies—the Los Angeles that much of the country envied.

Saeed offered a brief review of his conversation with his son.

"As you know," Parsky said, "we take a keen interest in any behavior by Muslims that's the least bit odd, and you're right. It's a little peculiar that this Assaf woman is so worried about David's going to New Mexico this summer. But maybe it is nothing more than a lover's concern. What about her boyfriend? You say his name is Rosincourt Sadr?" Saeed nodded. "What do you know about him?"

"Not so much. Soroya told David he's an engineer. I'm not sure what he does."

"And you say they are in El Paso, but she's worried about your son going to New Mexico?" Parsky asked.

"That's what David told me. It's probably nothing. Talking about it makes me feel like a foolish old man."

Parsky waved off that concern. "We always hope these things turn out to be foolish worries. Then we can all laugh about it, pat each other on the back. But we don't know," he added seriously. "That's why we check."

"Thank you," Saeed said. "I don't have an address for these two. I'm—"

Parsky interrupted Saeed. "We can find them in minutes."

It didn't take that long once Parsky turned it over to a colleague. Within a week, operating totally outside US law, the Mossad wired Soroya and Rosincourt's Festival Street apartment for sound. On the first weekend they uncovered chilling indications of something terribly amiss. Those concerns were funneled immediately from a garage listening post in El Paso to the Mossad headquarters in Tel Aviv. Israel's embassy in Washington received a copy:

FLASH PRECEDENCE
Top Secret
To ISEMBWASH

Surveillance of the living quarters of the two US citizens, second-generation Iranian targets (Code Afarsek & Banana) in El
Paso provides clear evidence of a major engineering and fabrication effort. There is every indication, but no proof, that this
effort, known as Project 853, has nuclear dimensions. Parties
within Mexico appear to be aiding and abetting this process.
Surveillance continues.

Within an hour the Israeli ambassador to Washington requested
an urgent meeting with the American director of Central Intelligence
(DCI). The men were associates of long standing. The phone message
was concise.

"General, we believe you have a very serious problem. We need to
talk."

Just two hours later, the DCI met with the Israeli ambassador and the
Mossad station chief in a secure conference room within the intelligence
community building on F Street.

As soon as the DCI heard the subject was Iran, he summoned his Ira-
nian-desk man.

The Mossad's operative came to the point, knowing no matter the
assurances, he *was* being recorded. "General, we have reason to believe an
American couple, US-born citizens of Iranian ancestry, are involved in a
complex plot to assemble and possibly detonate a nuclear device within the
western US. We further believe there is Mexican involvement. We do not
think this is an immediate problem—their efforts may not reach completion until this summer. They may not succeed at all, given our other dis-
ruptive efforts, but this is a clear and present danger."

Pro forma attempts by the DCI to determine Mossad's sources, or
whether the foreign intelligence agency had violated US laws, came to
naught.

"My advice, General," the Israeli ambassador said, "is that you acquire
the appropriate FISA warrant." The Foreign Intelligence Surveillance Act
permitted surveillance warrants against suspected foreign agents inside the

United States. "We think you should put Mr. Rosincourt Sadr, Ms. Soroya Assaf, their residence on Festival Street, and their factory on Doniphan Road all under immediate surveillance."

The Mossad operative handed the director a card with the names of the targets, along with their addresses. All four men then shook hands and left the bubble.

Within minutes the Mossad agents in El Paso had been instructed to pull their bugs from Festival Street. Now it was up to the Americans.

CHAPTER 17
CONVERGENCE

March 2012

The Director of Central Intelligence and the National Security Advisor hurried into the Oval Office, where the president barely glanced up from signing documents. His tall chief of staff, Bob O'Brien, hovered over him. When the president put aside his pen, O'Brien carefully assembled the pages and stepped back, lowering an imperious gaze on the two visitors.

"Iranians in El Paso?" the president said in the mellifluous voice that had charmed millions. "How long is this going to take?"

The DCI delivered his message to the president. The National Security Advisor confirmed the general's findings: serious concern was warranted. The president smiled.

"So it's"—he glanced at his watch—"eight thirty in the morning and I'm dealing with radical twenty-somethings in El Paso? Gentlemen, it sounds like another amateur hour. Bunglers in ski masks. If I had a dollar for every time I've had to listen to this stuff." He shook his head. "Are we looking at another taxi bomber?"

"No, Mr. President, we are not," the DCI assured him.

"Then get all the players involved. CIA in Mexico City. Homeland Security should take over the El Paso surveillance, assuming we get FISA to approve. Any issue there?" the president asked.

"I can't imagine that will be a problem," the DCI replied.

"Good. What about NSC?" the president asked his national security advisor. "You guys developing an action plan, should the need arise?"

"Yes, Mr. President."

"Fine. Go to it." He turned to O'Brien. "What's next?" he asked as the visitors made their exit.

The Homeland Security chief had Elizabeth Mallory flown in from El Paso. For four months she had been investigating the Pueblo Canyon bombing that had taken the lives of Dr. Sig Antonovitch, Dr. Simon Hall, and their driver. During the winter just passed, the Agency and/or the Mossad had struck back. Their men on motorbikes attached a magnetic bomb to the Peugeot carrying Natanz chemist Mostafa Ahmadi Roshan to his office in Tehran. But back in the U.S. Elizabeth's El Paso anti-terrorist task force had made little progress. Even so, when news of a possible Iranian-Mexican nuclear plot emerged from the FISA courtroom, Elizabeth was the logical candidate to oversee the case. She had defeated Iranian nuclear smugglers once before, in Kazakhstan, with derring-do that still overshadowed her recent setbacks in the New Mexican bombing murders.

She was also fluent in Farsi and had demonstrated considerable coolness under fire while running the Predator squadron in Qatar. The FBI and CIA both thought this thirty-nine-year-old professional was right for the job.

Her first meeting with Justice Department officials produced a sobering flash of recognition for Elizabeth when she heard the names of the key targets in the nuclear bomb building case: Rosincourt Sadr and Soroya Assaf.

"I know about those two," she told the two older men and young woman from Justice. Her statement got their attention. "Assaf's been on my personal watch list for six years, and Rosincourt's cousin was Mehdi Banisadr of *the* Banisadr clan."

"The *late* Mehdi Banisadr?" the most senior Justice lawyer said with a mildly amused look.

"The one and only," Elizabeth replied soberly, without noting her role in young Medhi's demise or that she had taken great pleasure in the assassination; Flash Gourdine's memory never rested easily for her. "Nukes in El Paso?" she went on, eyes narrowing. "That sounds like the perfect wave."

"What do you mean?" the young woman who'd been doing the briefing asked.

"We've got Hezbollah cells in Mexico," Elizabeth responded. "Blood-lands for a border that's more porous than your average sea sponge, and—all apologies to law-abiding Muslims—a lot of engineering know-how in the Islamic community down there. A lot of them went to UTEP and were good enough to land work with the oil companies. Or Los Alamos," she added with a knowing nod.

"So the know-how's there?" The senior Justice official no longer appeared bemused.

"Absolutely," Elizabeth replied. "And based on what I've just heard, the know-how is not just there. It's getting applied even as we sit here."

During the next twenty-four hours, Elizabeth made the rounds, meeting a man from Mossad, experts from the Department of Energy's weapons labs, and two Iranian academics. The latter were exiles with sharp axes to grind, but she wanted to hear from a broad spectrum of sources.

As Elizabeth was finishing her round of Washington meetings, Colonel Ashkan Gharabaghi settled down with Rosincourt and Soroya in another anonymous room in the ongoing series of Juarez hotels. Speaking only to Roz, the colonel delivered explicit instructions on the handling of the fissile rings.

"First of all," Gharabaghi ordered, "you must always lock these pieces up. They cost a quarter million dollars each to produce, but in the global struggle for justice and power"—he raised his eyes, as if to the heavens—"they are priceless."

Rosincourt nodded. Soroya watched the colonel stare only at her room-mate, which was how she'd begun to think of Roz. They no longer made love. They hadn't even kissed in weeks. Roz's interest in her had begun to wane as soon as they were ushered into Project 853, and now she had no interest in him either. They were no longer joined by love, only by murder and terror. And at night, while he slept, she pined for David Borookhim.

"Secondly," the colonel went on, "you must treat the rings with the utmost care. Uranium metal is pyrophoric. You know what that means?" Roz nodded. Soroya shook her head no. "It means"—Gharabaghi stared fiercely at her—"that it will spark or burn if any of the protective layers of nickel are removed and the metal under them is scratched."

To Soroya the colonel sounded like he resented every breath he took in her presence.

"Most important of all," Gharabaghi warned, "these components are fissionable. They will go critical if you store them close to one another. You must place each one in a special box or cage designed to avoid a critical assembly and to prevent any damage. Then you must store these packages in your personal walk-in safe. You've got one at Bradley Brothers, right?"

"Yes," Roz said.

"Make sure that vault is under surveillance twenty-four hours a day. There must be a night watchman. Do not share the combination for that safe with anyone other than her," he added with a passing glance at Soroya. "Did you change the combination as I ordered?" Roz nodded. "Then no one else, not even the owners know it?"

"Right," Roz said. "And they haven't even tried to use it in months."

"Take nothing for granted," the colonel said. "At the end of June, when all fifteen plugs and rings are on hand, Dr. Hout will be here to supervise the cleaning of each component with a solvent. The thin nickel plating will not be removed. It will not seriously degrade the nuclear performance of the weapon." Gharabaghi smiled for the first time when he said that. "Once they're cleaned and inspected by Dr. Hout, the discs will then be ready for insertion—and use."

He concluded with windup orders. "These fifteen rings are to be installed into Akhbar-I during the weekend before shipment under the direct supervision of Dr. Hout."

Soroya realized the colonel was addressing Roz as a junior officer, not as an engineer. It frightened her to realize this; just the change in tone made the detonation of the nuclear bomb seem ever more inevitable and imminent.

It really is inevitable, she reminded herself. *The countdown's begun.*

Before leaving Washington, Elizabeth shoehorned in a night at her father's home. It seemed like precious little time with him but it was enough to look in his bright-blue eyes, see they were as clear as ever, and notice he'd gotten over his limp.

"All healed up?" she said.

"That's right, and I was hoping to leave you behind on a ride along the Potomac."

"No can do, Dad. Next time. That's a promise."

"Things getting hot south of the border?" he asked.

"That's one way of putting it."

"Can you give me a little more information to keep this old hand in the loop?"

"Sorry, Dad. You know the game, and you know the rules."

In the morning she was gone, so quickly it seemed she'd never really been home. And as her father waved good-bye, she wondered, as she often did, if she'd ever see him again. The death of her mother had filled Elizabeth with regret for a relationship that never was; but she knew, as she waved back to her father, that someday his death would flood her with the loss of all the riches they'd ever shared.

Armed with all the approvals, funding, and technical support she needed, Elizabeth set out to determine what the Assaf woman and Mehdi Banisadr's cousin were up to, both in their apartment and at the Bradley Brothers shop. She had Jack Barry down in Mexico City to keep her apprised of the savagery south of the border. She asked her FBI technicians to wire the Festival Street apartment for sound.

"How much time do you need?" she asked the bureau's electronics supervisor. "I can tell you that most days those two come home for lunch. Other than that, you should have clear sailing."

"Half an hour is all we need. We'll be putting a compact microphone in every wall outlet. The copper wiring already there takes the signals to a router that we'll put in the power panel. We'll establish a second cable account for the residence so we can collect everything over the Internet. By the end of the week, with the appropriate passwords, you'll be accessing those voice communications from your laptop."

That's consistent with the evolution of electronic surveillance I've seen over the years. Elizabeth asked the FBI's man to get the job done as soon as he could. "We'll watch the shop to warn you if they head home. You'll need to wire up Bradley Brothers as well—the office and the main assembly area. I'm assuming that's going to be a black-bag operation."

"No need." The team leader smiled. "We go into places of work with telephone company credentials. Nobody seems to mind. They're too busy these days." He added a postscript: "Other good news, Ms. Mallory: We've started using voice-activated mikes. The intercepted information goes to a central server, and all the dead time gets ignored. Only the product you need is stored until you access it. Saves a lot of time."

"That sounds great," she said as she watched the young geeks leave.

Forty-eight hours later, an FBI agent delivered a sealed envelope to Elizabeth in her windowless ATF office. She had just come in from a run along the Rio Grande.

Elizabeth thanked him and found a message inside advising that the bugging of Festival Street was complete. A separately sealed card provided the password and PIN needed to access the product.

She grabbed a cup of coffee to gird herself for a dull morning listening to shop talk and family news. But at 10:15 on the morning of March 22, her coffee hit the floor.

"Holy shit!" she shouted to the walls. Her ears were locked into a stunning exchange between Rosincourt and Soroya.

Rosincourt: "Getting my hands on that first ring made it real for the first time. I'm building a nuke with my own hands! And we're going to get to shoot it."

Soroya: "Great. I still think Gharabaghi's a creep. And every time Hout sits next to me, he *accidentally* brushes against my leg. What a slob."

Gharabaghi! Elizabeth hit "pause," then had to prop her elbows on the table to hold herself upright. *That son of a bitch from Kazakhstan*, she told herself, remembering how the sun had blinded her on the evening she'd brought down the Antonov-12. Now the sun would be at her back. *He won't even see me coming until I take him down.*

In the next instant, she recalled the photos of the brutal maiming and murder of Gunpowder and the friendly old Kazakh farmer who'd bought the gelding.

Much as she hated Ashkan Gharabaghi, a good part of her was happy to have him so firmly in her crosshairs once again. She'd gotten even with Mehdi Banisadr, and now she would settle old scores with Gharabaghi. She was not surprised to find the colonel was running the show south of the border. He was, after all, a high-ranking member of the Quds, and they were busy working to structure Hezbollah in Mexico.

It could have been predicted, she said to herself, still genuinely pleased to have the bastard in her sights. Yes, she knew she was driven by revenge and someday it would be nice if loftier aspirations dominated her life, but not before the business of old blood had been settled.

She resumed listening to the recording. Rosincourt said he was going to bed. Elizabeth didn't hear Soroya respond. The couple's nighttime parting sounded neither sweet nor loving.

Sitting back, Elizabeth took out the earbuds. *Nukes. Just what the Mossad warned us about.* She felt like she was finally in the right place at the right time. No more busy work. The Pueblo Canyon bombing no longer felt like a puzzle. Gharabaghi had reached out from Juarez to even some scores for Tehran. She would return the favor if she possibly could.

After a few minutes of reflection, she reported her findings to her director:

> There can be no doubt this couple is involved in a plot to assemble a nuclear weapon within their shop. The two principals are second-generation Iranian-Americans with a very strong anti-American belief system. This operation is part of a broader Iranian plan with some sort of support from within Mexico. It appears only the fissile materials for this weapon are to come from Iran. The rest of the weapon components originate with commercial suppliers, for the most part in the US although one key piece came from China. It is not known how this weapon is to be used, but it is clear it will not be ready for detonation until sometime this summer. I cannot see where any major US laws have yet been broken, but we need to keep a close eye on this one.

She also added a personal postscript for the director's eyes only:

> This is going to be interesting. From the transcripts I find that bloody bastard Gharabaghi at the center of all this, including Pueblo Canyon. I only got his airplane last time. I'll do better this time around.

The formal report, minus the personal postscript, was passed along from FBI headquarters to the White House Situation Room. From there it moved rapidly to the National Security Advisor for discussion with the president, who was busy reviewing the results of primary elections and counting delegates with his campaign manager, a middle-aged woman who looked ready to bite off the head of anyone who encroached on her time with her only boss.

But when the president spotted the DCI and National Security Advisor, he waved them in. The two men stood before his desk, waiting for the campaign manager to leave. The Secret Service agents who protected the president had nicknamed her "Hardpan."

"Go ahead," the president said impatiently.

"I am not permitted to divulge this information to anyone but you," the DCI said curtly.

The president stared at him. "Come back in five," he said to Hardpan, who scowled at the men from the intelligence community as if they carried communicable diseases.

The president's national security advisor then briefed him.

"So if I'm hearing you correctly," the president responded in his eternally unruffled voice, "no American laws have been broken, General, except by the Mossad. I can't tell you how sick I am of hearing about these ham-handed, two-bit terrorists. If these clowns even manage to get their hands on any radioactive stuff, they'll just end up irradiating their own underwear. What else do you have?"

"We think that's plenty, Mr. President," the DCI said. "We have active conspirators with the technical knowhow to build a nuclear device working in concert with a high-ranking member of the Iranian Quds."

"But they're months away from taking any action, right?" The president didn't wait for a reply. "And they don't have their hands on the radioactive materials yet. Gentlemen, I hear this every other week from you guys. Quit crying wolf on me."

"We are not crying wolf," the DCI countered. "These people are capable and have a supply chain, a purpose, and a clear-cut goal."

"So let me know when there's a clear and present danger and you have a clear-cut plan," the president responded. "We've got bin Laden. The rest of them are pikers. They're already dead. They just don't know it yet. And I'm busy. The Senate race polls have a lot of my one-time friends running for cover. Suddenly they've never heard of me." He sounded like he was about to swear, but his famous self-control reasserted itself, and he merely shook his head.

Down on the border in El Paso, Elizabeth Mallory held a far different view of the threat facing her country. This time the US would be playing for keeps. Somebody was going to win and somebody was going to lose.

Nuclear hardball had begun.

CHAPTER 18
NIGHT VISITORS

March–May 2012

Elizabeth found the owners of her target company in Hobbs, New Mexico. Bum and Hiram Bradley appeared to run an old-line oil-field services firm with shops in Midland and El Paso. On paper it was a successful if not particularly notable outfit—except it employed Rosincourt Sadr and Soroya Assaf.

Using the company's purchase of cordite gunpowder as an excuse, Elizabeth downgraded her credentials to appear as a lowly bureaucrat with the ATF. There were many legitimate uses of cordite in construction and mining, so the purchase by Bradley Brothers provided an innocuous excuse to contact the owners.

In mid-March she drove over to Hobbs, climbed the dusty, wooden stairs to the Bradley offices on the second floor, and greeted Bum Bradley, the company's chairman and treasurer. The man, she realized with a glance, was much more casual than his title suggested. She hadn't seen a rangy cowboy like him in years. He had deep laugh lines in his cheeks and crow's-feet radiating from the corners of his clear, hazel eyes.

"What gives me the honor?" he boomed, laugh lines flexing. He nodded at a stuffed chair in front of his desk.

When she sat she smelled dust in the fabric, or maybe it was everywhere in the room. It was difficult to reconcile the funkiness of the office with the disturbing evidence of sophisticated bomb building that had prompted her unannounced visit.

"We at the Bureau of Alcohol, Tobacco, Firearms, and Explosives noted your company bought a little cordite, Mr. Bradley. No problem with that. It's not a controlled substance, and we know it's used in excavation work, but I've never heard of it being used in the oil fields. Don't tell me you guys are going back to the days of nitroglycerin. You fracking wells with grenades or something?" The suggestion was ridiculous, of course, but she wanted to catch the old cowpoke's response.

He smiled and shook his head. She had a feeling he didn't see too many women walk into his office. This was a man's world. A quick glance at the framed photos on the wall told that story. Some showed oil wells blowing out, others were of Bum and a guy who looked a lot like him posing with a variety of game trophies. But the one that really caught her eye was the most dated: a black-and-white snapshot of a rakish air corps officer in his mid-twenties, a handsome man with dark eyes and a daredevil smile that looked a lot like Bum's. He was wearing a flying suit; his hat displayed the coveted fifty-mission crush.

Her subject caught her looking. "My father," he said laconically. "World War II. Pacific. Never came home. Never got to hold Hiram or me."

She wondered immediately if he was trying to distract her, then realized she had distracted herself with these photos. But not for long. "What about that cordite?" Still friendly in tone and appearance.

"To tell you the truth, my brother and I have been wondering the same thing. We've got a new manager running the show over there in El Paso. He's a great engineer, salesman, everything you want. And he's bringing in terrific new business I'm sorry to say I don't even remotely understand. But it delivers big numbers to the bottom line."

"It's your name on the door," she said, holding her smile. "Why aren't you trying to find out what's going on over there?"

"I have." Bum sighed. "You ever hear of a magnetohydrodynamic generator?" She shook her head. "Me neither. And that's just one of the things he's got going over there. Makes me feel put out to pasture, and it's my company. It's all that computer stuff now," he said, shaking his head.

She let silence swell between them; like most investigators she'd found saying nothing often pried loose the most difficult answers. It also gave her a chance to read some other photos on the wall. One showed Bum and a lookalike—Hiram, she presumed—at an airfield in Southeast Asia. Another showed a towering oilrig fully decorated for Christmas. Then there were memorabilia, including a collection of handsome ceramic mugs from beer halls in Germany. A tattered American flag hung on another wall. The thirteenth stripe had three bullet holes in its red fabric and distinct gunpowder burns. She figured it had come back from 'Nam or somewhere nearby. She already knew Bum was an Air Force vet, as his father would have been if he'd survived Ie Shima. Her guess? Bum was a patriotic guy, not some A-bomb building religious nutbar. But she would never stake the health of the investigation on a guess.

Bum broke the silence, but not with a confession. "You don't miss much," he said.

She smiled. "I learned long ago that looking at a man's photos can tell you a lot."

"Like?"

"Like you're a patriot. Like you served. Like you or your brother took the time to rescue a flag, maybe in battle, and if you did that you'd have taken the time to rescue a whole lot more. That you cared about your father, but you didn't have a family of your own because there are no kids' pictures up there."

"You see a lot when you look at a man's wall," Bum said. "What about when you look at a woman's?"

"No matter what you see, be careful about making too much of it. Women are a lot more complicated."

He laughed. "My sentiments exactly! But you know what? I'd have no problem with you taking a walk around our El Paso operation. You see a lot. Maybe you'll see something there too. It's on Doniphan Road."

"Oh, I know where it is," she said, realizing in the same instant that she liked Bum Bradley. Most times she was a professional skeptic, but he struck her as the real deal. He wore his slim-cut jeans and scuffed but well-polished boots with ease. No drugstore cowboy. "Why don't you come with me?" she asked. She'd like to see how he moved around his company now that he found his own holdings so foreign. And then she wondered if she'd made an unconscious play on words.

"Accompany a good-looking lady? You don't have to ask me twice."

He's flirting, she said to herself. But what proved most striking to her was she didn't mind. *How old is he? I like them older, but not ancient.* Still she looked at him closely and was struck almost numb by the fact that she was undeniably—well, maybe only slightly, but nevertheless... Lord, she could scarcely admit this—attracted…to…him. The last acknowledgement felt like it dribbled from a dry tap.

It's been a while, she reminded herself. Since Flash Gourdine. *Maybe too long, if you're looking at this old guy.*

Nope, I'm not letting myself go there, she told herself sternly. The old cowboy was too much of a leap in age—and she wasn't going to jump.

"How about if we keep this strictly business?" she replied.

"Long as we keep it," he said without missing a beat.

It was like he'd read her every thought. "I think we'd better make it an after-hours visit," she said. She already knew Sadr and Assaf were never in the shop on Friday afternoons and evenings. Off to Juarez every time.

"I'll tell you what," Bradley said through a sheepish grin. "You live in El Paso, right? How about you get out of that government costume, get dolled up, and join me in a visit to my old friends over there at the shop? We'll drop by in the evening and you can pretend to be my new social friend."

"You are an operator," she said, smiling herself. "How soon can we do it?"

"You in a rush to see the shop or to see me again?"

"Has anybody ever told you, Mr. Bum Bradley, that you are an incorrigible flirt?"

"I think I might have heard that a time or two, but not lately."

I should say not. "To answer your question, it's to see the shop, And just so you know, you're old enough to be my father, even if you are easy on the eyes."

"'Even if' is sometimes just enough."

She rolled her eyes and handed him a generic business card, then headed back to El Paso feeling giddier than she thought healthy. *How am I ever going to explain this one to Dad?* The very fact that she asked herself that question made Elizabeth recognize more than she wanted to, and it had nothing to do with the kind of fireworks that had brought her to Hobbs.

Bum draped his legs on his desk and watched her drive off. Then he noticed the dusty tip of his Tony Lama boot swinging back and forth like a pendulum.

"Stop doing your damn desk dance," he said to his foot. "It ain't happening yet."

He got on the phone to one of his oldest friends, Fritz Burkhardt. Fritz had been the company's first hire. He'd made the move to El Paso seven years earlier, but he was still a good buddy.

After the "how's life treating you?" small talk, Bum got to the point. "Listen, you old coot, I'm meeting a new lady friend from El Paso Friday night. Least I think I am. She's seems eager to go. I want to stop by the plant just to say hello. You can check her out. She's a keeper. Little younger than me, but—"

"She'd be petrified if she were any older, Bum. Last girlfriend you had was complaining about her old-age pension and bitching up a storm about them nickel ice cream cones disappearing on her."

Bum laughed. "Fritz, you haven't changed a bit."

"Yeah, I have. I've gotten older, but I'm still younger than any girlfriend you'll ever have. When are you going to write your theme song—"Wasting Away Again in Geezerville"? Suits you to a damn T."

"You're a hard nut to crack, Fritz."

"'Specially with those teeth you got. I remember you breaking a molar on a hot dog."

"It had a stone in it," Bum said, playing indignant.

"The only stones were the rocks in your head, and from the way you're rattling on here they ain't gone away."

"So you'll be there?" Bum asked. "Friday night?"

"Sure. What else am I gonna do? I bet I'll hear her joints creaking from a mile away."

Three nights later Elizabeth rendezvoused with Bum a few blocks from the Bradley Brothers shop. She left her car parked on a busy street in an industrial section of El Paso and slid into his red Mustang convertible, thinking the car had first hit the road a good ten years before she was born. But it was in good shape, and so was the driver in his rakishly tilted cowboy hat and pearl-button shirt. She was pleased not to have overdressed when she slipped on tawny-colored slacks and a blue merino top.

"Cool car," she said, buckling herself in. "Fast?"

"It sure is," he said, laying a strip of rubber a hundred feet long.

Long as you're not, she thought, looking at him.

It couldn't have been thirty seconds before they'd pulled into the parking lot of a structure large enough to house a zeppelin. As soon as they walked inside, she saw the cavernous space was needed to accommodate overhead cranes to assemble oil-gas separators along with other petroleum-processing equipment.

But the shop appeared deserted and eerily quiet except for a guy named Fritz. He looked shocked when he saw her; he had trouble responding when Bum introduced them.

"Cat got your tongue, Fritz?" Bum joked.

"Yeah, I guess so," he managed. "Nice to meet you," he gulped when he took Elizabeth's hand. His was unpleasantly damp.

Bum gave her the full tour. Fritz tagged along. The three of them stopped to chat about a piece of the strange-looking machine Rosincourt was building for Compagnie Talleyrand.

"Can't say much about that Talleyrand stuff," Fritz said. "Pretty proprietary, you know, Bum."

After a half hour, Bum suggested he and Fritz retire to a couple of canvas chairs.

"Elizabeth, you seem interested in all our toys. You're welcome to keep walking around while we have a cigar."

"I'd love to," she said, struck by his evident openness.

As she walked off, the men lit their stogies in full violation of the signboards on every wall.

The prerogatives of ownership, she said to herself.

She strolled through the whole plant, making detailed notes on access and layout. With her cell phone, she photographed the walk-in safe, which she found locked or she would have had a look around in there too. Then she snapped pictures of the controls for the security system; she sensed Bum wouldn't have minded in the least if he'd seen what she was up to. Clearly the old guy wasn't completely at ease with the goings-on in his own shop.

Satisfied with her reconnaissance, she decided to look for the two-legged security. As she moved deeper into the warrens of the factory, she detected the unmistakable sounds of lovemaking in the executive suite. It had large windows looking out over the shop floor, but the blinds had been lowered. For good reason, from what Elizabeth could garner. She wondered if she'd just walked up on Hiram, the older brother; she realized she hadn't determined whether he was married. *Could be a paramour.* She shook her head. That would be awfully frisky for a guy in his late sixties.

She no sooner stopped to listen than the noises ceased. She thought she heard some scurrying, and though it was outside her purview she tried to see around the edge of the blinds. Right then the door opened. She stepped back as a man in his fifties, dressed like a night watchman, stepped out. His hair was mussed and his face was red.

"Who are you?" he asked, but not with authority. With fear. The sound of a man who had "busted" printed across his burning cheeks—the ones on his face.

"I'm Elizabeth Mallory, a friend of Bum Bradley's."

"Oh, no," he groaned. "Is Bum here?"

She nodded. The guard looked anguished, which pleased her immensely. It never hurt to have something on the security staff when you were checking out a place.

"What's your name, and what's going on in there?" she asked.

He stared at her as if he didn't know whether to confess or try to lie his way out of his delicate predicament.

"Just tell me," she said. "I'm not going to bite."

"I'm Jack Daniel, Ms. Mallory. I have a friend who visits me on Friday nights. Everybody else is usually gone, and the electronic security is good. I can count on it for an hour or two while we sort of slip away." He nodded at the suite. "For drinks. And...stuff. Please don't tell Bum. And where is he?" he asked, perhaps realizing Bum could appear at any moment.

"Don't worry. He's talking to a guy named Fritz."

"Fritz is here too?" the guard said. That news appeared to shock him even more.

"Why are you so worried about Fritz?" she asked.

"He'll never let me live this down. He'll make jokes about this for as long as I live."

"I won't tell him. Bum and I will be leaving, and I think Fritz is there so Bum can show me off." As soon as she said that, she realized how immodest it sounded.

But before she could correct herself, Jack said, "I can understand that."

"We'll be gone soon," she added, "but you might want to keep it down in there."

"Okay," she heard from inside the suite. She wasn't entirely sure the voice belonged to a woman. Didn't much care either.

When she walked back to Bum and Fritz, they were finishing their cigars—along with a few beers that had magically appeared. As the three of them left, she caught Fritz giving Bum an approving wink. *Guys never change.*

"How about a drink? Or a steak?" Bum asked her. "Or I could drive you to a nice, quiet place for a view of the city."

"You really are Mr. Incorrigible, Bum." But she laughed as she said it, then agreed to one beer. "How's that sound?"

"Great."

He drove her to a brewery short on atmosphere and long on taste, which were the proportions she favored most. And yes, one beer turned into two, and the conversation proved more interesting than she was comfortable with. That was because she realized once she got past Bum Bradley's age, he was everything she appreciated in a guy. For starters he was genuinely curious about her; she had to watch that she didn't say too much. And he had a roguish quality she admired in men. Kind of like Flash Gourdine in that regard. So she put on the brakes after her second frosty mug had disappeared and took the ride back to her less sporty Honda.

In a courtly manner, he hopped out of the Mustang and opened the passenger door, then escorted her to the Accord. She thought he'd try to kiss her and prepared herself to duck if he dived. But he didn't. What he did was take her hand and give it a nice, warm squeeze, and that sent a delightful—and surprising—tingle down her spine.

Still smiling, she drove away, her night's work just beginning. Back in her apartment, she methodically transcribed every observation she'd made at the Bradley Brothers shop and printed out every photo. She also noted Friday evenings would be a good time for her to return with an FBI security expert to penetrate the facility.

Seventy-two hours later, Mike McKinney walked into her office. She knew him by reputation as a world-class Navy locksmith and electronics expert. After she informed him of what she'd observed, including Jack Daniel's liaison, McKinney agreed Friday night sounded like their best bet.

As dusk settled over El Paso exactly one week after she'd first toured the plant, Elizabeth and Mike hunkered down on the roof of a nearby bottling factory. Both were dressed in black, loose-fitting sweats and well-padded, dark tennis shoes. No iridescent runners for them. When Jack Daniel's lady friend arrived, Elizabeth used binoculars to spy a light in the executive office suite. Clearly Jack had been telling the truth when he'd said he trusted the electronic security. He shouldn't have.

It took McKinney only three minutes to disable the plant's electronic eyes and sensors. Then he and Elizabeth accessed every corner of the facility, photographed all the drawings they could find, and penetrated the vault already housing the first five fissile rings. She noted Rosincourt was a long way from having a full load of them for Akhbar-I, but the inventory concerned her.

She and McKinney completed their survey in less than an hour and vanished back into the night.

Elizabeth sent an encrypted report to her director, then considered the implications of what she had seen. The headline was that she was now certain Sadr and Soroya Assaf were building an atomic bomb in a factory not fifteen minutes from where she sat—and it would be ready to explode into a massive mushroom cloud in a couple of months. Wasn't it time to intercept or disrupt the shipment of the fissile materials? Though it wasn't her role as an investigator to insist upon a course of action at this point, she added a postscript to her formal report:

> Addendum: Five fissile rings have arrived in El Paso. Would it not be appropriate to find the courier within Mexico and have our CIA associates terminate him? How about knocking off Gharabaghi at the same time? We know he's the kingpin. May I communicate directly with Jack Barry on this one?

The director's office responded abruptly.

> The fissile materials courier has already been identified, but he's a drug overlord with an impenetrable phalanx of bodyguards. No, we cannot go around knocking off every foreign national we do not like. We've taken enough grief with the hit on bin Laden in somebody else's country. No, you may not discuss this matter with Jack Barry.

Elizabeth countered quickly:

In the matter of the courier chain, that's why we have Predator aircraft. I know something about how well they work.

The response from Washington was even more abrupt.

Elizabeth, you have got to be kidding. Fly Predators over Mexico? Blow away Mexican citizens on the streets of Chihuahua? Please keep us posted on activities in El Paso. We'll take care of Chihuahua.

A day later the Washington office tried to calm Elizabeth's frustrations while assisting her analysis of the Assaf-Sadr plot.

Mallory: You are now granted full access to NSA intercepts of Tehran-Chihuahua traffic. Courier will deliver. This should facilitate your penetrations of the assembly plant.

Elizabeth thought she should check with Bum Bradley on the off-chance Jack Daniel or someone else had determined there had been an unauthorized entry into the building. She decided to do this even though she considered it unlikely that Sadr or Assaf would have told Bum if they had noticed anything amiss. They'd have been much more likely to launch their own quiet counter-initiative than to risk any action that could reveal their bomb building.

But for Elizabeth, contacting Bum was a good excuse to hear his voice—a recognition that didn't register fully until he answered.

"So good to hear from you," he said right away. "I thought maybe I scared you off with all that factory stuff. We need to keep current. Every week those birds are buying more strange hardware."

If she'd had any suspicions about his involvement in building a bomb, they disappeared during this conversation. She let him detail Sadr's latest purchases and learned nothing she didn't already know from the intercepts and her own forays with McKinney.

The conversation eventually drifted from parts procurement to contrasting his life in Hobbs with hers in El Paso. Bum clearly preferred country living, which Elizabeth could well understand. She certainly wouldn't want to spend her final years fighting traffic in a congested city. The call ended with Bum suggesting they stay in touch.

"Sounds good," she responded. And it did.

But Elizabeth did not call him, and just when she felt she might have put thoughts of a sixty-plus-year-old man behind her, Bum rang her in early May to report that invoices for cadmium plating had come across his desk. That engaged her attention, but so did his lighter note that bluebonnets were blossoming all over Texas.

By May a much darker kind of phenomenon was coming to life on the border. Six enriched uranium rings had crossed into the United States. As expected Talleyrand's air freighter made it into Chihuahua every week on schedule. Miguel Acuña and his band of gunslingers were always stationed at the foot of the stairs, helping with the paperwork and accepting small gifts.

Both Rosincourt and Colonel Gharabaghi were unhappy with the week it took to make the transfer from the Chihuahua airport to the El Paso mailbox, but the parts showed up and the dimensions and packaging were always correct. Besides, Acuña wouldn't even offer an excuse for his tardiness, and his glare alone made Roz grateful the man wasn't disemboweling him. The younger man had seen videos of what was happening to people in Mexican torture houses, and that was enough to silence him forever.

Armed with the Assaf-Sadr travel plans to Juarez gleaned from the intercepts, Elizabeth and Mike McKinney fine-tuned their visits to the Bradley Brothers plant. With every entry they searched for complete layouts of the items being assembled but found none. There were dimensioned shop drawings of components but no master schematic. On the other hand, they found the specs for the cell phone system to be installed in Akhbar-I. Among the details was a notation that a sister unit was to go to Colonel Gharabaghi. Learning that Gharabaghi was the likely trigger man was a coup that made Elizabeth savor the thought of killing him.

But even that couldn't compete with her discovery of the delivery schedule for the enriched uranium rings. She found it on the inventory control sheet and waved over McKinney, whispering what she'd found. "A new one seems to show up every week. If those deliveries continue, these guys will have their needed fifteen rings by the end of *June!*"

On May 31, Elizabeth e-mailed her director:

> Penetrations continue. Fissile inventory buildup suggests required materials will be on hand by the end of June. They seem to transit Mexico but there is no indication of Mexican government involvement. Do you wish to initiate arrests before there is a critical mass on hand?

The director responded with caution. Both he and the White House wanted to hold steady until all the people in the terrorist network could be identified. Arrests would warn the plotters of a breech in their security. He ordered Elizabeth to identify the communicators and technical experts on Akhbar-I, wherever they might have been, and he expressed confidence in the NSA's ability to sabotage the weapon's electronics. She and locksmith Mike were to assist by adjusting the Akhbar-I firing circuits.

Elizabeth was much less sanguine. She had seen progress on the atomic bomb firsthand. Week by week Sadr and Assaf were building a nuclear device that could kill millions. To wait felt like a perilous strategy, but the orders came from on high. And it didn't take the skills of a Kremlinologist of old to read between the lines: The White House wanted irrefutable evidence of a real atomic bomb *and* uncontestable links to Iran, not the phantom WMDs that still haunted—and hindered—American foreign policy.

Soroya Assaf's work on the bomb was nearing completion. She had become Rosincourt's gofer, which didn't suit her at all. A biophysics major and now an errand girl? For someone she didn't love? For a bomb that would, at the very least, kill the real love of her life? She could have screamed every time those questions assaulted her.

David e-mailed to say he and his friends were planning to camp in the New Mexican Rockies that summer—after he helped his *zeidy* move. So now he was planning an even longer sojourn. Soroya decided to try to lure him somewhere far, far away, even though it risked her own role in Project 853. She hit "reply" and said she could get away starting the second week of July. "Will that give you enough time to move your *zeidy?* Then you could rendezvous with me someplace cool like Sand Point, Idaho, or Vancouver, BC."

Inshallah, he'd say yes. She almost added a blatantly suggestive sentence about what she'd do to him night and day if he'd only meet her and give up on his notion of returning to his summer playground in New Mexico. She remembered how innocent it had sounded back in high school when he talked about helping with the sheep herd. How romantic.

Who ever would have thought—she didn't want to finish the sentence but couldn't stop herself—*that someday I would become a creepy bomber who would take part in the most horrendous act of domestic terrorism in US history?*

Creepy. That was the part that really bothered her. It made her realize that from a historical point of view she would soon be keeping company with bastards like Timothy McVeigh, who'd killed *kids* in Oklahoma City, and the Unabomber. She remembered pictures of *that* bearded scumbag's old shack and realized her Festival Street apartment would soon be plastered all over the Internet. So what if she got to live out the rest of her life on the Caspian Sea? She'd be with Roz, the very sight of whom had come to irritate her. And who was kidding who? The Mossad or CIA or Navy SEALS would find them and kill them. They got bin Laden, didn't they? And the drones sure found Mehdi.

You are so dead, girl.

So if I'm dead, she said to herself, *what should I do with the time I've got left?*

Bum's legs were resting once more on his old desk, one booted foot atop the other. The fancy, perforated-leather tip was moving back and forth again, and an old Roger Miller song played in his head: *"England swing like a pendulum do, bobbies on bicycles two by two…"*

Bum had noticed his desk dance started every time he thought of that filly named Elizabeth. He figured he'd die if he ever saw her in a ponytail. That was his favorite look—long hair tied back, swishing side to side.

Something truly playful about a woman in a ponytail. And he swore it had nothing to do with his love of Ford Mustangs or the real four-legged critters.

His musings were killing him. He jerked his boots off the desk and grabbed the phone. *Hell, I'm too old to play hard to get.*

"It's me, Bum," he said when he heard her official voice. Sounded kind of hard, but it changed quickly.

"Really? How nice to hear from you," Elizabeth said. "What brings me this pleasure?"

She's either toying with me or she's interested. Even saying this to himself didn't make it wholly believable, but nobody had ever handed anything to Bum. He'd had to earn it all.

"I was wondering if you'd like to come visit again." That was it. No excuse like "I think I've got some weird crap going on in my business." *Nope. Just me.* Which made him pessimistic about her answer.

"You got something else going on in that shop of yours?"

"Well, maybe. But that's not why I called." *Just do it*, he said to himself, remembering that line from a T-shirt. "I was thinking you might enjoy an old-time"—*Damn, why'd I have to say "old"?*—"Memorial Day parade and cookout."

Silence. Or was that a quick intake of breath he heard on the other end of the line?

"Tell me more, Bum."

Hell, she didn't say no. Buoyed, he went on. "I'm a Cold War vet, so I'm riding in the parade. It's kind of a big deal around these parts. They even give you a front-row seat. And then the Rotary will be doing their big annual barbeque—with great music. Really. It's as good as anything you'll hear out your way. I can put you up at the Hampton Inn. Nice place. Can you make it?" He could hear his heart in his ears and could not remember the last time *that* had happened.

"Bum, that sounds really nice. I'd be delighted."

They finalized plans, and Bum put the phone down and his feet up. Noticed that boot tip back in motion.

"Oh, go ahead, you old fool. Have your fun."

"*Westminster Abbey, the tower Big Ben. The rosy red cheeks of the little children.*"

❀ ❀ ❀

Elizabeth pulled into Hobbs on Saturday evening, in time for dinner at the steakhouse. Turned out Bum Bradley did have some business for her. He produced copies of purchase orders for tungsten carbide discs from China, gun parts from different dealers in Texas, and cadmium plating for what, in another context, would appear to have been a harmless rod. He also provided documents detailing the cordite purchases that had nominally drawn Elizabeth to Hobbs in the first place.

She was aware of all this but she didn't let on; instead she remained openly grateful for his cooperation. The professional agent never knew when a contact might turn over something that all the government's digging had failed to uncover.

But mostly Elizabeth was pleased to drop the charade in favor of other talk. Bum sure seemed eager to bring up his plans for the next day.

"Ever ride a horse?" he asked over an after-dinner beer.

Elizabeth smiled. A real rugged and—dare she admit it?—handsome cowboy was asking if she, an equestrian of some note in the intelligence community, had ever ridden a horse. She shaped a coy response.

"Oh, I've been on one or two." Said in a way that wouldn't have fooled a child, much less an old cowpoke.

"Well, in that case, would you like to ride in the parade with me?"

"I'd *love* to."

"We could get you outfitted, no problem."

"No worries. I've got jeans and boots. I was coming to a Western parade, right? I sure wasn't going to show up in my government costume, now was I?"

They both laughed over what he'd said a few weeks earlier.

After breakfast the next morning at the Hampton Inn, Bum drove Elizabeth out to his place in a sharp-looking, blue pickup truck. She steeled herself for an old ranch-style house in town, but they headed right out of Hobbs. He didn't stop driving till he they passed through a wide gate framed by big timbers on the sides and overhead. Strong but unpretentious. *Kind of like him.*

They drove for a few more minutes, the truck kicking up a dust funnel behind them, and then reached the corral. He had seven horses in there. She stepped past the gate to look them over.

"You don't need to pick one too quick," he advised unnecessarily. "You can take your time."

"Thanks," she said, though her thoughts already had leaped all the way back to seeing a critter named Gunpowder for the first time. He'd been in a corral filled with horses snuffling her pockets, just like these friendly guys. Most of them had walked away too—as much as saying, "What? No food?"

She had to force aside the last memories she had of Gunpowder—the gruesome photos that had been delivered in a parcel. A lively, young mare helped. She walked up and peered closely at Elizabeth, making her smile.

"I'll take this gal right here."

"She's a handful," Bum said.

"So am I." Elizabeth smiled.

"Yeah, I figured you were one and the same."

Elizabeth pulled her hair back, banding it in a ponytail, then noticed Bum staring at it. She checked to make sure she hadn't left a clump hanging loose.

"Do I look okay?" she asked him.

"Are you kidding?" he said.

She put on her felt hat with a nice, seven-inch brim for the leisurely ride to the parade grounds. She heard music from a credible high school band before she spotted folks starting to assemble. She found the music stirring—"Halls of Montezuma," "America the Beautiful," and classics from George Gershwin and Aaron Copland that sounded as magisterial as they were wistful.

The music stopped for mercifully short speeches. Then the band and dozens of equestrians and horse-drawn wagons assembled behind wide banners heralding the memories of those who had served. Elizabeth noticed some of the more senior ladies along the parade route. They were looking in her direction and whispering. She could have read those lips a mile away: "Who's *she*?"

Come sundown she and Bum sat by themselves at the edge of the barbeque crowd. The whole town had moved to an enormous, red barn a few miles outside town. Eight-foot ventilating fans were set in the spacious doors at each end to keep the summer air moving. A stunning country-western singer named Leslie dominated the stage, backed up by a traditional country band with acoustic guitar and a stand-up bass. A natural beauty with chestnut hair brushing her shoulders, she strolled around with microphone in hand, performing all the classics, pausing only to chat easily with the audience. Elizabeth felt the singer's authenticity all the way across the barn. Leslie knew how to connect—and she could sing.

When she started George Strait's "I Just Want to Dance With You," Bum took Elizabeth's hand.

Just what I was thinking, Elizabeth said to herself as Bum escorted her to the dance floor. Soon enough they were two-stepping as if they'd been at it for years.

When Leslie finally lay the mike aside, Bum and Elizabeth sat down to resume their conversation. Not a breath about bombs or Rosincourt or Soroya Assaf. They were talking about music. Elizabeth wanted to know if he'd ever seen *The Bodyguard*.

"Can't say I have," Bum replied.

"Well, there's a scene in a bar, kinda like this place. Anyway it rings a bell because it reminds me of us."

"Really?"

"Yes. The Whitney Houston character is a rock star, the Queen of the Night. She lives in Hollywood, delivers loud rock music without much in the way of words, and makes a lot of money. She's got millions of fans but one of them is trying to kill her. The Kevin Costner character is her bodyguard. A good guy like you, Bum." She nudged his arm. "He's older, a Secret Service veteran. He carries a gun, and his music is country-western all the way.

"So one night, to get the Queen of the Night out of harm's way, Costner takes her to one of his country-western haunts. She's never seen anything like it, right? She's an African-American woman from the city. But she likes it. She's sitting in a booth, drinking beer and listening to music. When they get up to dance, the Queen of the Night is reduced to tears by the lyrics of a Dolly Parton song."

"I'll bet I know which one," Bum said. "'I Will Always Love You.'"

"That's right, but how'd you know that? You sure you didn't see the movie?"

"Nope. But it's one of Dolly's best, and I just love it."

"So does the Houston character. For her it's a song from a different world, and at the end of the movie she just blows everyone away when she sings her own version of it."

"I'll bet that's a moment to remember."

"It sure is. But here's the thing, Bum. You're the bodyguard. You're showing me something I haven't seen in years." She paused, wondered if she should risk going on, then knew she had to. "And I'm not just talking about the parade and the barn and all this really nice stuff."

He took her hand. They were still on the edge of the crowd. The night cloaked them, and none of those ladies who'd been whispering could see them now. Not that Elizabeth thought about anybody but Bum, because he was kissing her. And she was kissing back.

Just as they separated, Leslie returned to the stage and sang lyrics as smooth as a shot of good tequila:

Jose Cuervo, you are a friend of mine.
I like to drink you with a little salt and lime.
Did I kiss all the cowboys? Did I shoot out the lights?
Did I dance on the bar? Did I start any fights?

"Would you look at that moon, Elizabeth?" Bum's eyes were already on the night sky. "They say youth is wasted on the young, but I'm not so sure. I think it's wasted on older people who won't keep living while they can."

Her hand rose to his cheek, and she ran her fingertips over his laugh lines, thinking he was probably right.

It felt like only a few minutes passed before Leslie said it was time for the last song of the evening. Elizabeth wondered if it would be "Save the Last Dance for Me," but the singer surprised her by breaking into Kris Kristofferson's "Lovin' Her Was Easier" in a soft voice breaking with emotion.

Bum took Elizabeth's hand again, and now that he had kissed her his touch felt like nothing she'd known before. He guided her to her feet but didn't lead her to the dance floor. He led her to his heart, pulling her close, then moved his feet slowly. Elizabeth felt as if the rest of the world had slipped away. She felt the strength of his arm around her and his hand holding hers next to his chest. She settled her face into the soft spot of his neck, between his stiff collar and his ear, breathing in the masculine fragrance of his sun-weathered skin.

They strolled slowly to his pickup hand in hand. Bum didn't drive much faster when he took her back to the Hampton Inn. They didn't say a word till he pulled up in front of the hotel.

"Elizabeth, who *are* you? And what are you doing here? You're *not* some bureaucrat checking invoices. I've been around the block too many times to believe that."

She put her index finger on the tip of his nose. "How about we table that question and you just trust me?"

"I can keep secrets, Elizabeth. That's a promise."

"And so can I." She smiled demurely. "So that's what I'm going to do."

"Would you like to come back again, Elizabeth? There's a Fourth of July parade next month."

She nodded in the dim light of his pickup. Then she took his hand and gave it a gentle tug. "But we still have some time, don't we?"

It was his turn to nod, and indeed he did.

With dawn's first light, Bum made coffee, then moved to the deserted Hampton Inn lobby. Most of the holiday weekend crowd had left the previous day. He was studying the grounds in the bottom of his second cup when he heard Elizabeth's lilting voice.

"Jose Cuervo, you are a friend of mine… Did I dance on the bar? Did I start any fights?"

Bum never missed a beat. "I'm just looking for my lost shaker of salt. I guess it's my own damn fault."

Both of them burst into the most comfortable laughter, the kind that comes after the deepest intimacy. They hugged again and collected breakfast from the buffet.

Sitting side by side, they radiated the happy glow of teenagers. *Those feelings just never change*, Bum realized.

"So you're really going to keep me in the dark about what might be going on in my own company?" he asked gently.

Elizabeth took his hand and looked in his eyes. "Bum, I'm going to tell you something. For your ears only. Not even your brother can know."

"Sure, go ahead."

"There's a nuclear dimension to this. Those kids . . ."

"Whaaat!" he blurted. A white flash appeared before his eyes. It was as if someone had just rolled a grenade under his chair. In that instant he returned to Christmas Island.

"You okay?" she asked. "Maybe I shouldn't have—"

"No—no, I'm fine," Bum insisted. "But are *you* okay? If there's a—"

Now she interrupted him but by shaking her head, warning him about saying anything that could be overheard. He buttoned up, nodding back at her.

"I can't say anything more," she added, "and please don't you say anything."

"First of all, I can't. Secondly, I won't. You have my word."

"I know I do," she said.

After breakfast he carried her bag out to her Honda in silence and placed it in the trunk. Then they stood and kissed, teens all over again.

A glow warmed Elizabeth as she drove alone back to El Paso on Route 62, rushing past endless miles of sand and stone. She had to let the lovely experiences of the past few days slip aside because a homicidal Iranian colonel still lurked south of the border. She looked toward Mexico as if she might spot him, recognizing that sometimes she loathed the very words "chain of command." What she wanted most right now was to hunt down and kill Gharabaghi. He'd maimed and murdered a Kazakh farmer and a marvelous horse, then blown up Dr. Sig Antonovitch, Dr. Simon Hall, and the poor limousine driver who'd had the bad luck to draw the wrong duty.

She pulled into a turnout. Anguished, she sat for several minutes, hands and head on the steering wheel. Then she kicked the car door open and stomped through the sagebrush, riffling her hands through the dry shrubs. A sharp, pungent fragrance filled her nose.

What a contrast. She was thinking of the demonic man just south of the border and the wonderful cowboy back in Hobbs. *The man I love.*

The fact that she'd said those words even to herself was astonishing to Elizabeth. *How did* that *happen?* she wondered. She could have itemized a lot—his hazel eyes and hard-work hands; his love of riding, dancing, and music—but no single attribute or feature could have captured the man himself. They were all mileposts that had led her to his heart, and to her own at the same instant. That was love.

In a dangerous time.

CHAPTER 19

GILHOOLEY'S

June 2012

As Bum walked down to his corral he recognized two things about Elizabeth Mallory. After the best weekend he'd known in many years, he knew she was worth every ounce of his love. But he also had to acknowledge to himself that he did not know who she really was. Only that she'd told him that there was a "nuclear dimension" to what was taking place in his shop. That had triggered recurring visions of Christmas Island; they would not let go of him.

He filled the water trough and fed his horses, letting himself drift off to thinking about the moon in June and all that wondrous sweet stuff that had taken him by surprise so late in life. And he sure thought about her kisses too. You bet. But all those recent memories, much as they tickled him, still couldn't keep him from circling back to the most pressing question of all: who was she?

It didn't take him long to wonder if she were a spy of some kind. After joking to himself that she'd sure infiltrated his fantasies fast enough, he gave serious consideration to the matter. For starters they'd met because she was interested in what might have been taking place right under his nose with Roz and Soroya.

Maybe she's looking into arms smuggling. He hoped not. A lot of gunrunners were mixed up with drugs too. Anybody fighting them or the war on drugs down in Mexico was up against pure evil as far as he was concerned. He'd heard all he ever wanted to know about the butchery south of the border. Damn near every day there was more grim news, a lot of it with El Paso connections. He remembered when Juarez was a sleepy border town with the best cantinas in all of Mexico. Back then it wasn't a blood-splattered war zone where guys with Uzis and chainsaws terrified the populace with threats, murder, and the grimmest examples of mayhem.

Bum hadn't ventured south in years, and if that ravaged country didn't get its house in order he doubted he would ever cross that border again. The thought of Elizabeth working against gunrunners or drugs in Mexico gripped him with the worst fear—the kind you feel for the ones you love most.

The only other possibility made Bum feel bad because it was based solely on Roz and Soroya's religion: could it have something to do with Muslim radicals? Not that those two kids would ever get caught up in something like that—*Hell, they were born here*—but maybe they had some crazy relatives, and the feds were turning the spotlight on Roz and Soroya because of the bad doings of blood ties. If so that would have been no more fair, in Bum's estimation, than blaming him for something Hiram was up to. Of course Hiram was never up to anything surreptitious, unless it was keeping a quiet eye on Bum the same way Bum kept one on him. "Got your back" meant something for both of them and always had.

So when Bum ambled back to the house, he wasn't entirely surprised to find Hiram waiting there. His brother still limped from getting thrown by a horse in his late fifties and wore trifocals and hearing aids. But even Bum wouldn't want to fight him. He had the big, scarred knuckles of a man who'd known plenty of fisticuffs in his youth and the kindly eyes of an older gent who thought better of it now. Which did not mean he went easy on his younger brother.

"How'd it go, you old peckerwood?" Hiram asked. "Just don't tell me you're going to have to start buying Trojans again."

"It wasn't like that, Hiram. She's a nice lady."

"Yeah? How nice?"

"Nice enough that I'll see her again. And nice enough that I'm not talking to you about her, if you're going to talk like that."

Hiram put his arm around his brother's shoulders. "Sorry. Didn't know you were getting serious."

"That's okay. Neither did I." Bum lied to his brother. He'd felt serious about Elizabeth almost from the start. But it was one of those white lies, so he didn't feel unduly burdened.

"You had lunch yet?" Hiram asked.

"Not yet, but I'm fixing to."

"How about I do the fixing? Beef enchiladas and rice?"

"That must mean we're going down to Farolito's." A café in Hobbs.

"That's what it means."

They talked about Talleyrand all through lunch. The French firm had been logging wells across the Permian Basin for decades. Bum and Hiram had both serviced those wells, and the brothers had shared many a roadhouse beer with the good ol' boys from Talleyrand's Houston office.

After lunch, when Hiram sauntered down to a saloon to catch the Astros game, Bum thought maybe he ought to train his eyes on a different game in Houston. A different kind of hardball. If Talleyrand were somehow at the center of all this business—and his shop was damn sure building a strange contraption for them—checking in with his old friends in H-town seemed like a good idea. He did not, under any circumstances, want Elizabeth involved in a nuclear event. She was too young to understand; he had seen one.

Bum climbed into his pickup and flicked open his cell, pleased he could still recall the Talleyrand number. He'd always been good with phone numbers, but he found himself testing his prowess every now and again to make sure he wasn't losing his mental edge. He figured as long as he kept his mind busy, he might stay two steps ahead of his age.

"Gus, it's me, Bum." Gus Adams was an aging field engineer at Talleyrand. He and Bum had spent many evenings in the cafés of Odessa listening to old-time country fiddlers and the melodic strains of Texas swing.

"Well, I'll be goddamned. How you doin'?"

"I'm still on the right side of the grass, so it can't be too bad. You?"

"Ah, Maggie"—Gus's wife—"says I got one foot in the grave, but I think that's just wishful thinking on her part. What can I do ya?"

Bum told him he was coming to Houston and would like to get together with him. Sooner rather than later.

"How soon?"

"Tomorrow?" Bum said.

"That's six hundred miles, Bum. You gonna do that in a day?"

"Still got my ragtop."

"Well, why doncha come to the Goode Company? They're still spooning out the best barbecue on the planet. I could see you there at six when I get off. How's that sound?"

Bum left Hobbs at sunrise, knowing he could average seventy miles an hour with no problem. He'd always loved road trips, and he took all the outlaws with him—Willie and Waylon, David Allen Coe, Johnny Cash, Merle Haggard. Every one of those boys could make him feel young as dawn and old as dust at the same time.

After several hours of driving through drought-parched west Texas, he stopped in San Antonio just to gaze at the River Walk—and to grab the strongest cup of coffee he could find. Then it was straight back to the Mustang for the trip's last few hours.

Bum arrived at the Goode Company about five minutes before Gus walked in the door. His old friend had a little less hair and a lot more waistline but otherwise Gus looked tan and healthy, probably from working outdoors; he'd been logging wells all over east Texas and Louisiana for as long as Bum could remember.

They grabbed a table, ordered beer, and worked their way down a buffet brimming with more selections than Bum could ever handle, but Gus rose to the challenge. The two ate and talked about the good old days. Then it was on to who was dead and who was still alive. Some of the men merited remembrance; for others it was good riddance.

As casually as he could, Bum mentioned the new ELF geophysical system under construction for Talleyrand in his El Paso shop.

"Don't know much about the new stuff," Gus said, shaking his oversized head. "I'm still dropping rods down holes and running recorders."

After a few more reminiscences, Gus suggested Bum call Jim Deaver, a Talleyrand engineer. "He might know something. Tell him I sent you."

Bum didn't want the evening to end, but around eight Gus said he had to go. "Got Maggie at home. You should try it one of these days, Bum. Them ladies are nice to have around. Really. I ain't foolin'."

Bum laughed at the way Gus made women sound like exotic creatures or aliens from another planet. "Maybe I'll give it a shot," Bum said. "I've been thinking it's time to settle down."

"Ah, Bum. It's past time. Trust me."

Both men laughed.

Bum drove over to the Rice Hotel, a grand relic of the early oil field days, and grabbed a fine room. He helped himself to a nightcap from the minibar, caught a late-night newscast, and sacked out.

Next morning he phoned Deaver right after the Talleyrand workday began at 8:00. The conversation combed the territory of familiar names and mutual friends, but as soon as Bum started asking pointed questions about Talleyrand's work, Deaver might as well have pulled the plug on his wireless for all the information Bum received. He could have been talking to Rosincourt again for all the jabber about proprietary information coming from Deaver.

Bum ended the call on a pleasant note but sat in his room shaking his head, wondering what the hell was going on. *Either those guys live in the dark or they're hiding something. What?*

He had a pot of coffee brought up, along with croissants and fruit, and had just tipped the room service waiter when the phone rang. He couldn't place the accent right away but he had no trouble understanding the confidential nature of the message.

"Want to know more about the ELF system, Mr. Bradley? Meet me for dinner at Gilhooley's in San Leon down on Galveston Bay at eight tonight."

"Who am I meeting?" Bum asked, but the man hung up.

Bum stared at his grapefruit sections, wondering if he should make the trip. Somebody must have known what he looked like; a photo of him wouldn't be hard to find, what with the pictures of his company's people on its Web site. But Bum would be flying blind. He sure knew plenty about Gilhooley's, though. Back in the old days, he'd lunched there with some regularity. Best oysters in all of Houston but a tough neighborhood, and the place had a decidedly downscale clientele—your basic beer-and-shot-of-whiskey crowd. Now, if you wanted to mix with parolees and ex-cons, along with bikers, shrimpers from Southeast Asia, and a horde of illegals from every corner of the world, Gilhooley's was the place to go. But if you wanted to play it safe, Bum knew better than to show up after dark.

There was plenty of light left when he turned off Bay Shore Drive toward the roadhouse, so it was easy to see that the oil spill had left a lot of men unemployed. And the hurricane sure hadn't helped: debris still saddled the front yards of neighboring trailers, though it was hard to tell what was garbage and what was the everyday accumulation of defeat. Might have been late in the day but the guys in the parking lot didn't have the weary look of men who'd worked a hard week. They had the resentful glare of men who hadn't worked in weeks.

Bum wondered if he should have driven his pickup, which didn't stick out like his sporty four-barrel. Right about then he could have done without the "look at me" message of the Mustang.

The tires crunched oyster shells as he rolled past motorcycles and junker cars, finding a space off to the side shadowed by a couple of trees. The evening, suddenly alive with the roar of a Harley, gave Bum a start. As soon as he turned off Waylon, he heard over-amplified music coming from Gilhooley's along with the distinct sound of shattering glassware. It sure sounded familiar, but not knowing what might come next clouded his thoughts.

Least you got plenty of daylight. It was, after all, the height of summer. And if some Talleyrand whistleblower wanted to spill some beans, Bum would be all ears.

A cluster of men stood nearby as he climbed out of the car. He hadn't taken two steps when one of them, a shirtless and heavily tattooed Vietnamese man, approached him.

"*Goi bang ong*, Bradley?"

Bum spotted what looked like a knife scar below the corner of the man's eye. What Bum didn't see was the guy's buddy coming up from behind with a BB-filled sock.

The nasty weapon felt hard as a lead pipe when it smashed Bum's head. He collapsed onto the broken oyster shells, unconscious. Within seconds his body was hauled deep into the shadows, mouth duct taped, hands and feet tied. Then he was shoved into a big, burlap bag and dumped in the back of a faded, brown pickup truck.

Minutes later the rattly Ford bounced along remote dirt roads where a body could be dumped, dragged to death, or fed to alligators. This was a border, too, between swamp and sea, with its own brand of blood play, killers, and scores to settle.

CHAPTER 20
SUMMER SOLSTICE

Late June 2012

Unaware of the ghosts she had set loose over breakfast with Bum, Elizabeth returned to work in El Paso. She plunged right back into monitoring the listening devices in Rosincourt and Soroya's Festival Street apartment. She also combed through the latest NSA intercepts. Her two principal subjects continued to visit Juarez for meetings with Colonel Gharabaghi every Friday. Their links to the colonel made it ever more apparent to Elizabeth that at least Rosincourt had a hand in the Pueblo Canyon roadside bombing. Not enough to justify an arrest—yet—but the evidence was piling up. Soroya had probably been involved as well. Those two, she realized, had a dismal if not deadly future.

Elizabeth was consumed by work and the most pressing of deadlines with Akhbar-I, but she was also painfully aware Bum wasn't responding to her e-mails or phone messages. Surely he hadn't consummated their attraction only to cast her aside. But that thought did occur to her. How could it not have? It was classic male behavior. But he hardly fit the stereotype.

Give him some breathing room, she counseled herself. *He's been a single guy all his life.* So she gave him *lots* of breathing room and tried mightily to abide her impatience.

At sundown on Friday, June 29, Elizabeth and locksmith extraordinaire Mike McKinney waited across the train tracks outside the Bradley Brothers parking lot. Sure enough Jack Daniel's chunky paramour arrived on schedule. Within minutes the lights went on the in the executive suite. The private party had begun.

Yay, libido, Elizabeth said to herself.

She and McKinney, once more dressed in dark clothes, entered the plant fifteen minutes later, moving quickly to the assembly area where the bulky frame of Akhbar-I dominated the floor. Elizabeth was startled when she saw the bomb becoming ever more complete. It was one thing to imagine the progress of a terrorist plot—even monitor it in real time—but it was quite another to see an atomic bomb appearing piece by tangible piece.

Unfortunately the plans for the weapon, which would have been extremely helpful, were hanging around Roz's neck on a USB stick; Elizabeth knew this from the listening devices in their apartment.

Her frustration ebbed greatly, though, when she and McKinney found the cell phones, GPS receiver, and encryption gear Colonel Gharabaghi planned to use in firing Akhbar-I. They noted the makes, models, and serial numbers, all of which the NSA would need to disrupt the firing—assuming they *could* disrupt it. That was what worried Elizabeth most. How many times had she flipped open her cell phone only to find it wasn't working? *Shit really does happen.*

With so much at stake, she hated having to depend on electronic devices to stop an atomic bomb from being fired in the heart of her own country. But that was the plan, apparently. NSA would disable Gharabaghi's phone link to Akhbar-I. Then Special Forces would seize the weapon as it rolled through southern New Mexico, whereupon it would become exhibit A in America's war on nuclear proliferation. Voila! No tragedy. But as far as she knew, Murphy's Law hadn't been repealed. It felt like Washington was playing dice with the country's future—*loaded* dice.

If everything on the drawing board worked out—a huge *if*—the timing for the White House would be hugely advantageous. The seizure of an atomic bomb would happen smack-dab in the middle of the president's reelection campaign. Some people caught all the breaks. But Elizabeth knew the benefits that would arise from seizing the bomb would be good for the whole country: the breakup of Hezbollah in Mexico, the arrest or killing of Gharabaghi.

Her desire to take down the colonel and everyone associated with him grew even stronger when she and McKinney made an unnerving discovery: the fourteenth uranium ring had arrived. Gharabaghi and his crew needed only one more. With fifteen uranium rings, the Project 853 team would have the makings of an A-bomb that would surely work.

One more ring? That's it?

Elizabeth felt blood drain from her face as she recounted the inventory. She noticed McKinney watching her carefully.

"They're almost there," she told him. She watched him take a steadying breath before she added, "I can't believe Washington is going to rely on a bunch of fancy electronics to protect hundreds of families in New Mexico. If they screw up, or if Gharabaghi actually has his eyes set on Denver, a million people could die."

McKinney nodded. "I hear you," he whispered. "But you don't want them to." His eyes gazed at the walls and recesses where their own government's bugs had been planted.

Elizabeth knew he was right. She was far less certain of her ability to sit tight.

In a Juarez suite, a jubilant Colonel Gharabaghi presided over a true staff meeting. For the first time, most of the major players were assembled in one room, including Dr. Hout and the still-unnamed communications expert from Europe. The man with the German accent, pale-blue eyes, and steely manner sat without acknowledging anyone. He seemed like such a pro, Soroya thought. He must have made a living helping terrorists. *Like yourself,* she added in an accusing inner voice.

He wasn't the only person who remained nameless. A crisply suited, middle-aged Hispanic man whom Gharabaghi spoke of only as "our courier," also took a seat. Both Rosincourt and Soroya recognized him as the stuffed-tire expediter, a man who had been introduced as Mr. Acuña at the time of their last visit. But since the colonel did not wish to disclose his name to others, the couple maintained silence while the colonel pressed his visitor for assurances that the last uranium ring would make it to El Paso on time.

"Every delivery you've made has had a delay," Gharabaghi said. "This can't happen with the last ring."

The pressure must be on in Tehran, Soroya thought.

"If you think you can do better, call FedEx," the Hispanic man replied with a shrug. He looked completely at ease, even when the colonel leaned into his face.

"It *must* be on time," he growled.

"You will get it," the man said, barely blinking.

Soroya thought Mr. Acuña was courting death with his offhanded manner toward the colonel. Then she realized she was engaging in wishful thinking.

Gharabaghi turned to the other men, his eyes hard as hammers, dark as demitasse. "The supreme leader wants the shot date confirmed. The Revolutionary Guard Corps has political events. Everything must be arranged."

Soroya gleaned the subtext as easily as she could read a marquee: Iran had to demonstrate it was a lot tougher than the countries thawed by the Arab spring. Mobs were toppling dictators and emirs in the softer, pro-Western Arab countries. Armed insurgents had killed Gadaffi and others. And the Great Satan was routinely reaching into Pakistan to kill off al-Qaeda leaders, including bin Laden. To stop any imperialistic attempt like that against Iran, the country's rulers needed to display their nation's military might. Alizadeh and the others had learned the North Korean lesson well: nothing said "hands off" better than a nuclear weapon.

"We Persians also play with fire," the colonel said, almost echoing Soroya's conclusions. "Our Shia brothers collapsed those Western lackeys in Bahrain, but the crowds in the streets, from Syria to Libya, give our people in Ahwaz bad ideas." Ahwaz, an oil town near the Persian Gulf, had been a hotbed of insurgent attacks and bombings in Iran. "President Alizadeh needs Project 853 to keep power. The election is coming next year. Defeating the American president will assure our political success at home. It worked in Madrid." The train bombings that had led to the defeat of the pro-American Spanish government. "It will work for us."

"*No problema*," said the smooth, unruffled Hispanic man in the suit. "My network is working perfectly. Don't let a few shootings bother you." Soroya figured he was referring to a firefight on the streets of Juarez the previous night. "My associates took care of another gang. That is just the cost of doing business. That is why you pay me."

Gharabaghi glared at the man and when he spoke he didn't shift his eyes for a second. "Monday, July sixteenth, is the shot day. It is an important anniversary. It was chosen by our president. I can't let him down.

We can't make a mistake. If you let me down"—he shook his head at the man—"you will pay."

The neatly attired Hispanic man stood, his face no more than six inches from Gharabaghi's. "You dare threaten me? Do you know where you are? Do you know what I could do to you right now?" He turned toward the door, yelling, "*Aqui! Ahora!*" Here. Now! Two of his lieutenants burst into the room with their weapons raised.

"Gentlemen," Dr. Hout spoke up, "let's all calm down. We are all tense. Dis is no good. Calm down. Nobody treten anybody. We get de job done."

Soroya watched Gharabaghi step back. Only then did the man she knew as Acuña sit back down. He waved his bodyguards out of the room. She thought Acuña had major cojones, but then again it was his turf.

"Hout," the colonel snapped, "I want you to stay in El Paso. Stay with the weapon. Be ready to clean and inspect the rings when number fifteen arrives. Then report back to me when it's done." This time Gharabaghi never so much as glanced at his most recent nemesis, but he did turn his eyes on Roz.

"Here is a SIM card. The crypto material is embedded. Insert it into the phones."

He never once looked at Soroya—par for the course of late, but it always made her feel expendable. Killable.

By mid-afternoon she and Roz were back at Don Quintin's, drinking lemonade in silence. No more alcohol for him, which meant she didn't order so much as a beer for herself, not unless she wanted to hear some pious spiel from him. His steadfast abstinence told her more about his resolve than anything else.

On Saturday Elizabeth tried calling Bum again. She'd left several messages in the past week. When once again she didn't get an answer, she called his office in Hobbs. All she reached was a message service, and she realized nobody would be working on the weekend. That was when she called his brother, Hiram.

"We haven't met," she began, "but I'm friends with your brother, Bum, and I haven't been able to reach him for several weeks. I'm just checking to make sure everything's okay with him."

She listened to a long expiration and then an even longer expletive. "Goddamn! I thought he was with you, scooted out from under my watchful eye without my knowing it. This ain't good," Hiram told her. "Ain't good at all. What is it you said you do?"

"I didn't say." He was a quick one. "But I work for the ATF."

"Then maybe you can put out an APB from ATF to find my brother, 'cause this ain't like him. He's the responsible one."

"Do you have any idea where he might have gone?"

"I thought to you," Hiram repeated. "But we were talking about Talleyrand over lunch just before he took off."

"Talleyrand? Where? In Houston?"

"Most likely," Hiram said. "Listen, I know them boys down there. I'll give them a call and see what they can tell me."

She thanked him but didn't hold out much hope of help from Talleyrand, because she also knew *them boys*, and what she knew wasn't good. But a half hour later Hiram was back on the horn with her saying Bum had eaten dinner with an old friend named Gus Adams, who had told him to call a Talleyrand engineer named Jim Deaver.

"Bum never checked out of the Rice Hotel. Just *poof*, he was gone." Hiram sounded distraught.

"Did you guys have favorite haunts down there?" Elizabeth's antennae were now fully deployed.

"Not for a long time, but back in the old days we liked to go brawling down on the coast at a place called Gilhooley's." *Brawling? For fun?* "Actually," Hiram added quickly, "I should amend that last statement a little bit. I liked to go brawling. He liked to go dancing. Funny, I'm the one who ended up hitched."

Hiram sounded like he might start to wander. Elizabeth tried to turn him around by asking if he could make some more calls, gather as much info as he could, but the ramble continued.

"And here I was thinking he was making the most of his semi-retirement by getting himself all bundled up in some love shack."

Ai yi yi, stop already. "Can you do that? I'm in the middle of something right now and can't break away."

"Yeah," Hiram responded as if his brain had started to refocus. "I'm already planning on it."

More than planning on it. Hiram grabbed his .38 revolver and was out the door two minutes after he hung up.

Elizabeth's concerns turned to dark fears. Had Gharabaghi caught Bum's scent when he'd started asking questions at Talleyrand? Did that evil man who had murdered so many have Bum killed and his body dumped in the Gulf—or left to the gators in the marshes down near Galveston? Either way there wouldn't be a trace left of the love of her life.

She could hardly dash out and look for him. All she could do was alert the FBI and hope Hiram would remain focused. Frankly he didn't sound like he would. It might have been a measure of her desperation on all fronts—professional and personal—that she sent off another "free advice" e-mail to her director, warning him of the impending arrival of the last uranium ring probably the following week. She urged the immediate arrest of the conspirators in the US and the elimination—"with extreme prejudice"—of those in Mexico.

The director thanked her for her suggestions but reminded Elizabeth her assignment was to take care of the communication electronics.

Yeah, I know.

Despite the summer heat, after work she took out her frustrations with a hard run along the Rio Grande, grumbling much of the way.

Gonna to be one helluva October surprise this year if everything works out okay. They'll roll up Roz and Soroya and Akhbar-I and take credit for unraveling the biggest bomb plot of all time.

But what about them? She gazed at the scarred city south of the river, where Gharabaghi and Hezbollah felt free to roam. It sickened her to think they might get overlooked because the political pay dirt at home was so huge. She had the momentary urge to hunt down the colonel herself. He had it coming. But her father, the consummate professional, stayed her hand without so much as a cell phone between them; she didn't have to hear him say a word to know what his advice would be: "Stick with the ops order, Baby Bear. Be a professional."

While Gharabaghi sees off Bum?

"You don't know that," she imagined her father saying.

No, I don't. But she sure believed it.

CHAPTER 21
HIRAM HUNTS

Late June 2012

Through a buddy in the Texas Department of Safety, Hiram learned Bum's red Mustang had turned up parked on the very edge of the Gilhooley's parking lot. "You're lucky it didn't end up in a chop shop or Mexico," his friend told him.

"I don't know how lucky I am. There's no sign of my brother, is there?"

"Nope," the trooper responded. "No blood, either. Got any ideas what he might have been doing down there?"

"Don't know for sure, but I'm guessing if his car was in the parking lot, he was doing something in Gilhooley's. Doesn't seem like *too* much of a stretch."

And it was more than enough to get Hiram in gear. A day later he rolled over those oyster shells in a tin can he'd rented at the airport. The car was from somewhere in Korea. Hiram couldn't even pronounce the name of the damn thing. Well, it got him where he wanted to go. He parked it, turned up his hearing aids, took his cane, pocketed his nickel-plated .38, and made his way into the lunch crowd at Gilhooley's. From what he could see, most of them still preferred the liquid side of sustenance.

He plopped his arthritic hip on a stool and summoned the barkeep by pointing his crooked index finger at a spot in front of him, the universal sign for "fill it."

"What'll it be?"

"Beam is fine," Hiram said, watching the guy fill a shot glass. Hiram tossed it down like it was sarsaparilla. He couldn't fight like he used to but he sure could drink some courage. "Again." With the second one, he grabbed the barkeep's wrist. "Who's the biggest asshole in the place these days?"

"What do you mean?" the bartender said, jerking his arm free.

"Who says yes or no if something's going down around here?"

"You think I'm going to answer that?"

"I'm missing my brother," Hiram said. "You think I won't shoot your fucking nuts off? Last thing I heard, he was headed here." Not true, but Hiram was playing the only hunch he had.

"Talk to him." The bartender pointed to a Hispanic gentleman in a crisp, white guayabera shirt. He was standing at the end of the bar with three other men.

Hiram took his cane and walked over to him. The man looked like a pro linebacker. He barely glanced at Hiram.

"Listen, you, I'm looking for my brother. He looks like me. I hear you run stuff, so tell me if you've seen anyone who looks like me around here."

The big guy smiled, looked amused, then whispered to one of his thugs, who told Hiram, "Go the fuck home."

"You shove it up your crusty ass," Hiram replied.

The thug, with tattoos covering most of his neck and arms, advanced on Hiram, who appeared ready to pull on his oversized cane handle.

"What? You got a sword in there?" The tattooed one laughed.

"Come two steps closer and you'll find out."

The goon took it as a challenge, so Hiram pulled the handle, which turned out to be a custom grip for a Taser. A tattooed heap of flesh hit the floor in less than a second. The boss's eyes opened wide.

"Holy shit, old man. You're something. But I can't let you do that to my people."

"I don't give a rat's ass about *your* people. I want answers about *my* people. My brother?"

Hiram heard the approach from behind—just the reason he'd cranked up the sound on his hearing aids out by the car. He turned and zapped another hood only three feet away. The guy's reeling crash onto the bar produced a cacophony of shattered glass.

"It's not the only weapon I have," Hiram said to the big guy. "Think about something, José, or whatever the fuck your name is. I'm an old man looking for my brother. You think I won't kill you and all your friends? I'm riding the caboose of life, so don't push me."

When the big guy's remaining thug grabbed a barstool and started toward Hiram, the boss man intervened. "Don't start breaking up old men in here." He turned his gaze on Hiram. "Only reason I'm not killing you is you just taught my guys never to underestimate some old fuck, and I guess they needed one to show 'em. So when I tell you I don't know what those gooks did with your brother, I don't expect you to give me anymore shit."

"Vietnamese?"

"Call 'em what you want."

"My brother never had no beef with them."

"I do, so I'm telling you a Vietnamese shrimper crew took him down."

"What do you mean 'took him down'?"

"I mean knocked him out and dragged him off."

"Dragged him where?"

"I don't know. You think I keep track of everything down here? You think I'm chasing those people? *You* do it."

Hiram read him for the truth, then nodded. "Fine. I'm leaving. Anybody tries to stop me, I'll kill him."

"I believe you would." The big guy laughed.

Hiram skedaddled to his rolling tin can, but what really galled him was that years earlier his brother had damn near gotten killed *helping* Vietnamese. That was back during Operation Baby Lift in 1975. Bum had been the crew chief on a C-5 that flew out a hundred kids from Tan Son Nhut Air Base right near Saigon. It was hell. The North Vietnamese army was shelling the airfield and had brought down the plane that took off right before Bum's. Killed everybody onboard. Meaning kids. Bum raced through gunfire to pick up a boy with a broken leg lying on the tarmac. Kid was screaming, but Bum got him on the damn plane and saved his life. And *those* people took him down?

You guys just made one helluva mistake, Hiram vowed.

He headed down to the waterfront with the same determination with which he'd walked into Gilhooley's. But he made himself calm down just a little. He thought the big lug in the bar was telling the truth, but Hiram knew he'd catch a gaff in the neck if he started Tasering Vietnamese refugees. He would have to play a softer hand. And so he did.

He checked with the port manager to find out who the top dog was among the shrimpers. Hiram was hardly surprised to find another Vietnamese, a man named Thinh Phan, in charge. They all had come to the US after their war. They worked like dogs; Hiram always admired their grit. But the thought that they'd taken his brother? It made the old man feel murderous.

He vaguely recalled that *thinh* meant something like "makes money" or "prosperous," and this Thinh fit the bill. With a slight limp afflicting an otherwise muscular frame, the forty-year-old skipper stepped off his beautifully maintained boat. It was ready for the season about to begin. When the Vietnamese veteran disembarked he did a double take, shocked by the apparition striding down the dock.

"You're the big boss of the shrimpers?" Hiram asked him. The sun was a bastard, beating down so hard he felt faint. Or it might have been the aftereffects of the whiskey and all that adrenaline pumping through him after his *discussion* in the bar.

"That's me," said Thinh Phan, hard-looking as steel cable. He adjusted his white ball cap but never took his eyes off of Hiram.

"Can we get out of the sun? I got some pretty important questions. It's about my brother." Hiram played the kinship card, knowing it meant something to the Vietnamese. They *all* had friends or relatives who had died trying to keep their families intact in the hellfire of war.

"I heard you Tasered two men at Gilhooley's," Phan said.

"Word travels fast."

"Don't try that with me." His words emerged from an expressionless Asian face.

"I won't."

"But I'm glad you did it to them. I hate those Mexican bastards. Come on."

Phan led him onto his boat and into the galley. He poured his guest a cup of coffee. Hiram introduced himself, then told his host what he'd heard at the bar.

"Some men do odd jobs during the off season," Phan said indifferently. His tone as much as said to Hiram, "Tell me why I should care about your brother." So Hiram did—the whole story about the Baby Lift. Phan's eyes widened with every word.

"Tan Son Nhut? 1975?" Phan shook his head in open wonder.

"Why? Does that mean anything to you?" Hiram asked.

"It means *everything* to me, mister." Phan now spoke without hesitation. He pointed to a wrinkled photograph of a gray-haired man pushpinned into the galley wall. "That's my father. He's no longer with us. He took me, my three brothers, and my sister, to the Saigon airbase in April '75. He heard they were saving children."

"Then you might have seen my brother."

"I did more than see your brother, Mr. Bradley. He came back for me. I'd been hit by a jeep the day before and broken my leg. I'm still gimpy from it. My father had all he could do to carry my brothers and sister. I was eight, the oldest. He had to leave me lying on the tarmac to rush them onto the plane. Then the turbines on that C-5 started turning. The NVA was moving in. I knew they'd kill me—I was crawling, trying to leave. And my father was trying to push my brothers and sister onto the plane. It was packed, overloaded. You can't know what it was like unless you were there. It was crazy. Your brother saw me lying on the tarmac and jumped out of the cargo bay. There were bullets flying everywhere. He came running right at me. I thought he was going to die. I thought *I* was going to die. He scooped me up. My leg hurt like hell, but it was the best pain of my life. 'You're gonna make it, you're gonna make it,' he kept saying to me.

"He threw me in the plane's loading bay just as it started to taxi. Did you know he almost didn't get back onboard? They weren't stopping for anyone. One of *my* people reached down and grabbed his hand."

Phan looked away, and Hiram saw tears in the man's eyes.

Both of them sat in silence for several seconds. Then Phan said, "When you came down the dock, I thought you were him. Your eyes. After all these years, I thought that airman had tracked me down. I tried to find your brother many times, but I never knew his name. Now I do. I'll find him. I don't know what they did to him, but I'll find him."

It was Hiram's turn to look away. His throat ached, felt like cancer of the heart. *Goddamn Bum never told me the whole story. Made it sound like a cakewalk.*

But Hiram had always suspected the truth lay much deeper than Bum's account. He just never knew how deep until today.

"Thanks," he said to Phan. "I'd tell you that you don't know how much it means to me, but you do know, don't you?"

Phan nodded and got on his cell, speaking quickly and sharply in the diphthongs of his native land. Then he turned back to Hiram. "Don't tell the police anything about me. If the cops come around, I can't help you. You understand? It's our own world, even here."

Hiram nodded, grateful for the extended hand. It looked to him like one of those people was reaching out for Bum all over again.

CHAPTER 22
INDEPENDENCE DAY

July 1–July 6, 2012

Elizabeth reached Hiram, again by phone, on Sunday morning, the first of July. He sounded unusually taciturn when she asked him if he'd made any headway in looking for his brother.

"Maybe," he said, letting silence thunder on the phone line.

"What does *that* mean?" she asked.

"It means *maybe*. It means you gotta be patient. Me too. It means I'm workin' on it."

She didn't know how much faith to put in an old guy who used to go brawling for fun, but if he were cut from the same cloth as Bum, she figured she ought to give him enough room to operate.

"Just tell me, is there anything I can do?"

"Nope," was all Hiram said.

She didn't fight him on that point, but there was indeed something she could do: she followed up on a call she'd made to the Harris County FBI office two weeks earlier to make certain the chief himself knew Bum Bradley's disappearance was of personal interest to the special agent in El Paso. Meaning her. She wasn't going to badger Numero Uno, but she was going to make sure the Houston office still accorded Bum's disappearance the highest priority—even if that status hadn't brought him back yet. *If there's any Bum to bring back.*

Monday, July 2

In Galveston, Thinh Phan climbed into his blue Toyota Tundra and tried so hard not to open up a pack of Marlboros. He'd quit two years earlier but still couldn't go for more than a few hours without wanting one bad. He always left the butts behind when he went to sea and didn't allow his crewmen to smoke. So he escaped the immediate claws of nicotine for weeks at a time. Plus, the Gulf had a rhythm that comforted him. The road didn't.

He looked at his hand. Shaky. And why wouldn't it be? He was about to take a huge risk, and if he were going to die he might as well smoke, right? He'd always said the day the doctor told him he was dying was going to be one of those good news/bad news things. The bad news was obvious. The good news was he'd get to smoke again.

So he ripped the cellophane off the package and lit up, sucking the smoke deep into his lungs. He coughed like a fool. Didn't care. He didn't think he had a reason to.

Monday morning was busy at the Bradley Brothers shop in El Paso. Dr. Hout had reappeared, irritating all the mechanics with his nitpicking. He had returned to Project 853 as a quality control and final assembly inspector. His cover in the US was as an unclassified scientific consultant at the New Mexico Institute of Mining and Technology in Socorro, a post arranged by Irwandi Bereueh—the Adam in the couple dubbed Adam and Eve by Roz and Soroya.

With his British passport and unimpeachable scientific credentials, Dr. Hout could come and go as he wished.

Soroya had been reduced to organizing the catering and running messages across the shop floor. It left her torn between feeling grateful not to have any further direct involvement with the bomb and frustrated she was being treated like a gofer. *Because you are a gofer.*

Rosincourt looked ecstatic. *Why wouldn't he be?* she asked herself. He had fourteen enriched uranium rings, and the Mexican courier had assured him number fifteen would arrive within a few days. The only thing she'd seen him eat in the last week was starchy Mexican pastries. Oh, and coffee. Gallons of it.

Just as Soroya took a break to fix a sandwich for herself, she overhead one of the receptionists at the plant tell a mechanic Bum Bradley had disappeared.

"Are you sure?" the mechanic asked. The man had gray, receding hair— someone Soroya thought might have known Bum for a long time.

"Absolutely. I heard it myself from a sheriff's deputy. Nobody's seen him since he drove to Houston a few weeks ago."

Houston? Talleyrand? Stunned, Soroya laid her sandwich on a paper plate. She remembered Acuña, the Mexican courier, casually talking about the killing of American consular employees. If they'd kill American officials, would they even think twice about killing a man who was just an American citizen asking nosey questions?

Shit! She liked Bum. She wished she didn't, but she did. Just thinking about what might have happened to him tore another seam in the cheap fabric that was holding her together.

What was I thinking—she pushed her sandwich away—*when I went along with this?*

Tuesday, July 3

At Elizabeth's urging, the FBI identified Compagnie Talleyrand as an organization of interest. When agents questioned engineer James Deaver, he merely noted a Mr. Bradley had called him with questions about Talleyrand that involved matters of a proprietary nature. He volunteered only that Bum had contacted him on the recommendation of Gus Adams. That oil-field hand had been crushed to hear about Bum's disappearance and more than willing to talk. Alas he had little to say that proved useful.

The bureau kept Elizabeth in the loop. She did not reciprocate by telling them Hiram was up to something. She still had no idea what the older Bradley brother was doing, but whatever it was he was working on it from Hobbs. She knew because he'd called the previous night to see if she would like to go there for the Independence Day parade.

"I'm sorry, Hiram," she'd told him. "I'm caught up in the middle of something right now and can't get away." It would have felt too sorrowful for Elizabeth to go there without Bum even if she hadn't been mired in all the details of Project 853.

Now she looked around her sparse cubicle and ordered herself to stay focused. *This is what you can do. You can nail the bastards who grabbed him.* She had little doubt Gharabaghi somehow had a hand in Bum's disappearance.

That made Elizabeth worry. Those guys in Washington would never round up all the guilty players. She could hardly stomach the idea that the colonel might have gotten away. But those Washington idiots, as she thought of them, were focused only on building a photo op at the UN. It wasn't bad enough to be haunted by George W.'s blunders; now Colin Powell's ghost was haunting US efforts too. She shuddered when she remembered the general's speech at the United Nations back in '03 when, among other myths, he made much of nonexistent yellow-cake uranium from Niger. Very impressive then. Widely discredited now.

That left the current crew in the White House still hogtied by worries about world opinion. That was when they weren't chewing up time counting delegates. Meantime, a nuke was on the loose in New Mexico.

And an Air Force vet has been kidnapped. Maybe killed.

Wednesday, July 4

Thinh Phan spent the night in a cheap seaside hotel. On his adopted nation's birthday, he was heading into the dragon's lair. He knew the two men he was looking for only by their first names—Van and Nguyen—and reputations. They were said to be ruthless. They had been paid to kill Bradley and dispose of his body. By whom Thinh didn't know; he doubted Van and Nguyen did either. Contract killers weren't paid by certified check. But as soon as Thinh had heard the man called Bum had been targeted, he sent word through the émigré grapevine that he wanted Bradley alive and would top any offer to get rid of him.

Text messages had followed, and Thinh pretended to negotiate with Van and Nguyen. Mostly he was dubious Bum was still among the living and figured it was more likely the pair of hired killers were looking to score a second payday. Even so Thinh kept digging into the shadowy world of the Gulf Coast.

He'd also called in chits earned in the long ago. From a second cousin once removed he'd learned the location of Van and Nguyen's boat near Matagorda. Thinh's cousin worked the coast near the Louisiana border. At night Thinh checked and found Van and Nguyen's vessel still dockside. He wondered whether the man called Bum could possibly be aboard. Or his body.

They don't call a man by his name when he dies in America. They don't believe in ancestors, not like we do. We would talk to Bum. We would use his name even when he passed, the same way Father is always Father and Mother is always Mother and a friend is always a friend.

And an enemy never dies.

Not yet dawn. The sky had only a tincture of light. No one around. The start of shrimp season was still days away. Thinh carried cash in one pocket, a Colt revolver in the other. If possible he'd give the ones called Van and Nguyen a choice. Thinh would even pay for the body to give Bum's family peace. And to say good-bye to the man who had given him life in a new land. But it wasn't just a time to call in chits; it was a time to pay them back too.

He parked far from the boat's berth and walked along the seawall, smelling the salt and hearing the thrust and parry of the tide as it crept forward and receded. He saw it was rising now, gaining inches of sand every few seconds. *Like death creeping up on your life every day.*

He heard voices and stopped. Then he saw two men stepping onto the boat. He waved to them like a friend.

"Van?" His voice a gull skimming across the small waves. "Nguyen?"

They stared at him. He hurried toward them. "I am Thinh Phan from Galveston."

But already the one who responded to "Van" was reaching hurriedly into his pocket. Thinh pulled out his Colt. It glimmered in the first light.

"Put it down, whatever it is, and don't run," Thinh yelled. "I have the money."

The two Vietnamese stopped and stared at him, but Van had his gun in hand. So did Thinh. But both kept the muzzles aimed at the ground.

"We can talk," Nguyen said. He waved Thinh closer.

Thinh looked around warily but approached the men. Thirty feet, then twenty. Plenty close for pistol shooting.

"I need to see Sergeant Bradley. Alive," Thinh said.

Van, the man with the gun in hand, smiled and nodded toward the bow of the boat. Thinh spotted the hold covered by dark canvas. It looked funereal to him.

"Where?" he asked Van.

"Where we put the fish," he said.

Sleep with the fishes. The American expression for killing someone came to mind. Thinh had collected Americanisms over the years. Right now he wished he hadn't; it made him more certain than ever this would not turn out well.

"Let's put away our guns," he said to the two men, "and you can show me."

Van made a display of putting his gun in his pocket and raising his hands, but he never lifted his gaze from Thinh as he stepped onto the shrimper. Eyeing one another the three men moved to the hold. Nguyen pulled the canvas aside. Thinh saw Sergeant Bradley chained hand and foot, squinting at even dawn's modest light, his mouth duct taped closed. Two buckets sat next to him, one with water, one with his slops.

"You see he's alive. You want to see him dead, you don't pay us," Van said. He'd slipped his hand in his gun pocket without Thinh noticing.

"I'll pay you, but let me talk to him first," Thinh said.

"No, he's alive. You talk to him later," Nguyen replied.

While he spoke Van quickly drew his gun and laughed. "Now we get the cash. You can join him out there." He smiled at the sea.

"No witnesses," Nguyen added with a smirk.

Sergeant Bradley made a ferocious attempt to stand. When Thinh saw Van glance into the hold, he knew why Bradley had raised a ruckus: the old airman was giving him a split second to try to survive. Thinh dove onto the deck, rolling away even as he pulled his gun and heard bullets chew up planking all around him.

He crashed into the wheelhouse and came up firing—two, three rounds, *bam-bam-bam*—and hitting Van. The gunman spun from the force of the bullet and slammed down behind a barrel. Thinh heard the man's gun skitter across the deck. Nguyen had drawn and dropped below a big, wooden box near the hold, but he hadn't fired. Yet.

The boat turned strangely silent after the gunplay, and the sky opened with red streaks of dawn. It was as if Thinh had bloodied the sun when he'd shot Van, maybe killed him. That left Nguyen to hunt down.

The boat was about seventy feet long. Nets and rigging were draped near or over the gunwale. Thinh looked around. Still not a person in sight on the wharf. A breeze suddenly cooled the sweat on the back of his neck and sent a chill down his back.

"I don't want to hurt you, Nguyen. I shot your friend because he tried to kill me. Put away your gun. I just want Sergeant Bradley." Thinh doubted Nguyen would stand down now, but the odds didn't favor either man—not with blood on the deck and murder in the air—so he kept trying. "I still have the cash. I'll still give you the money for the sergeant—fifty thousand dollars, Nguyen. Not bad for a few weeks of work."

Nothing. Thinh listened closely. The boat creaked. He had no idea if the sounds rose from the sea's endless roll or Nguyen's steps.

"Cash?" Nguyen's voice rose from behind the box near the hold.

"Cash, just like you wanted," Thinh said. "You can take it all now." *No honor among thieves.* Another Americanism Thinh liked.

He studied the deck in front of the wheelhouse for any movement. The creaking continued. And then he felt staggering pain in the back of his leg. He turned to find that Van, only wounded, had crawled up behind him and sunk a gaff into his hamstring. The younger man had the wooden handle in his grip and was trying to drag himself up Thinh's body, ripping open the long, thick muscle.

Thinh shot him in the head, and Van fell away. The gaff did not. It was sunk inches into Thinh's flesh. His leg buckled and he fell to his knees, losing sight of the pilothouse.

"Van?" Nguyen said softly.

"I got him," Thinh replied in a husky voice, so different from the one he'd owned only moments earlier, but the pain was penetrating everything, clouding his eyes, gripping his lungs, leaving him feeling crippled even of voice.

Nguyen ran up, rearing back when he saw Thinh's gun. He kept moving backward as first one then another bullet tore into his chest.

With copious quantities of blood spilling from his leg, Thinh fought to stay conscious as he dragged himself toward the hold. He looked down. Sergeant Bradley, no longer squinting, nodded fiercely at a ladder.

Thinh didn't know if he had the strength to climb down without falling. *You have to.* He thought to call 911. But that came with a price too: Whose gang did Van and Nguyen belong to? What retribution would they want? He had emptied all six rounds from his revolver into the now-lifeless bodies on the deck. His shiny Colt had become excess baggage. *Are there more brothers?* Thinh knew the revenge they would extract, so he crawled to the ladder, the gaff still sunk in the meat of his muscle.

With the wooden handle smacking against the back of his knee, Thinh took deep breaths and lowered himself into the hold by gripping the ladder and hopping from one rung to the other with his uninjured leg. Each movement sent scorching pain up his body.

As soon as he reached Sergeant Bradley, he pulled the muzzling duct tape off.

"Thanks," Bum said. "Over there." He tried to point with his chained hand. "The keys for these things. Get them before you pass out and we both die."

Thinh marshaled the last of his reserves. So dizzy he felt like the shrimper was caught in a storm, he crawled to a hook where the keys hung and must have tantalized the sergeant for weeks. He brought them back and unlocked Bum's handcuffs. The sergeant took over, freeing his manacled legs.

"I can't believe you're still alive," Thinh managed.

"I wasn't going to be for much longer. I've been bargaining with those two pukes since they took me. I basically promised them the whole ranch and everything in it if they'd let me go."

"Me too," Thinh said.

"Why?" Bum asked.

"Just hold on," Thinh replied. Gingerly he pulled out his cell and dialed his nephew, Diem. "Diem's parents were boat people. He lives in Palacios now, not far away. The kid grew up on the Texas coast, joined the Marines and served as a medic in Iraq. Tough duty. Maybe the toughest ever with those Ides."

Diem sounded sleepy. "What is it, Uncle Thinh? What's wrong?"

"Bring your medical bag, son. I got an airman down." Thinh said nothing of his own wounds.

"Who? What?"

Hiram saw the grin on Thinh's face.

"Remember the story about the Air Force guy who saved my life at Tan Son Nhut? Pulled me off the runway when I was a broken-legged kid? Well he's here, he's hurt, and he needs help."

Bum, still sitting among harvested fish, looked at Thinh in stunned disbelief.

CHAPTER 23
THE JET ENGINE SCREAMS

July 5–July 6, 1012

Thursday, July 5

When the post office opened, uranium ring number fifteen sat waiting for Rosincourt and Soroya. She watched his eyes light up when he gazed at the parcel, thinking he looked as high as he had been when he used to smoke pot. She understood why: now he had a critical mass for Akhbar-I.

In scientific terms the rings actually provided almost two times the necessary critical mass. She had watched Roz assemble the casing and mechanical parts of the nuclear device. It lacked only insertion of the fissile rings, bags of cordite, and cell phone electronics. Roz had also welded extra pipes and cosmetic valves onto the exterior of Akhbar-I to disguise its true intent, though to Soroya the shape still appeared crudely bomb-like.

When they got back from the post office, she saw him stare at the ungainly looking contraption and nod approvingly. The bomb, Soroya realized, was at last ready for loading onto a flatcar. Her stomach seemed to fall away, as if she had just landed on an elevator to hell.

Just over the border, Miguel Acuña made arrangements for the security of Talleyrand's Gulfstream 650, scheduled to arrive at the private annex of the Juarez airport the following week. The Gulfstream would be the exfiltration aircraft for Colonel Gharabaghi, Rosincourt, Soroya, and Dr. Hout just after Akhbar-I went off.

From his actions it appeared Acuña knew security in Juarez was complicated and enormously challenging. At the airport it was even worse because of clashing jurisdictions, some legal, most not. The Federales tried to maintain safety for traveling tourists. Los Aztecas owned the streets but only after fighting back competing gangs. Nobody had central control of the city as a whole.

Acuña had spent a week negotiating a cease-fire for the weekend of July 14 and 15, which was to say he had paid off everyone and their cousins—in the most literal sense. But every day he had to pay off new players as they streamed into Juarez for unexpected bonuses. The courier had turned into a walking ATM. He would also have to deal with customs and immigration folks when his departing VIPs—the bomb makers—boarded the Gulfstream.

Friday, July 6

Colonel Gharabaghi presided over the last meeting of the Project 853 group in Juarez. This time he invited only Rosincourt, Soroya, and Dr. Hout. Soroya found it odd to have such a small group after the last meeting, which had been well attended. It felt especially strange because the colonel had moved the venue to the upscale Casa Grande Hotel near the Juarez airport. A nice place, but the jet noise was loud.

Gharabaghi asked them first about the priceless uranium rings. "Are you guys ready to clean them off and do the final inspection?"

"Yes," Roz said. "The solvent tanks are ready."

The colonel handed Dr. Hout a set of go/no go gauges, instruments for quality control. "Call me—use stolen cell phones—to confirm the dimensions of the cleaned rings." Gharabaghi paused for a jet takeoff. He lifted his eyes from his listeners, smiling and nodding at the noise before resuming his directions to Dr. Hout. "Tell me whether they're okay or not okay."

"Of course," the hefty South African responded. He sounded bored.

Next on the agenda was the schedule for the fateful final days: July 14 to 16. The colonel ran down times and locations. Dr. Hout responded by reciting the countdown for inserting the uranium rings.

"We'll do dat on Saturday," the physicist said, "and add cordite and communications links on Sunday, den ship and evacuate on Monday. No problem. Plenty of time in each day for dese tasks."

Soroya confirmed she was now the caterer for Project 853. That sounded bizarre to a young woman whose first associations with food service had been the renowned caterers in Beverly Hills. They attended to weddings, private parties, and film crews, not bomb builders. *Caterer to a bomb?* Sounded like the title of a badly conceived memoir. But she had never been assigned any role in the assembly of the weapon, for which she remained grateful.

"I'll leave with Roz as we've planned." Her comment drew a scary smile from Gharabaghi. She tried to ignore his feral grin, wondering instead how she'd slip farewell notes to her mother and the rest of her family.

The colonel turned from her and snapped at Roz, "Is the flatbed railcar ordered?"

"Yes," he replied. "It arrives early next week."

"Will a locomotive pick it up Monday morning?"

"Yes," Roz said again. "The other freight cars are to be assembled over the weekend."

"So the train *will* depart at dawn on Monday, July 16?"

"Yes," Roz said, visibly tiring of the harangue. "The Burlington Northern Santa Fe runs on schedule. That's their business."

If Gharabaghi caught his underling's sarcasm, he let it go. Soroya thought he looked satisfied. He should have been. Everything was in order.

Gharabaghi then asked Dr. Hout to leave and to send in Kabiz, one of the two Iranian security men who had arrived in the past twenty-four hours. That was when Soroya first sensed something was going terribly wrong.

Dr. Hout smiled at her—he'd never done that before; it didn't feel good—and walked out. The door never closed before Kabiz appeared, a shoulder strap holding his Uzi, a thick roll of black plastic tucked under his other arm.

"Stand up," the colonel shouted at Soroya.

She rose to her feet, glancing nervously from him to Roz. Her boyfriend never looked back.

"You think you are so smart. You think you can make demands. You say *I*"—the colonel pointed to himself—"have to do this or *you* will quit. You make threats and you think you can get away with it. I said nothing. I just waited, but I do not have to wait anymore. Who do you think you are?"

As he spoke Kabiz unfurled the heavy, black plastic.

"What are you doing?" Soroya asked. Her voice shook. She heard her fear and knew they did too. "Roz? What's going on?"

He *still* wouldn't look at her.

I'm dead. I'm dead. She thought of her mother. *She'll be all alone.* Strange as it seemed even to Soroya, she saw her mom watching movies by herself. The young woman filled with a sadness so deep, so final, it pulsed to her fingertips and curled her toes. The fear she felt was horrifying.

"I'm sorry. I never meant to disrespect you," she pleaded with the colonel.

"You disrespected *me*," the colonel said, then pointed to Roz. "And you disrespected him. Tell her."

Only now did her boyfriend lift his eyes to her. "You are a stupid bitch. Starting last month, I checked your e-mail. You think I couldn't access it but I could, and I did every day. You betrayed me with your Jew boy, David. You tried to keep him from coming to New Mexico. You would have blown the whole project to save one Jew. Well, guess what? Once I saw that we set it up so your e-mails never went to him. They went to *me*. I answered you. I came this close to killing you." Roz held his index finger and thumb so close together she could scarcely see light between them. "But you got to live because he"—Roz nodded at the colonel—"said you couldn't disappear then. So I just read your e-mails, and every day you told him you love him. But you don't love me."

"Roz, that's not true. Look, I'm here."

He shook his head. "And now you're a liar." He stood and reached toward Gharabaghi, who handed him a gun with a silencer. "The next time a jet takes off, I'm killing you. And when my bomb goes off, I'm killing your Jew boy too."

Soroya's tears spilled freely. "Roz, don't do this to me. I believed in you. I've been here from the start. Alright, I was wrong to do what I did with David, but—"

"So you admit this blasphemy with the Jew?" the colonel demanded. "Not just e-mail, but sex. Sex!" He sounded enraged. Soroya heard the turbofans on a jet engine start to turn. They grew louder. Roz aimed the gun right at her face. *No, not there.* She thought of her mother again. *Don't make her see that.* She put her hands up and crouched, and then tried to ball up where she lay.

But even when the engine screamed, Roz didn't shoot. Gharabaghi pulled the gun from him and pushed him aside. He grabbed her hair, jerked her head up, and shot her in the heart.

Soroya felt piercing pain. And then, of course, she felt nothing.

Kabiz raced over with the body bag. He picked her up easily—she looked slight and fragile, weightless in death—and laid her carefully inside the black-plastic bag. He paused before zipping it up and looked at Roz, but the young man had turned away.

Not a drop of Soroya's blood spilled to the floor. But it bloomed on her shirt, wider with every second. As the jet rose into the sky, the sound of the zipper seemed to fill the room.

"You are a coward," the colonel said to Roz, and for a moment he raised the gun on him too. "Do your job or you will not die so easily."

That evening Elizabeth and Mike McKinney made their last penetration of the Bradley Brothers plant. Jack Daniel and his girlfriend rendezvoused in the executive suite, as unwittingly helpful as ever.

Elizabeth located the communications equipment for detonating Akhbar-I and signaled to McKinney. He removed the SIM card in the cell phone to be used by Gharabaghi. Then he added a new card courtesy of the NSA. The pair of intruders adjusted the encrypting equipment attached to that phone before inspecting the GPS transmitter intended to remain with the bomb. They found it functional as anticipated.

The last item on their agenda was a farewell visit to the vault. They confirmed all fifteen uranium rings had arrived and were still gift wrapped.

In less than an hour, they had completed their incursion. After exiting the building, McKinney reconnected the security alarms.

"Good working with you," Elizabeth said to him.

"Same here," McKinney replied. "I'm guessing we'll be doing this again sometime."

"Maybe so."

"I just have one question," McKinney said. "And if you can't answer it, I'll understand. But what the hell have we been doing here? That's an

A-bomb in there. Why are we going home to dinner? We should be disabling it. That's what we usually do with discovered ordnance. That's what we're paid to do."

"I can't answer your questions, but it's not because of the security demands. I honestly don't know why, Mike. I just hope Washington knows what it's doing."

He raised a skeptical eyebrow. She nodded. They shook hands and fled.

Back in her apartment, Elizabeth poured herself a scotch straight up. A private ritual upon the completion of a mission, a silent salute to her father and her other forebears in the spy trade. Not that she always had a chance to raise a toast. There had barely been time to breathe years earlier when she'd brought down the Antonov-12 in Kazakhstan. But she raised the tumbler now and sipped twenty-one-year-old Glenfiddich, dearly hoping Murphy's Law had been repealed. Washington's plan, as she understood it, had more holes in it than a hair net.

She returned to her computer to review intercepts from the Festival Street apartment, intrigued by an intelligence report that Soroya had not returned from Juarez. Oddly she heard Rosincourt crying. Soft but insistent. She wondered why and what had happened to Soroya. But as she listened, Roz blurted "bitch" three times. Even then he didn't sound angry; he sounded drenched with sorrow.

What's going on? Elizabeth had her suspicions, and once more they revolved around Gharabaghi. Quickly she checked the intercepts from the plant, but not a clue emerged. She sent an encrypted message to the agents watching Festival Street, requesting details of any recent sightings. A response came back almost immediately, saying Roz had not left his apartment since returning from Mexico and no one else had entered it.

Then she received an e-mail from the FBI in Houston, which momentarily raised her hopes about Bum. But the missive was a routine update containing nothing new.

Gharabaghi killed Bum. Elizabeth would have bet a year's salary on that. She raised a toast to her cowboy lover. Her eyes closed, spilling a tear.

Then she returned to her computer. NSA intercepts confirmed Gharabaghi's plans to remain in Juarez for the weekend. Just thinking of him reclining on a bed while some miserably poor prostitute serviced him gave her yet another reason to want to shoot him. She started recounting to herself the man's crimes: The car-bomb murders of Dr. Antonovitch and Dr.

Hall along with their driver. The murder of a Kazakh farmer and the torture slaying of a horse. *Who tortures a horse, for Christ's sake?* And now Bum was missing. *And Soroya.* That had to be suspicious. Then there was the role Gharabaghi and all of his Quds agents played in Colonel Gourdine's gruesome and slow death. But all of it paled—even Bum's disappearance—now that her nemesis was on the verge of rolling a live nuke through the New Mexico desert while the White House dithered.

She downed the last of her scotch but felt more clearheaded than ever. She stepped out onto the balcony, then stared south toward Juarez, peering at the lights of that misbegotten city. Before her father's voice could warn her, she said to herself, *No, Dad, not this time. Sometimes you have to go with your gut. You said so yourself.*

She was going down to Juarez on her own. *What's the worst the agency can do to me? Fire me?*

But that wasn't the worst that could happen to Elizabeth. Not even close. More than 40,000 people had been murdered in Mexico's drug war—police, soldiers, mayors, teachers, children, doctors and nurses, judges, even military commanders. *A criminal insurgency.* Many of them had died from gruesome torture. Already her own government had started flying Predator drones over Mexican territory, like the ones she had commanded in the skies above Iraq.

But right now Elizabeth believed they needed boots on the ground on the other side of the border. She had a pair.

CHAPTER 24
INCUBATION

July 7–15, 2012

Saturday–Sunday, July 7–8

At first light the next morning, Elizabeth threw on Levis, a dark-blue jersey, and an oversized Army jacket emblazoned with the solitary star of the First Armored Division. Dressed like an Army wife off on a shopping spree in Mexico. But she also added a few items rarely found on the women she was attempting to resemble: a snub-nosed .22 caliber revolver loaded with hollow points that would scramble Gharabaghi's brain, a bogus ID, and a change of clothes in her shoulder bag.

She called a cab, but before leaving her apartment she darted to the bathroom to check her makeup and touch up her hair. She noticed distinct strands of gray just above her temples. With a grimace—and a vow to see her stylist—she pinned her hair away from her face with a gold barrette.

The taxi whisked her to the crowded Santa Fe Bridge. She'd paid her fare and taken three steps toward the border when a stout-looking Hispanic couple moved abruptly beside her. Both wore khaki work clothes and moved with the agility of pouncing cougars. The short, dark-haired woman trained her serious, brown eyes on Elizabeth and seized the agent's arm with an uncompromising grip. The man, bald and swarthy, mirrored her movements, moving swiftly to grab Elizabeth's hand when she tried to retrieve the .22.

"Don't," he said, furrowing his brow. "We're on the same team, but you've just committed a foul."

"Show me some ID," Elizabeth demanded.

"We can do better than that," the woman said.

The couple pulled her rapidly backward through a milling crowd of people who appeared to take no notice of the apprehension. Had the pair been trying to force her into Mexico, Elizabeth would have fought loud and hard, but she had a strong, sickening sense she'd been busted by her own people and knew that if that were so, the wrath of Washington was about to come down on her.

Perhaps worse: it turned out to be the wrath of an old friend.

As they approached a white van idling less than a hundred feet from where she'd climbed out of the taxi, the side door slid open, revealing Jack Barry, the CIA station chief in Mexico City. What he didn't look like at that moment was an old buddy. When the door slammed behind Elizabeth, he didn't sound like one either.

"What the hell do you think you're doing going over there? You're violating domestic laws against operating in another country. You would have been violating Mexican law by carrying a concealed weapon into their country if that"—he tapped the .22 in her pocket—"is what I think it is. And you've violated your own oaths by breaking the chain of command, which involves a whole series of criminal sanctions. Why, Elizabeth? Why?"

"Do you know exactly what is going on over at the—"

"Not here," Jack snapped. His gaze darted immediately to the van driver and a person in the shotgun seat, whom she presumed was a security hand.

They remained silent as the van drove to an underground garage below the bland-looking federal office where Elizabeth worked. Without a word they trudged upstairs to her windowless cubicle. Only when the door closed did Jack look at her.

"We're engaged in a very complex ballet here, Ms. Mallory."

Ms. Mallory? From him?

"This is the agency's biggest operation since the Glomar Explorer." The CIA effort to recover parts of a Soviet nuclear submarine, a long-term project that involved considerable subterfuge. "You have built a reputation for coolness under fire, from Kazakhstan to Al Udeid. And the agency has invested in your education. For chrissakes we sent you to the Defense Language School. We entrusted you with the Pueblo Canyon bombing, which, by the way, has produced no results so far. And now you've got a key role in this 853 affair and you've decided to freelance?" He shook his head in disbelief. "Washington's going to think you've lost it."

I think they've lost it, she almost said aloud but she understood, in the gravest terms imaginable, that she was in career-saving mode—or ought to have been.

"When the director hears about this," Jack went on, "he's going to want you fired. You'll be gone like *that*." He snapped his fingers. "No appeals, no employment rights, no due process. And you could be subject to a criminal investigation. Intent to commit murder."

"That would be tough to prove," she said respectfully.

"And most inconvenient to defend," Jack volleyed.

"With all due respect," Elizabeth continued, "Washington is screwing up again. I watched them dither while bin Laden scampered away from Tora Bora. Now they're going to let an Iranian nuke roll through the hills of New Mexico in hopes of neutering it electronically. Then they'll grab it for display at the UN as an October election surprise. But Jack, things never work out the way we plan. Do you really believe sitting tight is the right thing to do?" she asked, her voice growing louder.

"Calm down. What I think and what you think is *limited* thinking. We don't know what else is going on. You see something and believe you know everything. I see something and I know better—and you should too. What's gotten into you?"

Elizabeth collapsed into her desk chair and swore.

Brady changed tack. "What's your connection to this Bum Bradley guy? You told the bureau you had a personal interest in his disappearance."

"Just that: it's personal," she said.

"Really? You're involved with him? You, of all people, going off the reservation because of a relationship?"

Elizabeth looked around her at all the reminders of her trade and winced. "I screwed up." She sounded defeated.

Brady accepted the surrender with a concise, "You sure did."

"Who else knows, Jack?"

"Just me. For all those two in the van know, you and I were just engaged in a diversion of some kind. But I have to write it up, Elizabeth. I will go to bat for you. But only if you promise me there'll be no more of this. You could have compromised the entire case. And if you screw it up after this, it'll be my head, not just yours. You hear me?" He stared at her. She saw that his rubicund, Irish complexion had turned scarlet.

"I hear you."

"I'm putting a minder on you from now on."

Oh, Christ. A shadow. "Who?"

He shook his head. "You'll never know unless you screw up, and then it won't much matter."

"I'm sorry, Jack."

"*Can* you stay on track, given your personal involvement?"

"Yes," she said.

"Good, because it's absolutely essential you pay attention to business. Gharabaghi's telephone and the GPS aboard Akhbar-I are your absolute responsibility. They are the crown jewels. We *need* you for that. Beyond that we're counting on you to monitor Rosincourt Sadr and Soroya Assaf's every move, to track and account for every piece of hardware, to listen to their every word. Don't let me down. I ask you this as your oldest friend in the agency. Promise me."

"I do. I'm sorry."

He took a breath. "Look, most people worth having in the agency go off the charts at some point. Let this be your one and only time and your career might outlive it."

"Can we move on?" she asked. He nodded. "Soroya Assaf never returned from Mexico." He nodded knowingly. "And last night Rosincourt was crying. Then he got angry and shouted 'bitch' three times."

"I'll bet she's dead," Jack replied solemnly. "I wondered how long Gharabaghi would put up with an outspoken young woman. Soon as I saw that video of her with that poster about her bush I wondered how those two would get along. I'm sure she was too brazen for him right from the start. That's my guess anyway. Just keep monitoring them and remember the rules, Elizabeth. I have my piece of the puzzle—Mexico. You have yours—El Paso. Keep the director posted on *everything* you hear from Festival and Doniphan streets. And make goddamn sure Gharabaghi gets the right phone. Copy that?"

"Copy."

She was still debriefing herself long after Jack left. But she never had to ask herself why she'd violated agency rules, which she'd always held sacrosanct. She'd done it for love, as unfamiliar to her as going rogue on the agency. The wild currents that ran through both actions felt strikingly similar. *You better be careful*, she warned herself. *You could get addicted to both.*

Thinh Phan's nephew, Diem, the medic, carried his medical kit into his living room: time to put a fresh dressing on the deep gash in the back of his uncle's leg. Then the young Marine asked him to stand up and put some weight on it. Thinh winced.

"Uncle, you've got to go to a hospital." He glanced at Bum, sitting on a couch several feet away. "Sergeant Bradley, you should have gone to one a few weeks ago."

"Well, I was otherwise engaged," Bum replied with a laugh. "My noggin doesn't hurt anymore, but that thing"—he pointed to Thinh's leg—"looks like hell."

"We sure know what hell looks like, don't we, Bum?" Thinh said.

"We sure do and then some. It was called Tan Son Nhut."

"You might have had a concussion," Diem said to Bum. "How long were you out?"

"I came around before we were out of Gilhooley's parking lot."

"How could you tell?" Diem asked. "You said they had you in a big sack."

"Oyster shells," Bum said. "They talk back when you roll over them. And I don't need any doc. I'm fine." He stood up and turned around. "See? Good as new."

Diem shook his head. "You two," he said. "The school of hard knocks is gonna knock you down."

"And we'll get right back up," Thinh said with a laugh. "Besides I can't go to a hospital, Diem. My blood's on the deck of that boat along with a couple of bodies. How am I going to explain that?"

"The truth?" the young man said. "They tried to kill you. Look at that." He pointed to Thinh's leg.

"I'll tell them the truth once Sergeant Bradley doesn't have to worry about someone trying to kill him. We've got to lie low for the time being. You just go on doing whatever you do."

"What I'm doing," the young medic said, "is taking care of you. We're back in Fallujah." Diem glanced at a black, semiautomatic pistol lying on the nightstand next to Bum's bed.

"It shouldn't be too much longer," Thinh said to his nephew. "Let's just keep our heads low and our eyes open."

"Like I said." Diem nodded. "Iraq."

Rosincourt drove to the Bradley Brothers shop by himself for the first time, trying to shake the memory of Soroya's murder. He kept seeing Gharabaghi grabbing her hair and shooting her in the chest. Roz cringed like he'd been struck each time he remembered. But the worst memory of all was the way his whole world had seemed to turn black when she'd disappeared into that body bag. He hadn't expected to be haunted like this. He worried her ghost might be in the car beside him. He even reached to the passenger seat, worried he'd feel Soroya's presence. But he felt nothing of her, only horror.

When he parked he prayed to Allah, then hurried inside, telling coworkers Soroya had flown to LA because her mother had been hospitalized.

"I think she'll be gone all week."

After thanking them for their condolences, he and Dr. Hout moved to a secure area outside the vault, then arranged the glass containers for cleaning the uranium rings. Their work began with the use of a highly flammable solvent to rinse the first of six small discs. Each was four inches in diameter with a one-inch hole in the center; they were remarkably heavy for their size. Eventually they would be inserted at the far end of the gun barrel.

It took Roz the better part of an hour to clean each disc, so the work would take most of the day. He sustained himself with coffee, ever wary of Dr. Hout hovering nearby. The way the fat, old man had smiled at Soroya still bothered him deeply, like he knew she was going to be murdered and thought it was funny.

When he finished the sixth disc, Hout inspected them. Then Roz placed them back into their individual cages in the vault.

Sunday's work was a little more difficult. There were nine doughnut-shaped rings, almost twice the size of Saturday's discs. Roz's hands shook so badly he dropped a gauge, then spilled some solvent.

"Have you eaten?" Hout asked in a demanding voice.

"Yes," Roz answered sullenly.

"I see you drink only de coffee. Eat!"

Roz made his way over to the remains of the spread Soroya had put out Friday morning. He grabbed a single slice of bread, cringing once more at the memory of Soroya's murder. He washed down the dry bread with more coffee. Dr. Hout watched and shook his head.

By Sunday evening the vault was once again home to fifteen nickel-plated uranium rings, now shiny and protected by plastic wrappers in their storage cages.

Dr. Hout sat down in a canvas chair in a large bay adjacent to Akhbar-I. "Come over here, Roz. Sit."

Roz wandered over and settled across from the physicist.

"You are like me. A man of de bomb," he said proudly. "Dat girl... What was her name?"

Roz glared at him. "Soroya," he said emphatically.

Dr. Hout waved his hand as if she hardly mattered, much less her name. "You will see dat dere are others. Lots of dem for a man of de bomb. I can see you are sad, but you will forget her when you see de work you do."

"I'll see it?" Roz said, brightening at the prospect of witnessing the blast—from afar.

Dr. Hout shook his head. "No, but dere will be pictures. Dere always are. And you will say, 'I did dat.' You will tink nothing of her again."

Roz wondered if that were true. He hoped so, because every time he thought of what happened to Soroya he wanted to throw up.

Monday, July 9

Colonel Gharabaghi stretched out on a long couch in his suite at the Casa Grande Hotel and began the day by snapping open his encrypted cell and calling Miguel Acuña. He wanted to let his man know he was heading back down to Chihuahua.

"I will return Thursday, when the Talleyrand plane gets in. I will see you at the airport then. Be damn sure that G-650 is secured and *very* well guarded."

"*Si*, señor," the Mexican jefe responded.

"One more thing, Miguel," the colonel said in an irritated voice. "There is an obnoxious Anglo blond in El Paso. Her name is Elizabeth Mallory. She works for the government. I think the CIA, but they give her other titles. I first met her in Moscow, then Paris. A real bitch. Find out where she works. Once Akhbar is ready, I want to have one of Bereueh's people take her out. Can you arrange that?"

"Not much time, not much to go on, señor, but I will try. I think I've heard of her." Acuña replaced the handset, then laughed.

Gharabaghi also smiled at the thought that in the end not even Elizabeth Mallory would slip through his hands. Western women were infidels, even the ones like Assaf who claimed to believe. He relished the prospect of Mallory's death almost as much as he looked forward to the explosion of Akhbar-I.

He rousted himself from the couch and packed a small bag, checked the magazine on his semiautomatic pistol, and headed for the door, pausing when his cell rang.

The voice on the phone brought another smile to his face. This time it was Dr. Hout calling from an El Paso pay phone. The physicist's words were opaque but their meaning was clear: "The entire school of fish has been cleaned. They are of legal size, ready for delivery."

Gharabaghi did not respond. It was enough that he had taken the call.

By noon transcripts of those two calls were on Elizabeth's computer screen thanks to NSA diligence. She wasn't shocked to see that the colonel had called for her execution. *Fair is fair*, she thought, *because if I could have I would have killed you already.*

Just over the border, Miguel Acuña began a round of meetings with his Los Azteca associates as well as the customs officials on his payroll. He doled out *mordida*—bribes—to killers and bureaucrats with equal ease. He was a banker on holiday tipping with the depositors' money.

At the Bradley Brothers shop, Rosincourt and his machinists began their week filing the welds and tightening bolts on what was called the "ELF seismic device." The men who labored so diligently by Roz's side did not know they were working on an atomic bomb. Dr. Hout checked off every move.

Tuesday, July 10

In Tehran a high-ranking member of the Revolutionary Guard waited for Iran's new foreign minister to rise from his prayer rug. When the man with the gray goatee straightened, the officer handed him a cable confirming Project 853 was moving forward on schedule.

The minister removed his steel-rim glasses and pinched the bridge of his nose. This was the news he had long awaited. Before assuming his new post, he had been Iran's atomic chief, overseeing the country's nuclear program. His predecessor as foreign minister had been dismissed for being too accommodating: he'd declared a step forward had been reached when Secretary of State Hillary Clinton said Iran was entitled to a peaceful nuclear-energy program. The mullahs had no regard for moderation, a point not lost on the new foreign minister as he pushed his glasses back into place.

The detonation would take place on Monday, July 16, the sixty-seventh anniversary of America's explosion of the world's first nuclear device. The foreign minister smiled as he reviewed the update. Akhbar-I was to be fired adjacent to the Trinity test site in the US at 11:00 a.m. mountain standard time. Dinner hour in Iran. Multiple sources would confirm the detonation: electromagnetic sensors at Tehran University; seismic sensors in Sweden; a visual report from their man in Socorro, New Mexico; and, of course, the "send" signal from Colonel Ashkan Gharabaghi's cell phone.

The foreign minister dismissed the officer who had brought him the report, then walked back into his office and summoned a young aide.

"Move ahead with our plans for the evening of July sixteenth," he said curtly. The minister had called for a dinner with French officials. Nominally it was to be a Bastille Day party to thank them for their hospitality to Ayatollah Khomeini in the days before the 1979 revolution—and for all the courtesies they had extended in-country ever since. But the party could not take place on the holiday's actual date, July 14, because it fell on a weekend day strictly reserved for Islamic religious observance.

The minister began to draft a letter from President Alizadeh to his American counterpart, explaining the significance of Project 853. Because Iran did not maintain diplomatic relations with the US, he planned to hand this document to the Swiss ambassador at dinner, for immediate transmission onward to Washington.

Wednesday, July 11

Rosincourt stood to the side, watching the cranes hoist the four-ton atomic bomb in the Bradley shop. A small crowd of employees stepped back as the crane operator moved the bomb toward a train flatcar. The cables sang softly, almost like violin strings. Steel slings cradled the device and lowered it onto curved metal supports.

The crane operator settled it gently into place on the train. Roz looked around as the others drifted back to work. *If they only knew*, he thought. Three technicians strapped down the device with steel bands, then secured the bomb, front and back, with chains. Only the rear entry plate remained accessible. Once it was loaded, two women in overalls hurried to give the bomb a final coat of white paint, covering up the chain scars and shop marks with a glistening semblance of innocence.

Roz stared at the white paint, hoping it really would wash away the memory of the black body bag—and all it contained—as Dr. Hout had suggested.

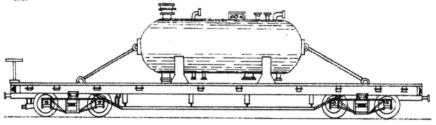

Akhbar-I, modified with decoy valves and fittings, aboard a BNSF flatbed.

Thursday, July 12

Heavily armed Federales surrounded a new, immaculate Gulfstream 650 owned by Compagnie Talleyrand. It had just landed at the Juarez airport. But the soldiers did not move forward to make arrests or attack the terrorists onboard the gleaming-white jet. They pressed close to provide their guests with security.

The G-650 had satellite phone and Internet service, making it the perfect airborne command post for those conducting a high-speed exfiltration. And with a range of more than 7,000 miles it could evacuate Gharabaghi and his cohorts to Tehran with only two stops—Caracas and Cairo—without once flying over US airspace.

The Federales weren't the only armed men; members of Los Aztecas lurked just outside the fence.

A charming and affable Miguel Acuña, wearing a bulky trench coat in the July heat, led a delegation of customs and immigration officials to the foot of the stairs. None demanded to see papers from the Talleyrand passengers and crew. Instead they appeared to be paying homage.

Acuña smiled, seemingly pleased with the results of his numerous payoffs. The officials toadied with the ease of men long accustomed to supplicating to wealth and power. For the next four nights, Acuña would sleep on the Gulfstream, armed and alert, for he had ample reasons of his own to make sure the jet's owners and passengers received the rewards they'd worked so hard to earn. Acuña also knew how to strike a servile smile. And he made sure a pair of his heavily armed friends stood guard under the aircraft's wings. He had negotiated an armistice with the gangs of Juarez; he felt worthy of a Nobel Peace Prize for his considerable efforts. After all the Juarez executive terminal was now a neutral zone in the gang wars. How long that truce would last was his principal concern, because if anything went wrong he knew he would be among the first to be shot.

Shot? he said to himself. *I should be so lucky.*

Friday, July 13

Despite its ominous reputation, Friday the thirteenth was a quiet day. Roz appeared at work but did little until late in the day, when he placed a phone and encryption gear for Colonel Gharabaghi in a box with a Bacardi rum imprint. Then he headed south to the border for the first time without his girlfriend. A Mexican border agent, accustomed to seeing Soroya with him, asked if she was okay.

"She's fine," Roz said, trying to keep his voice steady.

"Where is she?" asked Esteban, who was old but had always flirted with Soroya.

Roz swallowed, felt himself sweating, and managed to say, "She's visiting her mother in California."

"And you go party without her?" Esteban said, clearly disapproving. He pointed to the Bacardi rum box. "You take all that booze with you? *Into* Mexico?"

Roz shrugged, but he was petrified Esteban would search the box and find the encryption gear. *What am I going to say they are?* He was so nervous he wanted to floor the accelerator and race into Juarez.

"Taking rum to Mexico is like taking coal to Newcastle," Esteban noted, still staring at the box.

Roz didn't even know what the border guard meant. "What?"

"It means it's not *necesario.* Maybe you should leave a bottle or two for me." When Roz froze, unable to speak or move, Esteban laughed. "Go on. But if I see Soroya, I'm going to make my own party."

Roz was drenched in perspiration as he drove away, but when he glanced in his side-view mirror, Esteban was already waving up another car.

By the time Roz reached Don Quintin's, he'd calmed down. And when he entered the restaurant and bar he was greeted by a smiling Colonel Gharabaghi, dressed in a baggy hunting jacket, which seemed highly appropriate to Roz. The colonel was flanked by Kabiz and another security man. Roz figured both of them were Quds officers.

Moments after Roz sat down, grateful for an iced lemonade, Gharabaghi left with the Bacardi box in hand. Kabiz went with him. The other security fellow settled across from Rosincourt. Dr. Hout lounged a couple seats away with a margarita. He smiled at Roz. It felt like a curse. The only other time Roz had seen Hout smile was at Soroya—just before she was executed.

A few hours later, Roz drove back to the States, grateful to be crossing the border without highly incriminating electronics in his car.

Saturday, July 14

Rosincourt arrived at the Bradley Brothers shop at 8:00 a.m. He spent the first part of the day fitting the six smaller uranium rings onto the draw bolt, then inserting that loaded bolt into the far end of Akhbar-I. He could have used Dr. Hout's help, but the older man was far too portly to work in that cramped space. He did hand the pieces to Roz and made sure the final assembly met the specs.

After a taco lunch, which Roz managed to eat, the two men turned their attention to the nine larger rings that were to go into the rear section of the gun barrel. Again Roz did the hardest work while Hout handed up the parts to be installed. The pair worked efficiently, two master mechanics who had been well chosen by the Quds Force.

By the end of the day, Akhbar-I was hot. While not yet equipped with explosives or detonators, it had every other component of a real A-bomb.

Look what you've done, Rosincourt said to himself, honestly astonished by what his considerable skills had wrought. For the first time, he felt cleansed of the most gruesome memories of Soroya's demise. He was so taken with the raw beauty of the bomb he decided to spend the night at the shop, fearful someone might try to tinker with it. He pulled an old sleeping bag from the back of his SUV but slept fitfully, awakening throughout the night. Each time he gazed at the white wonder, he dreamed of a blaze brighter than the sun.

Elizabeth had little time for sleep. When she did lie down, memories of Bum invaded her thoughts. Better to work until she collapsed from exhaustion.

From her office on North Mesa, she had logged every minute of Akhbar-I's assembly with great care. All week she'd filed daily reports, but now, with the fissile rings and discs inserted into a real A-bomb, she wanted to summarize and remind Washington how serious the situation had become. Her report would also help focus her Monday plans.

TO: Director, ATF

SUBJECT: 853 Daily summary, week of July 8–14

Sun, July 8: Six discs, nine weapons-grade rings cleaned and returned to vault. G was so advised.

Mon, July 9: Machine shop work. Phones not moved. No sign of S.

Tue, July 10: BNSF flatbed arrived.

Wed, July 11: Akhbar-I lifted onto flatbed. Big job!

Thu, July 12: R travel preparations. Phones have not been moved. S still absent.

Fri, July 13: R picked up phones & GPS, took them to Juarez. Delivery to G confirmed.

Sat, July 14: All fissile materials inserted in weapon. Aside from HE & dets, it's hot.

Elizabeth sat back and sent the message, then checked her personal e-mail as she had every quarter hour since Bum's disappearance. Today was different. She lunged to her feet when she saw she had mail—from him. She tapped the screen on her smartphone to bring it up.

"I'm okay. I have to lie low to help others."

He's alive. "You're alive," she shouted, as if worried the message would vanish if she didn't give it a larger life. She wiped tears from her cheeks, only then realizing she was crying.

But "I'm okay" is all I get? And he's got to lie low to help somebody? She cleared her throat and called Hiram immediately. The old codger picked up on the first ring.

"It's me, Elizabeth Mallory. I just got an e-mail from Bum, but all it said was 'I'm okay.' And he's got to keep his head down to help some other people. What's that about?"

"I got it too. It means he's okay."

"Please don't stonewall me, Hiram. Tell me what you know."

"I don't know anything except I'm pretty sure he's okay. If my brother says he's helping somebody, he's helping somebody. And if I know him like I think I do, he's probably getting ready to do something too."

"Like what?"

"Well, I'm guessing he's pretty damn pissed at Talleyrand, seeing as he was fixing to see some Talleyrand whistle-blower before he got taken down. I'm sure he's not going to take *that* sitting down. Bradley boys just don't do that. Never have."

"No!" she shouted. "He can't start messing around right now. That's a really bad idea."

"Oh, he's full of bad ideas," said Hiram, as if he had decided of late she was number one on the bad idea list. Elizabeth ignored the tone.

"Can I reach him?" she asked.

"Try hitting 'reply.' I hear it works pretty good on these e-mail things."

Now he was playing the country yokel for all it was worth. She didn't have time for this. "Have you hit 'reply'?"

"Yeah, and it did wonders for my health. You should try it."

"Have you talked to him?" Trying not to sound impatient, which only made her sound more impatient than ever.

"Nope, 'cause my brother didn't just fall off the turnip truck. If he doesn't want to be found, he's not going to be found. He sure as hell ain't gonna be using his phone."

She...could...have...screamed. "Alright, I'll e-mail him."

"*Good* idea. Wish I'd have thought of that one myself. Just don't expect a quick reply. Wherever he is he's not getting his messages too fast, from what I can see. And Liz?"

"It's Elizabeth."

"Okay, *E-liz-a-beth*, from what I'm thinking you shouldn't be worrying too much about Bum right now 'cause I'm guessing you got more problems than a treed coon. Am I right?"

"You're guessing that, huh?"

"I am indeed."

"Thank you for the counsel."

"Anytime. Just call 1-800-SHRINK and you'll get me."

Argh! She hung up.

But hold on, she said to herself. *Hiram believes he's alive. That's the headline.*

So she did hit "reply" and said, simply, "Glad to hear it. Would love to talk to you. Love, Elizabeth." Then she sent it off into the ether.

Sunday, July 15

Roz awoke to find the fat, round face of Dr. Hout peering down at him. The physicist rubbed his hands together and said, "I make coffee. I bring it dere. We get to work. I bring you donuts too, in honor of de rings." He laughed.

Rousted, Roz crawled out of his sleeping bag and ate four sugared donuts. He was getting back his appetite. "Thanks!" he said to Dr. Hout, who stuffed a custard-filled, chocolate-glazed creation into his maw.

The two of them spent the day arming Akhbar-I, first inserting the cordite powder bags before closing the gun breech. After attaching detonators and the cell phone receiver to the powder train, they hooked up the GPS transmitter and safety circuits. Then they gave the batteries a final charge.

"No room for error," Dr. Hout said.

By early afternoon the two of them had bolted the rear panel of the device shut.

A mile away, in her fortified federal office building, Elizabeth listened to those clanging sounds on her computer along with the comments made by Roz and Dr. Hout. She reread Gharabaghi's announced plans to kill her once Akhbar was buttoned up. The threat made the clanging in the shop sound like alarm bells.

By secure e-mail she advised her director in Washington that Akhbar-I was fully loaded and armed. She despaired of preemptive action, yet she feared for the lives of countless Americans if the planners in DC hadn't thought this one through. There were so many ways things could go wrong. What if they hadn't checked and rechecked their communication link to the bomb? Gharabaghi's people must have been doing that on a regular basis. A thousand what-ifs cartwheeled through her mind.

She had kindred spirits down the hall, men and women from the FBI, Homeland Security, the IRS, and Border Patrol, but no one was cleared to know what she was doing. She had no one to talk to and no chance to relax. There wasn't even a sunset view from the windows because there were no windows. The nondescript office was in a standard tilt-up concrete structure, as personality-less as the cold-looking boxes that dotted the former Soviet Union. Only the bathrooms, thankfully, enjoyed ventilation. A retired police officer guarded the crypto-locked front door. Surveillance cameras tracked visitors and watched the unguarded fire door to the rear. But even with these protections, Gharabaghi's announced plans to kill her made Elizabeth dread the coming night.

Rosincourt slid into his sleeping bag, pleased by how little grief he now felt over Soroya. He had joined a cause much greater than himself and had lost the petty emotions that come from simple-minded attachments. Or at least that was what he told himself. Mostly he felt great gazing at the bomb.

He looked forward to getting on a private jet, flying to Ramsar, and becoming a revered figure in the ongoing Iranian resurgence. He thought of Jefferson and Washington and Lincoln, and all the other American heroes he'd read about at the St. John's School. He realized Persia would soon have its own pantheon of Islamic greats. Rosincourt Sadr would be up there with Cyrus the Great and Ruhollah Khomeini. As for his old classmates and friends, he wouldn't miss any of them. Not even his parents. None of them had loyalty to the new Iran, and they had no understanding of a real Muslim's dreams of justice for his homeland.

"No justice, no peace." That was what Soroya used to chant when she walked around with that stupid sign. He'd never thought much about those words, but they rang so true for Iran. For so long his country had been denied justice, so now there would be no peace. Only a brilliant act of war.

Rosincourt Sadr, a name for the ages.

CHAPTER 25
SUNRISE

Morning, July 16, 2012

During the long, hot days of summer, Texans start work early. At dawn on Monday, July 16, 2012, a locomotive arrived on schedule at the Bradley Brothers Company. It moved at a crawl toward a flatbed train car with a bright-white atomic bomb posing as a gas-oil separator. The locomotive's coupler appeared to reach out like a claw when it gripped its mate on the flatbed. Locked and loaded, the locomotive moved out. Rosincourt watched the flatcar with undiminished interest. *A hero of the nation.* Those words came to him unbidden, but not unearned. He smiled in the sunshine.

Within the hour the BNSF engine had added the Bradley offering to an already-assembled line of boxcars and tankers ready to roll north. From atop a nearby mountain, Elizabeth watched the procession begin to travel. Her minder, another woman with dark hair, perhaps twice her age, remained unobtrusive while shadowing Elizabeth to the trailhead. The minder watched as Elizabeth hiked off to an observation post several miles away. The assigned shadow parked about a hundred feet from Elizabeth's car, expecting, as any reasonable person would, that she would return from her remote desert perch when her duties were complete. Where else would she go? It was blazing hot, one hundred plus—and the day promised temperatures rising even higher. Truly deadly heat.

But perhaps the sharp-featured, older woman hadn't taken note of Elizabeth's slightly bulging daypack or her trail runners, and in all likelihood she knew nothing of Elizabeth's history of successful marathon competitions. The minder most certainly did not know of Elizabeth's professed skepticism of Washington planners. Perhaps the older agent even thought Elizabeth's contrite expressions to Jack Barry had been made in earnest and would trump her greater concerns for the country at large.

On all counts her minder was wrong. Dead wrong.

When Elizabeth saw the train moving, she drank more mineral-enriched water from a bottle. She'd been building up her body's reserves since rising at 4:00 a.m. Checking to be sure she was still alone, she created a false trail to a rise of boulders, shed her clothes, and hid them along with her water bottle. Then she put on dun-colored shorts and a sleeveless top along with an oversized ball cap that hid her hair. Next she snaked a clear-plastic drinking tube out of her daypack—really a shoulder-mounted Camelback, a widely used hydration system for endurance athletes. But she'd filled the water bladder only halfway so the pack had room for other tools of the covert world. She took a sip of water from the plastic tube and looked south to Mexico. Then she started to run at a strong marathoner's pace, expecting to cross the border in about an hour. Plenty of time to get to her target—a word she used advisedly.

Elizabeth wasn't the only person heading for the border, but Rosin-court was considerably more comfortable in his air-conditioned SUV. He exited the shop yard, crossed the tracks, and headed down Doniphan Road, thoughts alive with the special blessings fame would bring him. He would soon have a life of leisure in Ramsar on the Caspian Sea. He imagined the wonderful cottage that would soon be his and the beautiful Muslim women who would audition for the opportunity to marry a national hero. Pity the poor martyrs who had to die to have their virgins. He was among the blessed who would find heaven on earth. What delighted him even more was to know that as he flew into the clouds aboard the Talleyrand jet, Soroya's Jew boy would be consumed in a mushroom cloud and headed to hell like the woman who had betrayed Iran's new national hero.

At 8:00 a.m. he crossed into Ciudad Juarez, as he and Soroya had done countless times before. Border guards on both sides waved in surprise; on Monday mornings the pair was usually headed north, and now he was alone. He looked for Esteban, fearing the worst, but the older man was not on duty.

In a crowd less than 200 feet away, a woman in shorts and a ball cap, arms and face glistening with perspiration, was moving toward the border's pedestrian crossing. Roz never noticed and if he had, he would have thought nothing of her.

Elizabeth didn't notice Rosincourt either. Her thoughts were on her minder. She figured that lady had probably given her close to an hour to note the train's movement and return to her car before she became alarmed by Elizabeth's absence. Then she would have come up the trail looking for Elizabeth. The minder was no longer among the fittest members of the bureau so it might have taken her a half hour to get there.

Because Elizabeth had phoned in her observations to the FBI command post while on the march, the older woman wouldn't be in panic mode; there would be little fear of a deep betrayal or of a mole in their midst. The minder should have been far more concerned that foreign agents had targeted her ward. That was why Elizabeth had left drag marks for a quarter of a mile leading away from two things: the path she had taken and the place where she had buried her clothes under the boulders. When Jack Barry had told her she'd have a minder, she'd brightened inside because minders often gave higher-ranking officials a false sense of security.

But by then her bosses *might* have concluded she'd taken flight. That possibility spiked her anxiety as she arrived to find a long line at the border, which sparked a sharp memory of the Hispanic couple that had intercepted her only days earlier. But just when she thought she'd crawl out of her skin, the Mexicans opened another lane. Elizabeth dashed to it, not caring that she had cut ahead of more portly—and less patient—travelers.

The Mexican border guard looked at her phony passport and nodded solemnly. He appeared tired, too weary to check the hydration pack hanging by her side or its highly illegal—and lethal—contents. His eyes did fall down her body to gaze most openly at her bare legs. She never shifted to discourage him. He managed a smile when he welcomed her to his city, among the most brutally violent on earth.

She crossed into Juarez and knew, in the most critical sense imaginable, that there was no going back. She was putting everything, including her life, on the line.

Baby Bear, what are you doing? Her father's voice was so clear he could have been standing next to her.

I'm doing what you always told me to do, Dad. I'm doing what's right.

By the time the BNSF train was passing through Las Cruces, Irwandi Bereueh was enjoying breakfast on the porch of his home in Socorro. As he poured his second cup of coffee, he received a telephone call from Colonel Gharabaghi. Irwandi straightened in his chair as if his commander were actually standing before him. The stilted conversation was clouded with code words, but the message was clear. Bereueh listened carefully.

"Keep your eyes open for any unusual activity on the Santa Fe's tracks during the next few hours," Gharabaghi instructed. "Report any untoward events to the telephone numbers I am about to give you. Please note the 98 country code."

It was early evening in Tehran. Two Frenchmen and a Swiss diplomat were leaving their handsome Tehran residences for dinner at Iran's foreign ministry. Highly polished black cars waited for them. The night promised all the charms and perquisites of power and nothing of its dark underside.

As each stepped into his long limousine, 9,000 miles away Rosincourt Sadr, the scion of one of Iran's most famous families, climbed out of his SUV at the Abraham Gonzalez International Airport in Juarez. He pulled out his lone bag, then headed for the executive annex, beaming when he saw the spotless, white G-650 that awaited him. White like the sands of the beaches he would soon call his own. White like the bomb that would soon deliver justice and herald a new international order.

Much closer to Rosincourt was a Juarez cab trundling to the airport, but it wasn't close enough to him to satisfy Elizabeth Mallory. She sat in the backseat, carefully checking the gear she had stashed in her hydration pack. She saw the distance they still had to travel and urged *"Vamos!"* Then she waved a fistful of twenty-dollar bills in the driver's face. He began darting through traffic like a man possessed by demon speed.

She slipped loose-fitting pants over her shorts and a baggy shirt over her sleeveless top. The driver never glanced in his rearview mirror. He couldn't afford to—not the way he was driving.

Only a few miles away, Colonel Gharabaghi emerged from the door of the gleaming Talleyrand jet, twenty feet above Dr. Hout, Miguel Acuña, and Rosincourt Sadr. The colonel was wearing a black-and-white Adidas sweat suit and carrying a larger-than-normal cell phone in his left hand. His eyes, shielded by dark aviator glasses, scanned the tarmac.

Hout labored up the steps of the aircraft. Rosincourt followed him. Subservient Mexican officials bid the departing foreigners farewell as Acuña thanked them in the most meaningful manner possible—with US dollars. Thousands of them.

As they neared the top of the stairs, Hout, breathing heavily, turned to Rosincourt.

"Tell me de trut. Do you even miss her?"

Roz smiled and shook his head. "Not a bit."

Hout laid a heavy hand on his shoulder. "You have a bright future."

At 11:00 a.m. the BNSF freight train approached the ghost town of San Marcial, thirty miles due east of the Trinity test site in New Mexico, where the world's first atomic bomb had been fired on July 16, 1945.

Close by a young man helped his grandfather load sheep into a cattle truck. The herd's new owner nodded approvingly. The rumble of an approaching freight train formed a steadying backdrop to the occasional bleating of the wooly creatures.

In Tehran the foreign minister's dinner guests were toasting Iranian-French relations with champagne flutes filled with sparkling mineral water. The foreign minister's eyes kept darting to a doorway, then to his watch. His rise to the pinnacle of Persian power would soon be complete. He awaited word of his country's greatest coup.

The goateed minister excused himself, then slipped away to a private bathroom. After locking the door behind him, he took out an envelope containing the letter he would dispatch to the president of the United States as soon the foreign minister received confirmation that his bomb had detonated. He had written the letter for the signature of the president of the Islamic Republic of Iran. After a simple salutation to the US president, it read:

> I have the honor to inform you that earlier today the Islamic Republic of Iran detonated a nuclear weapon near your Trinity test site in New Mexico. We regret the losses inflicted on engineers and crew aboard that Santa Fe train. Consistent with the value you placed on the Iranian lives lost aboard Iran Air 655, we have deposited one hundred million Euros in the Tehran branch of Credit Lyonnaise for distribution by the International Red Crescent to the families of those injured or killed.

> I also have the honor to inform you that the Islamic Republic of Iran is now a nuclear weapon state. We have chosen to demonstrate this fact with a detonation at your nuclear test site on the sixty-seventh anniversary of your first test. Since you fired there, we must assume you have no serious objections to our use of your test site, just as you have allowed the British to test in Nevada.

> From this demonstration it should be evident we can fire a nuclear device anywhere—in your country or others—at the time and place of our choosing.

> As was the case during the Cold War, we view these weapons as a deterrent. We do not seek conflict with the United States, but please understand that any attempts to attack the Islamic

Republic of Iran, any refusal to remove Zionist settlers from Palestine, and/or any interference with the exercise of our sover-
eignty and authority in what you call the Middle East will be
considered acts of war. There are several more of our weapons
safely stored within your country.

We understand detonations of nuclear weapons in the heart of
Washington and New York, Los Angeles, and Chicago will bring
down a rain of devastation on the Islamic people, but your gods
are materialistic; they live in your cities. Our God holds a place
for us in heaven.

We look forward to a peaceful coexistence within our respective hemispheres.

Allahu Akhbar.

The foreign minister caught himself smiling in the mirror. He folded
up the letter and placed it back inside his suit jacket. He would hand it
to the Swiss ambassador as soon as he received word that the world had
changed forever.

Elizabeth shoved a wad of money at the driver and kicked open the
taxi door at the annex for executive jets. Her driver, carefully eying a sum
greater than a week's worth of wages, did not notice that she left behind
the hydration pack in favor of a fabric shoulder bag that had been carefully
folded next to the pack's water bladder. The bag now carried her secrets and
would appear far less eye-catching to airport personnel than a pack with a
plastic tube protruding from its top.

She didn't dare try to pass through security, but she had no need. She
hurried along a cyclone fence until she had a clear view of the Talleyrand
jet. It had taxied to within a hundred yards of the terminal. From behind
her dark glasses, she saw Colonel Gharabaghi talking to Dr. Hout and Rosincourt atop the boarding stairs. Soroya's body, she was now certain, had
been disposed of somewhere in the alleys or sewers of Juarez. The courier of

Akhbar-I's most vital elements, Miguel Acuña, stood on the tarmac below the aircraft door.

All of this had been as predictable as the BNSF train schedule. So was Gharabaghi's next move. As Dr. Hout and Rosincourt crowded around him, he carefully punched the keypad of his large cell phone, raising his hand in triumph when he finished like a maestro striking a final note at a grand piano. He looked up expectantly, as if the detonation of the nuclear bomb would be visible from his perch above the tarmac. All remained quiet.

That was when Elizabeth used her own phone and saw Gharabaghi's startled expression when his rang. He answered, looking surprised.

"Hi, Ashkan, it's me, your dancing partner from Moscow. I can tell by the way you were dialing just now you thought you'd just set off a big bomb, but guess what? We're two steps ahead of you, old man."

He was looking around frantically for her.

"Your bomb is still rolling peacefully through the desert, Ashkan. Doesn't it remind you of how you failed with that Antonov in Kazakhstan? The one that blond woman shot down?" She waved at him through the fence. "Over here."

When his eyes landed on her, he took off his dark glasses, staring in open disbelief as she pulled off her ball cap so her blond hair could cascade down onto her shoulders. "Yes, it's me. As we say in America, I'm back and I'm pissed."

Much to her surprise, the colonel laughed. "You are wrong, Elizabeth. We found what you did to my phone. We changed the code."

"Good for you," she parried, "but you couldn't have changed it in the bomb. It won't fire. I saw to that myself. And now I'm going to see to it that you never get off the ground." She raised a black, 9mm semi-automatic pistol with a four-inch barrel.

He looked stunned, as if the implications of what she'd done—and said—were only now sinking in. But he rallied enough to push Rosincourt and Hout into the cabin. He then shouted at the pilot in Farsi, "Take off!"

As he turned back, Elizabeth steadied her pistol against a fence post and clicked off the safety, then spoke into the phone one more time.

"It has incendiary rounds, Ashkan. And you are most definitely dead."

"Stop her!" Gharabaghi yelled at Miguel Acuña down on the tarmac. The nattily dressed thug was already fleeing. "I told you to take that woman down! She's right there. Kill her. Now!" Acuña disappeared into the executive terminal.

Elizabeth aimed for the Gulfstream's fuel tank. She fired her first hollow-point round, its central cavity filled with magnesium—a device intended to set fire to buildings and vehicles, including this Gulfstream-650. She had studied the jet's layout and knew exactly where to aim. The first round scored a hit, but it produced only a trickle of fuel spilling to the ground. No ignition. Undaunted, she aimed again. Out of the corner of her eye, she saw Acuña racing out of the annex on her side of the fence. He was heading directly toward her. She had only an instant to make the most critical decision of her life: kill him and save herself or hit the G-650 and stop Gharabaghi for good.

She fired at the plane. She had to hit the fuel tank a second time; there would be no chance for a third round. Bingo! The bullet tore into the tank. A flame bloomed as Acuña slammed her to the ground.

She fought him fiercely as the tank exploded. But then, to her surprise, a massive blast consumed the jet, its crew, and the passengers, including Gharabaghi. His mangled body rose more than a hundred feet into the air and landed in a ball of flames on the nearby runway.

The explosion shook the ground under Elizabeth's back. Chunks of the aircraft rained down around the struggling pair.

"That would be the plastique in the wheel well," Acuña grunted to Elizabeth as she tried to wrestle her gun against his chest. She was about to fire a deadly round into him when he added in a panicky voice, "I'm on your side, Mallory. For chrissakes, don't shoot." By then he was fully atop the struggling woman, shielding her from the flying debris. "Goddamn it, stop. We need to get out of here."

She hesitated, fearful she would be agreeing to her own death. But then the trench coat-clad Hispanic rose and extended a helping hand amidst the continuing shower of flaming fragments. Together they staggered to the terminal door to be greeted by a speeding SUV. With a squeal of brakes, the front passenger door flew open. A man's voice shouted, "Get in, both of you, now!" It was Jack Barry, again ready to haul Elizabeth out of Mexico. But with Acuña in tow? That made no sense to her.

Acuña shoved Elizabeth into the back seat and slammed the door behind them. Flames engulfed the twisted remains of the G-650, and huge plumes of black smoke billowed hundreds of feet into the air.

The driver of the SUV reached out his window, put an emergency light on the roof, and raced away as police cars, fire trucks, and ambulances sped past in the other direction, sirens blaring.

"Stop for no one," Barry shouted at the driver, pulling a large semi-automatic from a shoulder holster. "At the border flash our ID, but we're not stopping till we hit US soil. Understand?"

Elizabeth understood the immediate goal of getting out of Mexico, but she could not comprehend why Acuña was coming along for the ride. But he'd known her name when he'd told her not to shoot him, and Jack clearly welcomed his company. In her stunned state, the pieces of the puzzle finally started to form. Then Jack, grinning widely, made it official.

"Elizabeth, I'd like you to meet your newest best friend, my long-time associate, Mr. Miguel Acuña."

Locked in an armored car, hurtling up Mexico's Route 45 at more than sixty miles per hour, Elizabeth locked eyes with her seatmate. She shook his proffered hand.

"Good to meet you formally, Ms. Mallory. I've been working under-cover for ten years. It started with the Mérida initiative, penetrating the drug federation. Then the agency helped me make some new friends at Talleyrand. But after what we just did, my days south of the border are over. Adios amigos," he said with a glance out the window. As he turned back to Elizabeth, he went on. "Jack enjoys diplomatic status because he's the CIA's station chief in Mexico City. I don't. That's why he's hightailing me out of here."

"Me too," Elizabeth said.

"That's right," Acuña replied, his casual tone at odds with the SUV's frantic plunge through Mexico's midday traffic. The diplomatic tags helped. He smiled at his newest best friend and added, "When I saw you aiming at that plane, I can't tell you how happy I was that the colonel once again ordered me to kill you. I knew that G-650 was gonna blow."

"So you put the plastique in the wheel well?"

"My guys did. It was wired into Gharabaghi's phone. He was supposed to blow himself away. But his too-smart Germans found and disabled that link."

"Nice move," Elizabeth said as they careened through Juarez like well-armed drug kingpins on the run. Five minutes out and a quarter of the way to the border, she looked through the rear window to see a massive fireball erupting from the airport tarmac. High in the sky, the top of a thick column of smoke and flames flowed outward, forming a mushroom cloud. But the iconic shape was infinitely less damaging than the one planned for the New Mexico desert.

A hundred fifty miles to the north, a train with its impotent freight rumbled across the landscape. The only sound of anguish that David Borookhim and his beloved grandfather heard came from a truck full of bleating sheep rolling down a dusty ranch road, raising a harmless cloud of its own.

CHAPTER 26
BASTILLE DAY

Noon, July 16, 2012

As instructed, the Bereuehs watched the Socorro train depot. At 11:15 a.m., a BNSF freight was slowly shunted to a siding at the isolated desert station. More than a dozen rangers in hazmat outfits crawled all over what appeared to be an oil-gas separator. They unbolted the rear access panel and within minutes removed a handful of electronics, a maze of detonators, and a bag of cordite.

Irwandi dutifully called the designated telephone number in Tehran. With a few words he reported what he had seen. The recipient of his call sounded horrified. He asked Irwandi to repeat his report *slowly*. Once more Irwandi carefully relayed what he had seen. The phone went silent for several seconds before the listener cut the connection.

Ten minutes later Iran's minister of nuclear affairs entered an ornate dining room to interrupt the Bastille Day dinner. He apologized profusely before whispering into the foreign minister's ear.

"*Agha*, the Talleyrand jet was just blown to pieces on the tarmac at Ciudad Juarez. Our geophysics people report no unusual seismic activity in the New Mexico desert. There has been no EMP signal. Our agents in New Mexico report an American bomb squad boarding a stopped freight train at the Socorro station, well north of San Marcial." He finished by saying, "*Fecker mekonam ma moshkeli darem.*" I think we have a problem.

"*Nefreen bar tu. A y!*" the foreign minister said quietly: "Oh, shit," loosely translated. Then, with all the calm he could muster, his face devoid of expression, Iran's chief diplomat rose to thank his guests for the pleasure of their company. He offered one final toast.

"*Pour notre amitie continue.*" To our continuing friendship. "May the Talleyrand family forgive us all. May Allah reward our Persian patriots in heaven."

On leaving, the Swiss ambassador turned to one of the French embassy officials and asked, "*Quel etait-il au juste?*" What was that all about?

She received only a shrug in response.

When his guests were gone, the foreign minister took out the envelope with the letter to the president of the United States. He could not bring himself to read it again before flipping it into the large fireplace. Flames ignited the envelope quickly and the letter, so safe with its secrets only seconds earlier, curled and blackened and turned to ash.

In El Paso the white SUV pulled into the secured garage under the bland-looking federal building. Miguel Acuña turned to Elizabeth.

"Did you know Gharabaghi called for your execution?"

"Yes, I did. I heard about that."

"I thought so. I was supposed to arrange it. That's one order I did not pass on to the Bereuehs. One less problem to worry about."

"You really are my newest best friend," Elizabeth joked.

When the foursome made it up to her office, Jack Barry turned on a television. Cable channels teemed with reports about the Iranian plot. Pundits from across the political spectrum were already denouncing the planned attack against the American heartland.

About the same time those newscasts came alive with reports of the plot, and as screens filled with video of the charred aircraft on the Juarez tarmac, a pair of FBI agents from the Albuquerque office burst into Irwandi Bereueh's home. They arrested Adam and Eve. Each was escorted to a separate room in their Socorro cottage. The questioning was not cordial, and the suspects were not cooperative. An hour later they were led from their bungalow, headed for a red-eye flight neither would welcome. They were foreign nationals, accused terrorists, and members of JI, Indonesia's Jemaah Islamiyah or Islamic Congregation. That was the Shiite military group that had turned violent in the late 1990s. In short Adam and Eve were three-time losers in the war on terror. At sundown, wearing orange jumpsuits and black hoods, they boarded a Navy aircraft that would take them to Guantanamo.

At the same time, Mexican intelligence agents, with CIA technical support, combed through the wreckage of the once-opulent Talleyrand jet. They recovered a treasure trove of charred computers, discs, and hard drives that had survived the explosion.

Elizabeth and two FBI agents, armed with warrants and firearms, drove to the Festival Street apartment she had inhabited electronically for three months. They found an array of men's work clothes in the closet and a boxed-up collection of women's underwear, shirts, and jeans. Not what they'd come for. They continued to tear the place apart until one of the agents held up a USB stick he'd found under a couch cushion.

"That's it." Elizabeth smiled but was interrupted by her cell phone.

"It's me," a familiar voice said.

"Bum!" she shouted. "Are you alright?"

"Nope," that dear voice replied. "And I won't be alright till I can set eyes on you again."

Elizabeth turned from the other agents, who appeared too interested in her conversation.

"When's that going to be?" she asked quietly.

"Not soon enough," he replied. "Another couple of days on my end. How's it looking for you?"

"Crazy," Elizabeth replied. "But things should clear up for me about the same time. I'm so glad to hear your voice. This is going to be the longest wait of my life."

"I'll be heading your way just as fast as I can."

EPILOGUE

Early the next morning, Talleyrand engineer James Deaver walked into his office in Houston to find an older man waiting for him. The look on the gent's face gave Deaver pause, and for good reason: Bum Bradley was furious and he had two younger, formidable-looking Asian men backing him up.

Deaver's arriving assistant broke the silence with a query. "Should I call security?"

Deaver didn't respond to her. "Who are you?" he asked the man staring into his eyes.

"Bum Bradley."

"Call security!" Deaver blurted.

"It's not going to help you," Bum said. "You've got about ten seconds to tell me why a bunch of thugs just happened to bust me up outside Gilhooley's right after I talked to—"

Bum never got to finish his question because a swarm of FBI agents poured into Deaver's office. One read the engineer his rights while another cuffed his hands behind his back.

"You work here?" an African-American agent in a red turtleneck asked Bum.

"Not on your life," he answered.

"You two?" the agent asked Thinh and his nephew, Diem.

"No way!" the Vietnamese refugees declared.

The agent surveyed the three of them. "So why are you guys here?"

"We've got a beef with this guy," Bum said.

"The whole company," Thinh added.

"You're going to have to get in line, gentlemen."

The agents who swarmed Deaver's office were only a small part of the FBI contingent that sealed off the entire Talleyrand building, then herded the employees into an auditorium. Deaver was marched into the cavernous room as well, and he quickly identified the higher-ups to whom he'd disclosed Bum Bradley's queries.

Agents filed out of the building with boxes brimming with documents. Talleyrand's incriminated executives were marched out next—in handcuffs. Network and local media caught the perp walk live as the arrested streamed into waiting vans. There was a lot of loud chatter among the journalists about the company's connections to Iran and possibly to the atomic bomb plot against the United States. At about the same time the executives made their humiliating exit, the company's lobbyists began squawking in Washington.

Bum and his Vietnamese buddies watched all the action up close.

"What do you think, Bum? These guys gonna beat the rap?" Thinh asked as agents slammed and locked the doors on the last of the vans.

"I don't know if they'll beat the rap, but people are never going to forget what they were party to. But it's going to be tough to prove they actually knew what those Iranians were doing."

"How could they not know?" Phan said. It wasn't really a question.

"Maybe they made a point of not knowing. When the contracts get big enough, it's easy to look the other way," Bum replied.

"Well, it sure cost them this time, at least in PR. Look at that," Thinh said, glancing at a dozen camera crews trained on the vans's departure. Upwards of sixty reporters scribbled frantically in their notebooks. Then the crews turned for video of the company's huge and painfully familiar logo.

As the three friends walked back to Thinh's car, Bum's phone rang. It was Elizabeth, checking in under more tranquil circumstances.

"How are you?" he asked.

"I'm doing real well, now that I can actually talk to you. It was crazy yesterday. When you called we were tearing apart Rosincourt's apartment."

"You have my permission to tear that place apart as much as you want," Bum responded in a laughing tone.

"I've missed you so much," she told him, a message so heartfelt it made Bum beam like the desert sun. They made plans to get together as soon as he could get to El Paso, but they both had more immediate work to do.

Bum went with Thinh when the émigré turned himself into the Matagorda, Texas, sheriff's office. Thinh's blow-by-blow account of what had happened on the shrimp boat correlated neatly with what homicide detectives had reconstructed during their own investigation of the killing of two notorious gangbangers. The gash in Thinh's leg certainly buttressed his contention that one of the men had attacked him from behind, leading to the deaths of both assailants.

"Justice wins," Diem said to his uncle as he and Bum escorted Thinh from the sheriff's office.

"Sometimes," Bum said, not so confident in that point but quite certain he wanted to see Elizabeth ASAP.

Early the next day, he climbed into his Mustang and took off for El Paso. By the time he reached the city, the twosome had arranged a rendezvous at her apartment.

He couldn't move fast enough once he saw the familiar-looking building. He parked his Mustang on the street, and Elizabeth buzzed him right inside. She stood waiting in the open doorway of her apartment. Wasting no time, she pulled Bum inside with a kiss and hunger he'd never felt before in a woman. It brought out a fierce streak of his own desire.

They made it to the bedroom, where the minutes passed in a timeless hour of lovemaking.

When they rested Bum asked her what had happened. She explained how she'd taken the initiative to go across the border, which made him wince.

"By yourself?"

She shrugged. "I've been in worse situations."

"I don't think I want to hear about them."

"I had to, Bum. I didn't see any fail-safe built into the system. No plan B reflecting the hazards of the real world."

"What do you mean? You're talking to an old cowhand here."

"No I'm not, Bum. You've lived in the real world all of your life. You know there's always gotta be a backup, a 'what if?' All along we were depending on everything going right. And everything always looks perfect if you're designing an operation in Washington, but little things go wrong all the time. You go to climb up on a roof with a rocket launcher and some old ladder breaks and you can't get up there. Or you run around the building to shoot down a plane that's picking up a load of uranium and the freakin' sun is blinding the sensors in your rocket launcher. There's always *something* going wrong in the field."

Bum's jaw hung open. "Hold on, Elizabeth. What's this about climbing up some ladder with a rocket launcher? Is that something you actually did?"

"I'm talking theory here."

No you're not. But he let it go. "So you composed your own plan B?" he asked instead.

"The only plan B for stopping some truly awful men, as it turned out. The target, or his tech people, had found the triggering device that was supposed to blow up the plane—and the people on it. Fortunately they couldn't detonate the A-bomb on the train. I took care of that myself."

"Yourself?" Bum ran his fingers through her hair, enjoying the silky feel. "You okay? I mean what with blowing them all to hell?"

"I'm fine with it. Besides that, Gharabaghi *had* to go. I didn't know that those people in Washington were planning to take him and the rest of his despicable crew out with a stick of plastique. So when he went"—she chuckled—"he *really* went. Maybe it means I'm not all touchy-feely, but when I take out guys planning to nuke my country, guys who like to torture horses, for God's sake, I have *no* regrets."

"Oh, I think you're plenty touchy-feely."

Bum pulled her close to prove his point, and their lips played meet and greet all over again.

In mid-August, Irwandi Bereueh cracked after a month of unrelenting interrogation. Each of his evasions had been invalidated by data collected in El Paso and Juarez. So he talked. Marshanda, the dutiful Muslim wife even in Gitmo, spoke only after she learned of Irwandi's collapse. The pair unveiled the network built within the US to support the Quds Force terror campaign, and they documented the growing strength of Hezbollah south of the border.

August proved a productive month for Elizabeth as well. With those confessions in hand and more roundups underway, the director of Central Intelligence invited her to an awards ceremony in her honor. On a steamy Thursday, a small group gathered in his office. All had to carry clearances, as there would be discussion of Elizabeth's stunning achievements in some detail. She made sure Bum's clearance arrived in time so he could join her for the event. Elizabeth's father was there too, along with one of Bum's old friends from his oil-field days, a one-time drilling contractor.

The friend had become governor of Texas; he had served as deputy secretary of defense before running for state office years earlier. He had remained active as an intelligence advisor. But his link to Elizabeth on that sweet August day was through Bum, not the intelligence community. In the old days, the brothers Bradley had cared for the governor's drilling rigs, through hurricanes and sand storms, for a quarter century. The governor was another of Bum's many friends, all of them as loyal to him as the Texas summer was long.

The ceremony was informal but touching. The director described what might have happened to the US without Elizabeth's actions, then awarded her a second Intelligence Community Medal for Valor. The citation referred to her "extraordinary heroism, conspicuous fortitude, and exemplary courage."

When the speeches ended, the director pulled her aside for a private tête-à-tête. "I'd like you back in Langley, where I can keep a close eye on you." A veiled reference to her going rogue twice on the agency, even if her second initiative proved vital to the complete success of the mission. But the director smiled when he said it and added, "Your future is really bright. I think one day we'll all be saying we knew you when."

As soon as Elizabeth shared the news with Bum and the governor, the latter urged her to take the Langley assignment. "That's where you want to be, in the seat of power. You're going places, girl."

The governor turned to Bum. "Time for you to get civilized, you old coot. I've got just the place for you. Keep you sane while Elizabeth keeps the world safe. You still keep horses, don't you?" Bum nodded. "Back when I was at the Pentagon I bought a place out in Middleburg, beautiful Virginia horse country. It belonged to the Kennedys once. Jackie couldn't abide Camp David because she couldn't keep her horses there. It's only a half hour from here." He looked from Bum to Elizabeth. "You'll both love it."

Over the Labor Day weekend, Elizabeth and Bum joined her father for what was becoming an annual end-of-summer cookout. Now a master chef, her father treated them to oysters, clams, and ahi steaks, all grilled or roasted on the barbecue.

Bum rose from the outdoor table as if to propose a toast, but instead he made a formal request to Elizabeth's father: "May I have your daughter's hand in marriage?"

Her father responded with a huge smile, raised his wine glass, and said, "Here, here, Justin Bradley. Welcome to the family!"

The big event took place on Halloween, when Bum and Elizabeth were married in the US Naval Academy chapel at Annapolis. The venue had been requested—or perhaps demanded—by Marine Sergeant Diem, as adept with scheduling the wedding as he was with sutures. The October 31 date seemed humorously appropriate to all of Elizabeth's spook friends. There were practical considerations as well: Halloween was a weekday with no football crowd, and it came a week before the presidential election that would surely anchor the bride to her new desk.

Hiram served as Bum's best man. Elizabeth's father walked her down the aisle dewy-eyed, as she was when she noticed. As the service drew to a close, a chorus of naval midshipmen sang all four choruses of the Naval Hymn: "Eternal Father, strong to save, whose arm hath bound the restless wave…for those in peril on the sea."

A few days later the newlyweds held an open house at their new quarters in northern Virginia. Their landlord, the former Texas governor and Bum's lifelong friend, hosted the event and conducted an impressive tour for the guests. Both Elizabeth and Bum accompanied them.

In the first hallway, the governor stopped to show Thinh Phan a row of old photos, each in a simple, black frame. "Here's the Kennedy family at play out in the yard. Jack and the two kids." The picture was dated November 16, 1963—the weekend before the children's father was assassinated in Dallas. But the governor omitted that poignant detail from his talk.

He moved on quickly to another photo. "Here's Ronald Reagan practicing for the debates out in the barn. I let him use the place as his DC base during the campaign. I *liked* that man." The photo carried an October 1980 date.

Another president shot by a gunman. Elizabeth kept this observation to herself.

The small group then moved to the glassed-in living room, where a young pony peered at them from across a rail.

"I see you've already got your own horse out here, Bum." The governor laughed. "Good work. I think that gelding will like it here."

"Actually, he's not mine," Bum responded. "I got him as a wedding present for Elizabeth. Might get her to come home from the office before sundown."

"Really?" the governor said, turning to Elizabeth. "What's that pony's name?"

"Gunpowder, of course."

REFERENCES

Allison, Graham, 2004, *Nuclear Terrorism: the Ultimate Preventable Catastrophe*, Times Books, NY

Arjomand, Said Amir, 2009, *After Khomeini: Iran Under His Successors*, Oxford University Press, UK

Baer, Robert, 2008, *The Devil We Know: Dealing with the New Iranian Superpower,* Three Rivers Press, NY

Claire, Rodger W., 2004, *Raid on the Sun: Inside Israel's Secret Campaign that Denied Saddam the Bomb,* Broadway Books, NY   (The 1981 raid on Iraq's Osirak reactor)

Cockburn, Andrew & Leslie, 1997, *One Point Safe*, Doubleday, NY ("Nuclear warheads, cheap, while supplies last," Eric Schmitt, *N.Y. Times*)

Cohen, Avner, 1998, *Israel and the Bomb*, Columbia University Press, NY

Coster-Mullen, John, 2007, *Atom Bombs: The Top Secret Inside Story of Little Boy and Fat Man*, Coster-Mullen, Waukesha, WI

Glasstone, Samuel, 1962, *Effects of Nuclear Weapons*, U.S. Atomic Energy Commission

Hansen, Chuck, 1988, *U.S. Nuclear Weapons: the Secret History*, Aerofax, Arlington, TX

Hersh, Seymour, 1991, *The Samson Option: Israel's Nuclear Arsenal and American Foreign Policy*, Random House, NY

Hoffman, David, 2009, *Dead Hand: the Untold Story of the Cold War Arms Race and its Dangerous Legacy*, Doubleday, NY

Huyser, Robert, 1986, *Mission to Tehran,* Andre Deutsch, London (With intro by Alexander Haig)

Khan, Abdul Quandeer, 1997, *Dr. A. Q. Khan on Science and Technology*, Sang-E-Meel Publications, Lahore, Pakistan

Langwiesche, William, 2007, *The Atomic Bazaar: the Rise of the Nuclear Poor*, Farrar, Straus & Giroux, NY

McPhee, John, 1973, *The Curve of Binding Energy*, Farrar, Straus & Giroux, NY

Reed, Thomas & Stillman, Danny, 2009, *The Nuclear Express: A Political History of the Bomb and its Proliferation,* Zenith Press, Minneapolis

Serber, Robert, 1992, *The Los Alamos Primer: First Lectures on How to Build an Atomic Bomb* 1992, University of California Press, Berkeley (Lectures first delivered to new employees at Los Alamos, April 1943)

Shute, Nevil, 1957, *On the Beach*, William Morrow & Co., NY

Smythe, Henry D, 1946, *Atomic Energy for Military Purposes: a General Account of the Scientific Research and Technical Development That Went Into the Making of Atomic Bombs,* Princeton University Press, Princeton, NJ

ABOUT THE AUTHORS

Thomas C. Reed is a former Secretary of the Air Force, having served in that capacity during the Ford and Carter administrations. In the mid-seventies Reed was the youngest-ever Director the National Reconnaissance Office,[1] an organization whose very existence was held to be secret until the end of the Cold War. During the eighties, Reed was a Special Assistant to President Reagan for National Security Policy. His technical background includes nuclear weapon design at Livermore and low-temperature physics.

Reed graduated from Cornell University with a degree in engineering and an ROTC commission into the U.S. Air Force. He began his professional career at the Air Force Ballistic Missile Division in Los Angeles during the 1950s, the years of Sputnik and the missile gap.

After earning a graduate degree from the University of Southern California, he moved to Lawrence Livermore where he designed two thermonuclear devices fired over the Pacific in the Dominic test series of 1962.[2] On leaving Livermore, Reed started and ran a successful high-tech company making superconductors.

---

1   Responsible for all U.S. satellite intelligence systems, both photographic and electronic, during the Cold War.

2   Reed was on Christmas Island for the 1962 *Bighorn* event described in Prologue to *The Tehran Triangle*.

Thomas C. Reed, standing with a model of the W-80, the fractional-megaton-class thermonuclear warhead carried by most U.S. cruise missiles.

In 1973 Reed was recruited to manage certain intelligence projects at the Pentagon in connection with the Yom Kippur War then raging in the Mideast. A decade of involvement in national security matters followed. Reed left Washington in 1983 to return to business pursuits, but throughout the years of Soviet collapse, Reed continued to advise the Joint Strategic Planning Staff on policy and intelligence matters.

Reed was born in New York City. His first book, *At the Abyss: An Insider's History of the Cold War*, with an Introduction by Former President George H.W. Bush, was published by Ballantine Books in 2004. It delves into the lives of those who fought and ended the Cold War without a nuclear shot being fired. His more recent book, *The Nuclear Express: a Political History of the Bomb and its Proliferation,* was published by Zenith Press in 2009. It was favorably reviewed by William J. Broad of *The New York Times* on December 9, 2008.[3] Reed was the principal authority appearing in the National

---

3   www.nytimes.com/2008/12/09/science/09bomb.html

Geographic Channel's *Secret History of the Atom Bomb*, first aired April 15, 2010.[4]

Mr. Reed lives in Healdsburg, California, with his wife Kay.

---

4   http://channel.nationalgeographic.com//episode/secret-history-of-the-atom-bomb-4603/videos#tab-videos/08018_00.

Sandy Baker graduated from Penn State with a B.A. in English. She began her career as a technical writer and editor with a defense contractor. Later when stationed in Germany with her Army officer husband, she taught English grammar and American History to Army GIs. There followed a stint on a regional New Jersey newspaper as a reporter and columnist. Baker then spent 12 years as a university development director, writing funding proposals and speeches, plus managing colloquia and other university events.

A Master Gardener since 2000, Baker writes for the MG website and lectures on basic landscape design, lawn alternatives, drought tolerant gardening, and native California plants. She was co-chair of the California statewide Master Gardener conference in 2011 at the same time she published her first children's gardening book.

Her second in the series will be published in 2012. She has been a contributing writer for *Travel Host* magazine.

Also in 2012, Baker chaired the California Writers Club- Redwood Writers Conference held in Santa Rosa where she lives with her husband Warren "Bud" Metzger.